TARIQ ALI
REDEMPTION

Born and educated in Pakistan and subsequently at
Oxford University, Tariq Ali is a writer and film-maker
who was for four years producer of Channel 4's *Bandung
File* and now produces *Rear Window*. Well known in the
nineteen sixties and seventies as an international political
activist, he is the author of over a dozen books on history,
world politics and biography, including the recently up-
dated *The Nehrus and the Gandhis, Can Pakistan
Survive?* and *Streetfighting Years: An Autobiography of
the Sixties*. He has written two highly acclaimed plays
with Howard Brenton, *Iranian Nights* and *Moscow Gold*.
He lives in North London.

D1100860

TARIQ ALI

REDEMPTION

PUBLISHED BY PAN BOOKS
IN ASSOCIATION WITH CHATTO & WINDUS

First published 1990 by Chatto & Windus Ltd
This Picador edition published 1991 by Pan Books Ltd,
Cavaye Place, London SW10 9PG
in association with Chatto & Windus

1 3 5 7 9 8 6 4 2

© Tariq Ali 1990

ISBN 0 330 32004 1

Printed in England by Clays Ltd, St Ives plc

This book is sold subject to the condition that it
shall not, by way of trade or otherwise, be lent, re-sold,
hired out, or otherwise circulated without the publisher's prior
consent in any form of binding or cover other than that in which
it is published and without a similar condition including this
condition being imposed on the subsequent purchaser

For Susan Alice Watkins

Part One

1

A new idea takes shape in the mind of Ezra Einstein

It was Christmas Eve in Paris. The year was nineteen eighty-nine. Outside it was mild. No scarves or gloves to be seen, and many of the joggers, those disfigurers of modern landscapes, were running in shorts and sleeveless vests. Not that there were many of them. Paris, unlike New York or London, is not a jogger-friendly city.

The talk in France that day was not of food or gifts or mistresses or the disturbingly large number of votes the fascists had won in a recent by-election. Everyone, regardless of political affiliation, was thinking about the popular uprising in Romania. At the very time when a new common sense was emerging which consigned insurrections to the museums of Europe, the Romanian people had, through their heroism, made it impossible for things to go on in the same old way. It is almost a truism that when people lose their fear, they can accomplish miracles. The citizens of Romania had done just that by splitting the forces of the state and toppling the despot.

In France, where the nation was celebrating the bicentenary of its own revolution, they were all elated with the news from Bucharest. The Far Right dreamt of the return of the Iron Guard and a fascist strongman, the Right opined that the exiled King Carol, like his co-royal in Spain, might provide a bridgehead to democracy, the Left hoped that some form of social-democracy

3

would prevail and the Far Left dreamt of workers' councils and soviet power. There was another reason why France was happy. It had links with Romania which went back many years, French had always been the cultural language of the Romanian intelligentsia and, yes, there was one more thing. The new Romanian prime minister spoke French in the battered accents of Toulouse. Every time he appeared on French television, the whole country sighed with pride or amusement. They did not as yet know when or why he had been in Toulouse. When they found out their feelings were rather more mixed.

Inside his tiny apartment in the Twentieth Arrondissement, a few minutes' walk from the Porte des Lilas, the seventy-year-old Trotskyist leader, Ezra Einstein, was sitting at his desk, his weary fingers, alert and ready, resting on the keyboard of his fifty-five-year-old typewriter. He looked down on the old machine with affection. He had spent more time on it than on any of his three companions over the preceding half-century. His fingers had rested more often on the keys and body of this antique writing aid than on the more intimate sections of the female anatomy. It was only now, with Maya, that Ezra was beginning to appreciate one of the great pleasures of life. Her thick, glossy black hair stroked his body till every resistance had been broken down and he would lie expectantly, her prisoner and slave. The comrades smiled to each other when they saw them together. Maya's voluptuous presence was enough to suggest the most exotic forms of love-making. Of course this was a stereotypical response. Maya dressed and walked artfully, a Brazilian enchantress, a wood-sprite from the threatened rain-forest, so one should not blame the comrades too much. It was obvious that both parties were happy. That much was incontestable. The reasons which attracted her to the seventy-year-old, battle-scarred veteran of the world movement were unfathomable. Needless to add, a number of malicious tales giving totally different versions were in circulation, but none had any foundation. Some of Ezra's less pleasant associates, like the Cuckoo or Jim Noble, automatically assumed that Maya's head was totally subordinated to her sensuous body.

4

Ezra himself occasionally gave the impression that he shared this view. All three were wrong.

Ezra was now stroking his typewriter and muttering endearments as though it were a little pet. He had always wanted a dog, but his parents had denied him that simple pleasure. His mother loathed all animals. His father would not have minded a spaniel or even an Alsatian, but he refused to have poodles or corgis in the house, and these two were the only breeds attractive to young Ezra. So the typewriter became a substitute of sorts. With its help he had produced over two dozen books, several scores of pamphlets, innumerable newspaper articles for the bourgeois press as well as the myriad publications of the movement, and of course several thousand internal documents.

The latter were one of Ezra's specialities. A master chef in a *haute-cuisine* establishment can cook almost anything – even an omelette produced by his hands drips with magical qualities – but he has his special dishes. Likewise, Ezra could produce a stimulating study on modern capitalism which, to his own bewilderment, made him an immediate post-modernist favourite; it took him a week to produce a Marxist study of the detective novel, which received a rave review in the *Gambian Literary Gazette*; then there was the celebrated comparative essay on the operas of Mozart and Verdi which was reprinted in an élite, subscription-only Italian music journal, *Musica Rossa* – now, alas, defunct.

But it was the challenge of inner-party debates that brought out the artist in Ezra. Polemical squibs and pamphlets were his forte. He rattled them off like machine-gun bullets. Not all by any means found their target, but those that did tended to devastate the victim. Ezra thrived on polemics. This is not to say that the rest of his work was inferior. Far from it. In fact some of his pieces in *Le Monde* and the *Frankfurter Rundschau* were superb little essays and were later reprinted in the *New Life Journal*. His critical review of the first volume of Solzhenitsyn's *Gulag Archipelago* in the Frankfurt newspaper had attracted favourable comment and had made even the Voice of Mother Russia feel uneasy. Ezra had pointed out that the Hermit had got some of his facts wrong and had conveniently forgotten others. He hinted that the Stalinist school of falsification had left its mark even on the Hermit.

Einstein's stature can be judged by the fact that his entry in the *Encyclopedia Trotskyana* (*ET*) ran to almost fifty pages. Now if *ET* had been produced by Ezra's own faction, this fact would be without interest. But the original publishers of *ET*, in the days when it was issued in a limited edition of only one hundred copies and its very existence was treated as a state secret, were the special section of the Stalinist secret police, the NKVD, which had been created to combat Trotskyism. The first issue of *ET* was made available to the Central Committee of the Communist Party of the Soviet Union in 1930, and it had subsequently been issued every year. It was only in 1987 that the preceding fifty-seven editions were made public and the book discontinued, much to the discomfiture of secret services in Western Europe and North America which had shamelessly plagiarized its findings to update their own records.

All that seemed pretty remote on the twenty-fourth of December, 1989. Ezra had just watched on television the trial of the Romanian Stalinist dictator, Nicolae Ceausescu, and his wife Elena, which had been followed by images of the dictator's bullet-ridden corpse. It had been a classic popular uprising, he thought. The arrest of a Lutheran priest sparked off a demonstration. The dictatorship mowed down women and children in cold blood. News of the massacre spread and the country rose. The army refused to obey orders and went over to the people. A diehard wing of the apparatus fought back, but it was all over within a week. The loss of life had been heavy and now there on the television screen, for everyone to see, Ceausescu lay dead. He had refused to plead for mercy. Neither he nor his wife had recognized the military tribunal which tried and condemned them.

Their defiance interested Ezra. The arrogance reminded him of the behaviour of Mao Zedong's widow, Chiang Ching, during her trial in the late Seventies. Stalino-feudalism! That's what these people represented. The Socialist boat had been wrecked and battered by them. Were there enough carpenters to build a new one? If they started now, when would it be constructed, and what guarantee was there that it would not be destroyed by new squalls generated artificially but effectively from Washington? Carpenters! Yes, that's what was needed now. Carpenters! The image kept recurring.

Ezra wondered whether the Tsar and his family in Ekaterinburg on that fateful day in 1918 had pleaded for mercy before being killed. For Ezra the executions of the last Romanov Tsar and one of the two remaining Stalino-feudal potentates in Europe, at the beginning and end of this century, had been necessary to ensure in the one case that the civil war was ended rapidly and in the other that the counter-revolution remained headless. He had nothing but the most crushing contempt for the chanceries of the West who favoured executing Stalinist dictators but were totally indulgent towards pro-Western despots. He suddenly remembered that the West had backed Ceausescu against Moscow, and the Foreign Office in London had got the English Queen to knight him and put him up at Buckingham Palace. A tiny wrinkle, no doubt, which could easily be ironed out with the help of pliant media-moguls.

But these unfriendly thoughts, which challenged the eternal double standards of those who wore democracy's nylon stocking skin-tightest over their faces, were soon banished from his head. He kept seeing the image of Romanian soldiers crossing themselves before they executed the defiant old couple. The cross had outflanked the hammer and sickle. Both symbols were bloody. Both had been misused by butchers of one sort or another. Yet one had already triumphed in Poland, and then in Czechoslovakia (though here there were others in the field), and was now threatening Romania.

'We need more carpenters!' Ezra muttered to his typewriter.

Old Einstein realized that the new revolutions were bound to turn Europe upside down. New strategies and new tactics were necessary for what remained of this century and its successor. He had kept the movement going ideologically, almost single-handed it must be admitted, for four whole decades. He had synthesized the ideas of the Old Testament (Marx/Engels) and the New (Lenin/Trotsky), denounced heretics (Kautsky/Stalin) with exemplary zeal and offered a pure version of the Marxist-Leninist scriptures to the new recruits who were hostile to the systems in both West and East.

In his own person Ezra Einstein combined some of the qualities of an Old Testament prophet with the defects of a New Testament apostle, whose task was to interpret the words of the saviours in changing conditions. His sincerity and passion were accepted by people he regarded as his political enemies, in other words by social-democrats of all hues as well as reform communists.

All of the hatred, ridicule and bile so often poured on his head originated from the same quarter: factional opponents from within 'the world movement', Jim Noble in New York, Frank Hood, Jimmy Rock and Jed Burroughs in London, and that bastard Pelletier in France. Ezra had spent about 100,000 hours of his life just replying to their distortions. He agreed that this had been a phenomenal waste of time, but necessary in order to educate his own supporters. His motto, 'Don't be sectarian to the sectarians', was a good one, but more honoured in the breach than the observance. It was impossible to apply it in practice while he had lieutenants of the calibre of the Cuckoo.

The turns in Eastern Europe posed new problems. If the movement did not tackle them, then it was finished. Dead as a dodo. For a minute Ezra tried to compute the length of time it had taken the dodo to become extinct. He wasn't sure, but made a note to confirm his estimate with the comrades in Mauritius.

His fingers started typing, and he soon realized that they were out of control. He had been intending to write a tiny internal document on the factional situation inside the Sri Lankan section. It was not going to be more than twenty or thirty pages, since anything longer than that these days was considered oppressive by the rank-and-file, but something strange appeared

8

to be taking place. A problem had developed. It wasn't the typewriter. The strange sensation was emanating from Ezra's own body. His fingers seemed to be obeying a call from a different section of his brain. He had just worked out the definitive line on uniting the Tamil and Buddhist workers on that island, but none of it seemed to be pouring out on to the paper. With growing bewilderment he saw a strange missive taking shape in front of him. This is how it looked, when completed:

FROM: *Ezra Einstein, Paris.*
TO: *All sections, sympathizing sections, individual members, etc.*

URGENT   URGENT   URGENT

Dear comrades:
In view of the situation in Eastern Europe and its likely impact on world politics we are having an emergency World Congress in January 1990 (venue to be decided soon) to discuss the changes necessary in our own theory and practice. Given the importance of what is taking place, we feel that this should be an open Congress and you are therefore encouraged to discuss with and explore the participation of all other Trotskyist groups and currents, despite the fact that they have for many years been hostile to us. The future of our entire movement is at stake: this is no time for sectarianism.

Of course you will be immediately asked whether there are any documents for this special gathering. The answer is no. We do not wish to pre-empt any organization. We must all come with an open mind and discuss freely and frankly. What we are convoking is nothing more or less than a Grand Soviet of the World Trotskyist Movement. What we need is a period of Reconstruction. The Movement needs carpenters. Please reply within two weeks so that we can make all the necessary preparations.
Yours fraternally,

He had made three carbon copies of the letter, which he had written in German and then translated into French, English and Spanish. Now he took the best of these to the tiny photocopier in a corner of the room and painstakingly began to reproduce the letter in fifty different editions. He smiled as he recalled the days when ten copies would have done. Yes, the movement had grown. There could be no doubt about that. No one could take that away from them.

His computer brain recalled the number of sections in 1938 when the movement had first come together on the instructions of Trotsky. Quickly he went through the problems posed during the war years; then the awful but necessary split of 1953. At this point he began to fast-forward some of the images. Not all the memories were pleasant. He settled comfortably on the great revival of 1968 and then, alas, the decline. In the course of his reflections, an odd coincidence, or so he thought, left a very strong impression on Ezra Einstein. Every significant split in the movement had occurred during an eclipse of the moon. Ezra was, naturally, a rock-solid materialist, and yet this fact continued to haunt him. If it was the case that all the major crises of capitalism were related to the movement of sun-spots, then anything was possible.

Now he began to get worried. There was only a hard core of cadres left in the movement and unless they were reoriented the whole thing might just disappear. At this thought a frown disfigured his forehead. He mused on the fact that there were more ex-members than members. The latter were, if the truth be told, outnumbered by more than a hundred to one.

He quickly recovered from this self-inflicted blow. Cynics often laughed at the small size of the movement, but if they had had even fifty people in Romania, in ten different towns, the portrait of Trotsky would have decorated a few squares and town halls. The same applied to East Germany and Czecho-slovakia, not to mention the Soviet Union. Yes, Romania could have been the first victory for the veterans of anti-Stalinism. Suddenly his mental train stopped on that particular thought-track. Try as he might he couldn't break loose from his old way of thinking. He pinched himself hard to get out of this one, and the slight physical discomfort helped him to confront the new reality once again. The phone on his desk began to buzz. He picked it up. It was a familiar voice. Ezra spoke to him in French.

The caller was Jean-Michel from Lausanne, known to the ordinary members of the world movement simply as the Cuckoo. The reasons for the nickname were unclear. The political explanation, that he was as predictable and as boring as the cuckoo in the Swiss clocks, was unconvincing. The other version was certainly more colourful. In the days when he was still attempting to master the English language, Jean-Michel was on a learning visit to London, carefully timed to coincide with the New Year sale at Liberty's, just off Oxford Street. In the shop he struck up an acquaintanceship with a pretty young shop-assistant. One thing led to another and in the throes of passion while stroking her nipple later that week, Jean-Michel sighed and said: 'How happy I am to be the cuckoo on your breast.'

It so happened that the shop-assistant was a leading activist in the shop-assistants' trade union, USDAW, and a member of the Rockers, a rival political organization. When she discovered that she had slept with a leading Einsteinite, she made sure that this phrase was spread far and wide. Whatever the truth in that story, one thing was obvious. The Cuckoo was, despite appearances, anything but a chocolate cream soldier. He was stout, red-cheeked and of medium height, but the colour often vanished from his face, leaving behind a pallid, grey complexion and heavy shadows under the eyes. He was in his late forties, but appeared ten years older. He tried to disguise the fact, but it was obvious that his hair was beginning to disappear, revealing an odd, pear-shaped skull, the result, presumably, of wartime forceps.

The Cuckoo suffered a great deal, and this had made him very hard. The reason for the suffering was not too well known, but it was conjectured by analysts sympathetic to the movement that the Cuckoo was a victim of the notorious desk-power syndrome, a disease which often afflicts political activists who work in tiny offices. Deprived of real power in the real world they invent a world of their own. The desk and its position in the office becomes the site of a power struggle which, in reality, exists only in their imagination. The tiny office and organization are transformed into a total fantasy construct, a microcosm of the state they would like to control, a dystopian embryo.

Cuckoo had been the tough, no-nonsense organization man. If Ezra was the movement's brain, Cuckoo was universally acknowledged as its anus, and everything that was execrable in the internal life of the world party flowed through his desk. This he kept permanently locked, but, unknown to him, the Triplets had cut a set of spare keys. They ran the French wing of Ezra's enterprise, and since it was also the largest, they felt that they must keep an eye on all the covert operations being planned by Ezra's closest comrade-in-arms. The Cuckoo was always puzzled as to how the Triplets seemed to be one step ahead of him in factional manoeuvres. It never occurred to him that his holiest of holies had been penetrated. He had forgotten that the French triumvirate was heavily influenced by old Renard on all factional matters.

At the time of the phone-call Cuckoo had retired from the Paris Centre and returned to his beloved Switzerland to create a tiny sect in his own image. He had hoped that the clean air of his native country would de-pollute his brain, refresh his cells and make him ready for the new factional battles that undoubtedly lay ahead. It was not the Cuckoo's first mistake. Nor his last. He found that the Swiss air was now even more of a pollutant than his brain, and the doctors told him that they could not help him at all. He had insisted on being kept in an oxygen tent for a week, but nothing happened.

Cuckoo, in fact, was in disgrace. One of his Parisian operations had misfired badly. He had accused an Albanian member of the movement, a distinguished trade unionist in exile, of being in the pay of the KGB. An internal trial had taken place on Cuckoo's insistence, but the proof was non-existent and even the so-called circumstantial evidence had turned out to be a figment of the Cuckoo's paranoia. Everyone involved in the trial felt that something more than political differences was at stake. Could it be sexual jealousy? It could. The Albanian comrade, a handsome young giant, was an electrician from Tirana. He had organized the first genuine trade-union cell, but had been discovered and had fled the country. In Paris he had been befriended by a former mistress of the Cuckoo, and the pair soon became involved in an intense emotional relationship. The exiled Albanian was told every possible gory detail of the Cuckoo's politico-sexual operations.

On a number of occasions since then, the electrician had eyed the Cuckoo in a strange way, as if to say, hmm, you're not just a political pervert. The Cuckoo felt that his former mistress was in breach of confidence. He had other plans for her, but he wanted the Albanian out of the way first. To the Cuckoo's amazement, the trial had backfired. The judges, all handpicked by himself, acquitted his rival of any malpractice. Cuckoo, the principal instigator of the proceedings, had fled to Switzerland. But he still rang up Ezra from time to time and they talked, as old comrades often do, of the state of the world.

Cuckoo was just back from Israel, where he had spent Christmas with a delegation of young businessmen who were posing as trade unionists interested in ecology. Cuckoo had seen the Ceausescu execution footage in his Jerusalem hotel room. He had been a bit shocked by the character of the trial, and even more upset at the speed with which the sentence was carried out. After the failure of his own attempts to secure a conviction in the 'KGB' case, the Cuckoo had paid a great deal of attention to legal procedures in other parts of the world. It was his considered opinion that the trial of the Ceausescus in Romania left a lot to be desired. This was undoubtedly true, but it is difficult to believe that the Cuckoo was motivated solely by the desire to see justice done. There was a simpler explanation. He was once more insanely jealous. He had failed to secure the political execution of his Albanian rival. The Romanian insurgents had been luckier.

He had also just seen the latest news from Central America, and was ringing up to discuss the crisis in Panama with Ezra. The news was truly amazing. A corrupt gangster and former CIA agent, put into power by Washington, becomes too uppity for his masters. They fail three times to topple him from within and finally send in the Marines. The dictator seeks refuge in the Vatican Embassy, US tanks surround the Embassy – all this was old news. But Cuckoo now told Ezra that the Vatican had denounced the American occupation of Panama in somewhat stronger language than Moscow. They said that they would not tolerate any pressure to deny the dictator sanctuary. Ezra roared with laughter as he cleaned his spectacles. He knew it was all bluff. Wojtyla would negotiate the transfer terms.

'What a world we live in, eh? What a world. Within a few days Ceausescu is executed and the Pope pisses on the White House, eh? Jean-Michel, listen. I am convinced that, provided we drastically change our strategy and tactics, we could spearhead a world revolution. We are closer to it than we were in the Twenties, the Forties or the Sixties.'

The Cuckoo rapidly brought the conversation to an end. He might be a rogue, but he was often closer to reality than his mentor.

Ezra was excited by the news. He paced up and down, ignoring Maya's calls to come down and have some supper. He was lost in admiration of the political skills demonstrated by God's representative on earth. Ezra knew that the Vatican would be compelled to compromise very shortly, but the gesture of defiance would stand it in good stead throughout Latin America, where the Yankees were loathed.

He kept muttering things like 'the Pope', 'the bloody Pope', 'the shrewd old fox', 'the cunning bastard', till Maya burst into the room, took him by the arm and dragged him to the kitchen. She was only in her late twenties, but her striking beauty and sharp black eyes gave her an imposing presence. When she entered a room, a shop or a café, all conversation ceased for a few seconds as viewers took mental snapshots.

Ezra might have recently celebrated his seventieth birthday, but he was an extremely affectionate and active man. He kissed her all the way down the stairs, and stroked her gently, both during the meal and afterwards.

Later, in bed, she played a Mozart concerto on the flute for him, as a prelude to playing a somewhat different note on his flute. He fell asleep, embedded in conjugal bliss and dreamt evil thoughts about His Holiness.

2

Funeral in London

By one of those puzzling coincidences, at exactly the same time as the Ceausescus were being executed by soldiers drunk on glory, Frank Hood, the veteran leader of the Hoodlums, was also on the verge of departing from this life. The only difference was that whereas the Ceausescus were aware of the fate that awaited them, Hood who had turned eighty-nine on the first day of December, was blithely preparing to indulge himself as only he knew how.

Frank Hood's career intrigued everyone, including the redoubtable editors of the *Encyclopedia Trotskyana* in Moscow. Contrary to what might be imagined, the men and women whose thankless task it was to follow every twist and turn of the world movement were instructed to include all the facts and to avoid innuendoes or material manufactured exclusively to please their masters. The secret *Encyclopedia* was the only place where writers were permitted literary deviations and even, where necessary, poetic licence, which may occasionally have shocked those used to the staid jargon of more traditional Soviet publications. *ET* was designed to be read only by members of the Central Committee, and they had to know the whole truth. Exaggeration, however, was frowned upon. Not that, in this case, any were necessary. The fifty pages on Hood reflect the bewilderment of the miserable analysts in Dzerzhinsky Street.

It may seem odd to deprive the reader of certain choice gems, but the entries contain such ricochets of policy, such a mountain of personal betrayals, and such abstruse details of the further reaches of modern metal surgery, that a reader's sensibility might rebel, and that is a risk best avoided. The 1969 edition of *ET*, however, did contain an accidental entry which was deleted in the following year. This was an inter-departmental memo from an agent in London.

TOP SECRET. TO HEAD OFFICE, MOSCOW. FROM VK, LONDON

For the last two years my job has been to follow the activities of the Hoodlum sect and its followers in Britain. I write to ask that I be relieved of my duties forthwith. I am prepared to accept the job you offered me last year in Novosibirsk. My reasons for this are as follows:

(1) Observing this sect is like being caught in a time-warp. Their language, behavioural patterns, ideological stance, methods of dealing with oppositionists is very similar to that of our own party from 1932–35. It has become a surreal nightmare for me.

(2) Much of their activity is irrelevant. They are engaged in property speculation and Mr Hood uses some apartments for very special purposes. I would rather be engaged in ordinary divorce work.

(3) My advice regarding them is to recruit some of them so that at the very least we have parity with the British on their Central Committee. As far as their ideological twists and turns are concerned all we need do is follow the excellent material published by Mr E. Einstein in the internal bulletins of his organization.

(4) Unless I am removed from this assignment within two weeks, I will resign from the service.

Hood had woken up on Christmas Eve feeling on top of the world. His features had not altered greatly over the past three decades. He still possessed the face of a new-born pig, with half-closed watery eyes, though it was much more bloated than ever before. His belly, a vast rotunda around which even the loosest trousers always appeared tight, rested on clumsy, elephant-column legs. His torso was united to his porker's head by a pink stump of flesh, which, for want of another word, it is necessary to describe as a neck.

At meetings of the Hoodlum Politburo, the blood often rushed to his bald head and suffused the entire top part of his body. This was a sure sign that he was about to rant and rave. When he picked his nose, the other Hoodlums tried as unobtrusively as possible to remove all bottles within easy reach. The nose-picking was always a prelude to breaking a milk or a beer bottle and brandishing it suggestively before the face of a petrified colleague, usually a wimpish professor from the academy who was only too delighted to accept a proletarian rebuke.

Frankie Hood's paranoia had faded slightly with old age. He had even forgotten his usual practice of insisting that Politburo meetings took place under the table in order to avoid the battery of directional mikes which the security forces of the British state were pointing at him from the outside.

At midday the doorbell rang. He rushed to the door. His Christmas treat had arrived. The Hoodlums had not forgotten their leader's special needs. They had dispatched their usual treat for festive occasions. It was the same every year, except for the change of nationality. The Hoodlums were, after all, internationalists, and this year a bemused eighteen-year-old waif from the wilds of Patagonia stood at the door.

For some reason the Hoodlums had recruited a dozen Welsh-Argentinians in Patagonia after the Welsh National Opera's dazzlingly successful tour of Argentina with an avant-garde version of *Don Giovanni* in which Hood's most prized recruit, the charismatic and stunning Laura Shaw, had sung the part of Donna Elvira dressed in a Gandhian loincloth. Hood looked at his Christmas present with interest.

'Come in, Comrade, come in. What's your name?'

'Anna Maria.'

The girl entered the flat. She had been given her instructions for the day, but she had not realized that the creature could be so old and grotesque. She had been assured of a break in a new opera to commemorate the fiftieth anniversary of the assassination of Trotsky. The talented and ambitious Patagonian had been promised the part of a member of Trotsky's household who was seduced by the assassin and deceived into letting him into both her bed and, more disastrously, the fortified residence of the exiled leader in Mexico City. But the price for such a part was to satisfy the 'perfectly normal and natural carnal instincts of Comrade Hood'.

'Put him in a good mood, my darling,' said one of the Hoodlums, 'and he might even help with your libretto.'

The would-be-diva was not stupid. She understood what was being demanded of her. Once inside the flat she did have second thoughts, but the promises outweighed everything else.

Beautiful, delicate, tragic Anna Maria. This red-haired, milky-skinned, blue-eyed, perky-breasted woman was about to enter a private hell. She stood in front of Frankie and attempted a smile. He inspected her like a slave-master. The routine was by now well established. He possessed and rejected them on a heap of old cushions on the floor, with the blinds drawn and the room in total darkness. He nodded to her and she felt her throat tighten. Her stomach was clenched, but she began to undress. If he had looked up at that moment even he would have noticed that her large and limpid eyes betrayed a suffering advanced beyond her years. But he was too busy undressing, a procedure which resembled that of lowering the mainsail on a ship.

She was grateful for the dark, even though his naked flesh seemed fluorescent, and she shut her eyes as she waited for the inevitable.

Hood lay on her, almost crushing her bones with his brute weight. Unlike the numerous predecessors who had been too scared to do anything but await the blow with patience, Anna Maria felt that the process should be speeded up a little, and she gave Hood's organ a tiny tug. To her amazement she found herself shaking hands with a detached, fleshy, penis-shaped rubber prosthesis.

'You bitch. Now see what you've done.'

Anna Maria screamed and pushed him off her body. She rushed to switch on the light. Hood roared with anger and began to chase her. She hurled the rubber penis at his head. He tried to shield his skull with his hands, but this left his organ bare. Anna Maria could hardly believe her eyes. She stared at the iron object in front of her with horror. It was an artificial penis mysteriously attached to his body. It suddenly became clear that the rubber object was a sheath designed to make his victims feel it was the real thing, and she had pulled it off by accident.

It was her laughter which drove Hood crazy that Christmas Eve. She could not bring herself under control. He kicked her, but she was too far gone to care.

'You ugly old pig. Why don't you get an iron mask for your face as well?'

This provoked her to further paroxysms, while Hood went red in the face and dropped on to the sofa. He began to breathe heavily. This finally sobered her up. Then she heard him give a horrible choking sound and she sighed with relief. There could be no doubt. The man with the iron penis had expired. Anna Maria rushed to the telephone.

Within fifteen minutes Laura Shaw and her twin sister Myra were in the apartment. Panic-stricken Hoodlums had called them to the scene. Anna Maria hurriedly stuffed the Spanish edition of the path-breaking pamphlet, *The Myth of Vaginal Orgasm* by Ann Koedt, into her bag and told them what had happened, without missing a single detail, except for the laughter which had finally dispatched Hood. The twins wept without restraint as they looked down on the naked body of their dead leader. Then Laura ushered Anna Maria out of the flat.

'Remember, you weren't here. We can't have our enemies broadcasting this. So forget everything. You have a big future ahead of you.'

Laura Shaw was, by any standards, a striking woman. Her black hair was only now beginning to turn slightly grey. She was well-built and ample-bosomed, but not as fat as her two Italian rivals, and she radiated authority both on and off the stage. Myra, by contrast, though identical in appearance, was far more restrained and less extrovert. Her talents were those of a producer and librettist. She managed Laura and Laura managed the world. Both were in their early fifties. Laura's renown as a soprano had won her universal acclaim, and she had set up her own Flushpit Opera Inc., which now acted on behalf of four top operatic singers and a few hundred aspiring stars. Anna Maria belonged to the latter category. Within the Hoodlum organization, Hood had used Laura as the public face of the group, but relied far more on Myra's organizational skills. Apart from her other qualities, what Frankie prized in her was her indefatigability as a raiser of funds.

The sisters had by now recomposed themselves completely. There was no trace of the tears. They looked at each other.

'He must be embalmed. I will not have Frankie cremated or put under the ground.'

Laura had spoken. Myra pursed her lips and then bit the lower one, suggesting disagreement.

'Darling, there's got to be a funeral. It's a political necessity! And there can't be a funeral without a body.'

'Why ever not?'

'What . . . ?'

'You're the organizer, Myra. Make the arrangements. We'll have a funeral. We'll bury the coffin. I will sing Fauré's "Requiem" and then the "Internationale". You will make the funeral oration. A few more songs, a wake in Hampstead, and then goodbye. It's simple. Just get on with it.'

Myra was puzzled.

'But what on earth are you planning to do with the body?'

'I'm taking it to our villa in Siena. It will remain embalmed as long as I live.'

'But Laura . . .'

'I'm fed up with your vacillations. After all that Frankie's done for us. I mean, he made us what we are. Do you think I'd ever have been satisfied with just singing? Ghastly thought, my dear. It's the combination, don't you see? Mozart and Marx. Engels and Puccini. Beethoven and Lenin. Trotsky and Verdi! Therein lies the magic to change the world.'

'What about Stalin and Wagner?'

'Shame on you, Myra Shaw,' Laura cried and then laughed the deep-throated infectious laugh that had made so many tenors swoon and become her slaves for life.

Frank Hood's funeral took place on the first day of the last decade of the century. Rival groups of ex-Hoodlums had assembled outside the cemetery. There had been several splits in the Hoodlum ranks during the preceding decades, but many former members had decided to pay their respects to the dead man who had played a vital part in their politico-psychological formation. Myra had foreseen this possibility, and the Flushpit Opera Inc. had hired special guards to keep out the other factions. There was a fist-fight and a great deal of abuse, in the course of which a middle-aged nun was trampled and badly injured. She was Frank Hood's only child, who had come all the way from a nunnery outside Cork to pay her last respects. In the event she was taken to hospital and put under intensive care. Apart from these small hiccups, the funeral proved a success. The sound of Laura singing was a moving experience – all the Hoodlums present were agreed on that fact. Why it even silenced the barbarians who had not been allowed beyond the cemetery gates.

And Frank Hood? Where was his body? It had been embalmed overnight by two dedicated Hoodlum embalmers who had been sworn to secrecy. Laura was no believer in oaths, and it did cross her mind that the mean duration of Hoodlum loyalty had once been computed at six months, whereas stone-dead hath no fellow, but Myra insisted that this was too operatic a solution. The body was then taken to the Shaw mansion in Highgate. In the box-room there was a beautiful old carved-oak chest, which contained Laura's many costumes and accompanied her on her tours throughout the world. In it now there also lay the founding father of the World Hoodlum Tendency.

3

How different sets of initials in the USA responded to the letter from France

When Emma Carpenter came down from her New York apartment on that freezing cold January morning, the last thing she expected was Ezra's letter. It was the second day of the new year. Despite her fifty-six years she was, as she reminded herself every morning, extremely well-preserved. She had given up smoking a few weeks after her trial and expulsion from PISPAW (Proletarian International Socialist Party of American Workers), and she had never felt better. Her son, who had turned thirty-one last month, often told her that she looked younger than she had done ten years ago. Suddenly Emma felt like writing a poem. Perhaps it was the sight of Ezra's scrawl which revived old memories. Perhaps her subconscious wanted to expel something permanently from her brain. She grabbed her fountain pen, only used for scribbling poems, and removed the thick leather-bound book from the bottom drawer of her writing desk. The whole poem never entered her head. Just the first few lines. Then the rest poured out onto the paper, but never via a typewriter. Emma began to write. The complete poem puzzled her. She read it aloud to check the rhythm.

Friends and lovers,
Can the fractured sickle mend laminated hearts
of popcorn queens?
The answer found by other time travellers
who trudge over raisins and germs
Swim through fields of Indian corn
fly along currents of lead vapour
All hooked on journey's end like eels
find the destination is here
and sit down and smoke another joint.

Strange how much it reminded her of an acid trip in the south of France over twenty years ago. Meaningless, empty, and yet . . . She remembered trying to concentrate on the visual, sensual aspects, but failing miserably. Instead, all the people around her had become fainter and fainter and she had started quietly journeying inwards. She remembered swimming through a corn field. A man had approached her and smiled.

'Are you a gypsy princess?'

Emma was shocked.

'How dare you, Monsieur? Don't you know who I am? I'm Mother Courage!'

It must be Ezra's letter triggering off these tiny explosions in her head. How vacuous it all sounded now. She immediately changed course.

Earlier in the week Emma had asked herself whether this last decade of her century would change her life in any way, but now as she collected her mail, her mind, if anything, was concentrated on the maintenance payment from her husband, Sid, which was already two months late. Emma felt that this was a bad sign. Sid should have risen to the occasion and ensured that she did not have to begin this decade in debt. She recognized Ezra's scrawl at once. What could the old buzzard want after all this time? Emma had not spoken to or heard from him or anyone else in the movement for nearly ten years.

Ever since she had been witch-hunted out of PISPAW on charges of 'breaching proletarian morality', 'collaborating with the state' and 'betraying internationalism', she had felt rather isolated. One of the main prosecution witnesses was her former husband Sid, who had told the PISPAW Control Commission, a body modelled on the pattern of the Soviet judiciary as it existed during the late Thirties, of her numerous love affairs with 'non-comrades' and 'comrades hostile to the PISPAW leadership'. PISPAW was the American section of the world movement and should not be confused with many other groups of initials prevented by reactionary legislation in the States from affiliating to international bodies. Emma had, accordingly, appealed to the highest authority of the movement, its World Congress, to reinstate her as a member and to censure PISPAW for its appalling and unreconstructed Stalinist methods. But the Cuckoo, who secretly admired PISPAW's tough organizational methods and was engaged in behind-the-scenes negotiations with PISPAW Führer Jim Noble, had persuaded Ezra that Emma was unstable, neurotic, subject to persecution mania, and therefore not worth the fight.

All this was untrue, of course, but Cuckoo applied a watchmaker's skill to manufacturing falsehoods. Emma had dispatched hundreds of letters to Europe pleading for help. Few, very few, comrades had bothered to reply. PISPAW did not like horizontal contact between the European and American members of the movement. They had made a big fuss about the 'Polonsky Letter'.

John Polonsky was a former PISPAW member who had left them, moved to Europe and joined the PSR in France. One of his letters to a PISPAW dissident in LA describing various anti-PISPAW manoeuvres in the French PSR had been 'discovered' when an élite corps of PISPAW gangsters had raided the dissident's apartment after making sure that he was carrying out a PISPAW assignment to sell at least fifty copies of the party organ outside the lobby of the Beverly Wilshire. The 'Polonsky Letter' had been utilized to create an anti-European hysteria inside

PISPAW, and this had led to an expulsion of most of the hundred and fifty odd dissidents in the organization.

As a result fewer letters left Europe for America. A few did so, nonetheless, and one in particular had informed Emma of the things being said about her, including the allegation that she needed psychiatric treatment. Small-time apparatchiks in insignificant sects knew exactly what to learn from their role-models who actually ran states. Emma had replied to the solitary letter from Amsterdam:

Your letter, of course, confirmed what I already knew. The additional information about my 'sanity' gave me a good laugh, since clearly they were trying to drive me mad and had failed miserably. In fact I think sometimes that it drove them mad that I didn't go mad. But after all, Joost, it isn't as though I was put out of the Sandinista Army two days before they took power. I'm not exactly missing the taking of power by that wonderful democratic vanguard of the vanguard, the PISPAW. In fact, I believe that half their workers are laid off and are in hiding pretending that they are still on the assembly line.

I am dismayed by the gutlessness of the Paris Centre, but then the reaction to the expulsion of three hundred dissidents a few years ago, a much larger victimization, was equally chickenshit, so I certainly couldn't expect them to put on their Superman capes for one very energetic but slightly ageing woman! I asked Ezra on the phone the other day when they would do something about PISPAW's bureaucratic practices and he said 'Soon.' I laughed like Snoopy. Soon? Like the radicalization in the US when PISPAW called the student movements of 1968–70, the '1905' of the American Revolution?

By the way, tell Ezra that PISPAW has now banned breast-feeding at branch meetings! They say it's 'anti-proletarian' and 'puts off new worker-recruits'. Puts off? I thought it would turn them on! You know, Joost, there is something sick about these guys. They expel anyone who tries

*to organize against their political line. Then because we've been
expelled we're attacked for being dilettantes and
petty-bourgeois rabble and hostile to Leninism and you name it,
we are it. The tragedy is that the Cuckoo really wants to be like
them, but on his own political line. Where will it all end,
Comrade?*

But this had been the last literary exchange with a comrade in
Europe. So Emma had done the next best thing. She picketed
every PISPAW meeting to publicize her plight and sell her
provocatively titled pamphlet, *How to Organize a Show-Trial:
the Case of Emma Carpenter versus PISPAW*. Despite being
abused, spat on and, on one occasion in Detroit, shoved to the
ground by a very raw new PISPAW recruit (Emma had stood up
and kicked him in the balls), she had gained some adherents.

Within a year she had over a hundred supporters on both
coasts, concentrated, it must be said, in New York and the Bay
Area. They called themselves the Committee for Socialist Democracy (CSD), but became known within the movement, by friends
and enemies, as the Carpenterites. At first Emma had wished that
it had been her maiden name, but then she began to relish the
irony. Carpenter was Sid's family name. Sid was a PISPAW
full-timer, a paid hack, a cadre-killer. He specialized in wiping
out dissenters inside the organization, prided himself on keeping
the party clean, pure, and unaffected by any awkward questions
posed by the real world, and the fact that the one group in the
entire country which plagued PISPAW and whose members got
up and asked awkward questions about internal democracy, etc.,
was known as the Carpenterites drove Sid absolutely crazy. He
even offered Emma money to change her name, but it was a
characteristically mean offer which she could and did refuse. And
the name stuck.

Ezra's letter was correctly addressed: 'Ms Emma Carpenter,
General Secretary, Committee for Socialist Democracy'. Emma
sipped her first cup of coffee and smiled. And why not? She would
go to Europe and hear what they all had to say. Then she would

tell them a few things. She would meet a few old friends and come back. She looked at the letter again. No mention was made of fares. PISPAW had all the money in the world. They never needed aid. The Centre knew that the other groups in the States, and there were at least seven, would have to be subsidized.

She would give Ezra a ring from work later in the day. It would be nice, despite everything, to hear the old, familiar voice. Ezra's English, spoken in heavy Continental accents, always reminded Emma of her own Jewish grandparents, who had migrated from Tsarist Russia between the revolutions of 1905 and 1917. They had both belonged to the left wing of the Mensheviks and, though they had regretted not being in Petrograd in October 1917, the feeling had not lasted more than a few years. Both had died natural deaths, at home in bed, while in their eighties. Emma had often argued with them, sometimes ferociously, but her father, apolitical and loving, always insisted on a truce. She shivered at the memory of how, during her PISPAW trial, some hack had said: 'Menshevism runs in her blood.'

Grandfather Moshe always used to tell her: 'You wait and see. In the end they'll be toppled by the people. The whole bloody lot of them. States can't float permanently on seas of blood. Sooner or later there will be a storm. One day, my little Emmushka, you will learn that the much-maligned Mensheviks were not so wrong when they warned against the Bolshevik adventure.' Emma used to provoke him, point to the rubbish can in the corner of the kitchen and say: 'Grandad, that's where the Mensheviks went. Straight into the dustbin of history.' Then old Moshe would lose his temper, curse Lenin as an 'amoral adventurer', denounce Trotsky as a 'ruthless fanatic' and insist that taken individual by individual, the Menshevik leaders were far better human beings than their Bolshevik counterparts. 'Can you even compare Martov to Zinoviev?' he would shout, and before Emma could reply, her father would gently remove her from the room. That would temporarily end one skirmish in the ongoing battle between Bolshevism and Menshevism, which took place in quite a few kitchens in different cities of the United States.

Emma had thought constantly about her grandfather through-out the last six months. The total collapse of Stalinism in the wake of Gorbachev's bombshells had stunned and excited her. She had been euphoric when Solidarity won the elections in Poland; thrown a party to celebrate the fall of East Berlin; wept when Dubcek appeared in public once again in Prague; cheered the insurrection in Romania. It was during these epochal changes that she had contacted the rest of the Committee for Socialist Democracy and, via a computer conference, they had agreed to disband themselves as an organization. Emma just didn't care any more about the punks in PISPAW or revenging herself or anything that smelt of the past. The old politics was dead and the music of the future was being played in the cities of Central and Eastern Europe. And that would change everything. She only wished that her grandfather were still alive, cursing herself for not having learnt more from him while he was still around.

And yet she wanted to shout a last hurrah. She wanted to see the faces of her tormentors, and of their friends, the apparatchiks who stood passively by while she was victimized. That's why, even though the CSD had been dissolved, she would allow herself this one last jaunt down memory lane. Who knows, someone might even turn up with a few new ideas.

She rang to pass on news of the Congress to her friends in the Bay Area who produced a not-too-bad, sane, Marxist monthly with the imaginative title of *Against the Stream*. She spoke to Ted Spanner, who knew about the Congress and had already accepted the invitation. Ted was a great guy. He had been a Shachtmanite for a long, long, time. Even when Emma had run into him while she was selling the PISPAW rag outside SDS conferences, he had always been friendly. He was over six foot tall, of Central European Jewish origins, and always wore jeans and cowboy boots. Even now, though he was a senior academic, his boots still turned on every foot-fetishist on campus, just as they had twenty years ago.

Emma wondered how a guy like that could not bring himself to accept that the Soviet Union was a degenerated workers' state and could carry on insisting that it was bureaucratic-collectivist, a totally new social formation suspended between capitalism and socialism which existed nowhere else on this planet. But believe it he did, and they had argued the merits of their respective theses for twenty years. That long? Yes, it had been a long time. A lot of water and bad blood had flowed underneath the old arch of history. And now history itself, as if angered by the Fifty Year War between Trotskyist sects, was preparing to solve the 'Russian question' in a fashion which none of the sects had thought of as a serious possibility.

History was on the run again, and in its own irrefutable fashion it was putting many of the old theoreticians of the movement to shame. Ted now had his own Institute in Berkeley, which she jokingly referred to as the 'Spanner Institute for the Study of Edward E. Spanner Thought' and where many of the old Fifties theoreticians of the movement, now distinguished academics, were invited to lecture together with the new post-modernist, post-Marxist and post-political specimens of the Eighties. Ezra had spoken at the Spanner Institute on a number of occasions. Relations between Ted and Ezra were friendly. So of course, Ted would go to the Congress. They agreed to go together and she was relieved. A sane travelling companion was vital when entering a tiny world from one's past. And they could both giggle together at the death-agony of the dinosaurs. Even though Ted himself was a member of the dinosaur family, he was more prepared for evolution than the others. And that, as Emma knew only too well, made an enormous difference on a social level.

A twenty-minute walk from Emma's mid-Manhattan apartment was the PISPAW building, the headquarters of the oldest Trotskyist group in the world. On the top floor was the office of the General Secretary. It was not opulently furnished, with the exception of the antique desk shipped over from a sale of *belle époque* Russian furniture in Finland. A Finnish consortium had won the contract to refurbish, reorganize and run the old Hotel Savoy in Moscow. They had suggested that the old furniture be thrown into the bargain, and some philistine apparatchik in Moscow had laughed and agreed. The sale of the furniture alone had netted the Finns over two million dollars.

The PISPAW general secretary, Jim Noble, had been besotted by an amazingly crafted nineteenth-century desk which bore the imprint of the master-carpenter from Kiev, Marco Kravchenko. He became involved in a foolish bout of bidding with the local stringer for the *New York Times*. Noble won, but at a cost. Kravchenko's wood sculpture was exquisite, but the bid had reached seventeen thousand dollars. The PISPAW credit card had come in handy. It was, after all, a good investment for the party.

At this desk there sat a man in his early fifties. Jim Noble was dressed in a smart suit and tie. See him on the street and he would appear the perfect WASP American, a business executive who ran the Manhattan section of the Mafia or a United Nations employee or even a middle-grade bureaucrat in the State Department. His hair was closely cropped. His body could have been that of a lean West Coast millionaire. The PISPAW general secretary was very finely tuned. He played tennis or swam every day. On the days that he missed out on both these exertions, his long-suffering companion bore the brunt of his heave-to's in bed at night as he pretended to make love whereas, in reality, he was only completing his daily aerobics programme.

Noble was pacing up and down in his room. He was in a foul mood. Everything had been going wrong lately. Only the previous week, three PISPAW members who were all due for pretty big inheritances when they reached twenty-one had resigned and left the organization. His companion, Louise-Carol Sands, slightly younger, bespectacled, with short grey ringlets and dressed in her usual red woollen track-suit, was sitting on the desk making sympathetic noises. Louise-Carol had long experience in handling strong and powerful men. Her mother had died during childbirth, and while in her teens she had acted as official hostess to her father, a distinguished and hawkish Pentagon General, who had never married again. The domestic calm was shattered only when the Defense Intelligence Agency informed General Sands that his daughter was a 'peacenik' and had joined PISPAW. He wept in anguish, but relations were broken off. General Sands wanted to bomb the Vietnamese back into the Stone Age. His lover, a thirty-three-year-old pilot, had been shot down while bombing Hanoi, and Sands never forgave the Vietnamese. The tragedy had won the General a great deal of sympathy, and only the previous year the cult Hollywood director, Daniel Dodge Patroller, had made a movie, *Forgiveness*, loosely based on Sands' affair with the pilot. PISPAW picketed the Oscar awards ceremony, and Louise-Carol was seen on every network that night.

There could be no doubt about it. The letter from France had created a real panic in the PISPAW command centre. Jim Noble was taken totally by surprise. He read the letter several times, studied every nuance and suspected that something was afoot. His first thought was that this was a gigantic Einsteinian manoeuvre to expel PISPAW from the world movement, and he determined then and there to sabotage the Congress in every way possible. He saw Louise-Carol smile. She always smiled in that stupid way when she was nervous, and even after twenty-five years it still drove Jim mad.

'Well, Louise-Carol, what do you know?' he shouted. 'What do you fucking know? Tell me? Come on, tell me.'

Louise-Carol did not speak, but grabbed the corner of the desk and pressed her behind on it with such force that it hurt. The smile disappeared. She blushed and perspired. A sweat-drop wormed its way downwards before she could wipe her face and was trapped by the tiny, almost invisible hairs above her lip.

'Er, Jim, I think you should calm down. As it is you're turning grey before your time. I just don't understand why you're so worried.'

'Fuck you . . . !'

He turned his back on her. She of all people should have known that he had good reason to be worried. The fact was that PISPAW's antics had become a general embarrassment to the

Trotskyist movement. The latest in a series of sharp and inexplicable about-turns had been Noble's new-found passion for Fidel
Castro. In the Sixties, when the rest of the radical milieu in
Europe and America was fellow-travelling with the Cuban Revolution, Noble and his gang had denounced everyone else as
'petty-bourgeois revisionists'. Then when most radicals had
taken their distance from the Bearded One after he had supported
the Soviet invasion of Czechoslovakia and become a virtual
Brezhnevite, Noble began to have second thoughts, though he
did not share these with anyone, not even with the ever-loyal
Louise-Carol, nor with his unquestioning comrade-in-arms, the
gaunt and congenitally oppressed manic depressive, Jim Flock,
who secretly loathed Noble, but who had his eye on the
Kravchenko desk as well as Louise-Carol.

Noble had waited. That was one thing he knew how to do.
Patience was his only virtue. He had risen within the organization
from the PISPAW youth groups. He had certain organizational
talents, and it became known that Jim Noble could get things
done. Within four, or perhaps it was five, years he had become the
PISPAW general secretary. Slowly he had weeded out the old-
timers, scarred veterans of the class war in late Twenties and
Thirties America.

The old boys from Flint and Minneapolis had been formed by
the trade-union struggles of the Thirties, and their PISPAW had
been built in that particular mould. The old regime was characterized by a bureaucratic pluralism which was unsatisfactory, but
benevolent. Noble's young Turks had no time for sentimentality.
They divided people into two categories, hard and soft, and they
set about slowly destroying the links with the past and rewriting
PISPAW's history. They began to build their 'Leninist vanguard
party' on the pattern of pre-1934 Stalinism. Noble's distrust of
intellectuals, his constant ideological zigzagging, could go on
forever now that he had won his final victory and every member
of the PISPAW Politburo was either a crony or had slept with
him.

In the Eighties PISPAW had shrunk from two thousand to six

hundred members, but the size of the apparatus remained inflated. A hundred people worked in a full-time capacity for PISPAW and its various front organizations. This meant one full-timer for every six members, a record with which few social-democratic parties in the world, with their hundreds of thousands of members could compete. If one took into consideration that of these six hundred members, at least one hundred and fifty were FBI agents, then the proportion of apparatchiks to rank-and-file members became even more grotesque.

Whereas US and allied intelligence agencies infiltrate armed-struggle organizations by providing people who are expert in the use of weapons and who, for that reason, are rarely turned down by the guerrilla groups, the priorities for placing informers inside the sects are different. In fact the more monolithic a sect, the more authoritarian its regime, the more worshipped its supreme leader, the easier it is for an operative to enter and work his or her way up to the top. All she or he has to do is to work hard, pay generous financial dues, and inform on dissidents and anti-leadership elements, and promotion is not long delayed. The behavioural pattern of rising inside the FBI or a sect like PISPAW was not dissimilar. The language and goals were, of course, polar opposites, but the methods of organization shared a great deal in common.

Whatever else Noble was – and speculation in this field had virtually become a cottage industry on the Left – he was not an absolute fool. He had realized, after years of serious thinking on the question, that the chance of PISPAW seizing state power in the United States was remote. In fact the possibility was so remote that there was a real danger that the membership might soon realize this and decamp, as memberships had been doing for nearly fifty years. What made the situation very serious was that the overturns in Eastern Europe might finally bury the notion of a vanguard Leninist party on the Noble model. What if the membership deserted collectively, leaving the PISPAW headquarters looking like the *Marie-Celeste*? It goes without saying that the turnover rate was very high.

Noble decided that the best way to defuse the situation was through humour. At party congresses, which were modelled on gatherings of the now extinct Stalinist parties as well as the PR techniques of the Republicans, he would, in the middle of a peroration, break into a joke.

'Of course, as comrades no doubt realize, it's going to take a long time to put me in the White House, Louise-Carol in the Pentagon and Jim Flock in the doghouse . . .'

The first time nobody laughed. The second time, Noble paused, removed the cigar from his top pocket, sniffed it and then smiled at the comrades. Alerted by this display of slapstick they roared obediently. In this way the message that the leadership had given up on its medium-term plans to install the dictatorship over the proletariat in the United States began to percolate down to the members. It depressed them greatly, and many of them began to wonder if there was any point in staying inside PISPAW. After all, some of them reasoned, if they could not win state power in the foreseeable future, why not return to an everyday bourgeois existence, use their skills inside the Democratic Party and link up with the supporters of the Reverend Jesse Jackson?

The leadership had foreseen this development. Noble had discussed this very danger in bed with Louise-Carol on several occasions. In fact that was about the only thing they did in bed these days. Louise-Carol it was who had come up with the brainwave, which she felt could revive PISPAW's drooping virility. The key task in the United States was no longer seizing power, but merely keeping the PISPAW apparatus well oiled in order to prevent US military adventures abroad. Cuba was under threat. Therefore PISPAW had to back Cuba. Plucky little Albania had defied all the superpowers. So PISPAW had to set up special pro-Albanian solidarity groups. In other words, PISPAW was to transform itself into a revolutionary travel organization and take members on regular jaunts to Havana and Tirana. Both capitals had banned the subversive Soviet paper *Moscow News*, and there was no danger of the dreadful disease spreading back into the party. Noble loathed Gorbachev, who was the butt of constant attacks in the PISPAW press. Simultaneously everything Fidel did was defended uncritically. When the Cuban General Ochoa was executed for his involvement in the Colombian drug trade, the PISPAW leaders defended the act.

At the same time Noble refused to part company with the old-world movement and the Paris Centre. He found that there was a lot of resistance within the party to breaking all links with Ezra and that crowd in Europe. The Carpenterites used to say that the only reason for this anomaly was that the FBI cadres now had a majority inside the party and they wanted to preserve the links, since they thought it was a major source of information about subversives in Europe and Latin America. This was such a preposterous slander that Noble had decided, uncharacteristically, to ignore it, and had barely thought about it till he had received Ezra's letter. In it, Ezra listed all the organizations he had invited from the United States. When he saw that this included the Carpenterites, Noble went berserk. He decided to ring an old friend in Lausanne, and Louise-Carol got the Cuckoo on the phone for him. Noble's face was slightly flushed as he took the receiver from her.

'Happy New Year, Jean-Michel. What the fuck is Ezra up to? He's invited that cocksucker Carpenter to Paris. She hasn't even got an organization any more. You know who she's screwing at the moment, don't you? A Cuban defector! Some jack-off artist who writes poetry. What sort of Congress is this anyway? I don't believe you. I know you're stuck in Lausanne, but that was all part of the deal wasn't it? What's the old motherfucker up to? He hasn't thrown in his lot with the capitalist-roaders in Moscow, has he? This is no time for impressionism. The whole Socialist project is under attack and this gathering is badly needed, but only if real decisions are made. I'm not coming to a fucking talk-shop. Come on Jean-Michel, don't play with me. You know all the dickheads in the Paris secretariat. Just find out and give me a ring? What? Of course I'm fucking coming! Are you? Good. One more thing. I don't believe that Einstein hasn't got a document ready. Tell him to try that on someone else. I want a copy before I leave New York. You just tell him that, OK? See you soon. Ciao.'

Jim really liked the Cuckoo. He was wasted in the European organizations, a useless constellation of petty-bourgeois intellectuals, too squeamish to build anything and constantly complaining about the supposedly bad language used by the American Left. That annoyed Noble more than almost anything else. Swearing was part of the tradition, and he didn't care a fuck if Trotsky had denounced the use of bad langauge on the grounds that it was either the result of oppression or used deliberately to be oppressive. The fact was that the European Trotskyists in Ezra's movement were a bunch of weak, pampered, liberals. Too fucking soft. The very thought of them was enough to produce a set of infuriated and extravagant curses which poured uncontrollably from Noble's mouth. He hated them all. Everyone? All except the Cuckoo. Louise-Carol found Noble's fondness for the Cuckoo unbearable, but this had very little to do with politics. It was a case of plain and simple jealousy.

Exactly ten years ago Noble had decided on a master-plan to 'proletarianize' or, to call things by their proper name, PISPAWize the movement in Europe. He was fed up with just being the leader of a North American sect. He wanted to be the King of the Sects, and on a world scale. That meant removing Ezra from the scene. Ezra's strength derived from his ideas, and his capacity to marshal them into books which were then published in dozens of languages. Noble hated all these books and he hated the fact that Ezra's reputation in the States was much, much higher than that of any figure directly associated with PISPAW. So in order to dump Ezra and capture the leadership on a world level, it was first necessary to discredit the relative autonomy which ideas possess in relation to the day-to-day necessities of the class struggle. This became a PISPAW obsession, and like all obsessions it had a very unhealthy side to it: a campaign to get rid of the riff-raff and rootless cosmopolitans from the ranks of the movement. Guilt would soon engulf many innocents in these organizations, and guilt was what Noble and his crew were banking on.

It was a crazy plan, and what was even crazier was the timing. The start of the Thatcher–Reagan period was simply the worst possible moment to embark on such an adventure. Cuckoo had announced the 'proletarianization proposals' to a packed meeting of cadres and declared this to be the way forward to the final victory of Socialism. At the end of his speech his mistress, Julia Richelieu, a tall, languid beauty who claimed to be directly descended from the seventeenth-century cardinal bearing the same name, had stood up to encourage a standing ovation from the seventy-five people present. Hysteria became the order of the day. Naturally neither Cuckoo, nor Noble, nor their mistresses and close cronies made the 'turn to industry'.

Ezra had reluctantly gone along with the tactic, but had been marginalized, since his own role was somewhat superfluous. It was hardly a surprise that the whole plan backfired badly. The sects were drastically reduced in size. The entire organization in Luxembourg was wiped out in an industrial accident. This was followed by at least six suicides in North America and a sharp decline in the limited political influence any of the groups might have had in Europe. The few genuine workers left the sects in disgust.

The only thing that survived, apart from the reams of paper where the 'colonization' of the factories had been discussed in minute detail, was the friendship between Nobel and Cuckoo. Indeed both Julia Richelieu and Louise-Carol agreed that there was more to the attachment than was visible to the naked eye, but since most of the comrades always averted their gaze at the sight of these two monsters enjoying a joke at Ezra's expense or humiliating an oppositionist or eyeing some unfortunate woman comrade, very few knew what this remark actually meant. That they were both voyeurs was, of course, well known to their intimates. But orifice-explorers? No proof ever emerged, but then not all the FBI documents had yet been released under the Freedom of Information Act. Cuckoo had not been able to tell

Noble what Ezra was planning because he simply did not know.

That night Noble had an unusual dream, the first time he'd had a dry dream in years. He was reading Cervantes' classic on the edge of a beach, and he was reading it in Spanish. Simultaneously he was massaging a large, hairy, naked body lying on its front. The strange thing was that it seemed as if he did this every day. Read *Don Quixote* and massaged the big man at the same time and on the same spot every afternoon. Suddenly the man turned. Noble couldn't believe his luck. He immediately went into an orgasmic mode and nearly fainted. It was Fidel, who asked him whether he was going to the emergency Congress in Paris. Noble nodded, upon which the Great and Beloved Leader of the Cuban People spoke the following words: 'Make sure that both enemies are identified clearly. We are now facing a war on two fronts and you, my dear Yanqui comrade, have a heavy responsibility. Marxism-Leninism or Death!' No more was said. The dream ended with Fidel standing up and putting on his bathrobe, but not before Noble had caught sight of the region where the revolutionary penis should have been positioned. Instead he had seen his own face.

The sight of his own miniaturized self, standing permanently to attention between the great man's thighs, woke Noble up. He was very excited and shook Louise-Carol awake. Then he described the dream to her in minute detail. She applauded wildly.

'It's fantastic Jim! Don't you see? Thanks to you PISPAW has become a decisive weapon in the armoury of the Cuban Revolution. Surely you can see that. I know it's unorthodox, but given their machismo you had the place of honour.'

Louise-Carol had somehow managed to confuse a dream-sequence with reality. She was deeply moved and she sat up in bed, hugging her knees and staring in a half-lost sort of way at Jim's face, which she now began to visualize as a very special section of her Cuban hero's anatomy. Silently, she cast off her faded green nightdress and parked the most intimate part of her body on her companion's face. This stopped Jim's chatter, but his tongue continued to wag silently and spasmodically, which pleased her greatly. Her ears had badly needed a rest. Louise-Carol's sparkling eyes never left the wall above the headboard. It was an old poster, marking a time when the Great Man had been twenty years younger and saucier, and the cigar in his mouth was positively suggestive as everything slowly blended into the only orgasm that Louise-Carol had ever experienced during her long life together with the PISPAW stallion.

4

Ezra shares a confidence with the Cuckoo

A week had passed since Ezra's letter had been posted and already he was besieged with telephone calls, telexes and fax messages. He now felt that he had to prepare some preliminary theses on the present situation. Should he take the risk of a long, private discussion with the Cuckoo? He decided against it for the moment. Best to discuss it first with the Triplets on the French Politburo.

He returned to his breakfast and picked up his copy of *Die Zeit*, which he regarded as the most sophisticated bourgeois paper in the world, much cleverer than *Le Monde* and the *Financial Times*. He had a fixed routine, and it was the German paper over breakfast, the English during lunch and the French after supper. He suddenly began to giggle, nod his head vigorously and talk to himself. Maya never got up before eleven and he had got used to a lonely breakfast. Just then the phone rang. He lifted the receiver as he gulped down the dregs of his decaffeinated coffee. The person at the other end, who happened to be the Cuckoo, had barely muttered 'hello' before Ezra blasted off.

'Bonjour Jean-Michel. Have you seen *Die Zeit* this morning? Go out and buy a copy immediately! It's incredible! They have reprinted the *Der Spiegel* Opinion Poll in East Germany, but with *all* the details. It's incredible! It's the most comprehensive poll ever conducted anywhere and do you know the results? Seventy-five per cent of the population – did you hear that, seventy-five per cent – are opposed to reunification with the Federal Republic. It proves what I've been writing for twenty years before the Wall came down. East Germany has a social identity, which supersedes its national identity! All the flags and consumer goods and battalions of youth sent in by the Christian democrats to swell the size of the pro-unification meetings have backfired in their face. And those foolish social-democrats are caught in their own vice. They collaborated with Honecker for years. But now they are falling in line behind Kohl and the German bourgeoisie. Why? Why? Because to back the new regime would mean showing the people in the West that it is possible to have a socialist or social democracy not based on capitalism. If Gysi and Modrow succeed, the SPD will face a rebellion from its ranks, I am one hundred per cent convinced of that, but German capitalism is the strongest in Europe. They will try and gobble up the poor DDR. That's why we must do everything in our power to encourage trade-union solidarity with the DDR. I've drafted an appeal for the Metal Workers Union. Listen. This is only a temporary phase. If no help reaches the DDR and its economy continues to collapse, then the West German bourgeoisie will march in and enter every crevice of this state. Can you do something in Switzerland?'

The Cuckoo was used to Ezra's monologues. He muttered his agreement, even though he knew that it was all wishful thinking, promised to do something for the DDR in Switzerland and then came straight to the point.

'Ezra, why have you called a Congress?'

'Why? Why? Isn't it obvious? The whole of Eastern Europe is going up in smoke. The situation inside the Soviet Union is critical. We stand on the edge of either huge defeats or unimaginable victories. The whole epoch is being reshaped, our world is being remade and you ask me why we've called a Congress. I'm worried about your health, Jean-Michel.'

'I'm fine. But I'm worried about what we can do at such a

Congress. You've called everyone. Could be a recipe for disaster. It's bad enough when it's just ourselves. Noble is very angry that Emma Carpenter has been invited. He told me . . .'

'To revert to Noble's language for a moment, I don't care a fuck what he thinks.'

'Ezra, Ezra. Can we talk? I'm in Paris for two days.'

'Good. Four, four-thirty this afternoon. My place. I want to discuss something very important with you.'

The Cuckoo was delighted at his easy victory. Ezra was pleased that the Swiss was in town. There were some things he couldn't talk about with anyone else. He must make sure that Maya was out when the Cuckoo came. Ezra could never understand why none of the women he had lived with over the last twenty-five years had liked the Cuckoo. All of them shared a similar assessment. They found him menacing, sadistic, hypocritical, mentally unbalanced and an extremely sinister influence on Ezra. Maya had met him twice and had reacted unfavourably. In her case it must have been pure instinct, since on both occasions Ezra had been present as well. She had said that there was something horrible in the way he looked at her. She was convinced that he was a rapist. (In this view she was not quite right. Maya was not very interested in the politics of the movement. If she had been she would have realized that the rapist side of the Cuckoo was amply fulfilled in the politico-organizational sphere. What he could not do to people, he did to tiny sects all over Europe.)

Ezra had met Maya after an exhilarating meeting in the Brazilian metropolis of São Paulo, which had the largest car-factories in the world and where he had shared a platform with the workers' leader and presidential candidate, Lula. The opinion polls were showing Lula neck-and-neck with the right-wing choice and the crowd was in an ebullient mood. Ezra had spoken in a mixture of Spanish and Portuguese and thrilled both Lula and the audience with his incredibly wide-ranging political culture. The meeting had been a mixed event, and a troupe of Brazilian balladeers had regaled the crowd with newly written songs. One of these singers was Maya's father, who at sixty-two was several years Ezra's junior.

Maya was entranced by Ezra's enthusiasm, his appalling Portuguese accent, his vicious, but completely unfunny, anti-bourgeois jokes and, surprisingly, his appearance. Even though it was a warm evening, Ezra was wearing his pre-war suit and tie, but that did not move her as much as the amazing red braces which were exposed to the São Paulo proletariat when he finally took off his jacket before answering questions. The braces were a collector's item. Maya, a talented flautist, was also a movie buff, and she recalled all those old Renoir films from the Thirties. Ezra could have walked straight out of them. She was overcome by an uncontrollable urge to unbutton the braces. She followed him around from meeting to meeting, till he began to notice her from the platform. Non-verbal communications were established.

The next time she bought one of his books and asked him to autograph it for her. A few words were exchanged on this occasion. One evening, in Rio, she told him he looked tired. He needed some fresh air. Ezra was touched and flattered. Maya's soft, black hair came down to her buttocks. She was dressed simply in faded denims and a Lula for President T-Shirt. Ezra couldn't believe that such a beautiful young thing could be interested in anything else but his intellect. On the walk she first held his hand, then, in the moonlight on a deserted corner of Copacabana Beach, she embraced and kissed him passionately on the mouth, her tongue desperately searching for the gold tooth she had seen at so many meetings. To say that Ezra was surprised would be an understatement. He suffered a mild cardiac arrest and fainted. When he regained consciousness some minutes later, he was horrified to find that she had undressed him and was gently massaging his body. All she was wearing were his braces, no longer suspended as was their wont, but resting gently on her totally delectable nipples. Maya had aroused him without too much difficulty, then mounted him and made love.

The very next day Ezra had proposed to her and she had accepted. Her friends, not to mention her lover, were totally shocked. They just saw Ezra as a plump old capon who was also a Trotskyist. Maya could never explain to them or anyone else, but she was incredibly happy. She grew to like most of Ezra's friends, preferring those who were not in the movement, but she stiffened perceptibly whenever the Cuckoo was in the vicinity. She confided to a Brazilian friend how sometimes she felt that the Cuckoo was the devil with whom Ezra had made a secret compact, but she could never understand what Ezra got out of it in return. Lovely, innocent, Maya. How was she to know that the world movement needed someone to keep its latrines disinfected? The Cuckoo was Ezra's choice for every dirty job that had to be done. Wasn't that how Lenin had used Stalin?

When the Cuckoo arrived promptly on Ezra's doorstep that afternoon, Maya had been dispatched to tea with Father Pedro Rossi, a brilliant young Brazilian whose illuminating theses on liberation theology had brought him into serious conflict with the Vatican, but won him a Professorship in Theology at Vincennes. In reality, the academic post was the result of an old coincidence. He had been a student in Paris together with Régis Debray in the early Sixties. Both had studied under Louis Althusser. Pedro had then returned to Brazil and engaged in some wildly adventurous activities, such as kidnapping the West German ambassador only to discover that he was a cultured social-democrat who knew more about Marx than his captors and who provided them with numerous quotations from the classics which showed the hostility of the founding fathers to terrorism. Debray, too, had left France first for Cuba and then Bolivia, where he had made his way to Che Guevara's doomed guerrilla band. He had been captured, tortured and imprisoned.

Rossi had left the group soon afterwards and moved towards the more radical sections of the Church. After his row with the Vatican, his old friend Debray, now back in France and close to the new centres of Socialist patronage, had helped him obtain the position he now occupied.

Pedro was not in the movement, so to speak, but was regarded as a close sympathizer. This was a much more intimate category than fellow-traveller, implying that there were important undisclosed reasons which made it impossible for him to become an active and public member of the movement. He was, however, a close personal friend of Ezra's. Through him, Maya kept in touch with Brazilian circles in Paris.

The Cuckoo saw her leaving and attempted to exchange greetings, but she looked through him, crossing first herself and then the road in order to avoid him. Ezra greeted the Cuckoo as a prodigal son and then unplugged the phone, a sure sign that he was intent on a serious discussion.

Some fifteen minutes' banter followed before Cuckoo posed the question. 'What was it that you wished to discuss with me?'

Ezra blushed, stood up, paced up and down, tightened his braces, removed his spectacles and then sighed and sat down. Cuckoo felt that the confession was about to proceed. Within seconds he would know what Ezra was up to in calling this emergency Congress.

After what seemed a long silence, Ezra spoke. 'Maya is pregnant, Jean-Michel. And, as a good Catholic, she insists on having the child.'

The Cuckoo was stunned.

'But . . . but this is ridiculous. Crazy. Must be stopped. It'll discredit our movement. Surely you see that it's totally irresponsible. It's not just your age, though that must be a consideration. It will distract you. Think of Lenin. He liked children, but iron discipline prevailed. What will people say? I can hear them already. "Ah, poor old Einstein. Couldn't make the revolution, so he started making babies instead." As a friend I have to be blunt. Don't you know how much time it will take away?'

Ezra shrugged.

'If she won't have an abortion, send her back to Brazil.'

'Jean-Michel, Jean-Michel,' Ezra said with a sigh. 'It's very simple. She wants the child and I want her.'

Ezra was displeased by the Cuckoo's response. They carried on talking about the pains and joys of fatherhood that awaited him. At one stage the Cuckoo attempted to divert the discussion.

'Ezra, there will be plenty of time to discuss senility and child-bearing. What I want to know is why in God's name you've convened an emergency Congress. There is consternation everywhere. Even the French are upset that it was done without any consultations. Why? What can it possibly achieve? The timing's wrong.'

Ezra compressed his lips and frowned as he stared hard at his protégé. Could this be the man he had trained to be his successor? All of Ezra's very worst mistakes had been the result of ignoring his instincts and letting the wish dictate the judgement. He saw the Cuckoo's weaknesses, but felt that they were outweighed by his organizational talents.

'You know something, Jean-Michel? I feel very happy these days. You think I've got soft and careless. You want me to be stern with myself. Disciplined. Send my lovely Maya back to Rio. She is like a dazzling flame which rises all the way to the sky. You want me to put this flame out, don't you? Douse it with cold water so it dwindles and dies. I will not do that. The flame will be reproduced and will blaze with even greater passion. You are a cold man, Jean-Michel. Too cold. You have begun to make even me shiver.'

The Cuckoo tried to retreat, but the damage was done. When he left, some hours later, he was still nowhere near uncovering the father-to-be's plans for the emergency Congress. The Cuckoo's trip had been a total failure.

Ezra reconnected the phone and slumped in his armchair. The Cuckoo wasn't altogether wrong, but he lacked humanity. This thought had crossed the old man's head for the first time today, and suddenly he began to see why Maya, and before her Marianne and before her Angela and before her Bala, had all taken against the psychologically disordered Cuckoo. Ezra smiled. He was pleased with himself. The surprise he was planning for the Congress was safe. Instinct had warned him against trusting the Cuckoo this time.

He did not disagree with everything that the Cuckoo had said regarding children. But the fact was that three-quarters of old

Ezra desperately wanted a child. He had not succumbed to the temptation in previous years because he felt that Lenin was more correct on this than Trotsky. Children were a luxury for revolutionaries. It is possible that had his parents allowed him a corgi, this desire to reproduce might have been circumvented, but all that was too late. Now he wanted simply to continue the Einstein line, and if there was anything in genetic fingerprinting, he thought, the baby could turn out to be extraordinary.

At this point the phone rang. He was late for a meeting.

5

The Triplets interrogate Ezra in the presence of old Renard

Even though Ezra was late he couldn't stop himself from entering a pâtisserie on the way and purchasing three choice specimens from the cream-cakes section. Eating one of them, he walked towards the bookshop of the PSR – Parti Socialiste Révolutionnaire, the French wing of the world movement. He was frowning as he entered the office where the Politburo met. The bookshop manageress had informed him that over the last fortnight they had only sold one copy of his latest book, *Le pari Gorbatchévien*.

In the old days the PSR had been the organization with the most *élan*. Its publications were invigorating, its intellectuals dominated the literary pages of *Le Monde*, its prestige was high in the lycées and polytechnics, and it even had a nest in one or two Renault plants. It was strongest, needless to say, amongst teachers, technicians, hospital workers, etc. At its height it had several thousand members and sympathizers. It was the jewel in the movement's crown, the icing on its cake and so forth. Now it was a sad echo of its own past. Only a hardcore remained to remind France of its revolutionary traditions. Many of the PSR's former members were now in the Socialist Party of Mitterrand and Rocard. Most of them were still well-disposed to some of the old ideas, but were busy searching for replacements.

Most, but not Kosminsky. He used to be the prettiest member of the Politburo during the May Events of 1968, and had been photographed in heroic pose on the barricades, with an attractive woman by his side, for *Paris-Match*. Even then, the PSR old-timers used to mutter, and not in a very friendly fashion: 'That Kosminsky. Wonder where he'll end up?'

Son of a Jewish tailor, who had shown foresight and migrated from Poland in the early Thirties, Pierre Kosminsky was always worried by his social background. His father had not bothered to restart a small business in Paris. Instead he had become a worker on the railways, a trade-union activist and a district-level leader of the French Communist Party. Even in the days when he was proudly proclaiming his proletarian antecedents in a debate with the Maoists at the Sorbonne, there was a faint air of regret in his eyes. The inevitable happened. He found an heiress, fell in love with her, and moved in to her apartment and out of the PSR.

And why not? What right had anyone to deprive him of true happiness? Why shouldn't he cross class boundaries if that was what he desired? These questions were not even posed. Kosminsky was denounced as a renegade, pure and simple. Not that he minded the label at all. It improved his standing in the circles which he now inhabited.

Latest reports indicated that Pierre, always an imaginative impresario, was now a permanent fixture in the ante-chamber of a rising leader of the government. Pierre's wife, the beautiful Michelle Kosminsky, *née* Vidal-Séverin, was a frequent visitor to the minister's bedchamber. This was, of course, simply to ensure that the gallant minister's stock kept on rising. One evening, during a dinner, the minister introduced Kosminsky to the bosses, the patrons whom his father had fought all his life. The minister was in an affable mood.

'This is my aide-de-camp, Pierre Kosminsky. You may remember him from the barricades. We were all there in those days, weren't we?'

Laughter followed and Pierre basked in the resulting

bonhomie. How civilized everything was these days. People he had regarded as the class enemy were generous, ready to forget and forgive, open to new ideas as to how to deal with working-class dissatisfaction and prevent strikes. Kosminsky was amazed to discover how generous and cultured they were, and how intelligent.

Later, in bed, he shuddered at the thought that he could ever have demanded workers' self-management. They could not run modern economies. The patrons were the embodiment of our civilization. He turned over to confess his adolescent naivety to Michelle, but, as usual, she wasn't there. The thought that, as he was lying there alone, his Michelle was busy with his ministerial boss, excited him. By the time Michelle returned, during the early hours of the morning, however, Pierre was fast asleep. He woke the next morning totally distracted from all matters connected with musical beds by Ezra's invitation to attend the Congress. Pierre was totally dumbfounded and, if the truth be told, a tiny bit flattered. Someone out there in the wilderness still cared. His own parents had died soon after the events of Sixty-Eight. Ezra had become the father-figure from whom he often sought advice on non-political matters. Till a few months ago, Pierre would ring Ezra just to hear his voice. What he did not realize was that Ezra had filled in his name and address out of habit. It wasn't a conscious choice, but an accident.

Kosminsky rang up his old friends at the PSR headquarters and accepted the invitation. The Triplets were livid. They felt that Ezra should have consulted them before taking such a major decision, and one which could compromise the entire organization.

The PSR leadership was large and unwieldy, but essentially three full-timers ran the show. They were male triplets, Paul, Jean and Simon, born to two Jewish doctors just before the Occupation. Their parents had joined the Communist resistance and the Triplets had been left at a farm, where they were brought up in a simple but friendly environment. They all developed different interests, but maintained the same politics. All three joined the Communist Party Youth at university. The Cuban Revolution and Guevara's internationalist pamphlets pushed them in the direction of the Trotskyists. There were two or three groups to choose from, but the Triplets found Ezra's circle to be the most intellectually stimulating.

Then during May Sixty-Eight all three helped build the PSR, which had grown from fifty-three members to three and later six thousand. For Ezra and his close comrades-in-arms, this was a gigantic leap forward. They had dreamt of the PSR replacing the French Communist Party, winning over the workers and preparing, after the dress-rehearsal of Sixty-Eight, for the real seizure of power. Things went a bit wrong in the late Seventies and Eighties. Noble and the Cuckoo hadn't helped much, and then the whole of France moved to the right and elected a Socialist government, simply in order to give the fascists a new lease of life.

Paul was a mathematician, Jean a chess grandmaster, Simon a chemist. It was well established that if any one of them had persisted in his profession he would have risen to the top. Jean had defeated every chess baron in non-competitive encounters, falling only to a sixteen-year-old Hungarian girl. Paul's thesis on Pythagoras was still a fixed textbook for the baccalaureate, and two of Simon's former colleagues had shared the Nobel Prize for Chemistry with some Russians a few years before.

The Triplets often thought of the different course each of their biographies might have taken, but they had no regrets. Paul ensured that the organization's finances were kept in order. Jean was a superb faction-fighter and had played a decisive role in defeating PISPAW's numerous attempts to take over the world movement. And as for Simon, he was a brilliant forger. Half the present government in Nicaragua had travelled back from Europe on his meticulously crafted passports. There had been only one major cock-up in Simon's career, and that was not his fault. In 1976 an Argentinian revolutionary, a veteran of the Junta's torture-rooms, was on his way to a meeting in Paris. Simon had provided him with a British passport on this occasion.

Unfortunately the plane crashed. Two British policemen who had turned up at the front door of the passport-holder's flat to express their condolences to his wife were shaken stiff to see the owner of the document staring them in the face. (He was a teacher in the East End of London and had voluntarily donated his passport to the movement in order to help Latin Americans fighting against the dictatorships backed and funded by the Pentagon.) He expressed surprise when asked for his passport at two a.m. in the morning, but kept his cool and pretended to go and search for the travel document before appearing again, perplexed, and reporting it gone. While he was having breakfast and reading about the air-crash, there was a knock on his door. It was Simon, who had flown over to warn him but had arrived five hours too late.

The Triplets had been discussing the situation in Eastern Europe. For once they were not in agreement. Simon, who knew Eastern Europe well, realized that the old game was up. Ezra's line of the impossibility of a restoration without fierce resistance by the workers seemed like a cruel joke. 'The reel of reformism cannot be run backwards,' he used to argue, suggesting thereby that since capitalism had been overthrown violently it could only be restored violently, since the working class would defend the system against any capitalist-roaders. Alas, history had disproved this thesis. Poland and Hungary, panting for restoration, had provided the unkindest rebuttal of all. Ezra had proclaimed Solidarity to be one of the purest examples of a self-confident and combative working class which would exercise class power in the purest sense of the phrase.

Simon argued for accepting reality and making a massive turn in the way the Far Left thought and functioned. He did not accept that the changes in the East were a ringing endorsement of neo-conservatism and the theories of Robert Nozick.

'What is happening is a social-democratization of the East. Their model is neither Bush nor Kohl. Austria and Sweden is what they think they want to be like. Anyway, whether we like it or not, the masses in the East are not moving towards us. Now, within a few years, this process could dramatically alter mass consciousness in the West with unforeseeable results. There won't be insurrections, but there will be turmoil. The signs are already present and if . . .'

'I don't agree. It's a flash in the pan. If capitalism is restored in Hungary, Poland or Romania, it won't be of the Scandinavian sort. More a Third World variety, with the military in a strong position and mass unemployment, with an end of all state subsidies. The workers, I'm afraid, will learn the hard way, through their own experience, which will be better for everyone.'

Jean was very angry. He hadn't heard of Nozick or John Rawls or any of these new-fangled names, and he did not wish to be enlightened. He was worried by the developments in Eastern Europe for one principal reason. They could demoralize the PSR cadres. The organization might haemorrhage. Therefore the basic theses enunciated by Trotsky in the founding document of the movement, *The Death Agony of Capitalism and the Tasks of the Fourth International*, known internally as 'The Transitional Programme', had to be defended till the end. There was much in there which had prefigured these developments. Trotsky had spoken of the hatred of the masses for the bureaucracy, of the necessity to drive the bureaucrats out of the soviets, of the desire of the people for revenge. Romania showed all these tendencies in motion. 'And how do you square that with the Peasant Party demanding the return of the monarchy?' mocked Simon. 'It might not happen, of course, but if it did what would be our *transitional* approach?'

The triplets were sitting in the gloomy inner sanctum of the PSR with a fourth much older man, Antoine Renard, who sat upright on his uncomfortable metal chair as they all waited for Ezra to finish reading the latest news from Romania in that day's *Libération*. Ezra folded the paper and put it down on the rickety wooden table between them.

'Ezra,' Renard began, 'tell us why you've called this special Congress. Is it to organize solidarity with Central America? Or to dissolve ourselves? Or to make a turn to the Animal Liberation

Front? What is preoccupying you these days, my young friend, apart, of course, from your beautiful child-bride? Tell your comrades all about it.'

Ezra looked at Renard and roared with laughter. Then he slapped him on the back in a show of fake heartiness which fooled none of those present. Renard reacted angrily.

'Don't you dare patronize me in that fashion. When I was your age I was ferrying arms in my hand luggage from Buenos Aires to Montevideo every week. The Tupamaros made me an honorary member. And all that time you and that Sardinian joker were at your typewriters talking about continental guerrilla warfare and armed struggle. People like you always forget that Trotsky was not just an intellectual. He was also the Commissar for War in 1917. He built the Red Army. He went into the field himself and addressed the soldiers. Bah!'

Ezra ignored this outburst and proceeded to put on his most serious businesslike air.

'It's no good pretending that everything has happened as we predicted, and yet I must be frank. I have not felt as happy as this since the defeat of fascism. Now Stalinism is dead and the East European masses are delirious with their new-found freedoms. The cold war is over. The two camps will never be the same again. The slate has almost been wiped clean. True, Stalinism has damaged the Marxist project almost beyond repair, but that does not mean that we can just sit back and forget the task of human emancipation. When the people move, it behoves all theoreticians to be silent for a moment and inhale the fresh air. That is the reason for calling a Congress. We need an open debate on the way forward to complete the processes which have been started in Eastern Europe. If we fail, we are finished. And if we are finished then you can say farewell to any idea of world revolution.'

Renard was fast asleep. The Triplets looked at each other. Then Paul spoke, quietly and without emotion.

'Ezra, why did you invite Kosminsky to the Congress?'

'I don't think I did.'

'You did. He rang us to accept the invitation.'

Ezra frowned. He realized it must have been an accident. He must remove Kosminsky from his address book. Aloud he defended the decision.

'He is a social-democrat now! We don't agree with him. Good! But let us hear him, and if he wants to attend that in itself is a good sign.'

Renard opened his eyes.

'What are you going to say at the Congress?'

Ezra was taken by surprise.

'I will defend our line, of course,' he stammered, 'but, er, but I will point out that some readjustments are necessary. I hope all of you have noticed that religion has played a major role in every mass upheaval of the last ten years. This fact can no longer be ignored.'

Renard and the Triplets stared at him in amazement.

'YES? . . .' they all shouted in unison.

At this point there was a knock at the door and Maya, laden with bulging shopping bags, entered the room. The Triplets smiled at her. Renard looked her up and down and whistled in amazement. Ezra beamed with joy.

'I'm sorry to interrupt, but Ezra I need you urgently. I'm sorry.'

Ezra looked apologetically at his four comrades, but they nodded understandingly when he began to pack his briefcase. As he took a few carrier bags from Maya, a small packet containing a pair of pink and blue baby-grows fell out of one of the bags. Ezra blushed as he reclaimed the incriminating item. The Triplets stared in amazement. Nothing whatsoever was said. Ezra and Maya said their farewells and departed.

For a few minutes, they looked at each other in silence. Then Simon roared with laughter as Renard spoke.

'I foresee trouble ahead on both political and domestic fronts for that young man. I remember the day when Ezra joined the movement. It was November 1939. He was nineteen years old. A kid. He wrote his first internal document the same year. It was a call to resistance, attacking those in the movement who thought it was just another imperialist war. Then in 1948, when Stalin assimilated most of these Eastern European states and quite a few people saw it as the inexorable advance of Socialism, this boy wrote another document. I still remember it, *All That Glitters Is Not Gold*. Later on he changed his mind and thought that perhaps it was silver, but religion? I can't believe this is serious. Is he losing his marbles, or is it that nymph with a crucifix whom he seduced in Rio? Better prepare for the battle my young comrades. The Congress will be a catastrophe.'

'Perhaps not,' muttered Simon. 'Perhaps it could be our redemption.'

6

Antoine Renard's last stand

As Renard walked out of the PSR building towards the Bastille he smiled at the sky. It was an incredibly mild winter. He had spent so much time in Latin America during the preceding decades that his memory of European weather patterns had become somewhat blurred. He now thought that this was the warmest January he had ever known in Paris. Since he was a year older than the century, this was unlikely. Renard had simply forgotten. He hailed a taxi. Even though he was ninety-one years old, he did not give an impression of great age. He was about five feet six inches in height, plump, with a fleshy face and a strikingly thick and big nose. He was dressed in an olive-green check overcoat which he had bought at the Harrods store in Rio in 1961. His manner was still vigorous and there was no indication of senility having gripped his brain.

Renard was the son of a train-driver, born during the early hours on New Year's Eve in the year 1899. He now had a house in the Angel suburb of Mexico City, another one in Buenos Aires, and he still maintained an old but elegant apartment in Paris, a few minutes walk from Les Halles, now a fairly chic district of the French capital. It was to this last address that he now guided the white-haired Algerian taxi-driver.

'Did you fight with the FLN?' Renard asked in Arabic.

The Algerian froze and looked at his passenger closely in the mirror. He wondered whether this old man was a fascist. Renard caught the look and smiled.

'I fought on your side. Smuggled arms and counterfeit money for the resistance.'

The taxi-driver relaxed and roared with laughter. When he dropped Renard at his apartment he refused to accept any money. Tears came to his eyes. 'I couldn't. Accept the ride as a gift. A small token of thanks for Frenchmen like you.'

Renard shook hands with him before turning to press the numbers on the entry-phone to the apartments. It always worked. A few words of Arabic, reference to the war, and you got a free ride. Renard had never been near Algeria, except in his dreams. But what the hell. At his age, and with his class war record, mixing up fiction with reality was a very minor offence.

Renard was frowning as the old lift slowly ascended. More than anything else he hated faintness of heart. He knew that Ezra and the Sardinian regarded him as an unstable adventurer, but he wouldn't change places with them for anything in the world. It's true that he had been expelled from the movement more often than anyone else, but he had always fought to get back in and succeeded. At the last Congress he had been given a standing ovation by the comrades. He smiled at the thought.

Renard, a founder-member of the French Communist Party, had been expelled with dozens of others in the late Twenties for defending the ideas of Trotsky and the Left Opposition. The Party had been reluctant to lose its most capable trade-union organizer. The secretary summoned Renard to his office and pleaded with him to keep his views to himself and remain inside.

'We have to make the revolution in France. What difference does it make whether Stalin is in power or Bukharin or Trotsky? Tell me that, eh?'

Renard smiled in that slightly patronizing fashion which infuriated even his comrades, and replied pompously.

'It makes a very big difference, Comrade. You see, Stalin is the gravedigger of the revolution.'

The secretary sighed and they parted company. Gravedigger of the revolution! Trotsky had called Stalin that to his face at the fateful Politburo meeting in 1927. It had turned out to be one of his more prophetic insults. When, three years later, Trotsky was expelled from the Soviet Union and deprived of his citizenship, Renard and several other French Communists joined him in his enforced exile on the island of Prinkipo in Turkey, where the Byzantine emperors had imprisoned their rivals. Renard fell under the hypnotic spell. He decided from that day on that his entire life would be devoted to the world revolution.

It was his imaginative interpretations of this vow that often got him into trouble. In those early days of exile when the organizer of the Red Army was working on his *History of the Russian Revolution* there was a desperate need for funds to maintain the household and publish the Bulletins of the Left Opposition, which were being smuggled back into the Soviet Union. Renard went back to France and set about raising money. This was his first business venture for the movement, and he astounded himself by his remarkable successes. Only one of his comrades, Alain, was unsurprised. They had been schoolfellows together and Alain recalled Renard's remarkable ability to provide food and drink whenever it was needed. But Alain was wrong this time. Renard was not raiding banks or robbing the rich.

It had started off quite innocently. Renard had bought a discarded Citroën, stationed himself at the Gare du Nord and offered his private taxi services to individuals or couples who seemed to be in trouble. Within a month he had acquired a regular clientele. Within three months he had a fleet of four cars. It was then that his career took a slightly different turn.

One evening when he was eating with his employees, none of whom, incidentally, were political in any sense of the word, a woman entered the café and asked one of the drivers to join her for a few minutes at the next table. She was smartly dressed, with only a discreet hint of make-up, and though Renard raised his eyebrows and observed them closely, he assumed she was either a relation or a girl-friend. When the man returned to join the others, there were knowing nods and winks from his colleagues. Renard smiled at them, but not with his eyes. As they were leaving he detained the man who had spoken to the woman.

'Well? Who was she and what did she want?'

Much to Renard's surprise it turned out that the woman was a senior prostitute, in the process of organizing a minor rebellion against her agent, who insisted on a 70 per cent cut per customer. There were three other apartments in her block, all of them housing two prostitutes each. She had been informally elected to find ways of getting rid of their pimp, an awkward-looking ex-butcher from Rouen. She had occasionally used the Renard Taxi Service – known locally as RTS – and found it extremely reliable. Her proposal, as it turned out, was a revolutionary one for Renard's tiny enterprise.

She proposed a two-tier deal with RTS. In order to avoid any ambiguity and subsequent conflict she had asked a notary, who was also a reliable and regular client, to draft a written proposal, which would be binding on both sides. It read as follows:

In the eventuality of an RTS employee ever being asked by a customer for the address of a safe and healthy whorehouse and the aforesaid employee bringing the said customer to one of the agreed apartments, RTS and the Prostitutes Collective will share equally in the resulting remuneration.

Where the Prostitutes Collective utilizes the services of RTS to collect or deliver clients to or from the agreed apartments or where members of the Collective have to be collected and delivered at another address and the RTS is required to provide minimal protection against any attempts by former agents of the Collective or by rival gangs to break the ethos of self-management propounded by the Collective, the RTS will be paid 20 per cent of the monies received by the Collective in addition to the normal taxi fare.

As a former trade-union leader, Renard had to admit that it was a model co-operative agreement. He had no qualms of conscience.

The situation was crystal-clear. A group of oppressed working women had asked him for help against their oppressors. The pimpocracy was an evil institution which had to be smashed. The RTS alliance with the Collective could be the torch that would light the way for other groups of women workers in the same condition. He signed the concordat.

The agreement altered the character of the RTS overnight. Renard's first experience in the purchase of illegal weaponry was a result of this deal. Every taxi-driver had to be armed and known to be armed. The contacts acquired during this period (1929–31) by Renard served him well into the late Sixties, when he was arming the Tupamaros in Uruguay, and even the late Seventies, when he was doing the same for the Sandinistas in Nicaragua. More importantly, it has to be said that as the RTS grew in strength so did the size of its turnover.

Back in Prinkipo, the comrades were incredulous. Even Trotsky, totally engrossed in writing his epic *History of the Russian Revolution,* took a few minutes off one day to inquire how the quality of life on the tiny island had suddenly changed. Who was responsible? Where were the funds coming from? His two French secretaries replied with one voice and more than a tinge of pride: 'Renard! He has been sending more and more money every month.'

Trotsky, imagining that this money was being raised through factory collections, smiled with delight. The two Frenchmen on the island basked in the reflected glory of Renard's successes. The shorter of the two, André Gaul, knew Antoine well, and therefore had his doubts from the very beginning, but even he could never have imagined the reality. He knew about the existence of the RTS, but thought it was a job like any other. And so it might have gone on indefinitely had it not been for a totally unforeseen accident.

One day, in 1935, a Latin American historian, Manuel Vital, and his comrade, Juan Edwardes, arrived at the Gare du Nord in Paris. There was nothing very striking about them except that Manuel's hair had too much oil on it and Juan carried a parrot on his left shoulder. Trotsky had by now left Prinkipo and was stranded in Europe, unsuccessfully pleading for asylum throughout the Continent. The Latin Americans had arrived with a message from the Mexican President Cárdenas, who wanted the exiled revolutionary to know that he was welcome to stay in Mexico. Manuel and Juan had been travelling by sea for many weeks. Sexual inactivity had begun to weigh on their minds. Before meeting their contact, they thought they needed to exercise their genitals. They got into a taxi and Vital went straight to the point.

'Do you know of some place where we could . . . ?' and he made a suggestive gesture with both his hands which is universally understood by cab-drivers throughout the world. Renard smiled and drove them straight to the Collective. After they had emptied their sperm bags, they were sent into the next room to pay the money. Once again they saw Renard, who was sitting recording payments in a small black book. He apologized for not being able to transport them to their next destination, but he had urgent business and he signalled to another taxi-driver to escort them to wherever it was that they wanted to go.

Half an hour later, Manuel and Juan were waiting at a secret rendezvous for their contact with Trotsky, who would give them further directions. To say that they were horrified when they discovered that the much-trusted comrade was none other than Renard would be a euphemism. Juan began to twitch rather violently, which in turn excited his parrot, who was screeching the filthiest abuses imaginable.

Renard was equally shocked but did not permit any sign of it to show on his face. Not a word was said about their previous encounter. Then Renard gave them a safe-conduct and an envelope bulging with money. At this point he could not resist a gibe. An evil grin covered his face.

'When you hand this envelope over to Comrade André Gaul you may, if you wish, inform him that it contains a substantial contribution from the pair of you.'

Manuel's face paled. He did not speak, but nodded curtly to Renard and left the room. Juan had gone red with embarrassment and anger and had almost throttled his poor parrot when, without any prompting at all, it squawked: 'Viva Lenin, Viva Trotsky!' It was Juan who blurted it all out one day to Trotsky's son, Sedov. The son told the father. Trotsky refused to believe the story. It was confirmed. The old man was livid with anger. He insisted that Renard be disciplined.

'Just imagine,' he roared. 'Just imagine what would happen if the Stalinists got hold of the story. It's indefensible.'

'If they did,' muttered Gaul under his breath, 'we could say it was such an outrageous slander even for them that we refused to even comment on the issue.'

Renard was heartbroken at being expelled from the movement. He sold the RTS to Juliette, now the *grande dame* of the Collective. In return he got the apartment which he was just entering and a large amount of money, most of which he donated to the movement.

Renard made himself a cup of boiled water and sat down in the ancient armchair in front of the fireplace. The apartment always brought back happy memories with Juliette, who had died only ten years ago. She had retired a wealthy middle-aged lady. Her savings from the old Collective days had provided her with much more money than the meagre state pension. He sipped his water as he stared at the large photograph of himself with Trotsky on Prinkipo.

'I wish we had parted friends, old man,' he whispered to the image above the mantelpiece.

Only after Trotsky's assassination had Renard been readmitted to the movement. It was Ezra who fought most vigorously for his reinstatement. He valued Renard's skills and needed his support in the crucial factional battles for the soul of the movement that lay ahead. Renard had not even been asked for a self-criticism, since it was felt that his period outside had been enough of a punishment. Susceptible as ever to the excitement of a clandestine life, Renard left France after the war. He had fought in the Resistance and had been sickened, though not in the least surprised, by the decision of the French Stalinists to collaborate with de Gaulle.

In disgust he left for Argentina. There he once again ran into Juan and his parrot, but the Argentinian looked through him and Renard began to build his own organization. At a World Congress of the movement in the Fifties, Juan came up with an interesting theory. He had written a lengthy text defending the view that flying saucers existed and going on to argue that it proved conclusively that out there somewhere, in the depths of outer space, there existed a Communist civilization. The reasoning behind this rather original extra-terrestrial view was a blind faith that a civilization which could produce the technological means to enjoy inter-planetary travel must be more advanced than our own planet and, *ipso facto*, must represent the highest stage of Communism. This deviation was not new to the movement, many of whose leaders had often confused the forces of production with the social relations of production, but Juan's variant was the first indication that the veteran Argentinian was himself heading towards the stratosphere.

Juan was somewhat disconcerted at the response. The younger comrades, but not Ezra or Gaul or the Sardinian, had doubled up with mirth and left the hall. Even Diablo, one of the more capable theoreticians of the movement, was unable to restrain himself. It was the smile on Diablo's face that enraged Juan more than anything else.

Renard, poker-faced, did not help matters when he inquired politely whether in Juan's view the flying-saucer people had solved the problems posed by male sexuality. The reference was obvious. Juan went bright red again and his left ear twitched. That was the signal which alerted the parrot, who roared: 'Viva Lenin, Viva Trotsky, Viva Juan Edwardes!' At this point the delegates who were still in the hall rose in a spontaneous standing and laughing ovation. Juan, his parrot and his delegation walked out in anger. Juan may have been a trifle zany, but he was definitely not an imbecile. He could see that they did not take him seriously. He would show them one day. Like so many others, he never did.

Renard was preparing to retire for the night. As he slowly began to undress, his mind returned to Ezra. The man must not be allowed to make a fool of himself. Renard was not thinking here of the biological changes affecting Maya's body. He was not in the least scandalized at the thought of Ezra becoming a father, though he did despair at the uncontainable sentimentality of his old comrade. He could become obsessed with the baby, over-power it with his affections and, knowing Ezra, he could easily become an expert in child-care. Renard suddenly started giggling like a child. What if Ezra were to sit down and write the definitive Marxist work on the early stages of child-care? An *Anti-Spock* or *Child-Care Under Late Capitalism* which would become the bible of the Left and the post-modernists.

Renard became serious again. He did not look forward to a public row with Ezra at the Congress, but it might come to that if he attempted to impose an unacceptable strategy. Noble and his gang would be there. So would the British groups. In the past Renard had backed Ezra against the more extreme exponents of Anglo-Saxon sectarianism. He did not want to change sides now. He must go and talk to Ezra. Perhaps he would also talk to Maya and explain the facts of life to her. Renard simply did not care about what happened to Europe. In this he was very unorthodox. His passion was Latin America, and there the struggle would go on as long as poverty, exploitation and the United States of America continued to exist. So he did not see any reason for wholesale panic in the face of the overturns in the East.

At his age, Renard also knew that one had to persist in the long view of history. He simply refused to accept that what the people of Eastern Europe were opting for was squalid housing, soaring crime rates, a massive increase in the number of servants, a new deprived under-class sympathetic to fascism, a public transport system on its last legs, privatized medicine and a widening gulf between the poor and the rich. This was the legacy of Reagan and

Thatcher, and he did not believe that even the free-market idiot who was the finance minister of the new Czechoslovakia, and resembled Trotsky in appearance, would be able to stuff all this down the throats of the Czech workers.

His inner thoughts were interrupted by a knock on the door. He frowned and then remembered it was Thursday. It must be Reinette.

'Come, come,' he shouted.

The key turned in the door and a tall, well-preserved, middle-aged woman entered the room. She was dressed in a grey silk suit and a matching scarf with red spots. How well he knew those clothes. There was even a resemblance to her late aunt. Juliette's sprightly forty-six-year-old niece had come to fulfil one of the bequests in the old lady's will. Not that Renard would have prosecuted her if she had decided to forget all about it, but there was still a warm feeling attached to the presence of this old commissar of the red-light area.

'What? Not ready?'

'I forgot. My mind was on other things.'

She smiled and helped him finish undressing. Then she gave him a friendly push on to the bed. After that she divested herself of her clothes, walked to the cupboard and took out a bottle of her special olive oil. She was fond of old Renard, but she had not imagined that he would live for so long. Gently she massaged his body, and he wriggled with pleasure as he stroked her breasts. Then, as she was nearing the end of her ordeal, she rubbed his genitals gently, a signing-off gesture in their routine. To her absolute amazement Renard's member suddenly stiffened and rose in a mocking farewell salute. This hadn't happened in over ten years. She rubbed it some more, wondering if she could squeeze out a little ink from Renard's old pen, but the moment had passed. The organ had reverted to its normal shrivelled little self. They smiled at each other.

She covered him up and tucked him in properly. After she had dressed and reorganized herself, she kissed him affectionately on the head.

'Au revoir, Antoine. I think that may have been your last stand!'

'No,' Renard muttered to himself after she had left. 'My last stand will be at Ezra's Congress.'

7

A few pages from Ezra's journal

4 January 1990: I have had to stop all work on my memoirs. I find it difficult today to summon the ghosts and spirits of my past. The voices are there and the sounds, some of them only too painfully acute. So much has passed before my eyes that at times like these they refuse me the power of recall, reducing my memory to a blank wall. It is the noises of time present which keep intruding, and even I begin to wonder whether the price being paid for what we have gained means that much of what we thought we had gained was nothing but illusion. Mirages in our minds and a living hell for those who supposedly gained. Surely this can't be so, for the gains of 1917 were spread all over the world: decolonizations which otherwise would have been delayed or bloody or both. The welfare states in the West would probably have been far less effective had it not been for the 'barbarians at the gate'.

This morning, for instance, a long letter from Otto in Berlin and the German translation of Igor Shagarevich's article. There is no doubting that it is an effective piece of writing, like some of Goebbels' filth in the early Thirties. It is a horrible little essay. Reading it has depressed me a great deal. It was first published during the last days of the old Brezhnevite regime, but it's become a sacred text for the nationalists. It's grotesque, unbelievable. This great Soviet mathematician is a vulgar anti-semite. The Soviet Union is not in crisis because of the crimes and disasters of

Stalinism, but because of the 'criminal intrigues' of the 'lesser people'. First the 'lesser people' were Zionists. Then they became Yid-Masons and now they are the Jews. Poor Shagarevich! But why are the songs of the Black Hundreds finding a new audience? Have all the gains of the Revolution disappeared? I suspect that this might be the case, but I cannot believe that the USSR will slowly lapse into capitalism. That is the sinister side of Shagarevich and his slavophile friends. They are hostile to modernity. Hence, too, their nostalgia for Stalin and the Tsar. I fear that Gorbachev could be overthrown if and when elements in the party and army link up with the slavophile intelligentsia. All this talk about love for Russian culture is nothing but a mountain of shit. And all this on the eve of the third millennium. Poor Russia! Are Pasternak and Mandelstam and Grossman not part of this Russian culture?

Otto's letter was a tonic. What an excellent comrade he is! And yet even Otto doubts if we can salvage something from the wreck.

I am very late with my new book answering the German revisionist historians on the origins of fascism. Unfortunately all this proto-fascist material in the Russian papers, *Molodave gvardia*, *Nash sovremennik* and *Moskovsky literator*, will help their thesis and not mine.

Last night Maya asked me to explain how it was that despite all its crimes, its inquisitions, its wars and its present backward positions on the liberation churches in Brazil, the Roman Catholic orthodoxy and its Pope have held out much better than Marxism. My answer was simple. We never were a religion. She laughed in my face. It was impossible to convince her. But I must confess the question has been bothering me since 1979.

7 January 1990: Long phone call today from the British comrades early in the morning. I hope they didn't hear Maya being sick in the background. It would be awful if they think she pukes every time they ring up. This would be the third time it's happened. Want me to go to London immediately. They say that my proposal for an emergency Congress without preconditions

has created a problem for them. They are still a tiny group. They fear they'll be totally swamped by the Rock and Burroughs organizations. The whole business is ridiculous, but part of the wretched English disease. For a country whose bourgeoisie has rarely split and whose labour movement remains the most unified in Europe, the continuing factionalism and splits in our movement is perplexing. Hood's old empire has splintered dramatically and there are three groups even within our own ranks. It would be ridiculous if Rock and Burroughs turned up but our comrades stayed away. Points in favour of going to London: (a) Maya likes the town. I could show her the Cemetery at Highgate and the Zoo. (b) I could meet Jemima Wilcox and the *New Life Journal* comrades. Find out why the *NLJ* publishing house is not reprinting my last three books. I wonder whether this tardiness is due to the fact that I referred to them as centrists and compared them to Kautsky and *Die Neue Zeit*? Perhaps I was too harsh! (c) Meeting with the RSG and LSD comrades to be restricted to two hours. (d) A nice hotel.

There is no way I can go this week. Warsaw gets priority.

8/9 January 1990: 2 a.m., Renard has just left us. He charmed Maya, who wishes I was more like him. Of course his advantage is that his Spanish and Portuguese are excellent. What she did not understand was that the whole point of impressing her with stories I have heard ten times over and jokes which I no longer find funny was to clear the decks for a lengthy session with me on the Congress. By the time we began to talk seriously Maya had gone to bed, but in a happy mood, not at all grudging about our 'shop-talk'. Renard is worried that if I do something totally unpredictable the pseudo-orthodoxy of Noble might win the day. He reasons like this: Noble's love-affair with Castro has made the whole gang totally hostile to Gorbachev. Within our ranks there are many who see Gorbachev as the main enemy today. They believe that 'illusions in Gorbachev' must be smashed. On this Renard is undoubtedly correct. There is a lot of delirious 'third-period' nonsense doing the rounds. But Renard's gentle hint that we should postpone the Congress indefinitely is unacceptable. He calls it a period of masterly inactivity, but the next result could be worse. It could lead to another round of splits with one side totally caving in to Gorbachev, losing all sense of critical perspective, and the others heading for outer space. I explained to my ninety-one-year-old fox, who still has more understanding of the world than the sectarians or the centrists, that to delay the Congress would not be masterly, but a slightly sordid bureaucratic manoeuvre. I did agree that we should at the very outset of the Congress push through a self-denying ordinance. It was not a decision-making body, but a consultative conference. We could take consultative votes which were not binding on any one. For me the Congress is the only way to reorient the comrades to meet the needs of the new situation. Otherwise we're finished. Kaput!

8 a.m.: Unfortunately just as I was telling Bob Beirut that I could only get to London after and not before my planned trip to Warsaw, Maya woke up and rushed to the basin next door, but she was so loud today that it disrupted our conversation. I think I will have to explain the real situation discreetly to Bob. I don't want them to think that the noises of Maya vomiting are in any way pre-planned. The one thing we don't need in that organization is another split!

I'm beginning to get the feeling that Renard is pressing the PSR to get the Congress delayed. Simon rang to ask me to attend the meeting of their Politburo tonight where they will be discussing the organization of the Congress . . . accommodation arrangements, translation facilities, funding, etc. And I have two meetings of the International Bureau before that: one with the Sri Lankans and one on the recurring problems we face in Bolivia. What a pity the world revolution does not permit sabbaticals!

8

Fall-out in Shawsville

'Ladies and Gentlemen, in a few minutes we shall be landing at Heathrow airport. Could you please . . .'

The LOT flight from Warsaw was on time. Ezra opened his eyes and looked out of the window. Surprisingly it was clear over London. He looked at the familiar landmarks and pursed his lips. He was feeling depressed. The meeting in Warsaw had been an unmitigated disaster. There had been about fifty people, mostly intellectuals hostile to any form of Socialism. His attempts to demonstrate Trotsky's foresight in predicting, fifty years ago, the incapacity of Stalinism to solve the fundamental problems of the masses had not gone down too well. One after the other ten, or possibly fifteen, of these intellectuals had stood up and stated that Lenin, Trotsky, Stalin were one and the same thing.

'The Soviet Union is like a fish that was rotten in the head at its very birth. Lenin and Trotsky were the parents that gave birth to this monstrosity. Stalin was only their offspring.'

Remarks like this had finally enraged Ezra. He had mentioned Rosa Luxemburg.

'Leave her where she is and where she deserves to be . . . at the bottom of the canal.'

This witticism had been greeted with applause. In desperation Ezra had shouted at them: 'What you're doing is putting the executioner and the victim on the same level. I suppose you will soon tell me that there was no difference between the Nazis and the Jews!'

To his absolute amazement they all nodded. At that point Ezra gave up and left the hall.

He had known that things were bad in Poland, but not this bad. It was as if the experience of Stalinism had destroyed the entire historical memory of the Polish working class. He felt as if he was the sole survivor of Atlantis. History appeared to be repeating itself. Walesa had dressed himself up in the clothes of Marshal Pilsudski. Glemp was behaving like a functionary of the Third Reich. Ezra felt that if capitalism was restored in this country it would become a clerical dictatorship, a confessional banana republic.

As he walked out of the Green Channel at Terminal Two all these thoughts disappeared suddenly. He caught sight of Maya, dressed in a stunning, light brown suit and matching hat. She smiled as she saw him and they hugged and kissed, oblivious to everyone else. Passers-by saw them and smiled, a few of them remarking what a lucky old man Ezra was to have such a beautiful granddaughter.

Ezra was used to ageist comments, which he explained as one of the functions of culture under late capitalism. It was an attempt to conceal an inner decay that compelled the advertisers and the television moguls to build up a cult of youth. Not that he had anything against youth as such. Had he not defended virtually every manifestation of youth rebellion during the Sixties and Seventies? Had he not written the decisive text on *Sexuality and Post-Modernism*? The fact that he was senior, very senior, in generation to Maya was of no significance whatsoever, or so he thought. As they got into the taxi, he felt the bulge in her stomach.

'We must think of a name,' Maya said, holding his hand.

'There's plenty of time.'

'It's always better to have some ideas well in advance.'

'If you like we can start making a list of names. Then see if we can agree on each other's choice for a boy or a girl.'

'I want a Chinese name.'

'What?'

'They're such beautiful names.'

Ezra was not convinced, but instead of inaugurating a polemic on the issue, he fell silent, confident that when the time came he would be able to talk her out of it. He had a great belief in his own powers of persuasion, left surprisingly undented by the recent experience in Warsaw. Nor did he fully realize that Maya could be every bit as obstinate as he, and on this matter she had thought a great deal. Ezra had no idea of the storms that lay ahead and how they would bring their relationship to the very edge of the abyss. The figure of fate was hovering above the birth of Ezra and Maya's child.

In their hotel room, Ezra was casually flicking through a copy of *The Independent* when his eye fell on a striking photograph. It could have been the scene at the funeral of an old gangster. His curiosity aroused, he read the caption, and his face paled. He let the paper drop from his hand. Old Frank Hood was dead. He was an old factional rival, but prior to the big split of the Fifties, they had known each other. Ezra had spoken at youth camps organized by Hood. How amazing that rival groups from amongst his own leather-jacketed supporters had clashed at their former leader's funeral. As in life so in death. How apt that Hood was sent off in the midst of fisticuffs.

Ezra recalled the circumstances in which Hood had been recruited to the Trotskyist cause in the late Thirties. He had been a Stalinist at the time, and had got into an argument in a pub near King's Cross with a Scottish Trotskyist shop-steward, Jock Fraser. Hood, believing that Trots were fascist agents, decided to settle the argument in the time-honoured fashion. He stood up and aimed a punch at Fraser's head. This was a serious mistake. Hood was short, fat and nasty. Jock was short, lean and tough. He looked weak and his face was drawn, but in his case it was foolish to go simply by appearances. Some years back, he had been the amateur welterweight boxing champion of Glasgow. He had no difficulty in ducking Hood's swings or in deflecting Hood's knee from his groin. Then he had stood up and without further ado proceeded with two successive lightning left hooks to immobilize Hood till closing time. The barman had picked up the fallen man and put him on a bench outside the Gents. When Hood regained consciousness, Fraser had left. The next day he sought him out, shook hands and decided to become a Trotsky-ist. The argument preceding the knock-out may have had some-thing to do with it, but it was the superior force which had been the decisive element. Hood learnt his lesson. As he became totally bald he looked even more menacing, but he never made the mistake of fighting again. He had a trained team of thugs who made sure that order was always preserved or disrupted, depending on the circumstances.

Hood's conversion from one current to the other was accom-panied by a change in the content of his rhetoric, but the style remained unaltered. For the rest of his life he remained, in the words of one of Britain's leading radical historians, an 'inverted Stalinist'. As Hood had become the mirror image of the man who had knocked him out in the pub, so his organization became the mirror image of the Stalinism it believed it despised. The nick-name by which the Hood Group became known within leftwing circles in Britain lacked subtlety, but it was apt. From a very early stage of their political life, Hood's partisans were referred to as the Hoodlums.

And yet, thought Ezra, what else was there in Britain at the time, apart from the Communist Party? In the early days, Hood had scooped up many decent young social-democrats disil-lusioned by the failure of the Attlee government to maintain its reformist impetus, and more so by the decision of European social-democracy as a whole to become camp-followers of Washington and pillars of the cold war. Later, after the events of 1956 when Khrushchev had denounced Stalin's crimes for the first time and then invaded Hungary, a new ferment shook the Communist parties in the West. Their certainties challenged, many party members rejected Stalinism and turned to the only existing organization on the far left. The Hoodlums had grown in size and picked up a few Red Professors, hard-faced, hatchet-wielding men who now began to do for Hood what they had been previously doing for Moscow. Hood had, till then, been working from within the Labour Party.

Excited by the new entrants to his group, he began to dream of the time when the Hoodlums would be *the* party of the British working class. Even at the beginning of this dream it wasn't exactly clear whether, for instance, a Hoodlum victory at the polls, or the Hoodlums propelled to power at the head of a General Strike which became an insurrection, would lead to the establishment of a state with the Hoodlums as the only party. In later years this was spelt out in Frank Hood's internal memos, where he made it clear that the dictatorship of the proletariat would, in effect, be nothing more or less than a dictatorship exercised on behalf of the proletariat by the Hoodlums. For Ezra that was when the degeneration had really started, but then Ezra always liked to look on the brighter side of the more shady outfits that helped to make up the world movement. To this day Ezra sincerely believed that if only Hood had stayed with him and Diablo after the nineteen fifty-three split they might have saved his soul. Instead the old rascal had ganged up with PISPAW, who had promised to build him an apparatus. He had repaid them by proclaiming PISPAW to be the fount of orthodoxy. After this they both found a new enemy in Diabloism, a filthy revisionist current whose main aim was to discredit Trotskyism.

'Ezra! Ezra! Come and help.'

Ezra walked to the bathroom to find his wife sitting up in the bath and waiting patiently for him to soap her back.

'It is awful. They have no showers in this hotel!'

Ezra began to laugh and explain the origins of the English bathtub. It was the Romans who had taught the inhabitants of these islands to have regular baths. Prior to the Roman invasion, it was possible on a bad day to smell the English from Calais. Showers were slowly making their way across the Channel in the twentieth century. Of course, if Britain had been invaded by the Arabs during the eleventh and twelfth centuries, the shower might have reached these shores much earlier.

78

Maya was by now used to these impromptu history lessons, but she was in a carefree mood today and without warning she grabbed her lover by the arm and dragged him somewhat roughly by his braces into the bath. The look of sheer horror on his face reduced her to uncontrollable giggles. Nobody, not even his mother, had ever treated the principal theoretician of the world movement in this fashion. The more angry his expression the more she laughed, and it was only when a weak smile appeared on his face that she managed to control her mirth and recover enough energy to pull herself out of the tub in which Ezra still lay immersed, his spectacles floating sadly in the surface grime.

This episode left its mark on their relationship. Till now, Ezra had been blind to everything but her beauty, her vibrancy, her ability to make him feel spiritually happy. Now, for the first time, and admittedly in somewhat awkward circumstances, he began to dwell on some of her weaknesses. What she had done could not simply be excused as a display of youthful exuberance. She was too childish, almost wilful. He even began to wonder whether the uncanny timing of her morning sickness was a deliberate ploy to embarrass him in the face of English Trotskyism. What had upset him was not the fact that his trousers and shirt were soaked beyond recognition. It was the infringement of his dignity. He could not imagine Krupskaya behaving in this fashion with Lenin. In this thought he was probably correct, but what about Inessa Armand? Now there was a woman who could have dragged Lenin, fully clothed, into any old bath and heard him roar with laughter. But Ezra's vision did not extend beyond Krupskaya on this particular occasion. In any case, he did not sulk for long. By the time she had massaged and dried him, he was in good spirits once again, her frailties all but forgotten.

Later that day they travelled to Highgate where, after showing her Marx's tomb, disfigured by a socialist-realist sculptor, he took her for a walk on Hampstead Heath. Despite the fact that it was a Sunday afternoon there were very few 'governments-in-exile' out that day. For nearly four decades, Ezra, on his visits to London, had always enjoyed walking silently and listening to the conversations of the Poles, Romanians, Albanians and Russians who filled certain paths of the Heath on the day of rest. He wondered whether their absence was just a coincidence or whether they had returned to their countries of origin following the democratic revolutions.

Suddenly, just as they reached the imposing front of Kenwood House, Ezra caught sight of the Shaw twins walking towards them. He appeared slightly agitated as he trembled with excitement and pointed Laura Shaw out to Maya, who promptly insisted that Ezra introduce her to the glamorous phantom of the opera.

Maya adored Laura Shaw. One night in Rio, as they had passed a giant billboard announcing the soprano's schedule in Brazil, Ezra had boasted to Maya that Laura was a Trotskyist. He had omitted to point out, for reasons best known to himself, that both the Shaw sisters were Hoodlum linchpins or, more precisely, linchpin Hoodlums. Now he confessed this hurriedly to Maya as the two women, attired in mink stoles and followed obediently by two pedigree canines, swept past him. The sisters had recognized Ezra, of course, but since he and his friend Diablo had been the main obstacles in the path of the world revolution, they could not possibly have acknowledged his actual presence. Maya asked a simple question, often posed by philistines in the bourgeois press of Britain and the United States for whom there was no question of any link between culture and politics. Yet the query was pertinent.

'How in heaven's name did those two become Trotskyistas?'

Ezra sat down on the bench and gently pulled her down. Then stroking her hand with great affection, he began to tell her the story. It should be pointed out straightaway that Ezra's version was sanitized for Maya's benefit. After all he did not want her to think that the movement was full of weirdos. As it was, he was a bit worried lest they accidentally bump into any Trotskyists. He would then be compelled to introduce her, and she might get the wrong idea about the real nature of the movement.

'During the explosions of Sixty-Eight, Hood realized that he was isolated. Our tendency and the Jim Rock group were both recruiting heavily amongst the students. Burroughs was deeply embedded in the Labour Party. Hood asked a few television producers in the BBC, sympathetic to his ideas, to organize weekly soirées where he could impress the cultural intelligentsia and win them over to the cause of the proletariat. Basically he was, as always, after money. He didn't imagine he would win too many people.

'One day, much to his surprise, Laura and Myra walked in to the soirée and took their seats. Hood, not a bad actor in those days, put on for their benefit a tried and tested party piece. Something like, "I am the leader of the proletariat and everyone else is petty-bourgeois scum." This particular turn usually worked well with very young people of non-proletarian origin, mainly university students. He had picked up all this nonsense from the Stalinists, of course, who had used these methods to hound out any dissident intellectuals from their ranks. Stalin sent people to the executioners, but Hood, not having that power, could only abuse them and, when the occasion demanded, have them beaten up by specially trained Hoodlums.'

Maya was beginning to get restive. She wasn't the least bit interested in Hood or the Hoodlums.

'But Ezra, if Hood was such an evil man how come that a talented, brilliant singer like Laura Shaw fell for his act? Was this Hood a magician, who could cast some spell? It doesn't make good sense to me.'

'It was the noise of time. You are too young, of course, to remember the excitement of Sixty-Eight . . .'

'I was four . . .'

'Exactly! It was a good instinct on the part of the Shaw sisters that brought them to the house in Hampstead that day. They wanted to believe that Hood was genuine because they wanted to get involved in something. They were charmed and bewitched by the old rogue, and addresses were exchanged. I am told that Hood was invited to a weekend gathering at the Shaw villa near Siena. Once there he was surrounded by pretty faces and some say that it was there that he . . . but anyway whatever happened there is not very relevant . . .'

Maya dug her nails into Ezra's hand.

'I want to know. It's the most interesting bit for me and you're putting on your hypocritical show of morality. Tell me! I insist.'

'Those were liberated days. The Shaws had no idea what they were letting themselves in for. The Hoodlums laid on a forty-eight-hour sexual orgy – I think it was to commemorate the feast of Caligula – and the leader of the proletariat, Frank Hood, was the guest of honour. The Shaws couldn't stop it so they drove off into the mountains for two days and left them to it. Someone painted a banner which read: "AND WE SHALL TREAT THE PROLETARIAT TO THE PLEASURES THAT WERE ENJOYED BY THE EMPERORS OF ANTIQUITY." Hood, so they say, was passed that night from one pair of arms to the other, male and female. Of course the irony is that the Italian employees at the villa, the only genuine workers present, were not even allowed to watch.'

For some reason Ezra found this last remark of his very funny. He burst into a maniacal laugh. Maya stared at him coldly.

'And then . . . ?'

'Well nothing. *Despite* this episode the Shaws joined the Hoodlums and Hood milked them for as much as he could get. It wasn't just money. The Shaws were influential. Many young singers were recruited to the Hood cause. Most of them, of course, left a few months later, tragic, burnt-out wrecks who had fallen victims to a sinister operation. It's the same syndrome as the kids who fell under the spell of Indian charlatans playing the part of mystic gurus. Maharishis, scientologists, Hoodlums. The differences in ideology were there, I don't deny that, but the psychological types they recruited were very similar. Middle-class kids with a masochistic streak on a guilt-trip. Most of them saw through the charade sooner or later. But not all of them. Even in his last few years, when he was expelled by the majority Hoodlums for raping young women on Christmas Eve and Easter Sunday every year, there was a handful who defended him. They pointed out, with some justification it has to be said, that Hood was always having sex with young women in his organization, so why had it taken so long for the Hoodlum leadership to act on the matter? They even claimed that it was a political dispute. Who knows? They may even have been right. You know Hood died a few days ago. I'm a bit surprised that they buried him yesterday. I wonder whether that was just a ploy by one Hoodlum faction to deceive their rivals. It would have been more traditional to embalm him and put him on display, may be at the villa in Siena, which was after all the scene of his greatest triumph.'

Maya smiled. 'Oh Ezra! You think crazy things. But tell me one thing. Why did this Hood man rape on religious days only?'

'It's straightforward enough. His daughter, disgusted by her father's brand of sado-masochistic politics, sought refuge in a convent. She was his Svetlana. He never forgave her. His Easter and Christmas ritual was his way of punishing her by proxy! Simple.'

'Have you invited the Shaws to your special Congress or whatever you call it?'

Ezra nodded sadly. He felt that there was very little chance of them attending such a gathering.

The couple got up and began to make their way to the exit. Ezra's routine in London – and he was nothing if not a creature of habit – entailed a visit to the Zoo. In the old days he used to visit the Dolphinarium on the Tottenham Court Road. He thought that dolphins were the most intelligent animals on earth and he could sit and watch them for hours. He sometimes wished that he could recruit a few dolphins to the cause. Life would have been easier.

Maya had no desire to go to the Zoo, but she decided to humour the old man.

As they were leaving the Heath to get a bus to Regent's Park, the Shaw sisters were preparing a surprise of their own. Laura handed her furs to the chauffeur and decided to drive. Myra entered the front of the antique Armstrong-Siddeley. The car purred softly and then moved off. It was followed at a respectable distance by the dogs who were being transported in the newest Soviet version of the Range-Rover, which Laura had bought for the animals a few months ago.

'Do you think we were wrong to ignore him?' Myra asked her sister. Even though Laura was the more famous of the two, it was Myra who kept the Shaw faction of the Hoodlums in order. So when Myra asked whether it had been tactically inept to ignore Ezra, Laura realized that it was not a frivolous question. She had no answer, so she shrugged her shoulders and took the speed up to 85 m.p.h., which was quite revolutionary on the North Circular, even on a Sunday.

'I think we were wrong. I think we should attend the Special Congress.'

Laura put her foot on the brake and the car skidded to a halt.

'What? And Frankie barely dead a fortnight? What would he have said?'

'He'd have gone. There is nothing to be lost and much to be gained. Agreed?'

Laura did not reply. She released the clutch, pressed the accelerator and drove them home.

Laura did not speak for a few hours. Then she did a most uncharacteristic thing. She did not agree with Myra. She insisted that Myra summon a meeting of the Central Committee to discuss the question. The membership of the Hoodlums (Shaw faction) was, at the last count, fifty-three, not counting the ten members of the Youth wing, most of whom were Shaw children of one sort or another. Half the organization consisted of the Central Committee. This body included Myra and Laura's paramours at the time, as well as the cook, maid, chauffeur, the full-time gardener and the man who came to prune the roses. The Transport Workers were represented by the milkman. The others were all aspiring young singers and musicians, desperate for a leg-up in the industry. Their only function was to rubber-stamp any and every Shaw fantasy. The question of which sister they would back in the eventuality of a political or tactical difference had never arisen till today.

Myra, livid with anger, ignored Laura's request, which was both proper and constitutional. She used her powers as general secretary to convene an emergency meeting of the Politburo. This had consisted of Laura, Myra and Hood. With the latter now dead, there had not been enough time to elect a third member. The meeting took place that evening. Myra chaired and moved the following resolution:

'This meeting of the Politburo, having studied the invitation from Ezra Einstein to an emergency Congress, declares that our organization, the historic repository of British Trotskyism, should be represented. It accordingly decides to nominate Laura S., Myra S., and three other comrades to attend the said Congress.'

Myra was hoping that Laura would abstain and make it a *nem. con.* decision, in the best traditions of Hoodlum practice. Laura voted against. She had an untypically threatening smile on her face. Myra voted for the motion. Laura was exultant.

'No majority. The motion falls.'

'I'm sorry comrade,' said Myra, 'the Chair always has a casting vote. So it's two–one. Meeting adjourned.'

The very next morning, Laura, angry at being outmanoeuvred in this fashion and not having Frank's shoulder on which to shed a few tears, asked her sister to move out of the house. It was Laura, after all, who earned the Shaw millions. It was her earnings which provided the organization with a material basis. Myra, a veteran of numerous Hoodlum splits, initiator of countless expulsions and inner-party show-trials, was devastated by this division inside the family. Cynics might argue that Myra's grief was merely the consequence of being cut off from the Shaw bank-account. Subsequent developments, alas, do not vindicate this view.

Laura's petulance had not really been provoked by any intrinsic hostility to Ezra's Congress. It was more the result of a long-repressed resentment against her twin. With Hood no longer present to act as a mediator or masseur of the Laura Shaw ego, which was as large as La Scala, the old arrangement had collapsed. Laura mistakenly felt that she could handle the organization just as well as Myra. The latter had unwittingly precipitated a showdown which had played straight into Laura's hands. After the ultimatum to leave the mansion, Myra attempted a dignified retreat. She offered to withdraw the motion so convincingly passed by the Politburo till a more representative gathering could take place. Laura remained adamant.

When Myra became finally convinced that she could not change the mind of her twin, she packed her bags and left the house. That same night, in a seedy little room in the middle of nowhere, Myra Shaw sat down and wrote a long letter to her sister:

Dear Laura
It's past two in the morning and I ask myself what I'm doing sitting in this sordid, ugly room in the ghastly bedsitterland near Paddington Station. I know the answer, but do you? I've been thinking of you non-stop ever since you threw me out today. I left my luggage here and then thought I'd come back and make you see reason. I got as far as Hampstead, but no longer had the will to walk through the Heath to your place. What a night it's been. I've never known such a clear sky over London. I did go for a walk in the starlight. There were pitch-black parts of the Heath, but I wasn't scared at all. In fact I found the darkness incredibly comforting. Did you, perchance, sister, look upwards tonight? Did you manage to look at the constellation of Orion? I did, and for the first time I realized that the clarity was false. Orion is a hunter, but it seemed that his wrists had been severed and some of his features dismembered. The Orion I saw tonight was hunter and hunted. I could fathom his structure entirely. It must have always been like that. Orion is twins. Us. Hunter. Hunted. I can hear your irritated voice: 'What is the bitch trying to say? I wish she'd hurry up.' But this is my last communication with you Laura, so don't push me forward too

*fast. I have many things to say to you. Constellations are
profound and mysterious things.*

    *I wondered what I'd done to make you hate me so much and
I think I'm beginning to understand. Every time I helped you
through a crisis you must have resented it a great deal. I thought
that because you were the better singer (oh yes, Laura, I never
doubted that for a minute!), because you earned the big money,
all the opera barons were at your feet and every male lead
wanted your body and . . . and . . . and. I mean you got
whatever you wanted Laura. Alright, the break-up with
Humphrey was not of your doing. Not your choice, but what
else could be done? It's not every day that a hardworking young
woman comes home and finds her father buggering her twin
sister's husband on the marital couch. It was awful. Did you
hate me for telling them both to get out and never enter the
house again? Did you L.? I only did it for you. I wanted you to
be happy. I mean what else could I have done? There were no
children. The separation was pretty painless. Oh no! Laura, had
you known all the time? Had it turned you on? That never
occurred to me and I am prepared to swear to that on the
Transitional Programme. I suppose it must have been that, but
if it wasn't, what else could it have been? I never got off with
any of your men. Remember the black trapeze artist from
Brixton? When he made a pass at me that day, I told you
immediately. You stopped his standing order that very week
and told the filthy gigolo to get out of the apartment you rented
for him. Surely you haven't forgotten.*

    *Was it my superiority in the political domain? Well that
couldn't be helped. Someone had to write your lines. You didn't
have time to write them yourself. I mean, what if you said the
wrong thing while presenting a noble comrade with the Shaw
Award for creative writing?*

    *You remember what happened when I didn't write your
speech on that curious occasion in Baghdad? I was totally
knocked out with Baghdad tummy and instead of talking about
the anti-Stalinist struggle of the regime, you bored on about the*

bloody international banks. I'd told you not to mention the banks, since half the leaders of that country were on the payroll of a multinational lending institution. Was it that Frank took me more seriously as a proletarian activist? Surely not. You know how much he admired you and praised your qualities as the leading spokeswoman of the Hoodlums, especially after you correctly pooh-poohed those tell-tale fictions about his so-called sexual misdemeanours.

Laura, you know perfectly well that I gave up my own husband when he left our Party. For me the Hoodlum cause came above everything else! It was I who taught you that, Laura. Have you forgotten when you mocked my political affiliation to the Hoodlums? 'Oh, darling they're just a bunch of loonies who live in their own make-believe world.' It took six months of Frank and me arguing with you finally to win you round. And now you dare pose as the Leader of the Hoodlums. That's what drives me really mad, Laura. I wouldn't mind, but you really aren't up to the tasks. You could easily discard the whole thing and sell our machinery to the first bidder. It is because you have taken over the Party that I have to do what I'm going to do when I've posted this letter to you.

Can you still recall that wimpish weasel who runs the Royal Naval Opera in Greenwich and who always flatters you to your face, but bad-mouths you behind your back? You know who I mean, don't you? That fanatically middle-brow careerist, Spotiswood, who directed one of the ghastliest modern operas of the Eighties, 'The Woman Night-Cleaner's Dinner Party', which nobody actually saw, but everyone thought was radical and anti-Thatcherite because of the title.

I remember you telling me that he'd made a pass at you. Anyway, that very week I heard the awful creep denouncing you to a few clones, all of them dressed like him in off-white designer suits and rolled up sleeves. So I walked up to him, screamed, punched him in the chest and emptied my glass of tomato juice (with Worcester sauce) on his head. The clones saw the red marks on his chest and panicked. They thought I'd

88

killed him. Two of them grabbed me while the third rang the police. When Spotiswood recovered I warned him that if this ever happened again I'd inform his wife of what they really get up to in that theatre. And all that I did for you. How could your heart remain frozen and so insensible to your own sister?

If you wanted to go to Ezra's Congress on your own, why didn't you say so instead of faking an argument and breaking with me? I fear that you will not be able to handle it all on your own. You've always needed lines, and with Frankie and me gone who will supply them? Roger? Roy? David? No such luck. They abandoned us when the going got tough and the bourgeois media turned on us.

I've thought about it all very carefully. I could hang on and wait for you to summon me, but the pain and hatred is very deep this time. I used to love you very much, though love is a word which means nothing in the world of soapbox opera. It was for your own good that I wanted you to realize that you were not a born political leader. With me around you'd never understand that, not even for a single day. So what I'm about to do is really to teach you a lesson, Laura. I know you'll try to laugh it off, but I hope what you've done to me begins to gnaw your insides.

You never understood why I wanted to write the libretto for that Scottish number, did you? Well, it was Mary, Queen of Scots, who said 'In my end is my beginning.' For the first time ever I think I understand what she meant. You see, my dear Laura, people imagine that one has to be in a real state before one does what I am planning, but this is sheer nonsense. A case of literary stereotyping and totally counterposed to the example of the noble Queen of the Scots.

Remember me to the dogs and Mummy.
Your sister in transition from one world to another,
Myra

Myra read the letter over again and then sealed the envelope. Her plan was to disappear abroad for a few years and then, when

Laura was in truly desperate straits, to return and lead the Hoodlums in a revolt to topple her from her position of authority. She thought she would go to Argentina and stay with a cousin who owned a large farm and several apartment blocks in Buenos Aires. The cousin in question loathed Laura, albeit for the wrong reasons, and he would, she was sure, happily provide her with shelter and not reveal her whereabouts to the tiny Hoodlum sect in Patagonia.

Myra walked out into the early hours to post her letter. She was walking slowly to the letter-box, when she noticed three police cars zooming past her, disgorging a dozen uniformed men and driving away at high speed. The men hid in the sidestreet. Myra peered at the building and immediately understood what was going on. The building contained the branch of an exclusive merchant bank and the police were clearly expecting visitors. Myra started to walk past the building rapidly, but at that very moment a large Mercedes pulled up near the pavement and unloaded four representatives of the criminal fraternity. They stared at Myra. She smiled, undecided whether to warn them or not. One of them approached her and asked her for a light.

'I don't smoke,' Myra whispered in a strange voice.

At this precise point, the forces of law and order, tired of waiting, decided to exercise their impatient trigger-fingers. Guns blazed from both sides and poor Myra fell to the ground. The criminals ran with the bullets chasing them. The police rushed to the spot where Myra lay and lifted her gently, but it was too late. Unlike the criminals and their uniformed opponents, Myra had not taken the precaution of wearing a bullet-proof waistcoat before she stepped outside. Her body was taken back to an unmarked house in the locality, which had served as the headquarters for the abortive police operation. There the letter to Laura was discovered in her pocket, opened, read, re-sealed and posted. The body was never discovered.

9

The *New Life Journal*

While Ezra and Maya were lying on the bed in their hotel room, resting from the exertions of their day before getting themselves ready for dinner with the editorial *aktiv* of the *New Life Journal* (*NLJ*), the editor of the magazine, Jemima Wilcox, was on the phone, desperately ringing her colleagues to ensure that at least some of them showed up for the dinner. Till now the only responses that she had received had been stony and irritated refusals. The magazine had changed its name in nineteen sixty-three. Its founder, Richard Lysaght, had insisted on the more up-beat title because of his belief that it reflected the character of editorial meetings. Everyone who attended them was exhilarated, intellectually refreshed, had new life injected into their souls. This view, incidentally, was not one which was universally shared.

Since it was only a few hours ago that Jemima herself had remembered Ezra's presence in town and that she had invited him to dinner, and since the seven members of the editorial committee who lived in London had only just been informed, it was going to be a lonely dinner party. Jemima's husband, Gyorgi, a collector of stamps, rare books and illegal weeds, had returned to Hungary. He had left Budapest in nineteen fifty-six after the defeat of the uprising. Now he was returning to establish a chain of bookshops, privately owned by him, where, he had promised Jemima, he would make sure that the *Journal* was adequately stocked.

Jemima was dressed in black corduroy trousers and a thick, navy blue knitted jumper. She was of medium height and of a remarkably slim build, which she was delighted to see made her just as fashionable as her twenty-one-year-old daughter, Lavinia. The first year of the last decade of this century was also the fiftieth anniversary of Jemima's birth, still a few months away. Not that she had changed all that much in appearance during the preceding decades. Her hair was, of course, totally white, but it had been like this for thirty years. Her wrinkles were well disguised by a subtle use of makeup and her body was well-tuned, a fact not unrelated to the missionary zeal with which she jogged round the square at seven a.m. every morning, much to the annoyance of excreting dogs and their owners.

As she sat at her kitchen table, a relic of the Thirties now on the verge of being declared an antique, and grated some carrots for a de-luxe vegetarian salad which would accompany the lentil soup, she wished that Richard were in town. It was at times like this that Jemima felt her comrades on the *aktiv* were always letting her down, and then she yearned for her former husband, fifteen years her senior and the father of the *NLJ*. She often heard his voice in her head, but now she could almost see him, his fiercely burning eyes, their intelligence only slightly distorted by the thick glass of his spectacles. Why had he deserted her at the steering wheel of the vessel he had so painfully constructed, supervising every little detail, from the undercoat used to paint the mast to the quality of paper used in the toilets? Where are you? What are you looking for? Why no messages for several weeks? These questions arose angrily in her head. At that very moment she heard the bleeping of the fax. Could there be such a thing as telepathy? She smiled as she saw the familiar typeface of Ricky's portable on the thin sheet of paper. Eagerly she tore the message off the machine.

BRIEF COMMENTS ON EINSTEIN'S REPLY TO HIS CRITICS
Due to a freak storm the electricity grids were out of action. Hence the fax delay. Ezra is a valued contributor to the Journal,

possibly till very recently the most valued, but his text suffers from five major weaknesses:

(1) It is chaotically organized. The chronology is jumbled, the narrative is incoherent, there is a great deal of repetition. Rhetorical questions and truistic assertions dominate the essay.

(2) It is drearily written. This is unusual for EE and reflects a crisis of perspectives. It is difficult to make a piece on the USSR at the moment dull, but he manages to do so. The prose is lifeless, a litter of passive, anonymous constructions, without any colour or vigour. Ask him why.

(3) It is not very informative. He has collected a great many statistics culled from the Soviet press, but does not appear to realize that half of them actually disprove his own case. There is a litany of acronyms, with no real attempt to situate, assess and define the major political currents inside the unions. He asserts that the workers are for glasnost, but hostile to perestroika. This may be true. But where is the evidence?

(4) It is politically evasive. Is he for Gorbachev's reforms? Against them? What or whom does he himself support? The institutional dramatis personae are never situated in any intelligible ideological spectrum. On the central question as to whether capitalism could revive the Soviet economy or simply make it into another Brazil, he is silent. Clearly even posing the question is akin to apostasy!

(5) It is theoretically sub-literate. This is the most depressing feature of the text since it demonstrates the inability of Ezra to face up to the new problems.

Please raise all these points with him gently, as you play the piano, but without being too diplomatic.
R.

Mimi smiled. She loved these letters from afar. Ricky had solved her problem all the way from Papua New Guinea. She just couldn't understand why these personal letters to her from a former husband irritated the other members of the editorial committee so much. As she walked to the kitchen she muttered aloud: 'I wish you were here, Ricky! Here!'

Richard Lysaght had graduated from Trinity College, Dublin, and moved immediately to London. He was an anthropologist by training, but in those heady years following Fifty-Six he had immersed himself in French existentialism. Initially he had been attracted to Camus and Merleau-Ponty, but had moved on to the more profound writings of Jean-Paul Sartre, and it was these that had pushed him towards Socialism and Marxism. He became a regular reader of *Les Temps modernes* and determined to start an English-language equivalent. He had been married at the age of eighteen to a fellow student at Trinity. There were two children, only a year apart in age, but they stayed behind with the mother when in nineteen fifty-four Richard abandoned his native shores as well as his wife.

The years it took him to get a divorce made him extremely hostile to the institution of marriage, a view reinforced by the exemplary relationship (or so it had appeared at the time) of Sartre and de Beauvoir. So when he ran into a stunning black-haired beauty at a CND party, he was determined that whatever else happened, he would definitely not get married again. Poor Ricky! If he had waited another decade, there might have been no problems on this front, but it was still the late Fifties and Jemima had been presented at Court. Even that might not have posed an insurmountable problem, but there was a much more important consideration. Her parents would have cut her off without a penny if she had moved in with a disreputable Irish Marxist. And the pennies, they both agreed, were badly needed if a magazine was ever going to be launched, not to mention a hegemonic publishing house.

The salad was nearing completion when Jemima's mind re-called the wedding. For some reason she always remembered the event when she was feeling a bit low and the effect it usually had was to increase the depression. Ricky had insisted that they get married in a country where an overnight divorce was obtainable provided both parties were in agreement. She had felt that this was not the best possible way to start a relationship, but had agreed to participate in the research. It was Ricky, of course, who after a few days in the Reading Room of the British Museum had found the ideal place. The only country where marriage and divorce were equally simple was Iceland. Jemima's parents were a bit perturbed, but a story was manufactured for their benefit. Ricky's mother, who had died during childbirth, was, for the benefit of the Wilcox family, buried in the tiny Catholic cemetery at Reykjavik. And so it happened. Within a few months of their marriage, Jemima's hair turned snow-white. There was no surface reason to explain this amazing occurrence. Some of her female friends suggested that it was Jemima's unconscious sending a message for help to the outside world, but she did not take them seriously.

The noise of the doorbell panicked the hostess into pouring too much vinegar into the salad dressing. She discarded her apron, quickly brushed her hair and went to the front door.

'Hello Mimi!' said Ezra, shaking hands with her in the friendly fashion he usually reserved for trade unionists. 'This is my wife, Maya. Mimi Wilcox, editor of the *New Life Journal*.'

It took a few minutes for them to settle down with drinks. Mimi was staggered by Maya's beauty. She wondered how Ezra had landed this one. Perhaps there was something there that Mimi had missed out on, or could it be that she was simply Ezra-blind? She admired the old boy greatly, but found him totally asexual. His texts had been a vital part of the *NLJ* armoury since the May events in France, and they had all learnt a great deal from him. Mimi had, on Ricky's strict instructions, actually joined the world movement for a while, but had withdrawn quietly and without rancour when the instruction was reversed. Ricky, the bastard, had promised to follow her, but had left her stranded in there, on her own. The story of her life!

'Ezra, a drink? Sorry, sorry. I've remembered. No alcohol. Fresh orange juice is on the way. Maya?'

Maya pointed to the bulge in her stomach. Mimi was amazed again. Not only had Ezra married again at the age of seventy, but he was on the point of becoming a father, the Jomo Kenyatta of the European Left. Well, well, well.

'How incredible. Many congratulations. This calls for a celebration. I'll have a glass of champagne!'

'Mimi,' Ezra began plaintively, 'the other comrades. Are they . . . ?'

'Oh, sorry. Gyorgi is in Hungary. My colleagues on the *Journal* all had other engagements tonight. So I'm afraid you've got only me.'

'That makes me very happy.' Maya smiled at Mimi, who disappeared to fetch their drinks.

'I met her first husband, Ricky Lysaght, in Paris. It was during the Algerian war.' Ezra sighed as he explained all this to Maya. 'A brilliant man. Very sharp mind. He created the *Journal* and built a team around him, but a centrist. An inveterate centrist.'

Maya had often heard Ezra use this word, which, to her, meant someone who was neither a Conservative nor a Socialist. Now she felt confused. 'Ezra, what is a centrist?'

'You mean you don't know?'

'I'm not sure.'

'Someone who vacillates between reform and revolution.'

'Talking about Ricky?' Mimi had walked into the room with a tray full of drinks.

'Where is he these days?' inquired Ezra.

'In Papua New Guinea. Working on the last volume. We communicate by fax.'

'Uneven and combined development,' said Ezra shaking his head and laughing. 'It will backfire, you know. All these technological advances will implode capitalism. I may be dead when it happens, but when it does, please make sure that you reprint my books.'

Later, during the frugal repast which Mimi had so painstakingly prepared, Ezra became a little aggressive.

'Some comrades say the *Journal* is moving to the right.'

'I don't think that's the case, Ezra,' Mimi riposted. 'It's the world which has moved to the right. We have to analyse these developments, and often those who are doing so are not, well, the traditional sort of comrades. Most of the work is being done by liberals, social-democrats, Greens, feminists. Marxism seems to be at something of an impasse.'

This was very unlike Mimi. It was not that she didn't feel strongly about certain things, it was just that her upbringing had made her ultra-diplomatic. This chameleon-like quality often deceived her colleagues on the *Journal* and drove some of them completely berserk. But Ricky's fax had contained clear and stern instructions. Ezra had to be firmly encouraged to confront the new realities. Hence this rather strong statement at her own dinner-table. Without the spectre of Ricky, she would have said similar things, but sweetened the pill with references to Ezra's own *oeuvre*.

Ezra, who knew Mimi well, was taken aback by her tone. This was very unlike her, but then he smiled to himself. It was obvious. The organ-grinder had clearly been at work from afar. Once he had realized this, Ezra tilted his chair back, shut his eyes a tiny bit, deliberately to put Mimi out of focus, and replied to her as if he were answering a hostile interlocutor at a public meeting. Because he was not looking at her, he missed her gesture indicating that the chair whose legs he was stretching was notoriously unsafe.

'Of course the faint-hearts collapse at the first sign. Marxism at an impasse you say? I beg to disagree. It is Stalinism which is finished. Dead. Gone forever. Marxism is wounded, I agree, but the balm is already having its effect. Wherever the masses are in motion they will sooner or later understand the basic premises of Marxism. As you already see in East Germany, the workers are against Stalinism and with a vengeance. But they don't want to hand the factories over to the West German bosses. Even in Romania there will be some surprises on this question. Poland is another matter, but look at the Soviet Union. The miners at Vorkuta and in the Donetsk region are showing that they can manage the mines as well as their towns. They certainly want democracy, but not capitalism. What other answers are there?

Does your *Journal* have them? Perhaps you should change its name to *The Impressionists Bi-Monthly* and in small type below have a sub-title: For Worshippers of Accomplished Facts . . .'

'Now come on, Ezra,' Mimi stopped him in full flow. 'I'm not going to let you get away with that. We published your last essay on the Soviet economy very recently. We have been having a vigorous debate on the whole question in our pages. Ricky has written . . .'

'Ricky's two volumes,' interrupted Ezra, who was an expert in reclaiming any conversation, 'are brilliant anthropological studies. I have learnt a great deal from them myself, but they are not a substitute for revolutionary Marxism. In fact I think that his first book, *The Transition from Ape to Man*, is much more self-assured than *Non-Verbal Communication: A Preliminary Essay*. He makes too many concessions to the vulgar empiricists. But these are small points. They are first-rate Marxist books. Agreed. But I doubt whether they offer any solution to the problems of the Turkish minority in Bulgaria or the Albanians in Kosovo or the nationalities in the Soviet Union. But we still do. You can say that we are crazed sectarians, but, in general, I am proud of our record. Do you know that we have comrades in Prague and East Berlin who have won the respect of the broad masses because of their unremitting hostility to the bureaucracy and their absolute refusal to cave in to Gorbachevite centrism? Do you know that . . .'

Before he could proceed any further, the chair broke and Ezra fell on to the wooden floor. The event defused the crisis. Ezra laughed good-naturedly, stood up immediately to prove that no damage had been done and repaired immediately to the bathroom in order to wash his hands, dust his trousers and relieve himself. Maya took this opportunity to establish an independent relationship with her hostess. She whispered to Mimi: 'Do you think that was the final collapse of the dialectic?'

Mimi, who had been told that Ezra's Brazilian lover was apolitical, was so amazed that at first she could only stare at Maya in silent admiration and then, a few seconds later, she roared with laughter. It was genuine laughter and not the sort provoked by the needs of *Journal* diplomacy.

After this therapeutic exchange the evening flowed smoothly. Ezra had calmed down and discussed business matters such as new editions of his books published by the Journal Publishing House, and a new book which he was writing on Germany, and finally he broached the real question.

'Mimi, did you receive our invitation to . . .'

'The Special Congress? Of course, of course. We discussed it at the last Editorial Committee. Everyone agreed that we must attend as observers.'

Mimi did not point out that only four members had been present at the meeting and the decision had been taken when one of them had left the room to make a phone-call. Constitutionally speaking, therefore, the meeting did not have the quorum necessary to make any decisions. Nonetheless the decision had been minuted.

Delighted with the news, Ezra walked away from the dining table and started flicking through the newest books on Mimi's shelves. He picked up the latest offering from Journal Books Inc. It was an exquisitely produced volume, *What Do Women Chess-Players Do When They Are Playing Chess?*, by the Swedish psycho-therapist, Gote Ericson. Ezra turned to the index first, as he always did with a *Journal* book. The litmus-test was applied. He turned to the letter E and his expert eye, computerized for this particular function, whizzed down the entries. Ah, there was Einstein, A. Oh! He frowned at not being included. This Ericson fellow must have moved to the right, if he had not had the grace to refer to Ezra's long essay *Chess and Class Struggle* which had been translated and published, it so happened, in the theoretical journal of the Swedish comrades.

Despite this obvious structural defect in the Ericson book, Ezra appeared to find it a compulsive read. He conveniently forgot the two women he had left at the table and settled down with the book in the corner of the black leather sofa, which looked worn and battered, but was still very comfortable. Ricky had bought it after their Icelandic capers. He had been shattered by Mimi's hair turning white and had bought the sofa, partially as a penance, but also because whenever she sat on it, the contrast with her hair was very striking.

From a distance the two women observed him and smiled to each other. Mimi thought that he would never have disappeared like this if Ricky or some of the others had been present. Maya was not at all displeased. She had Mimi to herself.

'Mimi, my father has been a subscriber to your *Journal* for many years. The only time he hit me was when I was two or three and I pissed on a copy which he had left lying on the floor. Later he told me that he had been reading one of Ezra's articles on France and I had wet it beyond recognition. So, instead of becoming a Trotskyist he became a musician.'

Maya's peals of infectious laughter captivated Mimi, who smiled appreciatively. As if moved by a telepathic reflex, they both looked at the other end of the room and then laughed again. Ezra had fallen fast asleep, the book on chess perched precariously on his lap.

'Tell me about your life, Mimi. You have two children?'

'No, just one. Ricky has two boys by his first wife. I have a girl. Only a few years younger than you.'

'Please Mimi, I want to hear your story. Ricky. Children. The *Journal*. How you manage now with your man back in Hungary. All of it.'

Mimi poured herself a full glass of the bad Italian white wine, which neither Maya nor Ezra had touched, sighed and began her tale. She talked about her family, their shock when they discovered that Ricky was a Marxist. Initially she had told them that he was an existentialist, which for some inexplicable reason her father had taken to be a synonym for a gardener. An Irish gardener was bad enough, but a red digger was unacceptable. Relations had been restored after Lavinia was born and the doting grandparents had reconciled themselves to their daughter's choice.

'And when did you become editor of the *Journal*? I remember in our house there was a dinner party. Everyone was amazed that a woman had been made editor. Somehow it didn't seem in character.'

'I don't think we thought about that aspect very seriously. Ricky couldn't run it on a daily basis. He hadn't done so for some time, and his long absences in the Pacific made it obvious that a change was necessary. There was no fax in those days and so we had to take certain decision. By the time his letters arrived with contrary instructions it was too late. Naturally, this created problems.'

Mimi was charmed by Maya and delighted that someone should show an interest in her life. Ezra was snoring gently and Maya walked over to cover him with the dog's rug from the kitchen. Then Mimi resumed her story. She talked of how Ricky had been determined that the first Editorial Committee of the *Journal* must speak all the principal languages of the world. There were only eight of them on the Committee, but they had worked hard and within a year someone or the other was either fluent in or could read texts in French, Spanish, German, Russian, Serbo-Croat, Japanese, Chinese, Arabic and Persian.

'At the same time we published the first major article on women. I wrote the first draft, but Ricky rewrote it from beginning to end, giving it a coherence which I was incapable of at that time. I would never have admitted this even a few years ago, because that article made my name. But I've outgrown all that now.

'It's really very funny, because two women have just published an unbalanced book in which they accuse Ricky of not defending me when my article came under fire from others on the Committee. If they only knew. It was modesty that stopped him defending the text, since he'd written most of it in the first place. In these days of advanced computer technology there are simple tests. If we put Rick's essays and book into the computer and then my old piece on women, or rather his old piece, anyway you know what I mean, the computer would soon discover which bits were written by him!'

Maya found all this a bit bewildering.

'You know, Mimi, it looks to me as if your Ricky loves stepping back into the limelight. Am I right or wrong?'

Mimi was staggered by Maya's perceptiveness, but did not feel that there was much point in getting involved in a long session of Ricky psycho-gossip. So she returned to her central theme.

'What I'm really trying to say is that the *Journal* had become a big success and might have continued along those lines if it hadn't been for an unforeseen episode of the sort that can destabilize any tiny apparatus regardless of politics.'

Maya's eyes lit up in anticipation.

'I fell in love with another member of the Editorial Committee. And he with me.'

'Who? Who was it? What happened?' Maya was now utterly enthralled by the tale.

'It doesn't really matter. It didn't last long. I was hypnotized by the brooding sexuality of his Celtic voice and his dour humour, but I wasn't prepared for physical violence. In those days S&M groupings were known only in specialist parlours in Soho, which was a long way from our world. I ran back to Ricky and showed him the bruises. We became friends again, but not lovers. Lavinia was five at the time and I decided to send her to a convent. But it did effectively split the Committee. The tensions were so bad that very few people turned up to meetings. It was then that Ricky started writing all the articles under different names. Since quite a few of them were really brilliant their authors began to receive requests to speak at seminars all over North America. Then Ricky had a brainwave. His two boys in Ireland, Sean and Gerald, had graduated with excellent degrees in Philosophy and Literature. They adored their father, not believing any of the tales their mother had told them about his black moods, his uncontrollable fits of anger, his irrational obsessions.

'He put on one of his really seductive displays of charm, moved them to London and put them on the Editorial Committee under two of the pseudonyms he had used for some of his articles. Then he adopted a young American from the West Coast, a waif accidentally stranded over here. All the boys picked up his ideas, his mannerisms and even attempted to mimic his writing style. It worked all right, I suppose, though there were tensions between the boys when they vied with each other for Ricky's approval and the rare invitation to dine with him at his club. Then Ricky decamped to Papua and we had to elect a new editor. The boys, not unnaturally, thought that one of them should be offered the post. If Ricky had really wanted that I'd have gone along with it, but he insisted that I took over instead. At first the kids agreed, but when they thought about it afterwards they felt angry and used. They staged an insurrection. The Commune lasted a few weeks. They had tried to get rid of Ricky altogether, but he bounced back and set up a two-person Commission of Inquiry to investigate the causes and reasons for the deterioration of comradely relations inside the *Journal*.'

At this point Maya interrupted the story. 'Mimi, you people must have a lot of time to spare. Slow down a bit, though. I'm getting muddled. So who were these Commissioners?'

'The two Commissioners were, effectively, outsiders. One had only joined the Committee a few months previous to the Children's Revolt. The other lived in Yorkshire and was pretty far removed from the actual site of the conflict. Anyway he'd missed one crucial meeting because he refused to take even a single day off from the England versus West Indies Cricket Test Match. Neither of them had ever personally experienced Ricky's outbursts. They saw themselves as umpires and acted accordingly. It's true that they had found his insistence that they wear Judges' wigs when interviewing members of the Committee a bit quirky, but then everyone was capable of some eccentricity or the other. At least Ricky's were never hidden. Their decision was interesting. They declared Ricky leg before wicket, I think the cricketing metaphor was actually used in their report, but they refused to declare him out.'

Maya was desperately trying to memorize these details for her father's benefit. She knew that he would want to know everything, and she could almost hear him recounting these tales at select dinner parties of *Journal* readers in Rio.

'So what happened, then?' she asked, hoping there would be no more cricket, which baffled her.

'Divide and rule. Sean and Gerald walked out. The others limped on a bit longer. I remained editor and Ricky carried on writing his letters from afar.'

'One more thing, Mimi.' Maya was not in the least ashamed of her own curiosity. 'Whatever happened to Lavinia?'

'Oh well, she survived the convent, went to Oxford and is now in Ireland breeding horses. My parents left her everything, so she has no financial problems. Adores her father, of course, but she'll never join the *Journal*. There was a time when we needed cash and I toyed with the idea of commissioning her to do a piece on a day in the life of a groom, but Ricky vetoed the idea. Then I persuaded Rhum Straw-Berry, the distinguished oral historian, to go and interview a groom for his special series on toilers of different sorts. He agreed, but I forgot to tell him that Ricky was violently hostile to any such notion. He asked Ricky for the Irish address and that was that. I got a very severe wigging from him and gave up. I've told you enough. Now it's my turn. Maya, what on earth is Ezra up to? Has the old boy flipped his lid? I mean, calling every sectarian under the sun to a Congress in Paris to discuss politics! The whole idea's a non-starter. What on earth is going on? You simply *have* to tell me. There's a story doing the rounds that the whole thing is just a gigantic hoax to celebrate the birth of your child!'

Maya had no idea what the Congress was about, but she did not want to admit that to the editor of the *New Life Journal*. She felt that Mimi might not take her seriously if she confessed her ignorance. So she simply assumed that Mimi's never-ending question referred to the little big thing in her stomach, and embarked on a description of the first time she had told Ezra, his reactions, the argument on the name, Ezra's refusal, after the Tiananmen Square massacre, to have the child called Mao

Einstein, her insistence on the name and the final compromise on Ho Einstein, regardless of whether it was a girl or a boy. So it was that Mimi failed in uncovering Ezra's strategy for the Congress.

After they had left, Mimi sat down and typed out a fax for Ricky, describing everything that had taken place, but confessing her failure either to shift Ezra in his view of the world or to discover the function of the Congress and concluding:

I suppose it would be only fair to describe the dinner, if one was being totally instrumental, as a failure, though I do think you would have liked Maya a great deal. She is genuinely pleasing to the eye, intelligent and full of life and fun. She reminds me of your old girl-friend in São Paulo . . . Do you remember the one I mean? You won't be surprised to hear that not a single member of the Committee showed up at the dinner, even though I gave them ample warning. They are behaving more and more like Ceausescu's orphans. In fact something else has happened which I need to bring to your attention. Given the crisis of Leninism and the perspectives of 1917, which article do you think our Committee is raving about? A text by Havel or an interview with Dubcek? No! A superb analytical text by Pedro Rossi on 'Walter Benjamin and the Crisis of the Turkish minority in Bulgaria'? Wrong again, Rick! Our bunch of deluded Bolsheviks want to publish a text on 'Lacrosse, Hockey and Pornography' by that Canadian separatist Cathy Fox, who broke with Ezra years ago. I don't deny that the text has its merits. It's well-written for a start, and the line of argument is certainly original, but at this time and in our Journal, . . . I mean the entire Socialist project is going up in smoke and we should evade the problem by a fifty-page essay on the phallic symbolism of the hockey-stick and the vaginal characteristics of lacrosse? It's all deeply shocking.

Your continued absence in Papua New Guinea is seriously inhibiting my more creative functions as editor. Have you finished the essay on the green tree-python? It might well have some relevance to our Committee. There are times when I yearn for a green tree-python. Some of these sessions are really soul-destroying. I feel more and more that for some of our colleagues the Journal *has* become a substitute for everything: politics, real life, sex, marital discord, etc. The world is changing, but not in our tiny offices. The most recent episode is the sudden discovery of the virtues of East Germany. For years we've been denouncing that regime. Now suddenly the prospect of reunification fills some of C's orphans with utter despair. Grasping at straws. That's what it is, Ricky. I wonder what the citizens of Papua would learn from our editorial meetings? Would the ingenious minds who discovered 'cargo cults' be able to find an explanation for the antics that take place in our palatial offices? Do you have any suggestions? Could you please send me some green tree-pythons as soon as possible? I'd like to leave a few of them twisted around the chandelier above our table! Tomorrow I will fax over another text on which I'd like your comments. It is on punk and post-punk as a modernist corrective to the commercialization of Sixties music. The argument is that this new music, which I personally loathe, deliberately uses a primitive, disharmonious and vulgar idiom. Pure rubbish as far as I can see. Most of this music is a ritual celebration of a total hostility to ideas. It has fed some of the more lumpen *activities of the far-left groups in recent years.* What do you think?

J.

10

The Cuckoo flies to New York

Emma was in a cheery mood that morning. This was the result of
two phone-calls which had followed each other in rapid succes-
sion. The first had been from her agent, who informed her that
PBS had accepted the second draft of her television play, *Trial*,
and that he was now negotiating the terms. Then Ted Spanner
had called to let her know that he was in town for the monthly
meeting of MAB, and to ask if she was free for lunch? She
certainly was, and so the minute she got off the phone she hurried
into her track-suit for a morning run, which had now become
necessary since she was going to alter her routine and have lunch.
Ted was bound to order wine, she doubted whether she would be
able to resist the desert and a glass of Muscat, and therefore some
exercise became vital. She wondered what Bob and Co. actually
discussed at their MAB gatherings. They behaved a bit like the
Freemasons. The membership of MAB – Marxism Ain't Bullshit
– was restricted to Ted and some of his academic chums in North
America and Britain. She supposed that what they discussed was
a strategy for advancing their cause on the campuses and ensuring that their enemies were contained. But Spanner had got his
own Institute. What more could he possibly want? She must ask
him over lunch. MAB indeed!

Half an hour later she was jogging along the riverside in a
warm, purple suit, with matching gloves and hat. She jogged at a
reasonable pace when her stomach was empty, but she was

careful today because the path was treacherous. Patches of frozen ice had claimed a number of casualties already. Emma winced as she saw some of the tell-tale signs *en route*.

The snow had melted, but spring was still far away. A cold breeze had forced the more sedate imbibers of fresh air to dress in furs and heavy overcoats so that only their dwarfed faces were visible. Emma knew some of them, and friendly nods were exchanged. Often when she was jogging Emma concentrated on the day which lay ahead, on mundane but vital matters such as how she was going to pay the phone-bill. Today she was thinking elevated thoughts. Her future as a writer. Her impending trip to Europe. The vista of the Mediterranean where she had spent a number of springs and many summers in the old days. Images of slender cypresses, almond trees in blossom, Grecian sunsets, the fragrance of jasmine, the screeching cicadas and the ever-blissful tranquillity. Colours and space were so different in southern Europe.

She thought, too, of friends in Paris and London. She had been out of touch for a very long time, nearly ten years now, and so she was not fully aware that every single comrade who had defended her against the ravages of PISPAW had left the movement. During her last trip to Europe in 1976 she had met so many couples breaking up. Everywhere the story was the same. It was as if the men had returned home at the end of a long war and suddenly seen their partners as companions and shuddered with disbelief. Disintegrating egos mingled with self-hatred. Long all-night discussions about the awfulness of monogamy and the equal awfulness of promiscuity or open relationships. She wondered how and where they all were today.

She was running back to her starting point and dreaming of the nice hot shower, when she sighted two serpents. The shock made her motionless. It must be a daytime nightmare. What she saw revived memories of pain associated with a particular cycle of her life. Noble and the Cuckoo noticed her as well and exchanged looks. They were equally embarrassed, but for different reasons. They were discussing a possible coalition to marginalize Ezra totally and they now knew that news of their meeting would reach the Centre in Paris very soon. As they came very close, Noble walked on, ignoring Emma, and stooped near a bench a small distance away. Jean-Michel saluted her and grinned. A shiver travelled down Emma's back.

'Hi, Jean-Michel? Visiting?'

'Hello, Emma. Hello. Yes, yes. I have come to see my former wife Emily. You know she is here now?'

Emma gave him a smile so false that she almost felt ashamed of herself.

'Well, I will see you at the Congress. Yes?'

Emma nodded and smiled. She had now recovered her composure.

'Sure you will, honey. It's great, Stalinism crumbling everywhere, isn't it?' He smiled and nodded. She continued: 'Everywhere now except China, Cuba, and inside the Trotskyist sects. Your organizations, Jean-Michel, are the last suppositories of what they were created to fight. That asshole who still runs PISPAW. Your friend over there . . . how long can these people go on? Think on it Jean-Michel. That's the only thing I'm coming to discuss!'

She waved and resumed her jog, leaving the Cuckoo to ponder her remarks. Emma was pleased with herself. Despite the initial faltering she felt that she had handled the encounter remarkably well. This boosted her confidence yet further, and she picked up some speed as she ran to the front of her apartment block.

After Noble and the Cuckoo had finished exploding Emma's political and sexual reputation for the tenth time, they returned to what they had been discussing. The Cuckoo had not been lying when he told Emma that the reason for his visit was to meet his former companion. Emily Grass had abandoned two lovers to go and live with the Cuckoo during her tenure as a full-timer in the apparatus at Paris Centre. Finally she had found the Cuckoo's demands unacceptable. Wearing rosary strands around her neck while the Cuckoo mounted her was not too awkward a demand, since it suggested anticlerical flavours. It was when he insisted that she dress up as a nun, but without any knickers, that Emily began to rebel. She'd had enough of his dirty habits. Now Emily was suffering from cancer. She was being treated and was responding well, but had asked to see the Cuckoo. Emily was a member of PISPAW and so the Cuckoo informed Noble that he was intending to come to New York. It seemed too good an opportunity for either man to miss.

Noble had proposed a deal to Cuckoo. If Ezra came up with something that would, in effect, disarm and demobilize the ranks, then in order to save the world movement they must unite and introduce a plan that would enable them to keep their forces together.

'Haven't you any idea, Jean-Michel? I can't believe that he hasn't told you.'

'He's obsessed with sex. You know he has married a young Brazilian. Well, she has a child inside her. That's all he thinks about.'

'Great! Good! But why the fuck has he called a Congress? Does he want to Trotskyize the baby in front of the whole fucking movement? He can have as many fucking babies as he wants. Why a fucking Congress? Why?'

The Cuckoo shrugged his shoulders and laughed.

'I really don't think he's decided anything. Anyway relax. It won't be a fucking Congress. Only a talking one!'

'But it's two weeks away, man. We have to prepare. He's invited all our enemies. The whole thing could blow up unless it's properly organized.'

'Look,' responded the Cuckoo. 'We'll be there. If it looks dangerous we'll act. The Triplets don't want to lose their apparatus either, you know. There will not, there cannot be any liquidation of the movement. Don't worry.'

'Jean-Michel, if ever you want to move here, let me know.'

The two men began to reminisce about old times as they walked about to the PISPAW headquarters, the scene of numerous triumphs such as the 'great turn to the proletariat' in nineteen seventy-nine; the mass expulsion of dissidents in nineteen seventy-three; the refusal to permit a Special Commission from the Paris Centre, investigating breaches of democracy, into the room where all the tapes of speeches made by Noble to closed PISPAW congresses were stored; and, of course, the trial of Emma Carpenter, not to mention numerous episodes of a similar character on a lesser scale.

Interestingly enough, neither of these two leaders of the world proletariat thought fit, at least on this particular occasion, to discuss the state of the world. Even as they were walking back, momentous events were taking place inside the Soviet Union itself. The old Tsarist Empire, taken over lock, stock and barrel by the Bolsheviks and expanded by Stalin, was beginning to fall apart. The Soviet leader, Mikhail Gorbachev, was now beginning to discover the Abraham Lincoln syndrome: if you don't complete the reforms from above quickly, you face rebellions from below. Gorbachev had excluded Lincoln's solution by explicitly renouncing the use of force to solve the problem of nationalities. In this fashion, this incredible product of the system appeared to have signed his own death warrant. Every day brought new instalments of the drama taking place on the Soviet stage.

That very day the newspapers were full of reports of Gorbachev's visit to Lithuania. He had been seen on television engaged in vigorous debates with ordinary people. He was trying to convince them against secession, but it seemed obvious that he had already decided that he would not bind them to Moscow by force. His philosophy had been summed up in the phrase: 'Divorce is sometimes necessary, but its conditions and terms must be agreed by both sides.' This indicated that the Soviet leader had a strategy. He certainly had a precedent. It was Lenin who had granted Lithuania independence in 1920. It was Stalin who had done the deal with Hitler and got it back. There was little doubt that Gorbachev was going to claim that he was acting as an orthodox Leninist in order to defuse the conservative opposition in the Central Committee. The whole of Moscow was discussing the dangers that lay ahead. The entire Caucasus was seething with anger against Moscow. People were thinking that this would be the time to launch a coup against Gorbachev. In fact the eyes of the world were once again on the Soviet Union. Would he pull it off? Or would *they* pull him down?

Noble and the Cuckoo steered clear of such difficult subjects. The Cuckoo did not wish to raise contentious matters such as the Castro brothers, and Noble, for his part, was happy to avoid talking about glasnost and perestroika. He had disciplined two comrades in the preceding week for reading *Moscow News* at a PISPAW public meeting, and three veterans in the Houston branch in Texas had been expelled, for having stated at a private dinner party, thrown by some former members who had themselves been expelled in the early Seventies (for demanding that PISPAW send arms to the Sandinistas), that the leadership's line on Cuba was 'bankrupt'. The Cuckoo was aware of all this, but he did not feel that it was appropriate to embarrass Noble right now. Unless the two of them agreed on a united front against any attempts to liquidate the movement, Ezra might get away with his schemes. So politics were not discussed.

No such inhibitions were evident around the small table in the *sushi* restaurant in the Village. Emma had been a bit put out when Ted turned up with Helen Grove, a short, grey-haired academic whom Emma didn't know at all. She thought that if Helen were a MAB groupie, it might inhibit conversation about the forthcoming beano in Paris, but all was well. Helen had no connections with MAB, and was in fact a member of the *Journal*'s Editorial Committee, and as such knew all about Ezra, the Congress, Maya, the baby, Mimi and, naturally, Ricky Lysaght. Helen had just arrived in New York *en route* to the Spanner Institute in Berkeley, where she was going to give a series of six lectures on 'The Origins of the Democratic Idea'.

The lunch went on for hours. A great deal of *sake* was consumed. Those exquisite little flasks were very deceptive. Emma hadn't enjoyed herself like this for years. The democratic revolutions in Eastern Europe and the Soviet Union excited her a great deal. They talked about Czechoslovakia; about Havel and Dubcek. All three of them felt that it would have been far more symbolic if Dubcek had been elected President. Havel should have been more generous. They talked about the Marxist dissident Petr Uhl, who had been in prison for a total of nine years, five of these 'for Trotskyism' and five for 'human rights'. Emma insisted that Petr would not have survived inside PISPAW for more than a year. He would have been expelled as 'a petty-bourgeois liberal deviationist'.

Then they moved on to more profound and philosophical questions, the nature of Marxism and the future of the Socialist project. Helen drew their attention to Marx's obsession with the figure of Prometheus, who combines the features of Satan and Job, but who suffers and never assents. In *Das Kapital*, the mythical liberator of humanity who defied his peers and brought Light to Earth is introduced in chapter 23. For Marx, Prometheus is the modern proletariat, manacled to capital. Zeus sends an eagle to tear out the liver of Prometheus. Marx's father had died of cancer of the liver. All these images were jumbled in his head. He himself became Prometheus, bringing the message of human emancipation to the enchained proletariat. Would someone tear *his* liver out? The price would be worth paying if the result was human self-emancipation.

'The irony surely is, is it not,' Emma asked, 'that it's the proletariat which is tearing out the Marxian liver, grilling it on an open fire and swallowing it with the help of a dark red wine – the blood of Christ. One only has to look at Poland.'

Helen refused to accept this view.

'Surely not. Anyone can see that Stalinism cloaked itself in the language of the *Manifesto* and appropriated the messages contained in the classic texts, but its practice had more in common with the Byzantine Church.'

'But anyone can't see that, Helen,' riposted Emma. 'That's where the problem lies. For the people in those countries Marxist Socialism is dead. Full stop. Not for ever, perhaps, but for a decade or so till they've learnt new lessons. I must confess that I'm thrilled to bits. Let them come to whatever they want by themselves.'

Helen was not prepared to give in so easily.

'If we agree that these states were societies in transition. They had rejected capitalism, but they had not achieved socialism . . .'

At this point Ted, who had been listening to them talk with a somewhat bemused expression, decided to enter the debate.

'But I most certainly don't agree!'

'Let me finish, Ted.' Helen's voice was a decibel higher than before. 'I know what you're going to say. These countries represented a new social formation, namely bureaucratic collectivism. If any argument is being disproved rapidly it is that one. I think Ezra Einstein's general view on these states has been correct. Either they move forward to Socialism, by which he means democracy and social ownership of the means of production, or they revert to capitalism and are totally absorbed by the world market. Where Einstein is wrong is in believing that the masses would never tolerate the restoration of capitalism. On this point I think Emma is right. They might. Where I disagree with Emma is that I don't think the working class in these countries will abandon some of the decent things the system has given them. Subsidized housing, very low electricity and gas rates, full employment, universal education on a lower and higher level and so on. I mean it is a joy to go to a concert hall in East Berlin or Kiev or in most places and see workers enjoying the fruits of bourgeois culture. Opera, ballet, classical literature, poetry, music, etc. Will they give all this up?'

Emma felt that the horrors and atrocities of the system had outweighed the gains in social welfare. Helen insisted that these material gains would be a stumbling block for any attempts to impose a capitalist system à la Thatcher or Reagan. She agreed, however, that the post-authoritarian regimes could become genuine social-democracies. Ted disagreed with both of them. He did not believe that new modes of production could collapse so easily. He foresaw a recuperation of bureaucratic collectivism in a new guise. Helen made one last attempt.

'Look, is it or is it not the case that the first of the great bourgeois revolutions against Absolutism was the revolt in The

Netherlands in fifteen sixty-six?' Ted and Emma nodded duti-fully. 'The second bourgeois upheaval against late feudalism was England in sixteen forty-nine. Am I correct?'

Ted grinned. He saw the drift of her argument, but he couldn't restrain himself. 'Wrong! It was an upheaval, but not of bourgeois origin, and England was not a feudal state at the time, late or early.'

Helen did not rise to the bait. Spanner's theories on the origins of capitalism were well known within the academy and had stimulated endless debate among historians. She knew that if she started on this one they would end up by having dinner at the restaurant. So she exercised self-discipline.

'For the sake of argument let's accept your view. But let's just continue. Big upheavals in the Absolute states from The Nether-land onwards. They end with the American War of Independence and the French Revolution of 1789. Then there are the unifi-cations of Germany and Italy, again carried out by violent means, and finally we see the overthrow of the Shogunate in Japan. My point is that *all* the regimes that were born out of these violent class struggles were dictatorships of one sort or another. Cromwell and Napoleon are two obvious examples, but there are others. The Founding Fathers in America kept a fifth of their population under slavery, there was an Iron Chancellor in Germany, a Piedmontese royalist adventurer in Italy, an absol-ute monarchy in Japan. Democracy, by which I mean universal suffrage, arrived three hundred and fifty years after the Dutch Events. Speaking relatively, Socialism is in its infancy. A long view of history, Comrades. That's what's needed.'

Ted suddenly frowned and banged his fist angrily on the table. The two women looked up in alarm, but he was laughing.

'I think we should break this up. We can continue the dis-cussion at Ezra's Congress. If I stay any longer the *sake* will begin to talk. Emma, great to see you.'

They kissed each other with genuine affection and then Emma gave Helen an impulsive hug. As she was leaving she suddenly realized that she had forgotten to tell Ted about her surreal encounter with the Cuckoo and Noble that morning. For some reason this fact gave her enormous pleasure. She had kept a hold on her life. Noble and the nightmares of that past were over. She was free. Truly free. She felt an incredible urge to fly to Bucharest.

11

Could tedium possibly stifle the turmoil in the world?

'The question is this, Comrades: if we attend this so-called emergency Congress convened by Einstein it might blow our cover. You all know what Einstein's like. Schematic brain, ultra-left politics, impressionistic beyond belief. He always wants quick results. Never understands that the house we are trying to build has to be constructed brick by brick. On the other hand if we did not attend, our rivals would scream that we had abandoned the movement. Our rank-and-file is very uneasy and jittery at the moment. Perhaps we should go, after all. But then, I wonder . . . What do the rest of you think?'

The Shadow-Shadow Cabinet of the Burrowers League was in session. This was the High Command which would seize power when Labour failed the nation for the tenth time and the working class moved rapidly from a General Strike to an immediate insurrection, splitting, in the process, the police, army, navy and air force. When that happened, the men and one woman seated around this table would take over. The Shadow-Shadow Prime Minister, Jed Burroughs, had been talking for over an hour on whether or not to go to Ezra's Congress. Jed was seventy-five years old and about five feet and three inches tall. The exact measurements were never revealed since height became a sensitive issue, part of the struggle of the smalletariat against the largeoisie. His face appeared pockmarked, but when seen in close-up there were no actual marks at all, just tension spots and the odd rash. Thin white hair delineated the borderlands between his skull and his face. He was, as usual, wearing a dirty grey raincoat.

Jed Burroughs' personal life was a mystery to most of the Burrowers. Only a handful of people knew the torments he suffered. It was this repression that explained the tension which permanently racked his body and which could only explode in the thunderbolts of dogma he hurled down at the members from the podium. It did not matter whether he was addressing a tiny gathering of a few dozen defenders of the faith or several hundred white-collar trade unionists. The message and the medium was exactly the same. Burroughs had welded form and content to such an extent that it was impossible to separate one from the other. His voice had a melodious lilt and this, coupled with his monotonous, over-rehearsed gestures, often had a soporific effect on an audience. It was not unusual to find the slightly older comrades fast asleep during a Burroughs' rant. At more intimate gatherings, such as the meeting of the Shadow-Shadow Cabinet taking place at the moment, he was soft-spoken to a fault as he concluded his remarks.

'That, then, is my considered opinion, Comrades. I know Einstein of old. He's devious, sure. But the tone of the letter does not suggest a master-plan to me. I think our old Comrade Einstein is confused and disoriented by the changes in Eastern Europe. That means his members are ours for the picking. From the very beginning our press has been clear and precise. Precise and clear. We will now reap the harvest. We are going to Paris!'

His Defence Minister, 'General' Jo 'Noddy' Hensfeet, had been nodding throughout the Cabinet meeting. He had nodded when Jed had initially suggested they boycott the event and he had nodded equally vigorously when Jed had concluded that they should accept the invitation. Noddy was not an atypical member of the Shadow-Shadow Cabinet.

A three-hour discussion commenced during the course of

which there was no disagreement. The twelve shadows present had attempted bravely to prevent the slide into total tedium by searching for different ways of saying the same thing. At the end it was agreed that Jed and the Shadow-Shadow Home Secretary, Paul Potter, should attend the Congress. Potter had never been to Paris and was strongly in favour.

'I think it's an excellent idea, Comrades. I do have some bad news to report, however, on another matter. As you know we lost three members in Newcastle to the Rockers a few weeks ago. That miserable and unprincipled opportunist Jimmy Rock has now decided to redouble his efforts. As you know, comrades are a bit fed up with the way things are moving in the Labour Party. The Rockers could pick up more people. Vigilance is essential in this period. But there is more. As comrades are aware, we've been bugging the offices of the Rockers for several months. There is no doubt that they are attempting to sabotage the Paris Congress. They've rung people up in North America and Germany to tell them it's been cancelled. They're planning to fake a letter from Ezra postponing the event at the last moment. If we are attending we should inform Einstein of these manoeuvres.'

The entire Cabinet nodded sagely. Burroughs smiled as he leaned back to congratulate Potter.

'You know something, comrades. When we seize the power, our Comrade Paul Potter here will play a vital role in ensuring that we hang on to it, eh?'

This statement was greeted with applause. The Cabinet meeting was about to be adjourned when the Shadow-Shadow Chancellor demanded a hearing. Jed frowned, but she was insistent.

'Comrades, we have to decide on something very crucial. I insist. . . .'

'You insist! You insist!' Jed screamed at her. 'Comrades, I suggest that the matter our colleague here wishes to address is referred to a sub-committee consisting of her, the Shadow Home Secretary and myself. Security is paramount. Agreed?'

'Agreed!' they all shouted in unison. Poor Chancellor. She was a computer-wizard who worked in a relatively high capacity for a multinational banking conglomerate. Three other Burrowers worked in her department. Over the last five years she had manipulated the figures so effectively that the Burrowers League had benefited to the tune of almost two hundred thousand pounds.

Three days ago the crime had been detected. An inquiry was taking place and, understandably, the Shadow-Shadow Chancellor wanted instructions. There were no moral questions involved – milking a multinational was a sacred duty – but getting caught? Jed was livid. He did not want money scandals at this particular time. The sub-committee agreed to meet that same evening. At this meeting Jed ranted and raved, but finally authorized enough money to be transferred back to the bank from which it had been liberated to sow doubt in the minds of the investigators. This wasn't Jed's idea. It was his Chancellor of the Exchequer who had devised the scheme as a way of disrupting the computer checks by daily injections of small amounts of money. Jed blinked in amazement at her ingenuity, and then spoke in such a way as to suggest that it had been his idea in the first place. Since the Cabinet were used to this behaviour-pattern, the Chancellor merely smiled and nodded.

Had Jed Burroughs always been like this?

ENCYCLOPEDIA TROTSKYANA: *Date of entry:* 1986

Jed Burroughs (real name: Jonah Brink), b. Amsterdam, 5 March 1915.
[Compilers PJ, GM, MJ, QH, RM, TE]

Brink, the son of a wealthy jeweller, joined the Dutch Communist Party at age 15.

Files indicate he was very serious and dedicated to the extent of being totally humourless.

In 1933 he came under the influence of the Trotskyites. Began to raise questions about Comintern policy re Germany and Hitler. In September 1933 he stated at a branch meeting that Trotsky had been right on the German Question. He was backed by his lover, Job Segal. Both were expelled from the local party the next day. Brink's sister, Sugar Brink, married Chaim Bernstein, aka Jimmy Rock (*see* BERNSTEIN, C.) and followed her husband to Britain. Jeweller Brink, a conservative, disinherited both his children.

[The following report was specially edited for the present edition of *ET*. There was no longer space to include the forty-two pages which are still available in previous editions.]

Burroughs in London

[By PJ, GM, MJ, QH, RM, TE]
Jed Brink and Job Segal arrived in London penniless. After some inquiries they discovered a tiny Trotskyist cell in the South London district of Balham. The two men were there greeted by an engineer. They mistook him for a comrade. The heart of their politics was poured out to the stranger. They did not realize till later that he merely shared a flat with its other occupant, their contact. Since he did not enlighten them they had no idea that he was a staunch supporter of Stanley Baldwin.

[ET staffers in London, PJ and GM, interviewed the engineer, a Mr Uriah H. Ansorge, on three separate occasions. Transcripts of interview are in NKVD File No. 32: 4T: JB]

Uriah. H. Ansorge gave them some advice as to where they might find work. As for politics, he merely repeated what he had heard Big Jim, his flat-mate, say to others. They must adopt pseudonyms and enter the Independent Labour Party. They immediately put this plan into action and proceeded to adopt new names. Jed became Burroughs and Job became Jones.

After their first ILP meeting they were approached by a friendly-looking giant with blond curly hair. This was Jim Port, who had been told their entire history by his Tory flat-mate, Uriah. Jed and Job, both in their late teens, were embarrassed. Big Jim put them at their ease and bought them a few drinks. He had found work for them, not easy in those days. For the next six months they washed-up in virtually every hotel kitchen in central London. With what they earned, it was possible to pay the rent on a tiny room near King's Cross, buy one meal a day, a few cigarettes and still save a bit to buy theatre tickets for a couple of cheap seats once a month.

It took Port a few months to realize that Jed and Job were very dull kids. They listened to everything he said with an intensity which scared him. He then heard them repeating his words to new recruits to the ILP. Port found excuses to avoid their company. To his close friends he confided that he had nicknamed them 'twin evils'. The ILP's big campaign at that time was against the 'twin evils: war and fascism'. Jed was nicknamed 'fascism' and Job was referred to as 'war'. When Jim and some of the ILP veterans were in their cups they started calling the boys by their new names to their faces. At first the two Js were simply bewildered. After six months they understood the reference and were clearly not amused. Job left the movement and started a small business. [Segal Undertakers Ltd was established in 1934 in Brighton. Fifty years later it had become the largest chain of undertakers in the country. Job Segal's decision to offer lower rates to the unemployed and elderly singles was a master-stroke. Job Segal died in 1969 in London, but his partner, Uriah H. Ansorge, is still alive. Jed Burroughs/Brink did not attend his funeral. – ET]

Jed never forgot Port's insult and retained an implacable hostility to all humour. Humour was characterized as a 'petty-bourgeois deviation' and banned inside the Burrowers.

Sexual Problems

Jed is a homosexual. Job had been his lover. We in the Soviet Union know that homosexuality is very widespread, but in those days the movement considered it an unacceptable aberration. It is possible that one reason for the lack of friendliness which Jed and Job experienced was that their comrades suspected their sexual proclivities. [To be dull and a homosexual was, in those days, pushing toleration to its very limits, especially in the pubs near King's Cross Station – PJ.] Jed accepted the rules of the game and has remained a loner. When he left the movement, Job succeeded in suppressing his own instincts and married a young shop-girl. Job's wedding and the rapid appearance of children eased the social pressure for Jed. Many comrades felt that they had been unfair and too hasty in jumping to conclusions.

But Jed never got over Job's defection. As World War Two approached, he decided to form an independent group outside the ILP. His following leapt from twelve to fifty loyalists. Quality was transformed into quantity. Fifty young men and women were regularly attending his lectures. Their social composition was of some interest. Almost half were workers of some description, and Jed began to work hard at proletarianizing the remaining 50 per cent. He trained them in how to speak, what gestures to use, how to deal with opponents inside the movement, how to deal with enemies outside the movement, how to talk to workers, how to treat intellectuals, how to preserve a certain moral standing in their places of work and, most important of all, how to dress in order to appeal to workers. Anything smacking even mildly of bohemianism, such as an open collar or long hair, was frowned upon. [The pattern was not dissimilar to that practised by the Communist International during the Thirties.] The only person permitted to dress badly was Jed, since he was deeply attached to his filthy old raincoat.

The one aspect of everyday life which Jed Burroughs always refused to discuss was sexuality. When a young woman suggested that the Group discuss the writings of Alexandra Kollontai, Jed Burroughs lost his temper. He became incoherent. The woman persisted. Jed Burroughs took her aside and told her that she need attend these meetings no longer. The subject was never raised again. [The woman in question, Dorothy Towler, is now regarded as one of the outstanding Afrikaans novelists.]

Jed's followers were bewildered by this behaviour but

they put it out of their minds. They knew that their leader was already too much like Captain Ahab. Sex was his white whale. His comrades thought it might be a good idea to make sure that the two were always kept separate.

After the war, Jed reluctantly accepted a directive from the Paris Centre and led his tiny band into the Labour Party. He loathed this party beyond belief, but being a disciplined comrade he did as he was told. The postwar settlement made him angry. At a public meeting, he characterized the new Eastern European states as 'bureaucratic state-capitalism'. Jimmy Rock stood up and argued the opposite. They were extensions of the Soviet Union and therefore, like their progenitor, they must be 'workers' states', albeit deformed from birth. It was a ferocious argument and each convinced the other. The next day Rock became a 'state-cap' and Jed embraced the other thesis.

When all the others got fed up and left, Jed carried on alone. He described his new tactic as entryism *sui generis* and proclaimed that he would transform and split the Labour Party. What Jed Burroughs could not do to the pretty men he encountered every day, he began to do to the Labour Party. The Burrowers became part of the shabby furniture in most Party HQs. As the children of Jed Burroughs, they were immediately identifiable by their dress, hair-cuts, predictable rhetoric and the right arm swinging up and down speaking gesture, which became known as the disabled wood-cutter's movement.

Yet, despite his growing years, Jed remained a tormented soul. Unable to satisfy himself on a regular basis sexually he had begun to haunt certain public lavatories in the hope of instant gratification. This became the sum total of his private existence. He became an even sadder and lonelier person.

Burroughs in the Sixties
What Burroughs hated most about the Sixties, apart from Rock and Ezra's opportunistic adaptation to petty-bourgeois

youth, was the movement for sexual liberation. His own concealed orientation had made him a misogynist. The women's movement threatened the internal stability of his organizational regime. He denounced it as another 'petty-bourgeois deviation'. Then, to his horror and fascination, the Gay Liberation Front was formed. A wave of expulsions hit the Burrowers as all those who had succumbed to the new mood were removed.

What no Burrower ever discovered was that Jed Burroughs used to disguise himself and attend the odd GLF meeting. This could have been his time to come out. Homosexuality had been decriminalized and gay people were ringing in the changes every day. Not Jed Burroughs. He became even more 'security-conscious'. He made it clear via an oral instruction that homosexuality was a luxury that a proletarian organization could not afford.

One of Jed Burroughs' problems was that he had constructed the Burrowers in a very special way. Monolithism reigned supreme. [The method of organization was, of course, well known in our country till April 1985.] Dissent was discouraged and dissenters of any sort who attempted to organize against Jed's leadership were unceremoniously expelled, as was a young female comrade who had decided to undergo a sex-change. The official reason for this was that since the Burrowers were a clandestine organization inside the Labour Party, they could not afford the luxury of free debate inside their own ranks. At one stage it seemed that the leaders of the parent Party might expel all the Burrowers, but this threat receded as the Burrowers dug deeper and did their usual disappearing trick. Jed and a few others were expelled and complained furiously, much to the amusement of those whom they themselves had expelled from the ranks.

Conclusion
In the Fifties all the segments of the world movement were embedded in the Labour Party – Rock, Burroughs, Hood,

everyone. Rarely in history has a single party been entered by so many sects with such negligible results. The shock troops invaded its every orifice. Not that their combined seed have so far succeeded in germinating. Rock and Hood tired of their own sterility and decided to try their luck elsewhere. But Burroughs persisted, and after 45 years of consistent effort he resorted to artificial insemination. This provided him with a member in Parliament. The celebrations lasted a whole year and the Burrowers recruited a few hundred more kids to the cause.

[END OF ENTRY]

That night in the pub, Paul Potter decided to speak frankly to his leader.

'Er, Jed, what is the real reason for going to this pissawful Einstein Congress in Paris? I mean, we've got on pretty well on our own so far. They've got nothing to offer. You know I backed the decision. But are you sure? Let's not go!'

Jed sipped his beer and looked hard at his Home Secretary. Then he smiled unpleasantly.

'Listen to me, Comrade. The world is being turned upside down by maniacs of one sort or another. Einstein's instincts are usually right. I know he's a petty-bourgeis intellectual through and through, but he does think. I was part of his movement for a long time. We have many Comrades in common. People like you only understand Britain. This tinpot little island with its tinpot fucking institutions. It affects everyone. Even us. Look at you. There's another world out there. It won't do you any harm to see it. Do you understand what I'm saying?'

Paul Potter nodded, but did not pursue the discussion. He knew that Burroughs was not telling the truth, and the Shadow Home Secretary was also aware of something else. The fact was that some years ago Jed had developed an uncontrollable crush on an English Member of Parliament, then a minister in the Conservative government. In his public speeches, veteran Jedologists began to note, he was much softer in his denunciations of

Norman Tebbit than of virtually every other member of the Cabinet. On one occasion he even turned up at a Burrowers Shadow Cabinet meeting dressed exactly like Tebbit. The Shadow Defence Secretary remarked on this fact, and to his amazement Jed actually smiled with pleasure and replied: 'Well, the person in question is a very well-dressed man.'

Jed started attending all of Tebbit's political meetings until he was visited at home by Special Branch men who asked him why he was tracking a member of the Cabinet. Jed blushed and blurted out an untruth. He was, he told the police, working on a biography of Tebbit in order to explain the rise of a Tory leader from a working-class origin.

The Special Branch sergeant looked puzzled and asked him why Tebbit rather than Cecil Parkinson, whose father had been a railway worker during the General Strike of Twenty-Six. Jed shrugged his shoulders. That was the end, but, as a result, Jed was forced to restrain his activities. He was the only Burrower who, after years of not watching television at all, suddenly purchased a dish and watched Sky TV regularly. This created a scandal, since the Burrowers were still blacking all Murdoch products because of Wapping, but Jed refused to surrender. 'Best to know the enemy,' he muttered, or words to that effect.

It so happened that Tebbit was due in Paris to address a meeting of the Frenchmen Against the European Community group on exactly the same day as Ezra's Congress. Jed decided to accept the invitation, to the consternation of his Politburo.

Fuelled by the heat of his fantastical romance, Jed was beginning to ditch habits formed over a lifetime. For example, he had trained all his cadres to make notes before a public speech on foolscap paper, and it was a strict Burrower rule that only four lines were permitted on each sheet. Burroughs explained this quirk by asserting that workers were impressed with public speakers who they felt had done their homework. A sheaf of foolscap carried to the platform, the pindrop silence broken only by the noise of paper touching paper, created a good impression. Not that the orthodox technique was free of snags. Traineehacks often got their arm gestures confused with the way they had been instructed to make notes and turn the sheets, and this had led to some disasters. Then there was the occasion when Jed himself addressed a large audience of twelve miners during the nineteen seventy-four strike and got so wound up in denouncing Edward Heath that he brushed his speech angrily to the floor. This naturally disturbed the flow, and one miner in a state of advanced insobriety took advantage of the interval to pose a key question. 'Ish it true?' he asked Jed, 'that if you have too many kids in India they chop your goolies off?' Jed's inability to respond to this question, led to the collapse of the meeting. Jed raved and ranted afterwards against alcoholism, and savaged one of his comrades who timidly suggested that though the miner's question might have been framed rather crudely, it did suggest the spirit of internationalism. Jed banished the comrade in question from all his public meetings for a whole year.

Now Jed had decided to abandon the four-lines-only-per-page-of-foolscap scheme without any advance warning. He decreed a new style which consisted of a raised finger, all the notes on one card, and short, vicious sentences, repeated every ten minutes with a smile. Jed had adopted the Tebbit touch. The old system lived on in Labour Party and Young Socialist branches throughout Britain, not to mention the National People's Alliance in Zaïre, the dictator's ruling party. Two of Jed's boys had returned to their homeland, after studying metallurgy at Liverpool University, and risen rapidly through the party until they were advising the dictator on speech-making techniques. That's how high the stakes had become when Jed had decided overnight to dump the whole system. On top of all that came the decision to attend a revisionist Congress in Paris, the capital of sin. The comrades were, not unnaturally, puzzled.

The next morning, Jed Burroughs rang Ezra Einstein. The two men had not spoken to each other for twenty-six years.

'Hullo there, Ezra. Burroughs here.'

Ezra's voice sounded excited. 'Yes, yes. Hello, Jed. We got your fax today. I'm delighted.'

'Good. But I don't understand, Ezra. Where *are* the documents for the Congress? Surely there must be some documents?'

'No. None at all. It would be foolish to pre-empt the discussion. Of course I have some ideas, but I will spell these out verbally.'

'By the way, did our young Comrade Paul Potter inform you of what that unprincipled opportunist Rock is up to?'

'Thank you. We knew already from some comrades in Moscow. He sent Nutty Shardman all the way to Leningrad to tell them that the Congress was postponed till December. Fortunately they checked.'

'But, Ezra, why not withdraw the invitation to the Rockers? This behaviour is unacceptable.'

'You know me, Jed. Never be sectarian to the sectarians.'

Ezra's superior chuckle irritated Jed Burroughs and he rapidly terminated the conversation. 'Never be sectarian to the sectarians,' mimicked Jed. 'That's why you wrote three pamphlets denouncing me, you bastard!'

12

The chapter of learning and forgetting

The new year drew on. Ezra's mind was by now fully concentrated on the Congress, which had been postponed by two weeks because of the astonishing response from all over the world. Delegates were coming from Iran, India and Pakistan, Nicaragua, Guatemala, El Salvador and Mexico, Chile, Bolivia, Peru, every country in Eastern Europe, South Africa and Namibia, Nigeria and Ghana, as well as the usuals from Western Europe and North America. The PSR had booked the Mutualité for the daily sessions, but the problem was putting everyone up. In desperation Simon had rung up Kosminsky at the Hôtel de Ville and he had promised, for old times' sake and because he had been invited, to find accommodation for five thousand people, but no more. New letters were sent out giving the new dates and insisting that delegations be restricted.

Ezra was in seventh heaven. He was getting angrier and angrier with the West German SPD, cursing their pusillanimity in the face of these unprecedented opportunities. If the SPD would only make common cause with the reformist leaders in East Germany, Gysi and Modrow, the whole of Germany could be transformed. Not that Ezra was surprised to find them stalling. It was a big risk for the SPD because it would mean a clash with their own bourgeoisie and none of the factions was in favour of that at the moment.

Maya, meanwhile, was getting bigger every day. She was constantly surprising Ezra. He had been so overcome by the sight of her long black hair draping her luscious breasts and half-covering the crucifix round her neck that night on Copacabana Beach and many nights subsequently in Paris and elsewhere that he assumed that she was an apolitical Catholic. It is possible, of course, to be extremely critical of him for making such an assumption, but that is a matter for Maya to sort out.

It is perfectly true that she was not a Trotskyist or even a Marxist, but she took an interest in politics and in particular in the peculiarly Latin American mix of politics and culture. For this was the atmosphere in which she had been born and brought up, and it had entered every pore of her body. While still in Brazil, she had published a collection of short stories, *Carioca-Cola*, which had been highly praised, even by writers at opposite ends of the political spectrum such as Marquez and Vargas Llosa.

She was working on a novel in her head, but it kept being disrupted by Ezra's needs and by the constant intrusion of the movement. She had not told Ezra this for the simple reason that he had never asked, even though he knew she had written some short stories. Unlike many of her fellow writers in and out of Latin America, Maya was not in the least egocentric or obsessed with her place in literature. Nor did she believe that literature was a sacrament, that it transcended politics and that it had its own laws and hierarchy. She had been livid when Borges abased himself before the Chilean fascist leader. She was completely relaxed about it all. Ezra's lack of interest in her work might irritate her sometimes, but it never upset her.

Some weeks before, Maya had received a request from Brazil's leading literary magazine for a short essay on the Czech novelist Milan Kundera. Everyone was suddenly interested in Eastern Europe, and the magazine wanted her to go and interview Kundera and find out whether he was going back or not. Failing this, Maya should assess him in the light of the new mood in

Prague. Having never read the works in question, Maya had rushed to the bookshop and bought two of his earlier books. She felt, for some reason, that a writer's first novels are far more revealing than later works. Meanwhile Father Pedro Rossi had got her a file on Kundera from a cuttings library, and she had made extensive notes in the margins. Now she was waiting for her lover to leave the house so she could appropriate his typewriter.

Ezra finally managed to extricate himself from the phone. The Cuckoo had been on the other end, pestering him for more and more information regarding the Congress. Cuckoo was determined to get an organizational grip on the whole affair. On this he agreed completely with Noble. Any spontaneity would be a disaster. Ezra was going away on one of his speaking tours. He had agreed to meet the Cuckoo for dinner next week in Rome, where both were speaking at a seminar on Eastern Europe hosted by the veteran centrist, Norberto Bobbio. Ezra hugged Maya and kissed her. His travelling bag was ready and he promised to ring her every night for the next seven days.

'You seem distant,' he said.

'I've got to write an article on Kundera by tomorrow morning.'

'Kundera?'

'The Czech novelist. You know the one . . .'

'*The Joke?*'

'Yes.'

'Wait a minute. If you look in one of the back issues of the *New Life Journal* there was an interesting review about four or five years ago by a Pakistani comrade. Will you be able to find it or should I . . .'

'I'll find it, Ezra. I've got the whole evening ahead of me. Why don't you go?'

Maya flicked through the *NLJ*'s Index Volume and traced the review. Then she sat down at Ezra's bureau and while thinking of an opening sentence for her own piece she fiddled aimlessly with one of the tiny drawers in front of her. Suddenly it fell out. An official-looking document landed straight on the desk. She shuddered as she realized it was Ezra's will, but she frowned angrily as she read the name of the principal beneficiary. It was the Cuckoo. Angrily she took a felt pen and crossed out the name. In its place she scribbled: HO EINSTEIN.

The anger seemed to have jolted her brain into gear. She started to read the piece on Kundera in Mimi's magazine. It had been published in the autumn of Eighty-Two:

Kundera is a product of the defeated hopes of the Prague Spring of 1968. This and only this can explain the pessimism, nihilism, cynicism and deep introversion which colour his writing and his view of the world. In the new introduction to The Joke *(this remains his best work) he proudly recalls how, in the course of a TV discussion in France, when a participant described* The Joke *as an 'indictment of Stalinism' he protested vigorously, asking to be spared all 'homilies' and insisting that his book was 'a simple love story'.*

Now it is possible that Kundera was refusing to become a pawn in the cold war, and if this were the case then it would be entirely to his credit, but I feel it is something else, something that runs very deep in his work and his psychology. What could it be? Simple. It is a revulsion against politics per se. *A belief that literature/art is a sacrament which transcends all else. No other explanation is possible. If we take at face-value his own description of* The Joke *as a 'love-story' it is simply laughable, in other words, a real joke. The novel is explicitly a denunciation of Stalinism and implicitly of the social and sexual relationships that prevail under such a regime. In reality there is very little 'love' in* The Joke. *There is sex, but of a completely alienated and male-centred variety. Women are objects, nothing more and nothing less. Even in* The Joke, *Kundera reveals the strong misogynist streak which reappears with a vengeance in his subsequent novels.*

The Joke was written in 1965. It became a best-seller of the Prague Spring, selling two hundred thousand copies. If the spring had been allowed to blossom who knows what Kundera could or would have written, but one can say confidently that it would not have been The Book of Laughter and Forgetting. *For this is the work of an exile, written in exile and marred by an extreme self-indulgence. It is gossipy to the point of irritation, though again, it contains sections which are deeply moving. However, as the old Brecht song says, sexual obsession has him (Kundera) in thrall.*

Salman Rushdie has referred to the book as 'erotic.' I did not find it so. Here, much more pronounced than in The Joke, *sex is so stereotypically male-dominated that the book can only be offensive to many of its women readers. 'Strip,' says the Man. The Woman strips. 'Lie down,' says the Man. The Woman lies down. Then he fucks her and later he drops her. This is the sort of sex we read about in the books of Milan Kundera. Even the mild lesbianism portrayed in the chapter titled 'Mother' is the by-product of a voyeurist male fantasy fulfilment for the 'hero', the point being that Kundera, who is normally so adroit at distancing himself from events and individuals, does not and clearly cannot distance himself from the phoney eroticism in his books.*

In The Book of Laughter and Forgetting *Mirek finds Zdena nauseous after having loved her in his youth. He ponders on this for a while. He thinks it could be because of her unthinking Stalinism (she supported the Soviet invasion of Czechoslovakia) . . . No, no, no, interrupts the author-narrator. This can never be the reason for hate. It is far simpler. Zdena is incredibly ugly. Women, you see, can be ugly in a man's world, men never. Don't we all know that ugly men are considered to be sexually attractive to beautiful women?*

The Joke *was written prior to the irruption of women on to the political stage.* The Book of Laughter and Forgetting *was crafted in Paris during the Seventies, when there was a great deal of feminist literature in the bookshops and feminist novels were being published everywhere. This has had no impact whatsoever on Kundera. His one reference to this new movement is a journalist's cliché, when he refers to bra-burning* and topless beaches in the South of France, which seem to have given him a bit of a jolt. Again, the strongest sections are the far too few political vignettes culled from reality. Stalinist falsifications of history, for instance. Kundera describes Gottwald's bare head on that cold February 1948 morning, and Clementis who supplied him with a hat to keep his head warm only to lose his own head a few years later. Kundera savages the French poet Eluard for deserting his old comrade Zavis Kalandra and later defending his execution by the Stalinists. Yet he does not tell us why Kalandra was executed. Not because he was a poet or a surrealist, but because he actually was a Trotskyist, unlike the man who sent the postcard in The Joke. Kalandra was not fooling around.

There is something more than just symbolism at stake here. Kalandra believed in an anti-Stalinist Marxist alternative. Kundera now believes in very little, but that very little includes the exiled Pole, Leszek Kolakowski, the anti-socialist in residence at All Souls College, Oxford. If this is more than impressionism, then Kundera will become yet another dissident from the East who ignores reaction in the West.

Kundera can escape from the horrors of occupied Prague, but his compatriots cannot all flee to the West. They may be in a depoliticized mood at the moment, but nothing in this world is ever static permanently. History is unpredictable, and not a respecter of evolutionary time. Kundera may yet be taken unawares. After all, at the height of the show-trials during the Fifties, few in Prague would have predicted the Spring of Sixty-Eight. Kalandra, the Marxist poet, was executed by the Stalinists. Kundera was permitted to leave the country. That already marks a change. History may yet turn out to be on the side of the poet who haunts Kundera rather than the novelist who has become the chronicler of permanent despair, the conservative nihilist who no longer looks over the horizon.

In the margin, near the sentences referring to bra-burning, there was a note in Ezra's spidery scrawl which made Maya laugh and miss his presence. It read as follows: 'I sometimes wonder whether the reason for the obsession with women not wearing bras has anything to do with the gigantic profits made by the firms who manufacture brassières. Surely only this can explain the hysteria which greeted the decision of some women to publicly burn their bras (in itself a mimicking of the draft-card burning by conscripted men who refused to fight in Vietnam)?'

Maya had found the article stimulating. She too found Kundera's references to sex fairly revolting, but he was such a cult figure now, and the mood was so definitely *post*-feminist these days, that she had not intended to make such a fuss on that particular theme. The *NLJ* article revived her feminism and she began her own criticism thus:

As a woman reader of this great Czech novelist I must start by asking him a few questions. One: does he hate us so much that once our bodies have satisfied his lusts we can be flushed down the lavatory like the proverbial rubber? Two: why does sex in his books never, never lead to any children? Since it gives very little real pleasure, what other function could it possibly have if not the reproduction of the species? Three: now that his fellow writer Vaclav Havel is a major political figure in Czechoslovakia, what new themes will ensnare Kundera . . .

The phone started ringing. Maya cursed herself for not having unplugged it before sitting down to write. She walked over and picked up the receiver. Father Pedro Rossi apologized for disturbing her and asked whether Ezra was at home.

'Hallo Pedro. I'm afraid Ezra is away for some days.'

'There is good news from home. Can we meet this evening?'

Maya frowned and looked at her watch. She just about had time to finish her article.

'Yes, yes, Pedro. Come for supper. About eight-thirty?'

While she was preparing a meal for her holy friend, it suddenly struck Maya that Pedro always rang to suggest a meeting when Ezra was out of town. Usually they met in a café near Saint-Michel. He'd visited them many times and knew the apartment well. Today was the first time she had invited him here when she was on her own. His behaviour was always impeccable, so why was it that she felt slightly uneasy? The only slightly odd episode had taken place last summer. They had all been sitting outside enjoying the glorious weather when he had suddenly noticed her crucifix reflecting the sun. He had asked to see it, but before she could say anything he had moved very close, fingered the crucifix while it was still round her neck, and his breathing became a little bit heavy. The inspection over, he had returned to his chair. Neither Ezra nor Simon had thought this strange and so she had almost forgotten the whole incident; now she remembered that it had made her feel slightly queasy.

Her concern evaporated when she opened the door. Pedro was accompanied by a tall well-dressed woman with a face which was strong and pleasant. Her eyes had a hypnotic quality, and Maya found herself staring into her guest's face at regular intervals throughout the evening.

Pedro introduced her and the two women touched hands. Evangelina was a theology student from Bulgaria, who had met Pedro when he was invited in 1988 to lecture at the University of Sofia on Liberation Theology and the Vatican. To Pedro's surprise the lecture hall was packed out, but most of the audience were dressed in long leather coats and had the same hair-cut. He realized, of course, that these were the cadres of the Bulgarian secret police. The only genuine student who turned up innocently was Evangelina. When the talk ended she questioned him in great detail about the doctrines being expounded by the Liberation Church in Brazil, the writings of Boff, his own conversion and how the dispute with the Vatican could be resolved. He answered her in the polite, priestly tones which had become his trade-mark. Afterwards they discussed matters in a more informal setting in the lounge of his hotel. The policemen had asked not a single question. Not even a foolish one. Lina, as she was known, could not understand the sudden interest in the Vatican, but Pedro remembered a series of articles which tried to place the blame for the assassination attempt on Pope Wojtyla onto the Bulgarian regime. Then all became clear. They were looking for some ideological ammunition in their fight against Wojtyla. After some reflection, Lina sadly agreed that Pedro's interpretation was the only likely explanation for the grotesqueness of the event.

She had then told him another story of how she and the literary circle she moved in had, a few years ago, attended a lecture given by a leading English playwright, one of whose plays was titled *Poetry, Bloody Poetry*. The secret police automatically assumed that this must be an attack on poets and poetry and arranged for him to be invited to Bulgaria. They were having a bit of trouble with some underground poets at the time whose scurrilous attacks on the ruling Zhivkov family were being memorized and whispered throughout the country. One of the ditties bordered on the obscene, explaining Zhivkov's anti-Turkish obsession by the fact that his wife had fallen in love with a hubble-bubble which gave her greater satisfaction than her husband. The English playwright accepted the invitation. On that occasion too the police packed the meeting. Their reaction to Pedro's lecture, which was virulently anti-Vatican, had been very favourable but they were disappointed by the playwright's performance. Blissfully unaware of the reasons underlying his invitation, he blithely interspersed poems from Brecht, Mayakovsky, Mandelstam and Akhmatova throughout his lecture. There was an investigation after the lecturer's departure. It turned out that nobody in the 'writer's section' of the special police had read beyond the title page of *Poetry, Bloody Poetry*.

Maya had never laughed so much. Lina had an unlimited supply of Bulgarian tales from the Zhivkov era. They all consumed a great deal of wine. Maya's morning sickness had come to an end and she had discovered that she could start drinking coffee and wine once again. But she had not drunk too much to be unaware of the fact that Pedro had fallen completely under Lina's spell. Behind the spectacles his eyes were shining, his skin was gleaming with anticipation and he was suggestively and continuously fingering his own crucifix. He was not capable of keeping his eyes off the Bulgarian theologist for even a single moment. He laughed louder and longer at her jokes than Maya.

When Maya left them alone and went to the kitchen to put the finishing touches to the dessert, she wondered what would happen next door. Just as she was bathing the sliced apples in some brandy and sprinkling sugar on them, she heard a squeal of excitement, which had clearly emanated from Pedro. Then there was an eerie silence. Maya put the apples under a low grill and tiptoed to the door. Pedro was lying spreadeagled on the floor in his vest, underpants, spectacles, crucifix and socks. His face was full of ecstasy. His cassock lay crumpled in the corner. Lina was leaning over him fully clothed, stroking his dark brown hair and bending down once in a while so that their tongues could meet. Both of them seemed oblivious to their surroundings. Maya suddenly smelt the apples burning, rushed back to the stove and rescued them just in time. She tasted a slice. It was exquisite. Then she deliberately smashed a plate on the floor and emitted a scream. She heard scuffling noises in the next room and smiled to herself, but the smile turned into giggles as she imagined what Ezra would have done if he had returned without warning and found Pedro on the floor with Lina fondling his beads.

When Maya went back into the room with the apples, Pedro and Lina were back at the table, stroking each other's hands, their faces flushed. Maya smiled and served them. It was Pedro who broke the silence.

'I'm in love, Maya. I'm going to defrock myself and marry Lina.'

Maya smiled, but then immediately she remembered odd telephone conversations she had overheard between Ezra and a number of comrades. In all of these Pedro's name had figured prominently.

'Wait till Ezra returns, Pedro. Don't do anything hasty.'

'We already have,' interjected Lina.

'Really? I wasn't in the kitchen that long, was I?'

Lina laughed. 'Enough for us to savour the hors d'oeuvre. We are saving the first intercourse for later.'

Maya and Lina laughed. Pedro blushed. Then Maya gave him a friendly hug.

'Listen. Wait for Ezra. You can do what you like, just don't defrock yourself, in the religious sense I mean. What difference does it make? Are you a Believer, Lina?'

Lina shook her head. 'Not at all. Theology was a safe subject and provided a useful cover for what some of us were really doing. I did find Catholicism interesting, but only as a contrast. The Jesuits and the Stalinists have a great deal in common.'

'Not just the Stalinists,' muttered Maya.

Pedro appeared a bit shocked. 'But Lina, you never told me . . .'

'How could I? The situation in Sofia was awful at the time.'

Maya then insisted that Lina stay over for the Congress. Pedro agreed that it was an excellent idea. Lina wanted more details.

'What Congress?'

Pedro, who on this question was one of Ezra's confidants, began to explain the whole idea in some detail. Lina was interested, but she did make the point that it might be better if she returned to Sofia, where some of her former dissident comrades were now in power and needed all the support that could be mustered. She explained that the remnants of Zhivkov's apparatuses were mobilizing an ugly nationalist mood against the Turkish minority.

'You know, when I see the nationalist demonstrations in our cities I am reminded of German fascism. It's very, very, dreadful. It is the one thing that makes me despondent.'

Pedro embraced her and held her close. 'But one of the main discussions will be on nationalism.'

On hearing this Lina agreed to delay her return to Sofia. She had come over to meet some Bulgarian friends in exile and had succeeded in persuading them to go back, but they too could stay for Ezra's Congress and return with her. Pedro was delighted and both of them were in rapturous mood as they said their farewells to Maya.

It was past midnight when the phone rang. Maya had just

retired to bed, but, knowing it was Ezra, she took the call. He was in Turin, where he had spoken at a trade-union conference which was reassessing the sliding scale of wages, and he sounded exhausted. She described the events which had taken place in their apartment that evening. Ezra was unamused. He repeated a single instruction three times in the course of a ten-minute conversation.

'Please make sure you tell Pedro that under no circumstances, I repeat, under no circumstances, must he withdraw from the Church. Did you hear me Maya? Please make sure you give him this message. I will try to ring him myself, but in case I don't get him . . .'

Maya understood the message, but even she did not realize its importance, or why Pedro Rossi, of all people, was such a vital part of Ezra's plans for the future of the movement.

13

Renard gets ready for combat

The Triplets were now preoccupied with the organizational preparations for the Congress. These could be summed up in one word. Money. They needed the equivalent of a hundred thousand dollars to fly out comrades from the Third World, Eastern Europe and Britain. The Japanese comrades were paying for the South Korean, Philippines and Hong Kong delegations, which is why the figure wasn't higher. The PSR was no longer the wealthy organization it used to be in the Seventies, with several thousand members, many of whom made more than generous donations to the party coffers. Fortunately Kosminsky was helping out with the accommodation, but money was still desperately needed. Whenever there was a financial crisis and no other solutions were visible on the horizon, the Triplets became telepathic and shouted aloud in unison: RENARD!

The phone-call was made and an hour later Renard arrived. Having been told the nature of his mission, he was attired in a faded combat jacket with bullet holes and his Che beret. He came straight to the point.

'How much?'

He never asked what for or why or would the money be refunded. Old trouper that he was he just made sure that it was obtained and made available to the PSR. It helped that he trusted the Triplets completely. He knew that the money would not be spent on buying villas in the Pyrenees. Simon named the figure.

'A hundred thousand dollars, mainly for plane fares, accommodation, food, etc.'

'What sort of plane tickets?'

'Real ones.'

'All of them?'

Simon laughed. He knew how the old fox's mind was working.

'No. Not necessarily.'

'Give me a week.'

The Triplets beamed with pleasure. In the past he had always wanted more time. His confidence on this occasion pleased, but also surprised them. Was he up to something without their knowledge? Renard was aware that they were all fascinated by his colourful past, and he revelled in playing the mystery man. His quarrel with Trotsky over the RTS business had given him a legendary status within the world movement. Keeping up the tempo, Renard stood up, shook hands three times and, with his face assuming the most conspiratorial look imaginable, gave an enigmatic smile as he slipped out of the room.

From the PSR headquarters he went straight to see an old friend, a former leader of the PSR, still very sympathetic to the cause, but now engaged in somewhat different pursuits. In the Seventies, Pierre Savary had run the travel bureau of the movement. He had developed links with shady, semi-legal travel agencies all over the world. Now he owned his own agency, with offices in Paris, London, New York, Mexico City, Hanoi, Manila, Tokyo and Martinique. Pierre had learnt a great deal from Renard in the old days and he paid him a monthly retainer as his 'business adviser', which was, and both of them were aware of the fact, just a way of making sure that the old man ate two meals a day.

Renard explained the financial crisis to Savary, who listened attentively. He agreed to provide cost-price tickets for all the delegates. Then Renard learnt forward and whispered in his ear.

'It would help if you could liberate some tickets, you know, like we did in Seventy-Three. Possible?'

Savary laughed. 'Of course. It's always possible, but not for the

Third World comrades. That's very dangerous these days. They must travel legit. Agreed?'

'Agreed. But Noble has asked for fifty tickets for his people outside the United States.'

'Have they got fifty outside New York?'

Renard's throaty chuckle punctuated the conversation. 'Einstein's agreed the number and the Triplets say there's no way out. So fifty duds for them. Yes?'

Savary grinned. 'Fine, but I cannot use my own stock. The risk is too great. Is Janine still working at the old place?'

'I think so.'

'She should pick up fifty from there and we'll put the stamps on here. I've still got the old stamps.'

'You'll take care of that, now. For sure?'

'For sure!'

They shook hands warmly. Renard calculated that he had reduced the costs by forty thousand dollars, and he had a fairly good idea as to where he could find the rest of the money. He got home and lay down for a while, as he often did these days when he wished to think strategically. Three words began to repeat themselves in his head. Money. Vanity. Commitment. Money. Vanity. Commitment.

He thought immediately of old Diablo. What a rock that man was, and how stupid that he had been marginalized by the movement. Diablo's style, of course, had been very autocratic, a result of his Turco-Greek antecedents. For that reason Ezra, the Sardinian and yes, he, Renard, had seen his arrest as a blessing in disguise. Diablo had been caught in the act of forging French francs to send to the Algerian resistance.

After a year in prison he had been released, but by then Ezra had re-organized the movement and Diablo found that his office was now occupied by a PISPAW representative from New York. Ezra had united with PISPAW to try to end the split of Fifty-Three. Hood in Britain and François Pelletier in France had remained aloof till the last. It was they who had invented the myth of Diabloite revisionism, and Diablo always felt that he had been shoved out because Ezra was under their sectarian pressure. Diablo was a proud man. He heard the sound of the tocsin, understood its meaning, collected his loyalists and marched out of the movement.

For a time he became a member of the Algerian government, but after the *coup d'état* which toppled Ben Bella he returned and hoisted his standard in France. His twin message of Democracy and Self-Management seemed utopian and simplistic to some of his former comrades, but with Eastern Europe now on fire he could smile and say, which he often did: 'I told them so years ago!'

Diablo had inherited a great deal of money from his family, but he lived simply and the money was always spent, in his words, 'on the needs of the international class struggle'. He had backed the dissident movements in Eastern Europe as well as the guerrilla organizations struggling in Latin America. Renard decided to approach him. He rang him, stressed the importance of a quick meeting, and they agreed to meet that evening at an old café near Renard's apartment.

When Diablo arrived at Le Croissant, Renard was seated at a corner table, not far from the spot where Jean Jaurès was assassinated in 1914. Renard's costume was slightly altered. He had retained the jacket from that morning, but instead of a beret he was wearing a Sandino hat. He rose as Diablo approached and the two veterans kissed each other on both cheeks. Diablo was stooping slightly, but was still a foot taller than Renard. At eighty-two he was also a good deal younger. He was smartly attired in a suit and tie and gave the appearance of an Edwardian gentleman. He reminded Renard of the deceased English actor, Alastair Sim.

Both men were survivors, and it was this fact that provided the basis for their mutual respect. The first hour, naturally, was spent discussing Eastern Europe. Diablo was livid that the Romanians had bowed to mob pressure one night and agreed to ban the Communist Party. Of course the stupidity had been rescinded the next morning, but it indicated that bad times lay ahead in that country. Renard proudly informed him that Petri Roman, the new Romanian prime minister, was a product of the Sixty-Eight upheavals in France and was well known to the PSR comrades in Toulouse. It was Roman who had dispatched the students in Bucharest to the factories; it was Roman who had seized the time on the balcony after Ceausescu had been heckled off the stage and appealed for a new regime; it was Roman who had refused to renounce his brand of reform Communism and insisted on pushing through a date for general elections. Both Diablo and Renard agreed that the movement did have its uses and its indirect influence was not negligible. The niceties over, Diablo looked Renard straight in the eyes.

'How much do you want and what for?'

Renard had not mentioned money at all and his face expressed hurt and surprise. Diablo knew his old friend well and was not taken in by the look of pain or the Sandino hat, nor by the jacket with bullet-holes.

'Renard, you and I have been in it for far too long to start playing tricks with each other now. So please be frank and I'll tell you what I can or cannot do.'

Renard was surprised by this remark, since he had stung Diablo before, but if he had forgotten so much the better.

'Listen Diablo.' Renard lowered his voice and Diablo bent his head so that he could catch every word.

'I don't know what it's for, but yesterday I got a message from the Sandinista Directorate, which they are prepared to confirm in writing. They need seventy thousand dollars urgently for some vital purchase in Switzerland. They asked me to approach you because they need the money now. They can't wait three weeks for me to do the rounds with my Sandino hat.'

Diablo once again looked straight into Renard's eyes. They did not flicker. Instead Renard permitted a tiny smile to stretch his mouth. Diablo then stared at the table-cloth and sighed. He poured himself another glass of wine from the half-empty carafe and sipped it slowly. On the face of it Renard sat calmly, never taking his eyes off Diablo's face, but inside his heart was pounding. Finally Diablo spoke.

'I'm going to Managua myself next month. Why shouldn't I take the money over then?'

'Next month is too late. Besides the money is needed here. Don't ask me why. I don't know. Nor do I want to know.'

'OK. Come to my place tomorrow at noon. I will have it ready. And bring the official request with you in whatever shape. I must have it for my archives.'

Renard relaxed and ordered some more wine, but Diablo insisted on leaving. His wife was unwell and on her own at home. He did not like being separated from her for too long these days. Either of them could drop dead any minute. Renard murmured the words appropriate on such occasions and the two men parted.

Renard avoided the temptation of lingering for a few more cognacs. This café always reminded him of the old days. It had been a regular port of call during the days of the Taxi Service. Before memories of the past took him over completely, and at his age this was increasingly the case, he stopped and concentrated on his present tasks. He had work to do.

Renard walked back slowly to his flat. A group of students returning home stared at him in amazement. A very old man wearing a combat jacket and a Sandino hat did present an unusual picture these days, at least in Paris. In Managua he might have appeared in a completely different light. Once he was back safely in his flat, he rang Simon at the PSR headquarters. No reply. Renard grunted. In the old days, prior to Congresses, whole nights were spent in animated and often heated discussions. He rang Simon at home. The call was answered promptly.

'Simon?'

Renard's voice was recognized at once.

'Renard, are you OK?'

'Of course I'm OK! Wouldn't ring you if I wasn't. I'd ring for the ambulance.'

Simon smiled. He realized now that the old man had to be humoured.

'What I meant was . . . is the mission proceeding smoothly?'

Renard's hoarse chuckle, tuned by decades of Gauloise cigarettes and cognacs, gave Simon the answer he wanted.

'Mission accomplished.'

'You mean you have got everything?'

Renard swelled up with pride. 'Could it be otherwise?'

'When can you deliver?'

'Tomorrow afternoon.'

'Till then my friend. Sleep well.'

Renard walked to his bureau, where in times past he had kept the files of the RTS, the account books, the payment receipts. Now it contained headed notepapers and seals, a selection of passports and money. He found the FSLN paper and typed out an authorization for himself to collect the money. Then he paused. An important decision had to be made. Should the signatory be unknown or a member of the Directorate? After a moment's thought he copied the mark of Daniel Ortega. It was a small enough gesture, but it would please old Diablo, make him happy in his twilight years. Then he affixed the seal of the Directorate, which, incidentally, was genuine, a gift to him for services rendered to the cause a decade ago. The task complete, the old revolutionary finally bade farewell to the day and retired to his bed.

14

Father Pedro's dilemma

Pedro Rossi was in turmoil. After they had left Maya's place a few nights ago, he and Lina had spent the night together in his apartment. Pedro had not felt such passion for anyone since the Seventies. Elvira, whom he had loved and lived with for six years, had been captured by the army. He was still haunted by the image of her in prison, raped by torturers who were drunk with power. She had refused to reveal any names. The electrodes pinned to her temples and nipples had destroyed her mind completely. She had starved herself to death. It was that trauma which had sent Pedro to the Church. Since that time, love and sex had become so intricately entwined in his head with the fate of Elvira that they had become painful abstractions. That is till his fateful visit to lecture the Bulgarian secret police in Sofia.

Consumed by passion, Pedro had poured out his innermost feelings to Lina that night. She had listened patiently, wiping his tears and fondling his hair. She too, had fallen in love, but she wanted to exorcise the ghosts from his previous life. Conversation about the meaning of life rapidly turned to the meaning of love and, naturally, to the burning question of whether or not they should make love that night. Their collective libido appeared to be sorting out this problem at a speed which surprised Lina. Then, just as they were poised on the threshold of what Jed Burroughs referred to as entryism, a streak of fear flashed like blue lightning through her head. Much to his surprise, she moved off him suddenly, giving his eager, straining member an affectionate tweak. This well-intentioned but thoughtless gesture had the effect of switching off all desire.

Pedro was by now in a state of such agony that he was reduced to speechlessness. Few tortures are greater than the dry pain of frustrated lust. Lina asked whether he would like a glass of water. He remained silent for a very long time. Finally, despite the strain inherent in a situation of this sort, he managed, in a choked voice, to force out a single word.

'Why?'

She attempted to stroke him, but he demonstratively moved away to make it clear that he was in a sulk. Lina simply shrugged her shoulders and attempted to explain to him in a straight-forward but loving fashion that news of AIDS had reached even Bulgaria and that it was simply irresponsible these days to make love without the necessary rubber precautions. To pre-empt any other possible suggestions she also said in a sweet and affection-ate voice that the same reason excluded most forms of mutually enjoyable non-penetrative sex.

This was, in reality, debatable, and had the conversation taken place in different circumstances, Father Pedro would undoubt-edly have entered into the spirit of the debate. As his conflict with the Vatican had revealed, he did not shirk the necessity of vigorous polemic when circumstances so dictated. But he was not even thinking along those lines any more. What had shattered his morale was her assumption that he, Pedro Rossi, had been anything but celibate for the last eleven years – in other words, since long before the AIDS epidemic had dealt a severe blow to promiscuity. He was hurt and upset that she had not even bothered to ask him before taking such drastic unilateral action. It was, after all, a simple matter, which could have been sorted out through friendly negotiations under the quilt. Instead . . . well, what was the point of thinking about it any more? Perhaps he shouldn't have lost his temper.

If only he had kept quiet, the storm that had risen in his heart and rapidly spread elsewhere might have abated and then they might have had a reasoned discussion. He regretted his loss of control as he replayed the conversation, with his own voice in the lead.

'Why? Why did you think that I was a Catholic only in name? Ever since they killed my Elvira I have had no emotional or physical contact with any woman. So how could I have contracted any disease? Answer me that! How? I have never been to hospital or needed a blood transfusion. What right have you . . . you, a simple student from a simple country, to cast aspersions on me. My body is not profane. Do you understand that? Not profane. Now please go. Go.'

Lina began to feel that perhaps she had made a mistake, but his tone was so patronizing and priggish and his reference to the simplicity of Bulgarian students had annoyed her so much that she behaved in an eccentric and uncharacteristic fashion. Her normal instincts would have been to give him a hug, dress and depart. Instead she began to question him in detail in a voice which was deliberately kept very calm so as to increase the effect of what can only be described as her provocations.

'Pedro, I believe you when you say that no woman has touched you for eleven years. Excuse my asking this, but I do so as a theology student from Bulgaria, and I know the habits of our priests very well. I must therefore ask you whether you have been with a man in these eleven years.'

Poor Pedro. He was thunderstruck by the question. He looked at her closely. Her face was as fresh as before, but not so rosy. In fact she had paled. Could she be serious? He felt like screaming aloud. He felt like grabbing her and shaking her. Instead he decided to behave as though in a court-room.

'I understand your question. It's not just Bulgaria. Lots of young men are pressured to accept the amorous advances of some of our holiest men in the Vatican. Understand one thing. I do not believe that homosexuality is a crime, let alone a sin in the eyes of God. Not God as an All-Seeing Being, but as a Concept, a moral construct. In fact there is a great deal of circumstantial evidence to suggest that the noble carpenter himself was not averse to . . . but I digress. The answer to your question is No. No! *No!*'

Lina should have stopped there. Everyone who heard the story felt that Pedro's dignified reply and his refusal to take factional advantage of her description of the practices of some of the officials of the Orthodox Church was a clear sign that he favoured a *rapprochement*. Lina refused the overture.

'What about animals. Bestiality. Ever had a donkey or a sheep? Don't look at me like that. It still happens in the Balkans and Italy, and in some places it's reaching epidemic proportions. I'm not sure whether irresponsible sex is infecting the poor animals, but . . .'

What agony could hurt male pride as much as this? Pedro did not wait for her to finish. He simply went berserk, even though it was five a.m. He lifted her bodily and deposited her outside his apartment. Then he hurled her clothes at her and slammed the door. He imagined that he heard her laughing as she traipsed down the stairs, but in this he was mistaken. Lina immediately realized that she had been insensitive and regretted her impetuosity. She dressed hurriedly and rushed back to her hotel.

Pedro had been thinking about nothing else for the last forty-eight hours. He had left several messages for Lina to ring him, but till now there had been no response. The whole business had got out of control and he blamed himself for everything. When he sought to analyse his behaviour the only conclusion he came to was that the events in the East were weighing so heavily on the minds of Socialists in the West that they were beginning to have a psychologically destabilizing effect. It was an interesting thought, but a trifle far-fetched. After all, why blame the people of Eastern Europe for an evening which went off at half-cock?

· Lina, too, was unhappy about what had taken place. She had spent most of the following day walking the streets of Paris, going into bookshops, staring aimlessly at the Seine, unthinkingly eating three portions of the superb chocolate gâteau served at L'Ecluse on the Left Bank, but still not succeeding in exorcising the Brazilian Father from her mind.

This morning she had decided that she could not give him up and had gone over to see Maya. The whole sad story was retold, with every grievous detail embellished to do justice to the magnitude of the tragedy which had befallen the couple. To her surprise Maya burst out laughing. She laughed and laughed, till she was hammering the table, helpless to stop. She would try to explain why she was laughing but the words 'Pedro . . .' were barely out of her mouth when she found herself overcome by a new wave of hysterics. Tears were pouring from her eyes, till Lina, who had been antagonized at first, began to see the funny side of it and became totally infected by Maya's laughter. They would stop and one of them would again try to speak, but the laughter would block all conversation. Maya hugged Lina as they began to laugh again. There was a discreet knock on the door. Both women sobered up immediately. Maya looked through the peep-hole. It was Pedro, who knocked once again. Lina was pushed into the kitchen and told with a gesture to remain quiet.

Then Maya undid the catch and let Pedro, attired as usual in his black woollen cassock, into the room. He smiled. They shook hands. For a moment Maya thought she was going to collapse into laughter once again, but she made a monumental effort to control herself. Her voice shook when she asked Pedro if he wanted some coffee. He declined the offer, making it difficult for her to recompose herself. They sat down and Pedro did not waste any time.

'I'm sorry for bursting in like this, Maya, but something awful has happened. Lina has disappeared and I'm very worried.'

Pedro nervously twirled the corners of his light brown moustache and wondered why she was behaving in such a odd fashion. Maya was by this time struggling once again not to laugh, and did odd things like blowing her nose and hiding her face in her hands, but she managed to reply.

'What happened?'

'We had a small disagreement, nothing important you understand, but somehow it went too far . . .'

'But what was it?'

'Oh nothing. Lina really didn't understand my vocation.'

At this point the floodgates burst once again as Maya compared this version to the juicy tales she had heard from Lina. She wrapped her arms around her stomach to stop Ho Einstein shaking loose, tilted her head back and howled like a siren. Pedro stared at her in amazement and Lina, taking pity on the man who would be her lover, emerged from her hiding place and stood in front of him. Pedro trembled as he stood up. Lina embraced him and he held her tight. As she observed the pair, Maya sighed, smiled to herself and slipped out of the room, leaving Pedro and Lina to rearrange their lives. Ho felt the earthquake subsiding. Maya had finally recovered her composure.

For the last two weeks Maya had been feeling incredibly tired. Little Ho was moving a great deal and at the most awkward moments imaginable. It was clearly going to be a big baby. Moreover it was now obvious that Maya was eight and not seven months pregnant as they had all thought, and this meant, to be realistic, that it could come at any time. Ezra's whistle-stop tours around the world meant that Maya was on her own for weeks at a time. Pedro was her only regular visitor, and even he was embarrassed to accompany her on shopping expeditions for baby clothes in case their relationship was misunderstood. Mimi Wilcox had rung a number of times and they had talked about some of the problems, though once or twice Maya had felt that Mimi had really rung up to speak to Ezra on various philosophical and political matters and was simply being polite. On one of these occasions Mimi informed her that Ricky was returning from Papua New Guinea in order to attend the Congress and had expressed a great desire to meet her. Mimi appeared to regard this as very important, but Maya was simply bemused.

Who can blame her? She had yet to read *Non-Verbal Communication: A Preliminary Essay*, but had been put off by the fact that it was a five-hundred-page volume. Even Ezra had recommended that she start with chapter 32, the one titled, 'Grimaces: their Symbolic and Psychological Significance in the Ancient World'. Every time she attempted to do so, Ho had started jogging inside her. It was a strange coincidence, almost as bizarre as her vomiting when any British Trotskyist rang up Ezra, and she decided to postpone reading Ricky's book till after Ho was born. Maya began to stroke her distended stomach gently and talk to her child. She was so absorbed in this that she did not notice the figure of Ezra, who had entered the room and was standing very quietly listening to her.

'Ho, if only you knew what was happening in the world outside. Everything is in turmoil. Your father has even organized a Congress to celebrate your arrival. People are coming from all over the world, you know. From faraway countries they are bringing gifts for you. And my beautiful baby we will soon go to Brazil to see your grandparents and have you christened in the sunshine. It's a good time to be born, Ho.'

'I'm not so sure about that, *Liebchen*.'

Maya was startled. 'Ezra! When . . .'

'Just now, just now. A few minutes ago.'

They embraced, but he disentangled himself gently as he observed Pedro and Lina, their eyes shining, their hands closely interlinked, enter the room. When Pedro noticed Ezra's presence he blushed and twitched in embarrassment. Lina was hurriedly introduced as a 'Bulgarian comrade' staying on for the Congress. Ezra welcomed her warmly.

'What's the situation in your country? I mean with the Zhivkov family out, what is the balance of forces between the liberals and the nationalists inside the party? Is there any left current worth the name? What is the situation inside the working class? Do you think there is any possibility of an independent trade union within the next six months?' He paused for a second, but since his questions had forced her to reflect seriously on these matters she didn't immediately reply. Ezra then proceeded to amplify his previous queries by throwing in a few subsidiaries.

'The litmus test in Bulgaria is the question of the Turkish minority. I think the most useful orientation we could have is towards those who defend every democratic right of the minority. The self-management current has never been strong in

Bulgaria, but nor is there any real force present which is independent of the bureaucracy. The Church is insignificant compared to Poland. I am not so optimistic about the evolution in your country.'

Lina had listened to Brazilian football commentators less garrulous than this. She toyed with the idea of smiling vacantly and saying her farewells, but she couldn't resist a short reply.

'Of course you must forgive me. I do not know the political situation as well as you. Sometimes those of us who live inside lack the necessary distance to see things clearly. But one thing you should know. Your litmus test on the Turkish minority question. Within the intelligentsia, of course, there are many people who are totally opposed to the oppression of the Bulgarian Turks, but most of these people are also for the restoration of capitalism. It's strange isn't it?'

She looked straight at Ezra and gave him one of her naïve smiles, of the sort that deceived the bureaucrats who ran the University in Sofia. Then she shrugged her shoulders despairingly and accompanied the gesture with a sad smile. Pedro saw the tongue in her cheek, smiled proudly and stroked his moustache.

Ezra was not sure how to deal with Lina's intervention. He appeared totally exhausted, and Maya told him to go and have a shower and change into something less formal. Ezra removed his spectacles, shook hands with Pedro and Lina and excused himself. The priest and the student kissed Maya goodbye. Maya stroked Lina's face and saw them out with the injunction:

'I want to know what happens next in your story. All the details.'

15

A French-Canadian letter

Maya was preparing their supper. Ezra was sitting at the kitchen table with the post which had mounted in his absence. He put all the magazines, journals and circulars to one side and started to open the letters. Every one of them brought a new smile on his face. The response to his invitation was overwhelming. They were all coming. All the big boys would be there. He made a mental calculation and then shouted: 'It's unbelievable. Without exaggerating, I can say that the representatives of nearly one hundred thousand Trotskyists will be present.'

'Are you sure?' Maya asked politely as she crushed some garlic.

Of course he was sure, and he started running through the membership figures of the Rockers, the Burrowers, the Hood-lums, PISPAW and its satellite organizations, the Spannerites, the Carpenterites, the Mexican group, etc, but she stopped him and interposed a question.

'How many people did you count in Emma Carpenter's group?'

Ezra was amazed and impressed by Maya's new-found interest. 'She has a couple of hundred members and about sixty paying sympathizers.'

Maya smiled. 'Ezra! Emma no longer has any group. She dissolved it during the events in Eastern Europe.'

'How do you know?'

'You told me. Remember?'

Of course he remembered, but he was cross. She had exposed his creative accounting, and he still did not want to admit she was right.

Maya was laughing. 'I think you should revise your estimate.'

'Crazy! You're crazy. Emma may have formally dissolved her organization, but she still represents them. So we have to count her as the spokesperson for two hundred and fifty members.'

She laughed again, but this time Ezra ignored her completely. There was a letter from Montreal: a refusal from the Pan-Canadian Feminist League to attend the Congress. Why could they not have sent a simple two-line rejection, like the Australian renegades? This was a whole bloody book. His face shrank as he began to read the letter. Its author was Catherine Fox, a former leader of Ezra's International and now a prominent feminist writer in North America.

He had always regarded her as the most talented *woman* on the leading bodies of the movement and had been upset when she left. Why was she doing this to him? He wanted to throw the letter into the kitchen bin with the vegetable peelings and the onion skins, but it was compulsive reading. Maya knew it was no ordinary letter, and as he finished a page she immediately picked it up and devoured its contents. Supper was forgotten. Catherine Fox was supplying something far more spicy.

Dear Ezra:

Here I am sitting at my Apple Mac II working on the second volume of my book Sexuality, Pornography and Censorship, *when your letter lands on the floor of my tiny hall. In the old days we had manual machines, remember? Oops! I notice you still have one.*

Anyway it was nice to hear from you after all these years, and it would be even nicer to discuss the big events which are reshaping your continent at this very moment.

Given our old friendship and the fact that I still respect you greatly, it would be unworthy to dismiss your invitiation out of hand. *This letter could be titled 'Why I Will Not Be At Ezra's Congress'! I could get out of what I have and need to say by two simple sentences, which I believe to be true and which I will write in any case. Listen my dear old Comrade Ezra, just listen for a change! What is happening in Eastern Europe is the final settling of accounts with Stalinism. Agreed? But it goes much, much further. For the people of those countries Stalinism is identified with Socialism, with any form of collective solidarity, with many things which remain important and worth fighting for as far as I'm concerned. But all that is dead. Understand that old man? It's dead. Something will be reborn, of that too I'm sure, but how and when and in what shape it is impossible to predict. The whole world has to be remade.*

Alas, poor Gorbachev. He seems to have come too late. If only he had done what he is doing now in '68, eh? So there is not really much point in your decision to call a Congress. It can influence nothing and achieve nothing. Hell, Ezra, I'm not in the mood for bullshit. Even if I was convinced that you could win over something big in, say, East Germany I would wish you luck, but I wouldn't come near your gang a second time. Once burnt, twice shy. Do you know what I'm talking about? Let me explain.

In those long ago days in the Seventies when I was chosen to represent the Canadian group on the Executive in Paris, I was so excited and happy. From a distance we used to mimic what all of you were doing in Europe.

We used to joke about you . . . 'Our father who art in Paris, hallowed be thy name, thy will be done in Canada as in France and Britain and Germany and Belgium, but not, alas, the United States where the Great Satan Noble reigns, etc.' So I travelled to Paris with an eagerness that, in retrospect, appears grotesque. It was awful being the only young woman on your Executive.

Why do men think they can stare at a woman's breasts and not be seen by the person in question? After three months I began to hallucinate. Even at meetings I sometimes used to shut my eyes slightly and all of you were transformed into animals, making animal gestures, talking animal languages. That was normal. The worst person around you at the time was the Cuckoo. Is he still around or have they finally locked him up?

Do you know how he operates? His personal style knows only two methods. Incorporation and Disincorporation! He constructs circles around himself and permits you entry into the inner circle only on special conditions. He can bowl you over by his admiration for your talents, his respect for your intellect, his deference to your superiority, but it's all part of an act. The force which drives him is lust, pure lust and his relentless attempts to seduce. If you're a candidate for the inner circle then your defences have to be destroyed and by audacious methods. The Danton of the sex-maniacs!

One day he told me during a meeting of the Executive that he needed a long and serious discussion with me on the situation in Canada. He was concerned, he said, about the inability of the comrades to develop a balanced position on the national question. He flattered me into believing that I could help in drafting a set of theses for the world movement on nationalism. Could I go around to his flat after dinner that night? He couldn't meet me before because he had this meeting and that meeting, etc.

When I arrived he welcomed me warmly, gave me his document to read and went into the kitchen to make some tea. When he returned with the teapot he had divested himself of every single piece of clothing. There was central heating, but it still seemed a tiny bit eccentric. I forced a weak little smile. He claimed he had a skin disease and the doctors had told him to spend as much time naked as possible. In those days, as you will recall Ezra, liberation of every sort was in the air and I thought that my slight revulsion could only be a result of not being fully liberated. After all, what the Cuckoo was doing was the most normal thing in the world. He was discussing politics with me and if he chose to discard his clothes that was his business.

What we were discussing – Québécois nationalism – was, of

course, totally unrelated to his sartorial state. While he was talking he would absent-mindedly fondle his big, semi-flaccid penis and long, red testicles. (By the way, Ezra, did he ever do this when you were alone with him? I always wondered . . . !) He never made a pass that day and nor was there a hint of mutual sexuality. He was just playing with, mesmerizing with his prick. Sorry! Penis.

The aim of the exercise was clear. These hypnotic, auto-erotic reveries were designed to take me over. He said at one point that I should be flattered that he felt so comfortable with me that he could relax in this fashion. And in this way he incorporated me and at some stage, for a short time, the ego boundaries did dissolve, but only for the duration of the fuck. Here I go again. Sorry Ezra. I mean intercourse. He took me in like a snake swallowing a desert victim. The painful part was the digestion. Being thrown outside for long spells and then swallowed again for a while. Therein lay the nature of his charisma.

After I had seen through him completely I discovered, surprise, surprise, that exactly the same routine, the same phrases, the same jokes had been used on Joanna, Lucy, Wendy, Marie-Jo . . . He is a crazed misogynist who is badly in need of treatment. The cure I think is simple. The Cuckoo is in love with Noble and has been for years. Why don't they consummate the bloody thing? It might improve them both, or am I being too Reichian?

You might think that I am being priggish, slightly Victorian in my attitudes. Believe me, this is not so, Ezra. The best sex I had was with non-Trotskyists. It was so good with some of my lovers, and there were a lot of them two decades ago, that I used to feel (and I know it sounds corny and ridiculously counterculture, but it's true nonetheless) that I was making love with the world, with people, with the people, with all the people. But when it came to the eagle-eyed, leather-jacketed footsoldiers of our tiny International, the antagonisms overpowered the sex. Why do you think this was, Ezra? Any ideas on the subject? Is sexual alienation part and parcel of being a Trot under late-capitalism?

Or is it the case that many of our dear comrades only join the movement to escape from the other world?

How we admired your speeches in those days. I remember when you came to Toronto and we had a large meeting. You said that the International organized fifty thousand revolutionaries all over the world! I felt then that I was listening to Beethoven's 'Ode to Joy'. I responded to this information, dripping with all the libido so predictably cathected to all those internalized icons of patriarchal ideology, which, true to purpose, froze all too many of my reasoning and critical faculties, a real intellectual handicap.

One of the patriarchal icons was actually an image of myself, under the archetype of woman-empty-of-herself, woman-as-vessel. And all of this because I was young and ignorant, uncertain, unsure, afraid to stand up for feelings because I so strongly mistrusted them. All too often, what I felt was sheer terror, and my gut reaction was: run, abandon the ship before it takes you down.

I'm still amazed when I think how someone like me, so unsure of so many things, could simultaneously be so arrogant about so many others. It is a legacy for which we are all paying in Eastern Europe. Do you understand what I'm saying? Does it make sense? Sometimes iron certitude and self-righteousness reflect a poverty of inner knowledge.

Look Ezra, it wasn't all like this. I'm deliberately stressing the negative things so you understand why I don't want to be in the same room as those gauchos you're assembling. Our lot were bad enough, but I'm told there will be Pelletier from France and the PISPAW clones and the Burrowers, Rockers and Hoodlums. I mean, what do you expect from people like me? I can see it all already. I think Emma's a masochist for agreeing to attend.

Listen, there were positive sides. One thing in particular was that I gained relationships with women of such profound depths that I will never feel the same kind of existential isolation that I had felt before my life in fringe revolutionary politics. And of

*course, old friend, I learnt a great deal from your encyclopedic
mind, so I don't want you to write me off. I'm still a Socialist
and I note that none of the risings in Eastern Europe, not a
single one, have so far been accompanied by the birth of a
women's movement. It's got to happen, but it does make me feel
that Socialism and feminism do depend on each other even
though both sides seem not to be aware of this.*

*I hear you got married again. News like that travels fast.
Congratulations! And I hope she's happy and not subjected too
much to ageist taunts from her male friends. I would really like
to meet her. If ever you come this way, do call. Montreal is as
stunning as ever in the autumn.*

I'll sign off in the old way just to cheer you up!
Love and Leninism,
Cathy.

Maya was still reading the last few pages of Cathy's letter. Ezra
had undoubtedly been affected by some of the facts recounted by
Cathy, but he was clearly trying to find a distraction. The smells
of the food were stimulating his taste-buds. He moved to the
cooker and helped himself to some of the delicious meat and bean
stew which Maya had cooked the previous day, wondering why
it was that Brazilian and Burmese food tasted even more delicious
a day after it had been cooked. It was the sort of question to
which Ricky Lysaght would have an immediate answer. Ezra
wondered whether Ricky had ever had letters like that from
former members of the *New Life Journal*.

'Could I have some, please?'

Ezra smiled and served Maya, poured water in their glasses
and sat down opposite her.

'I would like to meet Cathy Fox.'

Ezra nodded, but did not say a word.

'So your friend and heir, Jean-Michel Cuckoo, is a performance artist.'

'Heir? What heir? What are you talking about?'

'Your will.'

'Oh that!' Ezra shrugged it off as a trivial matter.

'Now that we have Ho in my stomach, I think she or he should be your heir. No?'

'For heaven's sake, Maya, it's only my archives and my library.'

'So you think your child is going to be illiterate. Did you hear that, Ho? Your father is not convinced that you will be able to read. Don't worry, my pet, we will get our own books. We will go and meet new friends. You have a very intelligent aunt called Cathy in Montreal. We will write and tell her about Papa's last will and testament, won't we?'

Ezra sighed in despair. Cathy's letter had left a strange aftertaste. Some of the phrases kept recurring in his head, and now Maya was making a totally unnecessary fuss about the will.

'Maya, there are some things I possess which can only be the property of the movement . . .'

'Is the Cuckoo now the same as the movement?'

'Would it make you happier if I changed the name in the will to Simon, for instance, or Jean, or both? You see, my little one, I can't leave my documents and files to the movement as such.'

'Why not?'

'There are no guarantees that the best comrades will permanently maintain power. Suppose some lunatic sectarians took control. I don't want them to have my papers!'

Maya gave up. She suggested that the Triplets were a safer bet than the Cuckoo and Ezra promised to write to his lawyer and change the terms. He had begun to have second thoughts about the Congress. Perhaps he had been wrong to invite Pelletier and the British sects. Perhaps it should have been more restricted. Was it too late? The telephone rang, and Maya took the call. She was conversing in Portuguese. He supposed it must be Pedro. What was going on between him and that rather arrogant Bulgarian woman? Maya signalled that Pedro wanted a quick word. Ezra ambled to the telephone.

'Hello, Pedro.'

'Hello, Ezra. I have taken a rather important decision and

wanted to mention it to you. I am going to defrock myself and marry Lina. We have decided this today. I wanted you and Maya to be the first to know.'

'What? Are you serious? Please be cautious, Pedro. As you know the situation in the Brazilian Church is rather precarious. You and your comrades are in the middle of a ferocious faction fight with the Vatican. Wojtyla only likes dissidents in Poland or Russia. He does not tolerate them in his own Church. Have you seen his latest encyclical? Time to say farewell, he writes, to the sad utopias of the century. In that he means Socialism, probably feminism, and most certainly the liberation theologians of your continent. If you, a leading theoretician of this current, cast off your cassock, proclaim it to be soiled and marry a pretty young Bulgarian, the orthodox Catholic press will have a field day. Surely you can see that.'

There was a long pause. Pedro was not a fool. Nor was he thinking of abandoning the example of Camillo Torres for the theories of Wilhelm Reich. He had just happened to fall in love, and that was a direct consequence of the democratic struggles in Eastern Europe. If Zhivkov had still been in power, Lina would not be cavorting with him in Paris. This was undeniable. On the other hand he saw the strength in Ezra's argument. He must discuss the matter with the others in Brazil before making a hasty and irreversible decision.

'Perhaps you are right, Ezra. In any case I was not planning to do anything till after your Congress. But I will think about it some more.'

Ezra melted immediately. 'Listen, Pedro, I know exactly how you feel. After all, look what happened to me as a result of your countrywoman's initiative on a hot night in Rio! Eh? So if you decide that you have to marry Lina at all costs, then we can discuss the matter again. I mean there are some other possibilities. You could transfer to the Lutherans or even the Church of England. But let's discuss all these matters after we have got the Congress out of the way. How's your speech progressing?'

'Fine. Very fine.'

'Good. A lot will depend on your intervention. Take my word for it.'

'I don't know what you mean, but I'll try my best. Au revoir.'

'Au revoir, Pedro.'

Ezra was beaming again. This tiny victory in delaying the nuptials of poor Pedro and Lina had dispelled all doubts regarding the Congress.

Part Two

16

Pre-Congress discussions

Emma Carpenter and Ted Spanner arrived in Paris one day before the Congress. They had spent a couple of days in Mimi's house in London, but without the pleasure of her company. Ted was especially disappointed because he had been toying with the possibility of making love with her. They had done so once before, nearly twenty years ago, and Ted was a great believer in great historical events occurring twice.

Mimi, alas, was on a delicate mission to Ireland. Her horse-breeding daughter, Lavinia, had fallen in love with a man who was older than either of her parents. When asked on the phone about his profession and what he did for a living, Lavinia had at first prevaricated, and then muttered something about his being a writer. Mimi was suspicious. It was bad enough the man being three times her daughter's age, but if he was penniless to boot it could be dangerous. Lavinia had inherited a great deal of wealth from her maternal grandparents. And so Mimi and Ricky had flown to Dublin to investigate the matter further. They were arriving in Paris tomorrow morning and would head straight for the Mutualité.

Emma and Ted had got over their jetlag and met many old friends in London. Emma discovered that she knew nobody she liked who was still involved with the sects. The local PISPAW zombies were, of course, still there with their bookshop, selling the PISPAW line to the British workers. One of the Cuckoo's characteristic interventions had led to the disintegration of Ezra's group into warring factions. Emma managed to get hold of the people who had been producing *Alternatives in Eastern Europe: a Socialist Focus* for over a decade and spent an evening with the collective. In the old days they had smuggled material into Czechoslovakia and Poland. Now some of the people they used to supply illegally with clandestine literature were members of the government.

Emma remembered a meeting in a large room in a squat in Tolmers Square over ten years ago, when the magazine was first being mooted. She remembered the dimly lit and smoke-filled ambience, which only added to the atmosphere. There was Fred Shapinsky, Ukrainian dope-fiend and revolutionary, with his crusty plaid shirts and ragged jeans flapping on his skinny frame, looking like an Eastern European Jimi Hendrix, minus the curls, emitting some sort of vocalization between a giggle and a snicker at each of Oliver Fairfax's witticisms; his side-kick Paddy Miller, a big, greasy-haired, unwashed guy with a good natured donkey laugh following Fred's snickers with unfailing regularity; and sitting next to them, but a universe away, Stanley Trace, thin, raw-boned, repressed son of a wealthy antique dealer, with a small fortune at his disposal and one he could not but use to compensate for his own lack of self-worth.

Next to Stanley was his girl-friend, slightly overweight, whose rosy cheeks, well-cut clothes and attempts to disguise her accent only emphasized her private schooling. Educated impeccably in economics by Ezra Einstein, she had disappeared a few years later into the cool, well-dressed embrace of her own forebears and was now a crack economist for an ancient merchant bank. And there was Elena Troy, another Ukrainian and Oliver's companion, who typeset the magazine through pregnancies, childbirths, snowstorms, earthquakes, etc. Thin face, bespectacled and with a friendly demeanour, her infectious laugh was often the saving grace of these tiny assemblies. They had changed a lot, Emma thought, as she sat in Olly and Ellie's sitting room, constantly invaded by a pack of children wanting something or other. They were discussing the redundancy of their journal since everything was being published in Eastern Europe itself.

A tall German computer-freak, with long blond hair, unruly moustache and a three-day stubble on his face, just back from East Berlin, was regaling them with a set of extraordinary anecdotes and cursing the leaders of the West German SPD for their pusillanimity in not supporting the experiment currently taking place. The atmosphere was exciting, but very different from the conspiratorial Tolmers Square days, when Oliver Fairfax, chain-smoking, gravel-voiced supremo, directed operations from the depth of an armchair badly scarred by stubbed-out cigarettes. Emma noticed how, despite the grey hair, stooped shoulders and fat bellies, they had retained all their old characteristics. Times, too, had changed, as she was only too well aware, but it was still great seeing them all and reminiscing about some of the good old times. Hell, it was good to be sentimental about some things.

Emma was staggered at how they had kept their magazine going without any real help from Paris. She had sold a few dozen subs for them in the States to help out, but had been angered by the failure of the world movement to lift this magazine and give it a worldwide distribution. There had been nothing else like it in the days when nobody cared about what happened in those countries and German social-democrats were busy hob-nobbing with Honecker, Husak and Ceausescu.

When Emma had returned to Mimi's place that evening, she found Ted on a long-distance call to his companion in San Francisco. She wanted to tell him about her evening, but she got fed up waiting and scurried off to bed. He overslept the next morning, and it took a great deal of shouting and shaking to get him out of bed and on his way to the tube to Heathrow airport.

And now they were in Paris. Despite everything Emma felt a touch of excitement, which irritated her greatly and was inexplicable. Ted was feeling rich and so they decided to take a taxi to the

PSR headquarters, where they would be assigned rooms, registered and given their credentials. Security was going to be tight because of the growth registered by French fascism in the preceding ten years. There had been a few threatening phone calls already, and the PSR's *service d'ordre* was not taking any risks whatsoever.

When they arrived near the Bastille, they stopped the driver and got out. As usual Spanner had conveniently forgotten to change money, and Emma ended up paying. She couldn't get over how tight-fisted he had become. She recalled the time when he had been awarded the prestigious C. Wright Mills Memorial Prize for one of his books and had pestered the Trust for the prize money – a measly, token hundred dollars – for months. Most other winners had donated their 'prize' to some worthy cause or the other. Yes, Ted did have a very strong retentive side to him.

Emma had been assigned a room in the apartment of an old friend, one of the few who had defended her against the PISPAW school of falsification, and so she parted company with Ted and, her delegate's credentials safe in her handbag, made her way to the rue d'Aboukir in the Second Arrondissement.

She was greeted with open arms by Philippe when she had climbed four floors to his tiny apartment. She pushed him back so that she could inspect him. He was older, but otherwise the same, an impish mixture of Charles Aznavour and Woody Allen. When Philippe had been taken seriously ill several years ago, the Cuckoo had not wasted too much time. He had made sure that Philippe was discarded by the Paris Centre. After years of working full-time for them, travelling all over the world with the message and a lot else besides, his illness had proved politically fatal. Philippe had left the movement in sorrow and disgust, but had retained his sense of humour and maintained contacts with many of his old PSR comrades. A few months ago he had suffered a relapse and had only just come out of hospital.

'I had to get better for the Congress, Emma. So many monsters in one hell . . . er . . . I mean hall! How could I miss such a spectacle?'

Meanwhile in another part of Paris, a limousine was driving down the Champs Elysées. It had just collected from the airport an important personage with an equally important, surprisingly heavy carved oak chest and was cruising back to the Hotel George V. Laura Shaw had arrived to attend the Congress on her way to Siena, where arrangements for the Body to be displayed to a group of carefully selected friends of the late Frank Hood had already been made.

The rest of her party was arriving tomorrow, but could stay only one day. The maids had to prepare for the spring-cleaning of the Shaw mansion and the gardeners had to feed a special organic manure to the lawns which surrounded the house. Laura had been tempted to leave them behind, but felt it would be better if she were accompanied by her delegation. Black leather jackets and jeans had been purchased for all of them from the Selfridge's post-Christmas sale.

Laura loved this hotel. She had been staying there since she was a child, and even though the management had changed they treated her like royalty. Her suite was a museum-piece, with a four-poster and the most exquisite and tasteful eighteenth-century furniture. Anyone else would have thought it slightly over the top, but not Laura. For the first time since the tragic expulsion and subsequent suicide of Myra, Laura wished that her sister were by her side. Even though no body had been discovered, Laura assumed that her sister was dead. There had been a spectacular memorial service at the Royal Opera House only last Sunday. Myra had been given a grand send-off, half-operatic, half-political. Jacqueline Ansorge, the South African soprano, had sung Fauré's Requiem, while her brother Jeremiah gave a rendering of the Internationale. The effect had been a bit spoilt when Jeremiah broke into nervous giggles after the chorus, but the incident was soon forgotten.

The expense had been prodigious, especially after she had paid off the three thousand extras hired for the occasion and dressed, naturally, in Hoodlum jackets with a large badge, specially imprinted for the occasion. It was a variant on the old iconography, a silhouetted number, black and red, with Marx, Engels, Lenin, Trotsky and . . . Hood! Unsurprisingly the badge had immediately become a collector's item.

When word of this spread and all sorts of people – like those dreadful comics, as Laura called them, Alexei Sayle and John Sessions – were appearing on TV shows with the badge prominently displayed, Laura demanded that the extras return the button, but it was too late. They had discovered they could sell the icons for substantial sums. Laura was enraged when Sayle had pointed to Frank's silhouette and joked for five minutes trying to work out who it was before finally concluding, outrage of outrages, that it was the crazed Albanian sex-maniac and amateur rapist, Enver Hoodhoxha! Her lawyers sympathized but gently suggested that a suit alleging either libel or a breach of copyright would, given the circumstances, be inadvisable.

She had just rung the actor Gilles Danton, only to be told that he was in Prague pinning a badge on Vaclav Havel. Even though Danton had become a total turncoat, he and his wife Fanny Fléchet had remained friends with Laura ever since they had acted with her in a pilot for a shlock TV mini-series on Trotsky's life and death. This had been during Laura's short-lived attempt to become an actress and thereby raise political consciousness. *Coyoacán Blues*, which they had shot on location in Mexico City nearly fifteen years ago, had remained a non-starter. The pilot had been funded by Shaw Inc. and the script provided by Myra. They had made Danton and Fléchet an offer the couple could not and did not refuse.

The film had sought to prove that Trotsky's assassin had been aided by one of his secretaries, a veteran PISPAW leader from the Thirties and a particular *bête noire* of Frank Hood's. There had been only two viewings, both unknown to Laura, one at the FBI headquarters in Washington and the other in the KGB viewing theatre in the Lubyanka in Dzerzhinsky Square in Moscow. The film had caused immense amusement in both quarters, especially the final scene where Laura had exposed the character played by

Danton as a vile infiltrator on the payroll of both the KGB and the FBI.

Laura was, in reality, very worried. Her speeches had usually been written by Frank or Myra. Now both were gone. Suddenly she felt incredibly angry with her twin for having died. Her last letter had made it clear that she had committed suicide, and Laura felt that the only reason for this thoughtless and undisciplined act was sheer vindictiveness. Myra had wanted to punish and torment her. Yet how ridiculously petty on her part. Petty-bourgeois individualism was something they had all combated inside the Hoodlums. Myra had presided over the Special Control Commission which had expelled the 'idealist current' based in the Cowley car plant in Oxford, the 'democracy group' in Swansea and the 'feminist heresy current' in South London. For her of all people to have shuffled off in this fashion was unforgivable.

Laura had tried a few weeks ago to persuade some playwrights associated with the Hoodlums in the past to help out with her address. Although most of them had refused, Trevor had actually sent her a song, suggesting that she convene a Hoodlum choir and sing it to the Congress. She had not had time to get the other singers organized, and had not looked at the song till now, since she was still capable of learning lines very quickly. Now, in the privacy of her hotel room, she took out Trevor's letter and the song and studied the words, resting one elbow on the great oak chest that stood in front of the window, with her face no more than a few inches from Frank's . . . She stopped reading, and her eyes zipped back to the start of Trevor's song. Her sudden scream of fury set the chandelier to jingling. Alas, the time when her voice would have shattered every crystal drop was over.

'That bastard! After all I've done for him. First-nighted his fucking stupid plays. Got him on to Desert Island Discs and now he does this? I'll kill him.'

The sheet with the song and suggested music (to the tune of the hymn 'For All the Saints') was lying on the table. Laura was already on the phone to her solicitors in London. She wanted a letter sent out to Trevor threatening him with legal action. The solicitor patiently pointed out that since Frank was six feet under the ground, the laws of libel were not applicable, not even in England. Laura fought back. She insisted that the song was a slur on every Hoodlum. The solicitor asked her to read it over the phone. She was angered by this request. Was the fool not aware that his phone was bugged precisely because he was her solicitor? She didn't want a Special Branch recording of her voice reciting or reading the bloody thing.

The solicitor suggested in the softest voice he could muster that she should fax it over to him immediately. Laura reflected. Most of the workers in the hotel were North Africans. They probably wouldn't understand a word anyway. She agreed to the request and asked Room Service to send a messenger.

An old Algerian duly arrived and was handed the offending doggerel. As luck would have it, the Algerian was a supporter of Diablo's tiny group. He read the song in the lift going down and couldn't believe his eyes. It reduced him to hysterics and he faxed it first to the solicitor and then to Diablo, *Libération*, *Le Monde* and everyone he knew who worked in an office with a fax machine. The song was titled 'In Memoriam', and dedicated to Frankie Hood (1900–89). It went like this:

For all the Trots, who now have been expelled,
Because against their Leaders they rebelled,
And to resign were forcibly compelled
By Frankie Hoo-ood,
By Frankie Hoo-ood!

To defend Russia we were pledged to fight,
To her Red Army we would add our might,
But Russia's H-Bomb, that wasn't quite right
It hurt him real good,
Said Frankie Hoo-ood!

And then one day in nineteen fifty-nine,
Out of the blue, there came a change of line,

The workers' bomb was absolutely fine
Said Frankie Hoo-ood,
Said Frankie Hoo-oo-ood!

Now we are few, who once had lots and lots,
Such is the fate of all small groups of Trots.
But don't despair, we'll rape some tiny tots.
Said Frankie Hoo-ood.
Said Frankie Hoo-oo-ood!

Do not fear, comrades, that the cause is dead.
By Trots the movement some day may be led,
Now Time has stuck its icepick in the head
Of Frankie Hoo-ood.
Of Frankie Hoo-ood!

When the messenger returned to hand the sheet back to Laura, he couldn't resist making an observation in reasonably sound English.

'The fax was sent, madame. May I be so bold as to ask the name of the librettist?'

'You read it?'

'It was difficult not to, madame.'

'I'll have you sacked!'

'Sorry, Madame, didn't mean to offend. You see, in the old days I was a member of Comrade Diablo's group and so I . . .'

Laura did not let him finish. She knew she was sunk. A vile revisionist had seen the damned thing. She thought he was smiling.

'Get *out*!' she screamed.

Suddenly she heard a familiar calming voice. At first Laura thought it must be her imagination, but it spoke again.

'Laura, my Comrade Laura. How many times have I explained to you that anger must be controlled and put to good use?'

'Frankie . . . ! Is it really you?' Joy was written all over her face as she rushed to her oak chest and lifted the lid, her hands trembling with excitement and anticipation. She flung the costumes out on to the floor. The refrigeration unit built into the chest was working. Thank heavens she had remembered to bring an adaptor to plug it in to the hotel electricity.

Beautifully embalmed, Frank was lying peacefully, but there was no sign of life. Laura cursed herself. She had been dreaming. Then as she was turning away she heard the voice again.

'Now, should we prepare your speech?'

Laura fell to her knees and stared at the body. She nearly fainted. The iron penis was throbbing with light. Here was the source of the voice. It was as if the cumulative wisdom of Hood had been transferred to his amazing metal organ. Or was this some optical illusion, a Hoodogram? She shivered slightly. Then Laura reached out to touch the apparition. The contact almost sizzled. She burst into song. It was an aria from *Don Carlos*, an odd choice since it bore no relationship whatsoever to Frankie or his penis.

'Enough of that. Get some paper and take down your speech. Hang on a minute. I heard that fucking Diabloite. Let's get out of this place. Book a suite in the Crillon. We'll work there.'

'Say no more, Frankie. Just relax.' She packed the case gently and couldn't help stroking the radiant iron member before she sealed the chest. The charge it gave her almost knocked her off her feet. If Laura had looked into one of the room's many gilded mirrors — and the fact that she had not done so in the previous half-hour is a singularity worthy of notice — the image would have reminded her of Elsa Lanchester playing the pop-eyed bride of Frankenstein, her hair frizzled with electrostatic bliss. Not even her worst enemy could deny Laura's power to hold and move a crowd. Only Frankie Hood had ever produced the same effect on Laura. She was his ideal audience. Now in an ebullient mood, she rang up the Hôtel Crillon, booked herself a suite and checked out of the George V. Frankie was quite right. She couldn't get over the Diabloite working there as a flunkey. Naturally she had not complained to the management. The triumphant Diabloites would have gone straight to the stinking bourgeois press and the whole affair would have been in tomorrow's *Libération*. She had always known that the Diabloites were agents of the international banks. How else to explain their constant flow of funds?

Laura was gradually working herself up into a state, which did not augur well for her conference performance. Would the disembodied Hood organ be able to control her once she was out of range?

17

Jimmy Rock alias Chaim Bernstein prepares to hurl a few Rockers into the battle

A rather odd-looking trio had disembarked from a weekend charter flight at Le Bourget. The man and woman must have been in their seventies. She was at least two feet taller than he was. Both had white hair, though the woman was going completely bald underneath the black beret whose twin allowed her husband's white curls to escape. The ungainly fifty-year-old carrying their cases also wore a black beret, but had a permanently wild look on his face. As they passed an old-fashioned billboard advertising electric typewriters, he put down the cases, jumped up in the air and executed a few karate kicks at the representation of the machine. The old couple smiled indulgently and called him to heel.

Jimmy Rock, his wife, Sugar Brink, and his sidekick, Nutty Shardman, had booked into a tiny hotel near the Gare du Nord. Their plans to prevent the Congress from taking place had backfired badly. Nutty Shardman was depressed at their failure and was sulking. Rock took such setbacks in his stride, but Nutty appeared inconsolable.

'We shouldn't have come, Rock. I'm telling you this. And we could have wrecked the Congress if you hadn't caved in when

Einstein rang you up. These people are down. It's no time for being soft. We should kick some sense into their heads.'

Rock smiled, baring the growing number of gaps which surrounded his dark brownish-yellow teeth. Sugar mimicked his smile but could not match his haphazard dentition.

'Nutty, Nutty, incorrigible Nutty,' crooned Rock. 'Even Deng Xiaoping is cleverer than you. "There's more than one way to skin a cat alive." Think about it, have a drink and calm down. Sugar and I are going to have a little rest before supper.'

The couple adjusted their berets and disappeared. Rock's parting words were intended to be soothing and had acted like a tonic. Nutty Shardman felt greatly reassured. His politico-emotional relationship with his leader was uncomplicated. Nutty simply worshipped Rock. Deep down he understood only too well why Rock had decided to come to the Congress. It was all to do with the Burrowers. Rock had got one of his hard-ons about 'unity'.

Nutty knew that Jed was planning to launch a campaign of street demonstrations in Britain against the poll-tax. He also knew that the ultra-pacifist approach of the Burrowers was the most vulnerable section of that organization's armour, and he chuckled as he saw how the Burrower-led movement — if, that is, it ever got off the ground — could be hijacked by even more militant tactics. This made Nutty roar with laughter, to the great horror of passers-by.

It was when Jimmy Rock learnt that Jed Burroughs was going to Paris that he had called an emergency meeting of his Central Committee. Rock was waging a campaign of predatory seduction, known in the trade as a 'unity offensive', towards the Burrowers. The characteristics of such an offensive are straightforward. A show of real affection and understanding is put on towards the group being wooed, but underlying the pursuit is a deadly sectarian desire to break it up and win over the majority of its members.

The tactics employed are far from novel. Boardroom battles and multinational merger plans tend to be far more vicious, and even more harmful, since thousands of jobs depend on the outcome. The consequences of sect-wars, insulated as they are from reality, can never be as serious. It is, however, true that the relentless trench warfare can sometimes reduce the less hardy participants to a state of total shell-shock. Many individual psyches are left to cower in no-man's-land, bruised and defenceless, for several years. The latest war to be plotted by Jimmy Rock against Jed Burroughs was more in the nature of guerrilla raids than set-piece battles.

Rock had assumed that many Burrowers must be deeply unhappy inside the Labour Party. He had written them several open letters in the *Rocker's Gazette* advocating that they quit and join the Rockers, and there had been a limited success. Three Burrowers in Newcastle had surrendered. In these bad times their minuscule defection was seen as a major victory. So if Jed Burroughs was heading in the direction of Ezra's Congress there was no way in which Rock, having tried and failed to sabotage the gathering, was going to forgo it. The Central Committee greatly admired their chief's olfactory skills. He could smell success quicker than any of his rivals. They smiled appreciatively at their leader's effortless flexibility and voted unanimously to accept the invitation. Smiles were exchanged and hands went up as they all agreed with Rock and decided to throw a whole hecatomb of sectarians into battle.

Yes, thought Nutty Shardman, as he gargled three large cognacs to drown his tiny cup of café espresso, Rock was a true genius. He had yet to encounter a mind more attuned to the instrumental needs of the organization. Suddenly, for no apparent reason, an ugly grin took charge of his face. The poor *garçon* bringing another cognac was so startled by the transformation that his hands trembled and the tray shook, unleashing a storm in the balloon, but disaster was averted. Nutty Shardman regained his composure and paid the bill. He was dreaming evil thoughts of how to smash the Congress from within. Then he started to think about Rock once again. Nutty Shardman had not wanted Sugar brought on this trip. He had many problems to discuss with his leader.

ENCYCLOPEDIA TROTSKYANA: *Date of entry: 1986*

Jimmy Rock (real name: Chaim Bernstein), b. Johannesburg, 11 March 1919. [Entry compilers: RK, LF, SM, and JP]

Early Years

Chaim Bernstein is the son of a couple who migrated to South Africa from Galicia in 1914. Bernstein *père* had been the manager on the estate of a Polish count. A pogrom on the eve of the First World War wiped out all his family. Bernstein heard the news in Warsaw, where he was visiting his fiancée, and never returned to the village of his birth. In Johannesburg, far away from the pogrom-continent, he started a small stationery shop, which grew larger with the years. The family was not wealthy, but nor was it uncomfortable.

Chaim was a wild teenager. He laughed a great deal and was popular with the young things who gathered for weekend dances in the old Jewish quarter in Jo'burg. He got a young woman pregnant and her parents insisted on marriage. Chaim fled to Holland with the approval of his parents. There, at the home of his uncle, he first met Sugar Brink, the only daughter of one of Amsterdam's leading diamond merchants. They fell in love, but this time Chaim married her in secret. The angry jeweller, furious at the thought that Sugar, the only jewel in his heart, had married a shyster, disinherited his daughter. Having already broken relations with his son Jed, whom he had lost to politics and to Job Segal, the jeweller was heart-broken. He won the support of the Bernstein parents.

In order to avoid the wrath of the scorned father, the couple fled to Jaffa in Palestine. They moved to Britain after the Second World War. They had seen glimpses of the Zionist future and rejected them completely. On this question young Chaim Bernstein was solid as a rock. Immovable. It was for this reason that Sugar suggested the pen-name Rock in the first place. In 1948, Bernstein/ Rock left Palestine for ever and sought refuge in London.

In Britain, Rock joined the world movement and rubbed shoulders with Einstein, Hood, Burroughs and the rest of them. In 1950 he left the mainstream of the movement. He felt that he needed a hand-picked audience, and so like his brother-in-law Jed he began by organizing a discussion group. This enabled him to locate an initial nucleus of supporters. The only problem was to find something which could serve as a point of reference and separate him from the other sects. Jed Burroughs had convinced him in 1948 that the Soviet Union was really capitalist, and so he wrote a Talmudic text entitled *Rock's Guide to Soviet Realities*. That did the trick, and recruiting began in earnest. Fifteen years later he had two hundred and fifty members. His old book was now reprinted and distributed under a new title, *The Rocker's Guide to Soviet Realities*. Rock wanted to build a sect in his own image and on his own island, far away from the others. He would show the others how to build a proper organization.

Character and Related Information

Rock became a familiar sight at leftwing gatherings. For special occasions he wore a thick-knit black polo-neck sweater, which set off his grey, unruly locks. Like Hood, he was short in stature and well-built, but unlike Hood he had a human side, which he often used to demonstrate in public. Sugar, by contrast, was tall and slim, but it was not till she had aged a bit that her resemblance to Jed became unmistakable. She then had to admit that they were brother and sister, but had not spoken to each other since Jed had betrayed her trust by running away from the family and leaving her behind. Few believed that this could be the only reason, but neither sibling provided a more convincing explanation. Rock, when asked, used to shrug his shoulders and smile. It was obvious that he knew, but was not going to reveal any family secrets. Rock could afford to smile. Sugar's father had disinherited his son and daughter, but left all his money in a trust fund for his grandchildren. Jed was gay. No children. Sugar and Rock decided to engender four little things who, even as they rested in their mother's womb like tiny pebbles on the bed of the ocean, were already millionaires.

Sect-leaders are usually blind to the many-sided realities of everyday life, but very conscious of the uncertain tenure of inner-party despotisms. Larger sects are permanently tempted to swallow up the smaller, and yet the laws of war and statecraft do not apply here, for unlike modern states, the tinier the sect the more damage it can cause inside a larger constellation. Even the most minuscule sect has very great powers of resistance, because the Leader or guru has much more time to mould every member in his own image. The Rockers suffered some bad experiences at the hands of one such sect, which manipulated the Central Committee in such a way as to cause a bacchanalian outbreak of political ambition. Rock's own position became shaky for a few months, and it was Nutty Shardman who saved the day by expelling the intruders. It had been a salutary experience. Henceforth the Rockers never allowed themselves to be infiltrated by seemingly harmless members of a smaller organism, but instead, in Nutty's words, 'went after the big fish' themselves.

Despite their addiction to the *Guide* the Rockers, at least in the early days, used to be relatively open-minded and free of dogma. Their guru was Rosa Luxemburg rather than Lenin. As for Trotsky, they accepted a great many of his theories, but not the analysis of Soviet society contained in his classic *The Revolution Betrayed*. In fact, the *Rocker's Guide to Soviet Realities* was written precisely to counter the orthodox Trotskyist view. Later, after 1968, Rock rewrote his pamphlet on Luxemburg and embraced every dot and comma of Lenin. Scientific thought was now transformed into a religion. [These practices, which became institutionalized in our own country during the early Stalin period, can be traced in the practice of all the sects discussed in this Encyclopedia.] Rock's organizational practices changed accordingly, and features familiar from the practices of Noble, Hood and Jed Burroughs could now be noticed inside the ranks of the Rockers. For one thing they changed their name from the pleasantly unaffected Rockers to the Rockers and Workers Party (RWP) and Rock, like his counterparts, began to dream that he was the British Lenin. This was fatal because it ran totally counter to natural credulity. Of all the Lenins on offer in Britain, we feel constrained to note that Rock was the least convincing.

[*Nutty Shardman: a necessary footnote:*

Many of the best Rockers left the organization, but the hard core remained and ensured that history was falsified and Rocker politics presented to the new members as a continuum. Once again, it was Rock's veteran sidekick, Nutty Shardman, who played an important role in this regard. Nutty, as he was known to friend and enemy alike, was a product of the student radicalization of the Sixties. His black leather jacket enhanced the tough look which he cultivated. He used to strike terror in the hearts of lecturers and students alike. His style of intimidation bordered on violence without actually crossing the frontier. His battle-cry – 'All right, let's Rock and roll' – was the last coherent sentence many a Labour Member of Parliament ever heard before the storm of rotten foodstuffs burst. He had a powerful political brain, but it was overshadowed by his unending capacity for dissimulation and a disposition which can only be described as vengeful. He concentrated these talents in destroying his opponents both inside and outside the organization. In most cases these were Trotskyists of a marginally different hue. Naturally such activity made him the principal polemicist of his group and, unsurprisingly, Nutty Shardman edited the weekly *Rocker's Gazette* ever after Rock's turn to Leninism. – LF]

'What drives me mad is when people claim that the *Gazette* was great when Mango edited it. It's bullshit.'

Nutty Shardman banged his fist on the table, upsetting his tenth glass of cognac. The rising tide of alcohol had brought colour to his face, helping to disguise his sickly pallid complexion. The remark had been addressed to himself, since the Rocks were still in bed.

What Nutty said about the *Gazette* not having known a golden age was not as far from the truth as one might have thought. The Rockers' weekly organ had always been rather simplistic, and this had been coupled with a romanticized and idealized view of the working class, which had led it to ape the tabloids. This world-view, which emanated from Rock himself, had led the latter to reduce every major point in his speeches to the level of a vulgar, sexist joke. For instance when he was trying to explain the difference between essence and appearance he would start with a paltry joke.

'A beautiful woman is having a bath. There is a knock on the door. "Who is it?" she asks. "Blind man," comes a frail reply. "Come in," she says. Enter a young, healthy worker. "Nice tits, love. Now tell me where you want me to hang the blind."'

He imagined that this enhanced his popularity with the working class, but no evidence was ever produced to sustain this thesis. The *Rocker's Gazette* had, naturally, never resorted to publishing photographs of nude models, but its attempt to mimic working-class culture often resulted in painful howlers. Even Rock had to give up on his jokes in public after the birth of the women's liberation movement and its spreading influence inside his ranks.

What can be said truthfully with regard to the *Gazette* is that what had once been a paper with the occasional decent article had been reduced by Nutty Shardman to an unreadable rag. Shardman's personality was such that few attempted to argue with him. There had been the famous tantrum in the late Seventies when he had physically destroyed three successive typewriters by hurling them to the floor and stamping them to pieces. (All Nutty's boots had solid steel toecaps. There were people who claimed that his skull was similarly reinforced.)

All three machines were new, but Shardman did not know how to work them, and since he had been desperately trying to finish off a document for the Central Committee analysing the importance of the strike by public employees, he had felt it necessary to display some class hatred. Three typewriters were wrecked and the analysis was still incomplete. Later in the pub, surrounded by his acolytes, he joked about the episode:

'I did it to keep Alex Mango in the organization. You know what he's like. Soft as shit. Vacillating all the time between the working class and the bourgeoisie. It's his public-school background. They're trained to be like that in there. Only way to keep Mango in line is through fear. Fear of the anger of the class. What are three piddling little typewriters compared to our one and only Alex Mango, eh?'

The cadres had looked at him in awe as they downed their pints. If old Rock were suddenly to stop a bus, they realized that Nutty would hold them together.

There was another reason for this calculated display of rage. It was to make others who worked with him understand that he was not a figure who could be tampered with easily. Not that anyone had ever wanted to try. And Nutty had never been known to make sexual approaches to Rockers, male or female, although spending too long in his presence produced in women a rising tension difficult to distinguish from the early stages of a nervous breakdown.

Soon afterwards Nutty had instructed his partisans to close down the Rockers' special journal, *Women Rockers Speak Out*. He felt that it was getting out of control and its autonomy had to be terminated. This was done and two hundred women left the group over the next six months. The exodus inspired Jimmy Rock himself to put pen to paper on the 'women's question'. The result, in Sugar's words, led to a 'dreadful abortion' and a hundred more women walked out in disgust.

A siege mentality gained ground. Even the *Gazette*'s star

columnist, Alex Mango, succumbed to the mood and, aware that nobody who mattered read the stuff, had fed several old pamphlets and the *Rocker's Guide to Soviet Realities* into his specially programmed computer. To this heady cocktail he added a few of his more pacy newspaper articles. Then he pressed a special button and the computer had unfailingly produced his weekly column for the *Gazette* ever since. The Rockers were happy because good old Alex was still writing for them, and Alex was happy because nobody he really cared about read the stuff.

Mango, an extremely talented polemicist, made sure that he preserved his best material for the national press and the literary journals. He was the leading representative of Rockism with a human face, and his own features were extremely pleasing, even though the hair which covered his forehead and came down to his shoulders was by now completely grey. This only enhanced his attractiveness to the young middle-class housewives in the north-western districts of the capital. His appetite was legendary. It was said that Alex used to disguise himself as a milkman and service most of North London in a day; but this was probably a vile slander spread by someone less well endowed with bottle. Someone like Nutty, who needed Alex but also loathed him.

A sophisticated and cultured public speaker, Mango was responsible for winning over many young people to the Rocker ranks. Few stayed long, but that was hardly Mango's fault. Like a smartly dressed doorman outside the façade of an imposing-looking mansion, Mango bowed slightly and opened the door with a smile. It was only after the unwitting new recruit had passed through the revolving door that he or she realized that inside it there was no roof, no walls, no building, nothing but a cellarful of second-hand furniture, and beneath it the abyss.

Rock and Shardman had sided with the rebellions in the East, but they were secretly worried. This fear was expressed by regular and hysterical denunciations of Gorbachev. Their hatred for the Soviet leader was the by-product of his popularity inside the workers' movement throughout Europe. Overnight he had ended the cold war and was thus threatening the established order, East and West. He had forced new thinking on both the Left and the Right. This greatly hurt the Rocker leadership because they felt that Gorbachev, by attacking every certainty that had been established since 1917, was taking away their chance to seize power in Britain. He had to be combated, fought to the finish, destroyed ideologically, smashed into the ground, and all this before the eyes of all those who had illusions about him. Rock and Shardman knew that at Ezra's Congress they would meet many, many, like-minded comrades, left disoriented by Ezra's refusal to declare Gorbachev as the *main* enemy. That was an additional reason for the journey to Paris. They would pick up a few recruits.

Nutty Shardman was thinking about all this when he looked up and saw his leader and leaderene standing before him. Both looked refreshed. They had changed their clothes and headgear and were now attired in denim suits and white berets.

'Nutty, I think you should get the next plane to Romania. Don't bother about this Congress. Sugar and I will handle everything here.'

Nutty Shardman was immediately suspicious. Why were they trying to get rid of him?

'Why?'

'We received a call from the comrades in London. A group of former Securitate employees, all rank-and-filers, Nutty! Not a single officer among them. Isn't that marvellous?'

'Yes, but . . .'

'Well, Comrade Shardman, it appears that they read your book. You know, *Why Eastern Europe is Bankrupt and Everything Must Be Destroyed from the Top Down and Other Essays.* They liked the tone, they liked the argument, and they set up a Securitate study circle just around this one book. Then they read my *Guide to Soviet Realities.* Now they have set up a clandestine cell of our RWP in Bucharest. The problem is that they are still on the wanted list of the new government and so they have not come out in public. These bloody reformists in the government won't last long. After them will come the right wing. Then it could be our turn. Stranger things have happened, Nutty. They want to establish contact.'

Nutty's eyes were beginning to shine.

'When? Where?'

'They have seen a photograph of us in the Encyclopedia. So they'll recognize you. You must be in Bucharest tomorrow evening. A man wearing a grey suit, a brown raincoat and a maroon felt hat will meet you at the airport. From there everything will be up to you.'

Leader and lieutenant looked at each other. Nutty Shardman compressed his lips and nodded silently. Both men knew that this was their big chance. Within five years Romania could belong to them. A Rockers' and workers' state in the new Europe. A red base from which they could defeat all their opponents, destroy Einstein's pretensions forever, make Burroughs look like a complete fool, show up PISPAW for the impotent little sect that it was and, above all, prepare to extend the Socialist order to Scotland. These sublime thoughts went through the heads of leader and disciple. They did not need to say anything to each other. Telepathy had done it all.

Early next morning, Nutty Shardman boarded a TAROM flight from Charles de Gaulle airport for Bucharest.

18

The plotters thicken

After a simple but tasty meal at a nearby café, Philippe and Emma returned to the apartment where they had been billeted. They had spent the whole evening discussing the future of Europe and its impact on the rest of world. Just as they were about to leave they had run into Philippe's uncle, who had fought in the Resistance during the Second World War. He was very upset at any talk of German reunification.

'Neither of you can understand what it means to people of my generation. It wasn't just Hitler, you know. It was German nationalism. In 1933, when Hitler became Chancellor, there were only two members of his Nazi Party in the government. Who were the rest? German nationalists belonging to parties just like the CDU and the CSU. They thought Hitler was being too constitutional and soft. They wanted him to crush the opposition immediately. Only fools can blame everything onto the Nazis. Without the support of the German Right and the capitalists, Hitler could never have stayed in power.'

Philippe stopped the old man. 'We can agree on that, but what is happening all over the East is the death of Stalinism. What we believe in seems to be disappearing, but it will be reborn, sooner or later.'

The old man grew angry. 'There are plenty of fascists in East Germany today. They've been desecrating Jewish cemeteries in Thuringia. I'm very pessimistic. We will have the Republicans and Kohl's gang competing for the nationalist vote. Already the Frankfurt stock market is overtaking the City of London. Soon they'll promise a return to the 1937 frontiers, and then what? You tell me if you're so clever.'

Philippe had pleaded exhaustion and turned down his uncle's offer of a cognac. Now, as they returned home, they resumed the conversation. Could the old man be right after all? Would it all end in disaster once again, this time with planetary consequences? The conversation moved from Berlin to Prague, thence to Warsaw and Budapest, and finally settled in Bucharest. Philippe told Emma a story.

'You know that I am from Toulouse. Well in that town there lives an old doctor. He and his wife fought first in Spain, then in the Resistance. In Spain they had made many friends, but one person in particular impressed them a lot by his humanity and generosity. He was a Romanian, who moved to Toulouse after the defeat in Spain and later fought alongside his French comrades. After the war he returned to Romania and became a high official in the new government. In Sixty-Six he came out with his son for a long stay abroad. The doctor by this time had two children as well, both of them boys. We all used to go to the same lycée, where we were members of the Communist Party's student organization.

'Later that year I left the Party and helped to found the JSR, the Jeunesse Socialiste Révolutionnaire, in Toulouse. The old PCF doctor's sons joined me. In Sixty-Eight the movement erupted and the JSR became one of the main organizations of the youth. We were in heaven. Our young Romanian friend never joined, but worked with us every day. We would go to the factories and distribute leaflets, sell papers, paint slogans on walls, and he was with us.'

'Who the hell is he, Philippe? Come on!'

'Petri Roman, the prime minister! You know it was Petri who seized the microphone on the balcony after the crowd started heckling Ceausescu. It was Petri who the very next day told the students in Bucharest to go to the factories! We failed in France in

Sixty-Eight. They succeeded in Romania in Eighty-Nine. I don't think he'll last too long. The tide is against people like him and Petr Uhl in Prague, but who knows? It's all unpredictable.'

'But here you are fighting for Socialist revolution, there the struggle was for democracy. It is unpredictable, but that's what I find exciting. It turns me on. You know, Philippe, I have the feeling that it's all just starting. That even before we enter the new millennium we will see other changes. I can't say what they'll be, or where, but it won't be the same.'

'I agree. Our century is ending with an ironic crescendo.'

And on that philosophical note they kissed each other and prepared for bed.

In another part of the city, three men and a woman were approaching the final stages of a marathon discussion. Jim Noble and Louise-Carol had arrived that morning with an outsize PISPAW delegation from New York. They had booked two whole apartments, one for the delegation – who were ten to a room in sleeping bags – and one for Jim and Louise-Carol, where the high-powered summit was now in motion. The other participants were the Cuckoo, Jean-Michel and Pelletier.

François Pelletier ran a tight little group in France whose initials need not be recorded, since no one ever used any other name than the Robots to refer to this illegitimate offspring of Stalinism and Trotskyism, a mixture of Burrower and Hoodlum. There was nothing very original about this short, seedy, white-haired Frenchman, except that, like Hood, he was a natural demagogue. Like Burroughs he spoke with mechanical gestures, which the Robots mimicked with amazing ease. In the Forties, whenever Pelletier was asked an awkward question, the forefinger of his right hand would subconsciously begin to crawl up his nose. He wasn't aware that he was doing this, but it did have the effect of bewitching his audience. The questioner was isolated as the gathering wondered whether the finger would succeed in its aim or return without its quarry. More often than not it succeeded, to the great relief of the audience, and the difficult question was invariably forgotten.

It was bad enough Pelletier engaging in this public dislay of an unhygienic habit, but when every single Robot picked up the gesture the sight became unbearable, and very few non-Robots went to the meetings any longer. Once this happened, of course, there were no more awkward questions and the forefinger began to feel somewhat neglected. However, it was always on the alert in the presence of non-Robots, as at this moment.

One important feature which distinguished Pelletier from his celebrated British counterparts was the fact that he was a Freemason. This secret society provided a radical and anticlerical component of the French Revolution of 1789. One of its members, Combes, organized the celebrated split between Church and state in 1905, for which the Vatican never forgave the Freemasons. Whatever progressive role the society may have played now lay buried in the past. It became a secret network whose members embraced every political party and every layer of French society, strong supporters of French colonialism as a civilizing force *par excellence*! This should have posed some contradictions for Pelletier, if not for his Robots, but astute dialectician that he was, these were easily sorted out.

Thus, during the War of Algerian Independence, Pelletier backed a pro-French political leader, Messali Hadj, against the anti-imperialist FLN. As a result the latter organization, which regarded Hadj as a collaborator, sentenced Pelletier to death, and he was only saved by the influence which Diablo, Gaul and Ezra had with the FLN leaders. Diablo and Ezra pleaded with them not to carry out the execution. Far better, they explained, to expose him for what he was – a French chauvinist and opportunist. Pelletier lived to build his sect. In Sixty-Eight, he sent the Robots to dismantle the barricades and attack the students. This led to a decline in their influence and some Robots were heard asking difficult questions. This fact was uncovered because the famous Pelletier forefinger had started travelling again to zones it had almost forgotten.

In 1978 there was a tiny Robot rebellion. One of Pelletier's aides, also a Freemason, had decamped with four hundred followers and the funds to sustain a new sect. Pelletier called a special Council meeting of the Freemasons and won their support. The defector was instructed to return the money and censured for his behaviour. He subsequently led the dissident Robots straight into the Socialist Party, some of whose members in parliament were part of the secret order, among them Hernu, the Socialist Defence Minister who ordered the sinking in New Zealand of the Greenpeace ship, *Rainbow Warrior*.

Nobody was surprised, therefore, when Pelletier, more than a little drunk, boasted to his lover in bed that the idea of blowing up the ship had originated with him. All the same, the woman in question, an employee of the Socialist trade-union federation, SFIO, was horrified. She was a Robot, but not a Freemason. At first she thought that Pelletier was boasting in order to offset his failure, for the third consecutive occasion, to persuade his organ to rise and do its duty. She had tried, too, but with little success, and the forefinger had begun to travel, making her realize that this little localized difficulty was worrying him a great deal. At that point he told her the story, and even though she was suspicious of the new Freudians, she wondered whether he was boasting about blowing up environmentalists to conceal the fact that one part of his own body refused to be blown. Later, in the same week, she discovered that the bragging had been justified. She left the Robots in some anger because she thought that the destruction of the *Rainbow Warrior* had been an immoral act and something not to be explained by any reference to the Robot transitional programme for the seizure of power in France.

What was it discussing, this awesome quartet, assembled in a rented PISPAW apartment in suburban Paris? The newspapers on that very day had reported the dispatch of Soviet troops to the borderlands of Azerbaijan; the arrest of the Bulgarian Stalinist Zhivkov; the defection of the leader of the Communist Party in Leipzig; the resignation of the Czech prime minister from the Czech Communist Party; the decision of the Hungarian, Czech and Polish parliaments to ask for the withdrawal of all Soviet troops and the breaking-up of a writers' meeting in Moscow by a gang of anti-semites. One would have thought that this litany provided ample space for a serious political discussion. But these veterans of the great world movement were engaged in something far more important. In fact they had just reached agreement on a secret pact. The Cuckoo proceeded to make sure that they had agreed on the same thing, since differing interpretations of mutually agreed documents had led, on previous occasions, to unfortunate splits. If this happened tomorrow, then their plans would be worth nothing.

'Let me summarize. We are not yet sure of the surprise Ezra has up his collar. Is that correct?'

'Sleeve,' smiled Louise-Carol.

'Up his sleeve,' continued the Cuckoo. 'If it is nothing very interesting, or merely a new way of repeating our old ideas, then fine. No problem. But if he says something which any of us regard as unacceptable and which we feel might lead to the liquidation of the movement, then we meet after his speech and prepare there and then our counter-offensive. If we need more time, we can prolong the Congress. Agreed?'

They all nodded. Then Noble, who had not spoken throughout the six-hour session, but had left the talking to his wife, decided to break his silence.

'In fact, I would insist that if we feel the need to respond then we must, repeat must, delay the Congress. Both to prepare, but more importantly to ensure that the riff-raff and freelancers who that sentimental old fool has invited are made to feel they cannot stay any longer. That's where we professional revolutionaries have an advantage. All of us here as part of the PISPAW delegation work full-time for the apparatus.'

Pelletier nodded violently in agreement. 'Brilliant idea. My Robots will be here as well, and I could always mobilize some more overnight.'

The Cuckoo looked at them in admiration. He had been trying desperately to transform Ezra's ragbag army of malcontents into a trained and disciplined unit just like these comrades, but the prize consistently eluded him. They parted company and Pelletier insisted that his chauffeur-bodyguard drop the Cuckoo off as well. In the Robot Limousine, the Cuckoo buried himself deep in one particular idea. Perhaps, he thought, my time has finally come.

19

Ho Einstein delays the Congress

In the Twentieth Arrondissement, Ezra was in a state of great excitement as he worked on his big speech which would inaugurate the Congress. His spidery scrawl had covered several cards. It reminded him of the old days in the Fifties, when he and Diablo were working together and the contents of important speeches and articles were carefully discussed beforehand. Then, after the effervescence of the Sixties when Ezra had become a figure much in demand at campuses all over the world, he had got into the habit of scribbling down a few notes before, or sometimes even during, a meeting. It was partially the pressure of time, but also a growing complacency. He could answer all the questions. Water shortage in India? Famines in Africa? Deforestation in Brazil? Ecology in Germany? Sewage disposal in Zambia? Food queues in Moscow? The fall-out after Chernobyl? Automation on the Volvo production-line in Göteborg? Feminism in Japan? He thought he could crack all these problems.

It was simple. A combination of good will and workers' self-management, but all this of course in the global context of a World Federation of Socialist Republics based on Workers' Councils and subject to recall at any time by the electors. In fact the emergence of satellite television meant that workers in factories and peasants in villages throughout the world could be brought together whenever necessary. Ezra was a great believer in the gains of the Third Industrial Revolution – technology and electronics – being used to institutionalize a new forum of participatory democracy. Not all of these ideas were connected to outer space, but his presentations sometimes tended to be a bit abstract. Also, like Minerva's owl, Ezra tended to be much sharper after a particular thesis had been vindicated or rejected by history.

However, doubt had wedged itself into his head ever since the Christmas Day execution of the Ceausescus and the sight of the young executioner crossing himself on television. All through history, he thought, the mind limped after reality. Even Marx was not ahead of his time, but merely expressed his ideas on social evolution at a quicker pace than most of his contemporaries. He was also more humane. Ezra chuckled as he recalled John Stuart Mill's liberal demand that everyone who earned more than seven hundred pounds a year should be exterminated in order to make way for the greatest happiness of the greatest number. A veritable Pol Pot of the Utilitarian tendency!

Ezra wanted his speech to be remembered as a turning point in the fortunes of his movement by the historians of the next century. He was sure that it would be and that . . .

A loud, penetrating scream suddenly filled the air and stopped his thought processes. Maya's waters had burst some five hours ago, but the labour pains had not followed and she had gone to sleep. He looked at his watch as he rushed to her side. It was three-thirty a.m. The ecstasy had begun.

'Ezraaaa . . . ring for the ambulance . . . aah! They're coming in spasms . . . my back is hurting . . . Mamaaaa! I want you . . . I wish I was at home . . .'

The ambulance arrived within minutes and Maya, weighted down by little Ho, who had started to push and shove as he or she prepared to come down the trail, was helped down the stairs by Ezra and two attendants. Within ten minutes she was in the hospital and a nurse was rubbing the small of her naked back. Maya refused to lie down. She wanted to be comfortable and so she stood hugging a filing cabinet as little Ho began the long dive to freedom. The doctor was a comrade, a veteran of Sixty-Eight and a former leader of the PSR, now inactive in the movement but still very immersed in the health workers' union. Even as he stood encouraging her to take long deep breaths, she could hear Ezra discussing matters which were totally unrelated to the pain.

'Antoine, is it true that those Robot renegades actively sabotaged a strike call?'

Dr Artaud nodded as he carried on attending to the world leader's companion.

'It's a scandal. We must denounce them in our press. In fact it's an outrage.'

Maya grinned at the sheer incorrigibility of her husband. Then she screamed in pain, 'Ezraaaah!' She had been in labour for nearly four hours. She was exhausted. Sweat was pouring down her body. Antoine gave her some sugar lumps to stabilize her energy. Ezra went out to Antoine's office to ring the Cuckoo and warn him that he had been held up and that the Congress opening should be delayed by a few hours. Cuckoo wanted more details on the agenda, and by the time they had finished speaking it was already nine a.m.

Ezra rushed back just in time to see little Ho sticking its head out.

'Push, Maya! Push hard,' suggested Dr Artaud.

Maya gave one last push and she screamed again as Artaud neatly plucked little Ho out and handed her to her mother, who was weeping tears of joy. Ezra was deeply moved. He watched in amazement and semi-shock as Antoine snipped away the umbilical and the nurses took away the mess and began to clean up the mother and child. Ho suddenly began crying and a collective sigh escaped from Antoine and the nurses. They handed her to Maya, who immediately put her to her breast, and the infant began to suck away.

It soon became obvious that Maya's milk had dried up. In the preceding weeks her breasts had become so heavy that little driplets had emerged when she dried herself too vigorously after a shower. Where the hell was the milk? Maya was filled with panic, which didn't help. Antoine advised her to relax, Ho screamed, the nurses rushed hither and thither and then something very strange took place.

Ezra took hold of his daughter and sat down on the bed next to his wife. He had felt an unusual sensation inside his body. As if in a trance he undid his shirt and put the baby to his left nipple. To the amazement of all those present the child began to suckle and the milk flowed. Maya was so moved that she fainted. Dr Artaud stared at Ezra in amazement. He knew that what had taken place was biologically possible, but it was meant to happen in extreme circumstances.

Maya was revived soon afterwards and she asked immediately for her baby. Her milk had returned with a vengeance, and tiny Ho fed off her mother soon afterwards. Maya spoke to Ho and felt the baby's toes curling ever so slightly at the sound of a familiar voice.

'Lucky, lucky Ho. Only in this world for a few minutes and you've tasted the milk of both your parents. Eh, my little one? What was Papa Ezra's milk like? Will you describe it to me? A bit thin and watery was it? Just like his politics are these days, eh? Never mind. Don't you worry my beauty. Maya's milk will flow forever now.'

Ezra simply did not understand what had happened to him. Now that it was all over he looked very embarrassed. Word had spread throughout the gynaecological department and the corridors outside were packed with doctors and nurses and visiting parents and grandparents who wanted to see the Grand Old Lactating Man. Ezra wiped his nipples with a wet towel admiringly supplied by a young nurse, kissed his wife and child, buttoned himself up and left for the Congress. As he walked out of the room into the corridor, the crowds which had gathered to get a glimpse of him moved aside to let him pass. Some old women slapped him on the back. A few of them were laughing, but in general everyone gave him a tremendous cheer and applauded. He smiled sheepishly, wondering what sort of reception awaited him at the Mutualité.

20

The Congress commences with a little foreplay

Ezra arrived outside the Mutualité at the same time as Ted Spanner stepped out of a cab with Ricky Lysaght and Mimi Wilcox, whom he had just collected from the airport. Mimi was paying the cab, but Ezra could only pause for a few genial exchanges. They agreed to eat together after the Congress before Ezra hurried off and made his way to the platform. Simon was chairing the morning session.

It is a well-known fact that most of the real decisions take place outside the Congress, in the corridors or in tiny smoke-filled rooms. This Congress was not destined to be exceptional in that regard, and yet it had generated a certain frisson, because nobody knew what Ezra really wanted. The hall was full, with standing room only, and it presented a bizarre spectacle. The leaders of the movement were seated with their followers in different parts of the hall and the sartorial contrast was, in itself, not without interest. Even the tiniest sects had turned up. Nobody wanted to be left out.

Above the platform there was a bench of honour where the true veterans – thirty-six in number, men and women who had been present at the Founding Congress in 1938 – were seated. Old Renard had just arrived and was making sure to sit as far away from Diablo as possible. He was dressed in a combat jacket, but had come without any headgear. He had received a phone-call only yesterday from Managua asking whether Diablo was suffering from senile decay. The Nicaraguans told Renard that during his recent trip to Managua, Diablo had asked them four times a day whether they had received the donation which had been requested and accepted on their behalf by Renard. The old Fox had not lost his nerve for even a second. He told Managua that Diablo was hallucinating – a result of the cocaine which his doctors administered regularly for health reasons. The conversation ended amidst much laughter.

Diablo was leaning forward and glaring at Renard, who was aware of this and deliberately looking straight ahead, waving to old friends in the audience, desperate for the the show to begin and distract Diablo. However the minute Simon declared the Extraordinary Congress open, Diablo was on his feet. His face wore the look of thunder. The middle-aged comrades in the audience chuckled. They were not going to be disappointed. Simon wondered what all this was about, but deferred to the large, tall man whose presence here must be a novelty for so many of the delegates who knew of him only by repute because his name was associated with a supposedly revisionist heresy.

'Comrade Diablo has the floor.'

Diablo walked slowly to the podium, exchanged a nod with Ezra and waited until there was pindrop silence.

'Comrades, I apologize for starting this great conference in this fashion, but I have no alternative. There is a comrade present here sharing the bench of honour reserved for founder-members of our movement. I charge him with a breach of proletarian morality, a violation of the internal norms of our movement and its statutes, and unless a Commission of Inquiry is set up immediately to investigate my charges and a satisfactory reply made to my questions I will have to leave this Congress now and report the matter to the police. A lot of money is involved.'

A buzz travelled through the old chamber. A money scandal and at the very start of the Congress. Movement connoisseurs couldn't believe their luck. All eyes were on the bench of honour. Who could it be? Everyone sitting there was looking uneasy except Renard and the South African Jamie Gelder. Ezra realized at once that Renard was the cause of this and he passed a note to Simon with a few suggestions. He also sent a note to Diablo which read: 'It would have been more constructive if you had come to the Secretariat and we could have dealt with it there. Why did you do this here?'

Simon was speaking:

'Comrades, given the seriousness of Comrade Diablo's charges, I propose we adjourn for one hour and that a Commission consisting of Comrade Ezra, myself, Comrade Gelder, Comrade Louise-Carol and Father Pedro Rossi meets immediately with Comrade Diablo and the person he has accused in the small room upstairs. I hope we can quickly sort out a way of dealing with this problem. I hope you will agree. All those in favour?'

Every hand went up and every sect-leader placed a spy near the stairs to see who else would be going up in addition to the comrades already mentioned. There was no way now that the identity of the guilty party could be hidden. But before the conference adjourned Renard rushed to the podium.

'Comrades, I would request attendance of the Tribunal as an observer. I think given my experience I may be able to expedite matters.'

The conference agreed this by acclamation, and as the delegates stood up and began to move around, making new friends, meeting old enemies and enjoying this unexpected bonus, Diablo's face could be seen in the distance, purple with rage. Despite the faint drizzle Emma, Ted, Ricky and Mimi decided to walk around the streets of the city. Emma asked about Lavinia and Ricky's face clouded.

Mimi sighed despairingly. 'It's worse than we thought. I had assumed that he was a layabout farmer or someone connected with horses or an old hippy refugee from Thatcher's Britain, something like that, but no such luck. He's a . . .'

'Libertine!' muttered Ricky. 'A loathsome Lothario! Utterly amoral. He had the nerve to address us as comrades, with a twinkle in his only eye. Sickening Cyclops!'

Ted smiled. He had never heard any contemporary use the word libertine in everyday speech. It was redolent of such classics as Casanova's *Memoirs*, pre-cad, pre-bounder, but it sounded good on Ricky's tongue. Paternal anger suited him somehow. Was he really one-eyed, or was this simply a Lysaghtian code for some grave inner defect? Ted wanted to hear more.

'Who the hell is he?'

It was Mimi who replied in a sad, doomed voice. 'Terry Contraband. That is his real name. I promise. And Lavinia wants it desperately. Lavinia Contraband. Ghastly! Though it is true that we knew him a quarter of a century ago. At least I did, because we were all in Ezra's British group at the time. He was a leading figure in Irish circles in Britain. In those days he was quite amusing. I still recall the odd evening in the pub when he would tease the Irish Catholic plebeian element present with anticlerical jokes . . .'

'Like what?' Emma asked. She was a collector of anti-religious jokes. Ricky snorted in disgust, but Mimi continued. She was trying to exhibit the more attractive side of Contraband.

'Well you know the sort of thing. He would turn to a Catholic friend and say something like: "Gerry, why did the Saviour always turn water into wine when it was his round?" This was mild. He would follow up with a more risky one: "Listen to me Sean. Suppose you were on active duty for a year, when you came back you found that lovely Annie had a bun in her oven. Yeah, sure, you'd beat the truth out of her, but suppose she kept saying that it was the Divine Being himself who'd entered her and that she was bearing you the son of God. I mean what would *you* do?" This one usually led to some half-friendly fisticuffs. Anyway Contraband at that time was through his fourth wife. Then he disappeared for ages. Turned up about ten years ago as a Labour Councillor in Islington, but was suspended for publicly assaulting the husband of his fourth wife, who'd walked out on him after being brutalized. Nobody knew what had happened to him. It emerges that he'd set up a little second-hand bookshop in Dublin, which also sold contraceptives under the counter. It was only a cover for some crooked bookies who were into doping horses. One of them used to ride Lavinia's prize stallion Ayatollah ten years ago. She wanted some advice and went to the bookshop to find him. She met Terence Contraband instead.'

'Is he really one-eyed?' Ted still wanted to know.

'Yes,' came Ricky's severe response. 'The cuckolder claims that it was in the Algerian war when he was helping Diablo, but that is a falsehood. It was a pub brawl, and the angry husband in question not being able to lay hands on a stake to perforate his heart, found a large wooden spoon and jammed it through his left eye instead. Messy business. And unfinished.'

The Parisian drizzle had stopped, leaving only a parquet of puddles behind. A wind started to blow the clouds away and the patches of blue sky were being enlarged every minute. The editor of the *New Life Journal* and her party slowed their pace as they turned round and began to stroll back to the hall.

Back at the Mutualité the Commission of Inquiry, having heard Diablo's version in great detail, requested Renard to explain himself. Both Ezra and Simon now understood the origins of the money which was helping to fund the Congress. Ezra was cross, but Simon was secretly tickled at the thought that Diablo's cash had funded this event and, indirectly, the Commission meeting itself. He wished, however, that Renard had told them at the time. How would the old highwayman get out of it this time? Renard looked at Diablo with eyes specially moistened for the occasion.

'There is no elaborate explanation. I am an old man with not long to go. I have no need of money for myself. I have no interests any longer apart from the movement. The money was requested by the Sandinistas, but it never reached them. Do you want to know why? Because when I left Diablo's apartment, carrying the two hundred thousand francs in a carrier bag, it was raining and there were no taxis available. So I decided to go home by Metro. On the train I fell asleep. I must have been very tired. When I woke up I was far away from my destination and the carrier bag had disappeared. Just like that. You can imagine my panic. I rushed everywhere. It was my fault, of course, and I did not have the courage to tell you about it Diablo. How could I? You might not have believed me and . . .'

'I still don't believe you, you bastard. You haven't changed a bit. Trotsky was right to expel you. We should never have taken you back. Does anyone else believe this hen-and-cow story? Well?'

The members of the Commission looked at each other, then at the two sparring veterans, and shrugged their shoulders. It was Ezra who attempted to defuse the issue.

'Diablo, I can understand your anger. What Renard did was grossly irresponsible. But I think, on this occasion, he is telling the truth. He is capable of inventing less flimsy excuses and he has had plenty of time to do so. In fact if he had pocketed the money he could have been sunning himself on Copacabana Beach by now. Please accept his explanation, but we shall make a very serious attempt to raise the money amongst our own ranks and pay it back to you. I promise you that.'

Diablo was ten years older than Ezra. The two had known each other since soon after Ezra had joined the movement at the age of sixteen. He trusted Ezra, even though he was jealous of his pupil's success as a theoretician in the outside world. He decided to accept the offer for the sake of factional peace. Everyone breathed again. The crisis was over.

As the conference began to come together again, Simon noticed new faces before him. The late arrivals from Mexico and Sri Lanka were now present and there were no absentees. Even from his chair on the platform, Simon could detect the tension between the two tiny delegations from Sri Lanka, but he was not prepared for what followed as the conference resumed. A tall, wiry, serpentine, figure, his bald head gleaming in the artificial light, stood up on a 'point of order'. Simon groaned, but nodded his head. It was unavoidable. The old Sinhalese leader stalked up to the platform in a self-induced rage. Ezra's face showed the tension. He sat bowed with his head in his hands.

'Comrades, I would like to inform you that there is a member of the CIA present in this hall, masquerading as the leader of a trade union whose only members consist of him, his wife, an ailing parrot who can only repeat what he says, and his full-time employees, all of them, as you know, funded by the Ford Foundation. Can we have such a conference, discussing vital questions in the presence of this lick-spittle? I ask for a special Commission of Inquiry to determine the credentials of this charlatan and his crew . . . I . . .'

'Comrades,' Simon interrupted the Sri Lankan. 'As chair of this opening session I would propose that we delay the plenary session no further. The charges made by Comrade Spencer Abitmortoddy are very serious, and it would be frivolous in the extreme to imagine that we could unravel everything in a short time as in Comrade Diablo's case. So I would suggest we set up a Commission which meets this evening to consider the allegations. I would unilaterally propose three members, Comrade Diablo, Comrade Renard and Comrade Gelder. All three have been to the island in the past, know the history of the movement backwards – as we know there has been no forward movement there for decades – and I hope both sides will accept them as impartial referees.'

Both parties nodded. The person accused by Abitmortoddy was grinning all over his face as if he thought the whole thing was a joke. Being too closely involved himself, he did not appreciate the tragic component of this sorry affair.

Finally, Simon got down to the business of the conference. 'I ask Comrade Einstein to move the opening report at this Extraordinary Congress. Since this is an open conference of the movement, Comrade Einstein will be speaking on his own behalf and not that of our divided Secretariat. Comrade Einstein, you have the floor.'

Ezra looked up, adjusted his spectacles, pressed his upper lip on the lower and walked thoughtfully to the podium. He paused for a moment to let the audience settle and then began to speak.

21

What is to be done?

'Comrades, our movement is once again at the crossroads. The ideologists of capital are celebrating and proclaiming the end of history. Their eurocommunist mimics are saying the same thing, but with a designer's gloss: they try to prettify images of life under capitalism. What vicious foolishness. What floundering. They forgot that the message of these events is very clear. Institutionalized oppression can only be removed by revolutions from below. And do you not think that the working class in the West, cowed by unemployment and reduced living standards, watching helplessly as a new underclass is born and consumed by a hatred against its condition, but a hatred it seeks to vent on other sections of the underprivileged like immigrant workers instead of concentrating its ire on those who have made these conditions, will also learn some lessons?(*Shouts of 'Overheated rhetoric', 'Get on with it.'*)

'But as they watch the events in Berlin and Bucharest, Prague and Budapest, the workers in the West might pick up a few ideas. Television is an unconscious educator, a medium which spread internationalism everywhere. So don't despair. A few years ago, Eastern Europe too appeared quiescent. Its bloated bureaucracies exuded self-satisfaction and complacency. The bourgeoisies in the West have picked up the same habit. They think they have tamed history. Comrades, they are making a very big mistake. (*Applause.*) Within a few years their world, too, could be on the brink of a revolution, but they will not hand over peacefully. That's the difference with Prague and Berlin.

'The series of events in Eastern Europe and the Soviet Union are challenging every orthodoxy including our own. Of course many of the predictions of the Old Man are being fulfilled. He spoke, as you will recall, of the hatred and anger of the masses driving the bureaucrats out of power and denying them a place in the new organs of representation. He spoke of layers of the bureaucracy opting for a restoration of capitalism rather than any variant of popular power. But underlying his thought was an often unspoken assumption. The Old Man assumed that these transformations would be carried through by us, or at least by Bolshevik-style parties, to create which was the reason of our existence. We have grown a thousandfold since our founding moment over fifty years ago, but success has so far eluded us. I think the time has come to ask ourselves why.'

From this point in his address, Ezra felt that he was not in control of the messages his brain was dispatching to his tongue. It was like that day last Christmas when he had sat down to type an internal polemic and had ended up sending the now famous letter which had brought all these people here. Nor could he stop speaking. A mysterious force seemed to have taken hold of him.

'We are living through an amazing procession of scenes from a popular, anti-bureaucratic struggle, which is continuing even as we meet. Standing amidst these changing conditions of life we must strive to understand and assimilate the idea of the constant movement of men, women and things. We must let our minds travel rather than force them to stay in a particular blind alley.

'I do not wish to keep you in suspense any longer. Ask yourselves two questions. Which countries have witnessed the largest mobilizations of workers, students and the poor of town and countryside over the last decade? Which political organization has provided leadership to the disparate social forces in both these countries, an organization totally independent from the ruling bureaucracies and classes in these two instances? I will tell you. Poland and Iran were the harbingers of what is still going on in different parts of the world.

'Poor Poland. Poor, poor, Poland. Partitioned at every historical turning-point, Poland saddled its labour movement with the heavy heritage of a miserable past: a militant nationalism. The legionnaires who planted the red and white flag with the Polish eagle on the fortresses in Warsaw were the footsoldiers of the Roman Catholic Church. The Polish Jews, victims of every social crisis, had experienced pogroms under the Tsars, under the revolution, under the Ukrainians and under the Lithuanians, so they, not surprisingly, sought solutions in their own nationalism, which the world today sees in all its glory as the iron heel of Zionism. The victims have become oppressors. But I must not get sidetracked. (*Applause.*)

'The recent upheavals in Poland saw the largest working-class mobilization independent of the bureaucracy accepting the leadership of Wojtyla and Glemp. The Church again! This frail aqueduct which has spanned almost twenty centuries is still with us, Comrades. Isn't it worth thinking about this remarkable fact? Should we not be reconsidering some of our certainties? I will return to the Church in a minute, but let us turn to that other event which has left its mark on our century.

'The Iranian revolution which toppled the king of that country and destroyed his army also witnessed the most gigantic mass mobilizations of the twentieth century. Here, from the very beginning, the masses saw a Muslim cleric as the symbol of their liberation from a pro-imperialist ruler and from the whole modernist impulse, which in Iran went together. Despite the fact that this was an arbitrary and cruel regime which killed more liberals and Socialists than the deposed monarch and which fought a long and cruel war with its neighbour Iraq and lost over a million people, it is still in power. Contrary to popular myths, Khomeini was a theologian of talent and a diehard Muslim, but he was not a fundamentalist in the sense of standing by every dot, comma and intonation of the Koran. To give you one example, Islam forbids a clerisy. It does not allow any worship of images.

Khomeini relied heavily on more favourable interpretations and was a formidable interpreter himself, looking for sentences which tallied with his particular brand of religious populism. Like the Church in Poland, so to a much greater extent in Iran, the Mosque became an organizing centre of the struggle.

'I will give you more examples. In East Germany, where the Left is strongest, the role of the Lutheran Church has none the less been impressive, not least because it is the most radical religious current in Central Europe. The Catholic hierarchy in Czechoslovakia is actively trying to build a Christian Democratic Party. In Romania, the uprising was sparked off by the arrest of a Lutheran pastor. The pattern is very clear. Behind every reason for despair, we have to discover a reason for hope. The people turned to religion because the secular world had been identified with cruelties associated during the Middle Ages with religion. Then came the Reformation. A secular Reformation will come too, but not for another twenty years. The long waves of ideological shifts are as predictable as the spots on the sun and the movements of the stars. Are there of any of us who don't admire the liberation Church in Latin America? Why did the fascists in El Salvador kill Bishop Romero and the American nuns? To ask in this case is to answer, is it not? Why was there a price on the head of our Comrade, Father Pedro Rossi, for several years? (*Applause.*) All of us have been stuck in our groove, pinned down by cement. We have behaved exactly like Jesuits, but without the mass following of the broad Church. It must change.

'Listen, Comrades, even in countries which are ultra-secular in practice, like Britain, I have information which may surprise you. The youth organizations and clubs of the Anglican Church are growing at a much faster rate than the Young Conservatives, the Young Socialists . . . I was going to say Young Communists, but that has today become a contradiction in terms. I will give you a concrete example. In a Labour-controlled borough in North London, the Christian Youth Club in just one part of this district, known as Crouch End, has a membership of fifty. Seventy-five per cent of these kids, all under twenty, are practising Christians.

'What then is to be done? The answer is obvious. We must move into the churches, the mosques, the synagogues, the temples, and provide leadership. Our training is impeccable. In this regard I would say that the comrades of PISPAW, of the Burrowers, of Comrade Pelletier's organization, as well as many smaller groups here, are better suited to this than the French PSR or the Mexican PPRRS. Their style, and I say this as a compliment . . . their style of education, their recruitment practices, their apprenticeships are so close to some of the Christian orders that I am confident we could make gains very rapidly. Within ten years I can predict we would have at least three or four cardinals, two ayatollahs, dozens of rabbis, and some of the smaller Churches like the Methodists in parts of Britain could be totally under our control. Our aim is to occupy the Vatican and elect a Pope from our movement. Much better to move in this direction rather than to become tainted with the practices of Stalinist bureaucracies or the social-democratic charlatans, patchers-up of capitalism. Look at their German party. On its knees before the bourgeoisie promising they will try to topple the genuinely social-democratic government in East Berlin. They have no will to power. None. Give me the Church any day, or the Mosque, or the Synagogue.

'I realize that this means changing everything. Everything. But at the end we might come out stronger. I ask you all not to reject what I have said out of hand. I know it seems shocking. We, the vanguard of the vanguard, moving into religion? It sounds appalling, Comrades, but it's the only way. I warn you if we don't do this together you can forget about being the vanguard of anything. The only van we'll ever see is the guards van of these new revolutions as they pass us by.

'What I am calling for is that we go into these religions and fight to establish a connection between Heaven and Earth. And we must develop a critique of both Heaven and Earth. Christians believe that everyone is equal in Heaven, but unequal on Earth. Let us challenge this dichotomy. Muslims believe that in Heaven a Man (*sic*) will have every possible pleasure, but why not on

Earth, and why just men? Why should religion project the popular yearning for freedom on to another, distant, world? We have enormous opportunities opening up before us. Comrades! I hope that you will not take my remarks as a sectarian attempt to ram a new idea down your throats. It would benefit the movement as a whole. Onwards and onwards we go. Scattered by a historical cataclysm, we will reassemble sometime in the first quarter of the twenty-first century. The older ones amongst us may not be there to taste the fruits.

'I can see that many of you are shocked, but Comrades, there is one more fact we have to grasp. One of the weaknesses of Marxism and all the other isms descended from it has been a lack of understanding of ethics, morality and, dare I say it, spirituality. We propound what we know is false because our intellects persuade us that it ought to be true. Our dogmas liquidate our intuitions. That is where the religions have always been able to trump us. All this will change. We have planted the seed. Long live the World Republic of Self-Management based on Workers' Councils. I notice some of you laughing. Yes, laughing! (*Shouts from hall of "We remain true to Marxism-Trotskyism."*) You do, do you? Every great movement has had to contend with people like you. The Donatist heresy split the Christians two hundred years after the death of its founder. The Donatists, like you my dear comrades of the Satanist League, claimed that they were the only true believers. That they and they alone had a direct relationship to the divine law. To God! They dismissed any effort to relate to the problems of life on Earth. Just like you, my dear comrades. I will end with paraphrasing St Augustine's rebuke to the Donatists: "The clouds roll with thunder," he shouted at them, "the clouds roll with thunder, that the House of the Lord shall be built throughout the Earth: and these frogs sit in their marsh and croak. 'We are the only Christians.'" The similarities would, in other circumstances, be amusing. Today I find them extremely disturbing. Thank you comrades.'

Ezra sat down to no applause whatsoever. Everyone was shell-shocked. For a few minutes nobody could speak. Ricky Lysaght broke the silence as he whispered to a stunned Ted Spanner: 'The old boy's back on form. This is a master stroke!'

Then the dazed chairman managed to speak.

'Comrades, I thank Comrade Einstein for his stimulating speech. The proposals he has made are of such a character that a great deal of discussion is necessary amongst ourselves ... I mean our own organizations, before we can even begin a discussion.'

But Renard, realizing that unless he did something Ezra would be totally isolated and defeated by PISPAW, Pelletier, the Cuckoo and all the others, now played a card with such high stakes that he himself was shaken by his own daring. He asked for the floor and was invited to speak.

'Dear Comrades, I was looking at you when Einstein came to the most important part of his speech. You think he's gone mad. I could see some of you laughing. Fine, fine. That is your privilege. I will now tell you something that only four people knew, namely Trotsky, his wife Natalia, the Mexican carpenter who made the coffin, and myself. Natalia told me this herself. There are some letters which Trotsky insisted were buried with him. He did not want them to be placed in the archive. And they were buried.'

The conference had barely recovered from hearing Ezra's remarks. Now they waited, with everyone leaning forward slightly to catch every word. Renard was a legend and nobody wanted to miss the revelation. The old rogue lowered his voice even more, knowing that he had captured their attention.

'These letters consist of correspondence between Trotsky and the Vatican on the fate of the Jews in Germany, but they also contain Trotsky's advice to Pope Pius on how to get out of his Concordat with fascism. That advice, Comrades, is pure gold. But there is attached to it a codicil addressed to the movement on the possibility of religion outlasting science and our attitude. Two days before he was assassinated he instructed Natalia to bury these documents when the time came. I suppose he had changed his mind. In any case, given the seriousness of the world situation, I propose that I am permitted to leave for Mexico City tonight with whomever else you nominate. This Congress must confer on us the authority to open the grave in Coyoacán and return with the documents. Given the delicate negotiations this will entail with Trotsky's grandson, I suggest that it should be the veterans from the bench up there who accompany me. Comrade Diablo or Comrade Gelder or Comrade Wu . . .'

Diablo indicated his refusal, but Gelder and Wu accepted. Then the Sri Lankans demanded the conference elect two more persons to discuss the allegations. The Cuckoo was nominated, but rejected by both sides. Finally Simon and Jean from the PSR Politburo were nominated and accepted. The Congress adjourned till the following afternoon.

Ezra grabbed Renard before he left the platform. The two of them remained seated as the hall emptied. Ezra had never heard the story of the Trotsky correspondence with the Pope. Was it true? Renard smiled, but did not reply.

'Renard, listen. I appreciate your support, but are you sure?'

Renard knew that if he told the truth, Ezra would sabotage the entire operation. He couldn't understand why, but Ezra had always had a priggish side to him. So he chose his words with care.

'Ezra, Natalia herself told me that the Old Man insisted that some papers, including letters, were put in a small leather bag and buried with his ashes. Now I have not read them, and I told the Congress that, but we have reached the lowest ideological point of our ebb. The letters will not only help you, they could also rehabilitate the Old Man in a dramatic fashion. I told you didn't I that when I was in Moscow I was asked seriously by some excited young anti-semites: "Is there any truth that Trotsky was a fascist agent?" I was angry and said no and they were disappointed. If he had been, they would have fought for his rehabilitation! So you see, my friend, the dialectic of history is so very unpredictable. We need the letter.'

'But what if it isn't there? I mean . . .'

'Then I will just have to report that, won't I, but the very fact that I have raised the question has already resulted in your plan being taken seriously. So just wait. Wu is too old to travel, but Gelder's coming with me.'

'I wish you luck. The fate of our movement could depend on what you find.'

22

The same evening

While Ezra had been speaking Maya had discharged herself from
the maternity ward. She was feeling well, there had been no
problems, and she saw no reason why she should stay in hospital
for another few days. So she picked up Ho, walked out, got a taxi
and came back home. There she was now suckling Ho, who
seemed to be growing at an alarming rate, and listening to Emma
and Mimi's account of the day's proceedings at the Congress.
They were clearly stunned by the turn of events. Now they waited
for Maya's interpretation of what had taken place. Looking like a
Brazilian Mona Lisa, Maya contented herself with a smile. Mimi
wanted an answer.

'But Maya, surely you suspected, didn't you? I mean it was like
a thunderbolt from heaven . . .'

'Perhaps it was . . .'

'Please be serious. Ezra is one of our best-selling authors and
contributors. If he's making a turn to religion we will have to
interview him at length. Our readers will be shocked. Please
realize the seriousness of this . . .'

Emma had not spoken a word since the conclusion of Ezra's
speech. She had been very upset by Ezra's performance. If tactics
and strategy could be so elastic as to lose all connection with the
goals, then what was the point of anything? Religious means
could never reach Socialist or secular ends. How could we ever
accept this turn, thought Emma. Our minds were shaped by the

heat of distant bonfires. 1789. 1848. 1871. 1905. 1917. 1956. 1968. 1975. 1979. 1989. These dates, marking defeated and victorious revolutions from the French through to the Nicaraguan and now Eastern Europe, flashed through her memory. Were these rhythms to be discarded for ever and replaced by a heavenly hierarchy? Should critical reason surrender in the face of setbacks, themselves the result of weakness and cowardice? Should the pharmacies which had, for fifty years, been brewing revolutionary potions now turn to the distilling of religious balms? Emma voiced these fears aloud.

'Maya, I have been told that you are a very intelligent person. Won't you help us put the train back on the tracks?'

'But Emma,' Maya began in her soft voice, fingering her crucifix for psychological support. 'The whole problem arose because the train had been stuck in a tunnel for half a century. The tracks in front of it have been dismantled and used elsewhere. Those behind it have decayed and are unusable. The only thing left is to get out of the train and walk to the station, a few yards down the road. The problem is that all the trains from that station lead to the temple. So Ezra thinks that it is better to leave the tunnel and find the old tracks after a detour via the temple. It is logical, is it not?'

'But what if the detour is so long that you can never find the old tracks?'

Maya shrugged her shoulders as she stood up and carefully deposited the sleeping Ho in the wicker carry-cot. Then she lifted it and went into Ezra's study, which she thought was ideal as a temporary nursery. On her way back she saw a letter with a Canadian postmark amongst the pile on Ezra's desk. It was addressed to her. Cathy Fox must have replied on the very day she received the letter. Maya was thrilled. She had asked Cathy lots of questions about love and sex and life and the future of the planet.

'Emma, do you know Cathy Fox in Montreal?'

Emma cheered up at the mention of her friend's name.

'Do I know Cathy Fox? She's one of my closest friends. I'm

really angry she decided not to come, but she sent me a copy of her letter to Ezra. It was great. Did you read it?'

Maya nodded. 'I liked it so much I wrote her asking some more questions.'

Maya flashed the new letter proudly. Mimi decided that the time had come to leave. She knew the signs and was not in the mood for a consciousness-raising session. The baby was a sweet big thing. She had done her duty. Maya was in safe hands and Ricky was waiting. Mimi reminded Maya that they were eating together on the following night.

'And I will meet this Ricky at last?'

Mimi nodded as they kissed each other. The minute she'd left, Emma suggested that they read Cathy's letter.

'She's the greatest letter-writer of the movement. Very few people take letters seriously any more. The telephone has taken over, but Cathy won't give up. Do you know she's had her telephone disconnected at home so that her only method of communication is through letters? Her fax machine is something special, custom-built and specially installed by her Japanese lover, a genius at that sort of thing. Have you a copy of your letter?'

Maya shook her head.

'Pity.'

Maya slit the envelope and pulled out a thick wad of paper. Both women moved to the sofa to devour the letter.

Dear Maya:
It was a great surprise to get your letter. My letter wasn't designed to make an impact. Honestly! I just felt I owed your old man an explanation for not turning up to his Congress! I'm glad you've established contact and it would be good to remain in touch. Of course I understand the problems with your relationship, but don't think that only old men are like that. The young ones can often be worse . . .

You asked so many questions that I blush to reply. It really does take me back twenty years, and the fact that you were then

only three or four doesn't make it any easier. Ask my friend
Emma, who will be in Paris. She can explain many things
directly. But look at her closely. She's got very slim and
muscular. Her hair is curled and her clothes are well-considered.
As I write to you I see her at the peak of the feminist rebellion.
Baggy jeans, thick knitted sweaters, sneakers or work boots,
hair unfashionably dishevelled and a delightful if not aesthetic
indifference to weight. She had just kicked her pig of a husband
out and was enjoying life.

How did I get into the movement? Well, it got into bed with
me! And then there was some further movement. I'm not joking
now. It really happened. One night in Seventy-One I was
invited to dinner by Rosie and her lover Rhett, who lived in a
collective house with two other people. Rhett's mother was a
'Gone with the Wind' fanatic. Hence her son's name! Both of
them were activists in the New Democratic Party, which is our
version of social-democracy. It's not at all like your Labour
Party in Brazil!

Rosie was dressed in feminist uniform with her lumberjack
shirts and otherwise the same as Emma. These were meant to be
marks of rising consciousness (ones I never adopted for various
idiosyncratic reasons), butRosie just couldn't hide the raw
erotic energy that emanated from her like light does from a
steady, powerful, beacon. That night there were only the three
of us, but ten days previously when I had first met the pair there
had been lots of others there as well. Anti-Vietnam war
activists, Black Power militants, NDP far-lefties, some veteran
Communist workers, all of us greedily consuming Rosie's
speciality: an all-purpose liver and sour cream dish, poured over
liberal helpings of noodles. It tasted worse than it sounds!

On the big night, so to speak, dinner was served for the four
house members plus me, their only, and honoured to be so,
guest. I noticed that Rhett kept staring at me and attempting his
gross attempt at 'revolutionary education'. ('You think Lenin
was authoritarian' . . . this in tones of disbelief and contempt
. . . and then: 'Don't you know the difference between Leninism

and Stalinism?') It was not that these questions were unfair or irrelevant. It was the tone that got me. His recruiting procedure was equally subtle: 'God, how I despise those social-democratic cretins!'

By now dinner was over and we were sitting upstairs in Rhett and Rosie's bedroom, smoking grass, chewing the Sixties fat, checking one another out, or so I thought. I noticed Rosie moving somewhat provocatively only a few seconds before she spoke. Her words were sort of unusual. 'You two go on talking,' she advised Rhett and me. 'I'm going next door to masturbate.' I gulped hard and, no doubt, blushed and restrained the impulse to cry out 'No don't. I'll be leaving right away' when I saw Rhett look at her with a flicker of sensuality, then turn back to me and the conversation and say to Rosie, 'OK, see you in a while.' So we carried on talking, a bit self-consciously, since our political pow-wow was regularly punctuated by first the slow and then speeded up noises coming from the next room.

I was totally unused to this kind of talk about sex. I found it a bit shocking, but, alas, not in the least titillating. It was too crude, too obvious and upfront, too candid and biological. Humanity was missing. Am I making sense Maya or does it all sound like the rantings of a middle-aged feminist? The thing is that I preferred my sex clothed in dramatic ritual and innuendo, redolent at least of the all-too-recently-smashed-taboos that used to surround it. Yet I could not deny the impact of Rosie's statement, of her act, and the fascination that she and it exerted on me. She was the 'older woman' and so, so experienced. At that time, Maya, she was your age.

That's how I entered the movement. It entered me in the shape of Rhett Smirkovsky some months later, but by that time I was already hooked. For years after that, Lenin, Trotsky and masturbation were linked together in my consciousness. Of course I am overstating things. The key as my hero Spinoza used to say is 'neither to laugh nor to cry, but to understand.' I'm not sure I can answer all your other questions, but I will try and be frank about a few of them. No! I never slept with Ezra nor did he ever suggest such a possibility. He was our father-figure and though we were pretty wild, we weren't into incest at all! There were some Trots whom I did enjoy, but both of them happened to be women. On other things such as whether there was a psycho-sexual dimension to the hostility of Ezra and the PISPAW gang-leaders, I don't think so. PISPAW always hated intellectuals, that's all. And Ezra is the epitome of a rootless cosmopolitan, free-floating intellectual, isn't he? His tragedy has been that he has allowed his natural political instincts to be tamed by the instrumentalist needs of a tiny sect. He could have influenced very big social layers throughout the world had he not held himself back. From what you write it would appear that he only holds back in the political domain, which confirms my point. You see, the way men function in society at large is not unrelated to how they act at home. This applies to the big capitalists knifing each other in the front in boardroom battles whose outcome involves the future of millions all over the world as much as to bourgeois politicians or members of the revolutionary sects.

In the old days, after Politburo meetings, I used to take myself off to a massage therapist for a bit of yelling and screaming, then to a neutral analyst for a bit of psychoanalytic feedback. What a stereotypical North American eh? A bit of yoga, a touch of psychoanalysis, a little mysticism, some vitamins, nuts and herbal teas and we all feel better. I used to have an overriding sense of what a transitional generation we were/are(?), caught between the disintegrating infrastructure of capitalism and a socialism not yet even conceived. If it were closer, perhaps the disintegrated social tensions which play themselves out in our psyches would not have exacted such a heavy price. But it isn't. Rhett once described the relationship between the conscious and the unconscious as dual power in one's head. Sounded good, but it was even more complex. Because even the unconscious is not completely unaffected by our environment.

You may well ask, as you do, that if it was so weird and crazy *why did I give it the most important years of my life? The good things one takes for granted, you know! I know that I read an amazing amount of stuff in those years and learnt more than I ever could have in any university. Then there was the camaraderie, which I often miss and which was what almost convinced me into flying over to your old man's Congress, but then I remembered all the tormentors who would be there as well.*

Some friends are at the front door, Maya, so I had better pack up for now, but keep writing.

Love and sisterhood,
Cathy.

The front door was unlocked and then slammed again. Ezra ran up the stairs as his doctor had ordered. Maya hid the letter and was immediately ashamed of herself for doing so. Emma smiled and got ready to leave as Ezra charged into the room. He did not notice Emma at all as he kissed Maya on the forehead. Emma waved silently and left the room with Ezra's words ringing in her ears.

'My sweetest little thing. I went searching for you in the hospital. You should have told me you were coming home. My beautiful one. Where is little Ho?'

Maya took him by the hand and led him to the study. There in the tiny cot on the floor lay Ho, fast asleep and radiating serenity. Ezra embraced his wife.

'Maya, if only the world was like this . . .'

She took his jacket off and pressed his shoulders to ease the exhaustion she could sense in his body. Then she put her arms around him and gently stroked his chest, which she knew was welling with emotion. But not just emotion. To her amazement she felt two wet spots on the front of his shirt. At the sight of his little child he had begun to lactate again. As if in solidarity two tiny tears slipped out of the corner of her eyes and moved down her cheeks.

23

The same evening . . . II

The PSR Politburo had been in almost permanent session since the closure of the Congress, the Triplets having a hard time as one member after another assailed Ezra. Simon tried to argue that Ezra was speaking metaphorically. The Temple was merely a symbol for the outside world. But nobody was prepared to accept this explanation. The discussion was polarized between diehard atheists who refused to have any truck with what was being proposed, and equally intransigent materialists who felt that the tactical shift being proposed by Ezra, however unpalatable it might appear, was necessary in order to survive the next twenty years. Simon made a passionate plea in this regard.

'Ezra may be wrong, I don't dispute that for one minute, but think of what else is happening in the world. The changes we are witnessing are of an epochal character. The changing face of the Eastern bloc will determine the shape of world politics for the next twenty to thirty years. We can, of course, grow old around this table. We can provide impeccable analysis of the situation week after week, but we don't need an organization to do that. A few comrades alone would be sufficient. Look at what is being proposed as an adventure, an undercover operation of such daring that our success could create havoc in the ranks of the establishments everywhere. The sacred ministries, of course, will be horrified when they discover that they have been polluted by such vile company, but that will not be *our* problem. The women comrades, in particular, will have a very important role to play within Christianity, Judaism and Islam. Yes, yes, Islam. I do not propose we enter Buddhism, Hinduism, Sikhism or some of the other sects, with the possible exception of the Zoroastrians or Parsis as they are known. The Parsis sit on mountains of wealth and have infiltrated key institutions of the state all over the world. Access to all that could be useful.'

Simon went on to point out the dangers involved, the excitement. He painted pictures of the people around the table in priests' and nuns' robes, in Hassidic paraphernalia, entering a new world, but with old aims. He could see that his listeners were beginning to see the attractive sides of the proposition and so he threw in the fact that they would all need fake identities and forged papers. He told them that they would need to have clandestine assemblies of PSR members once a month, where they would exchange notes and experiences and discuss the whole question of how to facilitate the transition of new recruits won inside the religious orders to the closed world of the movement. As eyes began to sparkle and minds were distracted, Simon put the proposal to the vote. There were thirty PSR leaders present at this enlarged Politburo. Five diehards voted against, fifteen abstained and the rest voted to back Ezra. Simon smiled and introduced Father Pedro Rossi, who had been specially invited to attend the discussion. He was now asked to speak.

Jean had wanted Pedro to start the proceedings, but Simon, who knew the priest well from his days as a guerrilla, had felt that his dry, pedagogic style might only heighten antagonisms. Now things were different. The PSR was committed to the new line and Pedro could help to educate cadres.

Pedro cleared his throat, stroked his moustache and started by explaining his own move to the Church. His opening, as Simon had predicted to his siblings, was characteristically arid. He explained the divide in the Church, its continued resistance to modernity and its attempts to restore the past. But, he went on to argue the existence of another paradigm, which despite its minority character was a different contestation of modernity. It fought against the present by advancing revolutionary utopias inspired by religion. These were not regressive in character. They wanted a detour via the past towards the new word and a new future. This critique of modernity could be profoundly radical, and the messianic kingdoms of the future were, in theory, not so different from the stateless utopias advanced by Lenin in *State and Revolution*. Then Pedro totally changed style. Having impressed them with his knowledge, he went on to explain the sort of factional opponents they would encounter inside the orthodox Church.

'Most of the traditional hierarchy in Europe, not Latin America but Europe, is clever and corrupt. Their souls are clogged with putrid dregs, which cause spiritual ulcers. Let me mention just one name. Archbishop Z, for instance, an adviser to the seniormost cardinals in the Vatican. It is well known, even to the youngest of priests, that Z, who masquerades as a writer of holy verse and a knight of the spirit, is a rogue, a crook, a coward, a sponger, a lick-spittle, and all this is his essence. His intellect can never cross the boundaries of this essence. In public he is a liberal. In private sessions with the priests he talks of how the Jews still use Christian blood for their religious purposes. He cites the disappearance of numerous Christian Palestinians and says that their blood was sucked out for such a use. He is a wriggling, slippery, elastic, worm, happiest when he is in the middle of a dung-heap. (*Applause.*) I seem to have got carried away, but we know him well. He was sent out to destroy the liberation Church in Brazil. We have a big dossier on him. He may be the most extreme example, but there are many like him.'

The Politburocracy was delighted by this broadside. Even Roger, who had been in a permanent minority against the Triplets for nearly thirty years and who had voted against Ezra's plans, was smiling and applauding, but for different reasons. Roger was already dreaming of doing a deal with Archbishop Z against his factional opponents in the PSR. What a triumph that would be. He asked to have his vote re-recorded. Simon was the only one who appreciated the real reason that underlay this turnabout. The meeting adjourned at two a.m.

Elsewhere in Paris other plans were being hatched. The PISPAW apartment was filled to capacity and seething with righteous anger. They were all assembled and ready for action. The Cuckoo was still attired in the ghastly grey suit which he wore when travelling abroad. Pelletier was seated on the armchair in the corner, with two Robot bodyguards perched on each arm. Jimmy Rock and Sugar Brink were at the table with Noble and Louise-Carol. Jed Burrows was missing, but his second-in-command, Paul Potter, a dour, balding, bespectacled copy of the original, who did all the shit work in the office, was present with a permanent frown on his face. In addition there were PISPAW employees from London and Stockholm, who were making sure that the coffee and spirits flowed without any hindrance, and standing around the room were some of the lower echelon cadres from all the groups present. These latter individuals avoided all horizontal contact. They were there to listen to their elders, smile when their Leader smiled, laugh loudly at his jokes and back him up if it ever became necessary. Noble looked at the Burrowers.

'Is Jed absenting himself for the whole evening, Paul? Where is he?'

Potter blushed, which was an indication that he knew perfectly well where Jed was and found the whole obsession with Tebbit both repugnant and embarrassing. 'Er, er . . . no. I don't think so. He wasn't feeling too well and his sister lives here, you know. He went to see her and I think she must have kept him there.'

It was such an unconvincing lie, spoken with such little conviction, that nobody believed him, not even the rank-and-file Burrowers, who were loyal to the core but not total imbeciles. Noble smiled understandingly.

'I think we should begin. There's only one item on the agenda.

One more thing. Er . . . er there should be a comrade from the PSR Politburo here later who will let us know whether the French want to go down the plughole with Ezra or not. Who wants to speak first?'

Pelletier rose from his armchair and took his seat at the rectangular dining table. The old Freemason had been outraged earlier at the very thought of having anything to do with the clerics. His whole life and that of his father, grandfather, and great-grandfather had been determined by their Freemason connections. Yet he did not regard Ezra's proposal as demented.

'Einstein has had an idea. As we know well all his ideas are marred by an excessive schematism. This one is no exception. There is, nonetheless, a rational core to his irrational schema. The religions are not withering away . . .'

'And we are?' interposed Sugar in an unnecessarily aggressive fashion.

Pelletier stared at her with a cold hatred. He loathed the Rockers. 'We are here to discuss politics, Comrade, not psychopathology. It doesn't need a genius to see that we are at an impasse. Perhaps things are different in Great Britain – if so we look forward to your report – but elsewhere in the Western world these have been bad years for us. That is why Einstein's preoccupations are not foolish. His solutions are, of course, completely unacceptable and liquidationist in character, but I have a plan which could outflank Ezra, what we in France refer to as *débordement*. First, however, I would like to hear what all of you have to say.'

Before anyone could speak, Roger, the eagerly awaited factional warrior from the PSR, walked in. He knew he had important news so he put on a show of modesty and sat at the back of the room. Noble asked him to the centre table. Then they all stared at him. Roger loved every minute of this attention, which he was denied in his own organization.

'It was obvious. Simon spoke and then the PSR leadership voted for Ezra with many abstentions. They are for the Einstein plan. Because the turn involves very heavy security it will not be discussed in public as such. Instead they will use names of political parties as a substitute for the places of worship. That's all.'

Jimmy Rock was irritated and grunted angrily. It was Sugar Rock who spoke.

'I think everyone here is overreacting to the situation. We Rockers believe that it is only a matter of time before the working class in the West recovers and follows the example of its brothers and sisters in the East. Sales of *Rocker's Gazette* have gone up and we are busy making buyers into readers.'

Paul Potter stared at them. 'You should start by making your sellers into buyers. Most of the *Gazettes* are left under their beds! But Comrade Rock, why don't you speak yourself? Enlighten us. Why are you silent?'

'What's the point of barking when you've got a dog?' explained Rock, while Sugar cooed with pleasure. He did not often pay her compliments in public.

It was fortunate that the third member of this trio, Nutty Shardman, was already on his way to enlighten the Securitate rank-and-file. He would have been very upset at the suggestion that it was Sugar who was Rock's dog. Rock had used this endearment often, and every time Nutty Shardman had insisted that her gender suggested a different appellation. Nutty wanted Rock to feel that he was the more faithful of Rock's two top retainers. Perhaps Sugar felt this too, because she now felt obliged to take on Nutty's role at this meeting.

'I think we should leave. What these people are up to is no concern of ours. We have the Rockers in Britain and that's enough. I mean the point is, Comrades, that history has just totally vindicated Comrade Rock's theses as contained in his seminal work, *The Rocker's Guide to Soviet Realities*. I mean, need one say more? If you comrades want to learn a few things, read Rock. We have no time to waste. We are busy publishing our guide in every Eastern European language. Comrade Shardman is already in Romania in this regard. So we'll leave you all to your religion. We still have confidence in our books, our knowledge, our future. I think it's a fucking irresponsible waste of time.'

Everyone rocked with laughter at Sugar's performance. Would Rock speak and repudiate his wife? Clearly not. The Rocker couple rose as one and departed to a round of applause. Noble did not join in the laughter. He was a counter of heads. Without the Rockers they were left without fifteen hundred votes, and Ezra simply had to be defeated this time.

The Cuckoo, too, did some mental arithmetic. If a few more sects walked out, Ezra could win. He began to wonder whether it was worth the fight. The problem was that Roger had seen him here and the news would spread throughout the PSR by tomorrow afternoon. He had still not spoken and he could pretend that he had been keeping an eye on the opposition. With this in mind he raised his hand and Noble immediately recognized him. The Cuckoo, in keeping with his new persona, threw a nasty glance at Roger before making his voice heard.

'Comrades! Ezra is wrong on tactics, but perfectly correct in his strategic overview. The mass vanguard, that self-active layer of workers and students which exists throughout the world and which is to us what cowshit is to the insect world, has moved to the right. Its most radical current forms the most dynamic component of the religious groupings. The two key religions, Christianity and Islam, are badly split. The Protestant–Catholic schism and the Sunni–Shia divide are analogous in many ways. Yet they can still believe in the same God and prophets, albeit with different emphasis. The fact that these religions are not monolithic is their weakness and our opportunity, which we must take up without further delay and in the most imaginative fashion possible. The entry of women into the Church and their fight to have the same rights as the men reveals the dynamic of this ancient cult. It would be crazy to ignore the rich possibilities that lie before us. Now is the time for large monumental canvases. Let's throw the miniature tradition on the scrapheap of history. Let's not drown ourselves in a whirlpool.'

Noble was no stranger to political twists and turns, but the

Cuckoo's somersault annoyed him because it was completely unexpected. Till now the Cuckoo had been raving against Ezra's lunacies and proclaiming the need to topple him for once and forever. Noble could feel the loss of control and abandoned resistance. He turned on his former ally.

'You fucking dickhead! What are you talking about? The only thing you're drowning yourself in is a bucket of Ezra's piss! You think you can fuck around with me like that? You're worse than a whore. A least they do it for money. You're just a sick son of a bitch. Soft as shit. Just like the rest of Ezra's mob. It was you who proposed a deal. It was you who came and pleaded with me in New York. And now . . . !'

Noble was in a very polemical mood, and the Cuckoo decided that further debate was useless. He stood up, winked to his companion, and they left the caucus meeting.

After the Cuckoo's exit what restraint there might have been disappeared. Pelletier unveiled his plan. It was a stroke of sheer genius. Everyone looked at him in silent admiration. It was so radical and clever that it cheered everyone up. Even Paul Potter, one of nature's depressives, smiled, and this made all the Burrowers laugh with joy. Pelletier basked in the glory of his idea. What he had proposed was, in reality, very simple. Old Freemason that he was, he argued that instead of entering the other religions, which could be a very messy operation in some parts of the world, it would be far more dramatic to unveil a totally new religion, a synthesis of Islam, Christianity and Trotskyism as practised by PISPAW, the Robots and the Burrowers. The new creed would have its own places of worship, its own Holy Book, its rituals, its sacrifices and its evangelists. Its priests and priestesses would speak in the name of the Creator and accept Jesus and Mohammed as the two great ancient Prophets, but would challenge the legitimacy of both the Christian saints and Mohammed's successors. In their place the new religion, Chrislamasonism, would create its own hierarchy of Popular Saints which would include some of the great figures of history, Hegel being an obvious example. It was agreed that the paradiso and the purgatorio were useful concepts in the sense that they both projected a utopia and simultaneously restricted entry to it. How would Chrislamasonism project the idea of heaven? Noble was very hard on this point.

'Look, there is no way in which we should bend to populist pressures on this one. Paradise has to be a dictatorship of the Angelariat, which is, naturally, based on soviet power.'

Pelletier was worried by this libertarian trend. Without raising his voice he made his position very clear.

'The whole point about going in for something like this is that you accept the authority of a single Creator. This is where Christianity made an error, in my opinion. The Trinity appears pluralistic, so it prepares the basis for doubt. I mean what's the difference between Zeus entering Leda disguised as a swan and the so-called virgin-birth syndrome? It was a big error and the early Christians should have corrected it at source. Islam's obstinate allegiances to the supremacy of One God is its strength. The Prophet is only a Messenger, nothing more. If we want to be original we can say that God is a hermaphrodite, who exudes a sexual dual power, but I would not challenge the all-powerful Creator by any demagogy about the Angelariat. If we're going in for this sort of thing it's best to do it as professionally as possible.'

Paul Potter backed Pelletier and the Robots on this question, which was clearly of crucial importance if Chrislamasonism was to start recruiting. Reluctantly, and with the disapproval of Louise-Carol, Noble decided to opt for unity. It would be unthinkable to start a new Church with a split hierarchy. They agreed on a three-pronged offensive. Two continents were earmarked for the first offensive. Europe and America. They agreed on a name for their daily paper (*Material Religion*) and agreed it would be published in English, Spanish and French with a possible Russian edition in the following year. They aimed to recruit half a million members in the first year and a million in the second. Paul Potter got very excited and revealed that the Burrowers already controlled half a dozen Methodist chapels in

England and Wales, which could be put to use immediately as the preachers, who were all Burrowers, could publicly declare for the new religion. It was all beginning to sound exciting and realistic. Idols would be smashed. The divine will would be done. Children would be sacrificed. Tyrants would be toppled.

Just as they had reached an agreement on all the fundamentals, a loud knocking was heard at the door. Louise-Carol nodded to a second-string PISPAW flunkey who scurried off to welcome the late arrival. It was Jed Burroughs, but in a very strange condition. Paul Potter hid his face. He knew instantly what had happened. There had been a similar incident thirty years ago in Morocco, but they had managed to hush it up. Burroughs was attired in a wig of black curly hair and a long flowing Arab gown, and his face was painted in a strange brown colour. He was thoroughly drunk. The sight of Tebbit had, this time, overwhelmed the old entryist. He had hurried to the Algerian quarter of the city, bought his disguise and wandered round in search of young North African boys.

Now, as he saw familiar faces of veteran comrades, Jed realized that he was overdressed. He took off his gown, raised his fist and began to dance as if though he were possessed by demons, simultaneously delivering a guttural rendering of the Internationale. Unfortunately Jed had forgotten to put his own clothes on underneath the gown when he left the brothel, and on hearing the immortal lines, 'Arise, ye starvelings, from your slumber', his previously sleeping member suddenly woke up and rose in a librating salute to all those present as the ecstatic performer reeled by them. Louise-Carol seemed hypnotized. A few sniggers did spread through the room, but the Robot chief was watching the whole business very intently, without even the trace of a smile on his weather-beaten, pockmarked face. When Jed, exhausted, was about to fall, his aide Paul Potter and two junior Burrowers rushed to grab him and laid him gently on the sofa. Burrows was asleep. Then they proceeded to cover him with the Arab gown.

Pelletier smiled. 'It's clear,' he said. 'We have just witnessed the weekly ritual of Chrislamasonism. There was a strange beauty in the dance of this whirling Burrower. Let us adapt it for our new creed on our holy day, which shall be Saturday.'

24

The expedition to Coyoacán

Now that he had arrived in Mexico City, Renard was faced with a tiny dilemma. He wanted to ring up an old lady friend whose large apartment overlooked Chapultepec Park, but he thought she might not appreciate Gelder's presence. This was pure supposition on Renard's part. In reality he was jealous of Gelder, who was a spry, well-preserved seventy-five-year-old and might easily appeal to Tamarinda, who had celebrated her own seventy-seventh birthday last month. He thought of dispatching Gelder to the fifteenth floor apartment of Chico on the Paseo del Reforma, but Renard's more generous side won this particular battle and he instructed the taxi-driver to head for the Park.

Renard knew the city well. He had come many times after the Old Man's assassination to meet his widow, Natalia, and take his old, old friend Victor Serge out for a drink. In those days Mexico City was one of his favourite Latin American towns, second only to Oaxaca, which was a pure Indian city. Renard knew what a rarity that was in this continent. Mexico was still the only Latin American country where the Indians were not permanently burdened with pain. In Oaxaca they looked happy. It was Gelder's first visit and he was like a child, excited and slightly nervous.

'The pollution's dreadful, isn't it?'

Renard nodded in agreement, even though he regarded the observation as banal and trivial. Gelder was beginning to get on his nerves. Renard had last visited this city in nineteen seventy-four. It was getting bad even then, but not like this. Ezra had been in town as well and they had discussed the future of the armed struggle in the continent. Ezra had been very dubious indeed and had felt that the time was coming to legalize the movements and build Labour Parties in every country where some form of democracy prevailed. Renard had gone to spend a week with Tamarinda on her avocado and mango farm a hundred kilometres north of Mexico City and then boarded a special North Korean plane which had been sent to collect Latin Americans and transport them to Pyongyang to celebrate the sixty-fifth birthday of Kim Il Sung. It was an old military transport plane with propellers. The journey had taken three days with stopovers in London and Prague, to collect more victims, and in Sverdlovsk for refuelling. Renard had not wanted to go. He knew that North Korea was a parody of Stalinist Russia, but he had been instructed by the Tupamaros in Uruguay to negotiate an arms deal with Pyongyang.

Renard suddenly began to chuckle. The Birthday Congress had been unbelievable. The secretary of the Central Committee had in a one-hour speech mentioned Kim Il Sung, 'the Great and Beloved Leader of Forty Million Korean People', one hundred and sixty-four times, on each occasion to be greeted with thunderous applause. It had been a sickening affair, with a number of professors from Scandinavia and Algeria paid fifteen thousand dollars each for making a similarly slavish speech, to prove to the benighted citizens of North Korea how popular their leader was all over the world. At the banquet they had served delicately seasoned and grilled dog meat, which Renard had enjoyed immensely. The French Stalinist delegate, like Ezra Einstein, was a great lover of dogs. She was seated next to Renard and had appeared to be relishing the food as well till Renard had enlightened her. Then she left the table and was violently sick, much to his amusement.

The high point of the trip had been a compulsory visit to the Zoo. Renard, who saw the entire country as a menagerie, had pretended to be ill, so they had taken him alone on the following day. He could not see the point of going to the Zoo, since there were only a few monkeys, an obviously ill bear, a mangy llama and an unhappy-looking green tree-python from Papua New Guinea. But there was one more cage. His interpreter and protocol chief proudly puffed up their shoulders as they escorted him to a large cage which housed a single parrot, with a glittering plumage. It was a nice-looking bird and its keeper, standing there waiting for them, seemed equally pleasant. Renard's interpreter nodded, the keeper muttered something and the bird squawked a single message several times. The interpreter smiled and translated it as 'Long Live Comrade Kim Il Sung.' As the image reappeared in his mind, Renard started laughing loudly. When would that wretched regime fall? Why should the unfortunate North Koreans suffer this museum of horrors any longer?

As the taxi finally reached the Avenida Chapultepec, Renard asked to be deposited outside 598-201, the tall brick building opposite the food stand near the middle exit. Inside Tamarinda gave him a hug and a kiss. She wondered how he could keep going at his age. He introduced her to Gelder.

'Another veteran, my dear Tamarinda, whom I have brought to seek shelter in your house.'

As Tamarinda smiled and eyed the newcomer, Renard muttered in her ear: '. . . but not in your bed!'

She slapped him affectionately on the face and showed them to their rooms. 'Have a shower and relax. Then come and join me on the balcony for a tequila. Then we can eat.'

Renard had slept on the Pan Am flight, but he was exhausted nonetheless. He had his shower, but not having the strength to dress himself he went straight to bed, hoping that a little nap would revive him. He was wakened four hours later by strangely familiar noises. He got out of bed, covered his nakedness with a bath towel and tiptoed into the hall. He traced the sounds to Tamarinda's bedroom. Renard dropped to the floor and peeped through the crack. He was both offended and disgusted by the sight which greeted him. Gelder's naked posterior was bobbing up and down, like a plastic duck in the bath. Tamarinda was squealing with pleasure. Renard raised himself and walked back to his bedroom. He was livid. He cursed himself for not having sent Gelder on to the Paseo del Reforma, where he would have been treated with the courtesy the young comrades accorded their grandparents.

Renard couldn't go to sleep again. Funny how jetlag had started affecting him only since he had touched eighty. He went to the kitchen, helped himself to some food and drink and deliberately made a lot of noise, at one stage dropping some silver goblets on to the floor, so that they knew he was up. He certainly knew that Gelder was up. The noise from Tamarinda's room ceased suddenly. Renard smiled and returned to his bed. Guerrilla tactics had worked yet again.

Renard now began to plan the next twenty-four hours, for they were due to return to Paris before the end of the Congress. As usual he had a number of options ready. The simplest would be if Trotsky's heirs refused to allow the coffin to be opened. Mission would fail, but the diversion would have given Ezra the necessary time to get a majority. If Trotsky's family agreed, then Renard would put his hand in blind and drag out a little leather bag in which some papers would be found. These he had already prepared with the help of an old forger in Rouen. The paper looked authentic and the cyrillic typewriter had once actually belonged to Trotsky. Renard had been given it as a token present when they left Prinkipo. The only problem was Gelder. Everything became clear. Instead of being cross with himself for having introduced his Dutch colleague to a former mistress, he convinced himself that it had all been part of a master-plan. Tamarinda and Gelder could orgy away to their mutual satisfaction, while he carried out the will of the Paris Congress. He chuckled as he downed a large glass of cognac, which soon had the desired effect and sent him to sleep.

At ten a.m. on the following day, Renard was at Coyoacán. He wiped the dust off the official sign which read 'Museo Leon Trotsky'. He could never control a tear when he came to the Old Man's last refuge. Renard had convinced himself that if he and not PISPAW had been responsible for security a sticky little worm like the killer Mercader would never have gained entry to the household. He wandered through the familiar rooms, grunted pleasurably as he saw how many Russian names now appeared in the Visitors' Book. Trotsky's grandson was waiting for him. To Renard's amazement he confirmed that some papers had indeed been buried with the urn and perhaps the time had come to disinter them. Renard nearly passed out. He had made up the whole story to try to help Ezra defeat PISPAW, the Robots and the Burrowers. Renard loathed all three organizations. Now he could hardly believe his ears. There was a real last will and testament.

Both men went down into the overgrown and untended garden. A small group of Mexican Trotskyists, armed with shovels, had already begun to dig around the headstone with its stylish hammer-and-sickle, carved by Juan Gorman at the time. Renard was sweating with anxiety and excitement. A chair had been brought there for him, but he insisted on remaining on his feet.

Within half an hour they had reached the coffin. Augusto, a tall comrade from Oaxaca, lowered himself down. Everyone was breathing heavily. How would this necroromance end? Ever since he had been told that something really existed, Renard had given up the idea of substituting a false correspondence with Pope Pius on the question of religion. He was unhappy about this because a great deal of computer-work had gone into composing the letter.

A shout rent the air. 'I have it, I have it. It's here, compañeros.'

Augusto was hauled back up. In his hand was a wooden box. He handed it to the grandson, who thanked them, trembling with emotion, and escorted Renard back to the house. There in the Old Man's study, they gently prised the old box open. The top virtually disintegrated in their hands. Inside was a leather pouch. Renard took a pair of plastic tweezers from his pocket and lifted the documents out. There were only two of them.

Both men laughed at the same time. They had unfolded the larger of the two pieces of paper. This was thicker and consisted of a portrait of Trotsky in the nude. On different parts of his body, the artist had painted the mark of two sensual lips, which also ringed the Old Man's holiest of holies, his penis. Scrawled all round the painting was a love letter from the author. Of course, thought Renard, it had to be Frida Kahlo. They read the letter. Even Renard was impressed by her erotic vocabulary. He wondered whether the Old Man had replied in kind. Probably not, since Kahlo and Diego Rivera would have made the letter public when they joined forces with the Stalinists. Trotsky could then have also have been exposed as a sexual degenerate. But what was the second piece of paper?

It was a set of verses, unrelated to each other, but clearly in Trotsky's handwriting. The first three were bad examples of erotic poetry, composed to honour a woman who was obviously disabled – the painter Frida Kahlo. Attached to them was a letter to Kahlo after she and her husband Diego Rivera abandoned Trotsky and made their peace with Stalin and Moscow. In this diatribe Trotsky described Rivera as 'undoubtedly a great epic painter, but with the political courage of a mouse, whose character left a great deal to be desired'. But the bulk of the letter, which had never been sent, was a lover's reproach to Kahlo herself. Then there was another poem, which curiously enough compared Stalin to an ant.

Pity the poor ant,
Which cannot understand,
The beauty of the statue,
Over which it climbs every day.
Pity the poor ant,
For it can never understand that
Those projections and those grooves
Which it feels as it moves,
Are only the contours of an object.
Pity poor Joseph
Vissarionovich
Ant.

For a long time Renard and the poet's grandson, their heads cupped in their hands, sat and looked at the piece of paper on the table before them. Renard was disappointed by the verses. Even the ant poem, which he liked, did not make sense politically. Was the statue a metaphor for Socialism? Surely not. Socialism as a lifeless, pretty object? He could see why Trotsky had felt they should be destroyed. Nevertheless he copied them out, and shook hands with the Keeper of the Seal.

On his way back to Chapultepec Park he heard a familiar voice which froze him to the ground.

'What were you doing digging my grave? Did they let you back into the movement you rogue? Answer me.'

Renard thought he was going mad. It must be the sun. He felt the heat on his head.

'Answer me!'

'Where are you, Lev Davidovich?'

'Everywhere!'

'Well, I was sent here by the Special Congress. There was talk of secret testaments, you know. Times are bad, Lev Davidovich.'

'So what's new? History must be taken as she is and when she comes up with new outrages we must fight back with our fists. What's the problem?'

'Eastern Europe is falling apart. The Soviet Union might crumble tomorrow. Our world is exploding before the amazed gaze of their world.'

'Renard, you never understood, did you? Ilyich and I always said that 1917 was an adventure. If we were isolated for too long it could not succeed. We needed Germany desperately, but it went with Hitler. So it's over. Begin again. Tell them I said that. Begin again. No other way.'

'Easy for you, but we're still alive, you know. Where are you by the way? Upstairs or downstairs?'

The Old Man chuckled.

'Getting worried about yourself, eh? Don't worry. Heaven is Hell and Hell, Heaven. That's all.'

'That doesn't surprise me. Listen, why don't you come back

with me to the Congress? I mean just like you are. Invisible. But come back and talk to them. If they hear your voice they won't need Ezra to convince them that there is a spiritual dimension to life. Just speak to them. It will unite the movement and we will achieve miracles. Yes, miracles. Well? What about it Comrade Trotsky?'

But no reply came.

When he returned to the apartment, Renard was not in a mood for frivolities. Gelder and Tamarinda had just finished lunch and were about to retire for a siesta. Gelder looked up, half-embarrassed, half-eager.

'Did you? I mean was there . . . ?'

Renard shook his head. He was not in a mood to divulge anything. 'Are you packed? Our plane leaves in three hours' time!'

Gelder blushed. It was Tamarinda who replied.

'He's not going back. We've decided to get married.'

Renard did not react. He congratulated them and began to pack his bag. He shook hands with his hostess and let Gelder accompany him to the front of the apartment. 'Any message for your wife, children or grandchildren?' he asked.

'Oh I'll be back soon to wind up my affairs.'

'I don't think so.'

This last was deliberately said in a sinister voice. It frightened Gelder.

'What do you mean, Renard?'

The lift touched the ground floor. The Fox had not yet replied. As the doorman hailed a taxi, Gelder repeated the question. Just as he was about to step in, Renard turned and whispered in fearful tones: 'Her last three husbands all died. Heart attacks it was said, but in every case there were traces of arsenic in the body. Farewell Gelder. Happy hunting.'

The look of uncertainty and fear on Gelder's face was reward enough for the unscrupulous old liar who was giggling to himself in the back of a taxi that crept snail-like towards the airport.

25

The Satanists fight back

At eight-thirty a.m. on the morning of the last day of the Congress, Ezra was still fast asleep. Maya was lying next to him wide awake as she fed Ho, who was already a greedy little girl. She let him sleep for another fifteen minutes. Ricky, Ted and Mimi had stayed a long time after supper. Ted was arguing against Ezra's master-plan, but Ricky had given it total support and pledged that of the *New Life Journal*. Mimi was more circumspect, agreeing half of the time with Ricky, but often nodding vigorously while Ted spoke.

Maya liked Ricky and could not understand why so many people found him intimidating. He had buttressed Ezra's arguments with some new information.

'Surely, Comrades, you must be aware of how religion affected the tribes in Papua New Guinea? No? Hmm. I'm a bit surprised to hear that. Well, Ezra, you'll be pleased to hear no doubt that there are still "cargo cults" on the island!'

Ezra had appeared bemused. He had studied a lot of anthropology for his treatise on economic theory, but obviously had not read Peter Worsley's classic book.

'What are they, Ricky?'

'The islanders were essentially animistic. In the early years of this century, nineteen thirteen and thereafter, they came under German Lutheran missionary influences. But it was the Australians at Port Moresby landing their crates of cargo containing technology, weaponry and other power-devices, which made some of the islanders abandon their beliefs and start the worship of cargos. They became totally obsessed with Western technology as the source of all power.

'I'm being perfectly serious. When a nasty Australian General misunderstood them they sent an appeal to the cargo chief, Jesus, who they believed lived somewhere above Sydney and would come and lead the Papuan islanders in an insurrection against the bad General. Oh and another thing, Ezra. When the islanders saw the self-important colonialist administrators constantly handing chits of paper to each other, they made the handing of chits a part of their cargo-cult ritual. I'm sure there is a moral in this somewhere. In any case it totally vindicates your decision, which I whole-heartedly support. My comrades here are a bit lukewarm I fear.'

Maya had not understood Ezra's reply at all. He often talked like this and it annoyed her, especially now that they had a common new language in the shape of the Church.

'The laws of uneven and combined development. Ha, ha, ha. What a world we live in my friends, what a world.'

Maya had enjoyed the evening enormously, even though she couldn't understand why Mimi was behaving in such a deferential way to Ricky and giving the appearance of being a touch embarrassed whenever Maya tried to discuss Ho's breast-feeding habits with her.

Ho had now finished her feed and was in an active mood. Her nappy was overflowing and the pungent aroma had entered Ezra's consciousness. His nose began to twitch and within a few minutes of Maya holding Ho directly above his face, he had opened his eyes. She then repaired with the infant to the bathroom. Ezra frowned because it meant delaying his shave. At his age he felt unable to shave over a basin into which infantile excreta were being disgorged. The thought set his mind in motion. He wondered what horrors would be disgorged on to his pate at the Congress later today.

In a tiny office, a few kilometres from the Mutualité, John Justice, the leader of the International Satanist Tendency, was rubbing his hands in glee. This crazed hobgoblin and twitching bag of bones looked like a cross between an inbred Mormon and an Albanian mountain goat. He had built his tendency on a world-wide basis, but had developed a compulsive habit of coming into countries and blowing up, metaphorically speaking of course, his own supporters. Justice had decided that the new revisionists must be fought to the death. He had spent the entire night writing a ten-page leaflet which was to be handed out today thanks to dedicated cadres who had spent the whole night translating it from gibberish into English, French and German.

It was a typical Satanist intervention. Ezra now realized that the Satanists should not have been invited to the Congress, but it was too late. Comrades from the Tendency had been rehearsing their assault on everyone else for hours and had been permitted only four hours sleep. The headline on the leaflet was relatively mild: *Ezra Einstein: Trojan Horse of Clerical Capitalism*. Within the Satanist current, where Homer was not widely read, this appeared to a rank-and-file unaware of the original to be a clever invention – they simply assumed that it was part of their leader's curious addiction to bestial metaphors. John Justice was in the habit of describing the Balkan states as 'a region of goatfuckers'. His attacks on the late Ayatollah Khomeini were always intemperate and bestial in character.

The IST newspaper, *The Satanist*, had provided its readers with a remarkable scoop for the special edition which had been run off the presses last night. A former Einsteinian who had deserted to the Satanists some years before had shown them a secret memo passed by the International Executive Bureau in May nineteen eighty-one. The significance of that month lay in the mysterious and unexplained attempt on the Pope's life by an unstable Turk in Rome. This occurrence had coincided with a meeting of the High Command of Ezra's forces in a beautiful mountain-town in the Italian Alps. Even John Justice felt that the resolution passed at that meeting, but not published, was bordering on the offensive. In any case it went completely against the grain of Einstein's latest manoeuvres. So they ran it on the centre-pages of their organ:

AGAINST THE SHOCKING TERRORIST ATTACK ON THE POPE!
A Declaration by the IEB of the FFI

The IEB meeting this day at Santa Maria Maggiore deplores unequivocally the attempt to kill the Pope. Our differences with the Vatican are well known and need no repetition here. Our position on individual terrorism is also clear: we are against it. We reject it as a method of struggle. But we have to recognize that this was no ordinary attempt by an Italian lunatic who believed in the 'third secret of Fatima'.

The attack was carried out by a young Turkish industrial worker, an exile from a brutal and violent NATO military dictatorship. This young proletarian had recently been repulsed by his Italian Roman Catholic lover. All the contradictions of his predicament exploded in the young man's mind. The deranged man waited for the right moment. Just as the little finger of the

Pope was engaged in easing the itch of the Holy posterior, the Turkish worker demonstrated his false consciousness by firing several shots. God's representative on Earth crumbled as three of these penetrated his buttocks. The Holy Father was only saved by the advances of technology and the Third Industrial Revolution (see p. 167 of *The Twilight of Capitalism* by E. Einstein for this prediction).

The IEB of the world Trotskyist movement condemns without reservation the irrationality of a Turkish proletarian confronted by his lover's confessional obstinacy. However the centrists and feminists are wrong to see this act as an example of anti-gay prejudice. On the contrary it could be argued, though *we* are not doing so, that by wiping out a holy arse, the young Turk may have unwittingly liberated hundreds of young priests in the Vatican from sexual oppression.

We cannot help but note that the ease with which the Pope was punctured is a grave reflection on the incompetence of the mercenary Swiss Guards. We call for their immediate withdrawal and demand that they are replaced by a contingent of the Red Army.

Swiss troops out of the Vatican now!

Down with the Turkish military junta!
Support the 198 per cent wage increase for the workers in artificial organ factories!
Down with clerical oppression; liberate the young priests!
Build the Turkish and Italian sections of our movement!
For a united and socialist federation of Italy and Turkey!
Long Live the World Revolution!

14 May 1981

The Satanists were stationed outside every entrance to the Congress. They were chanting their anger as Ezra and the others arrived, with David and Deidre Spart orchestrating the rhythm of the chants.

'Down with God! Stay with Satan! Down with God! Stay with Satan!'

'Ezra Einstein is a Punk, Stay with him and You'll be Sunk.'

These alternated with 'Buy your copy of The Satanist here. Read about Ezra Einstein. The Satanist exposes the Trojan Horse of Capitalism,' and 'The Pope is a Dope. Read Einstein's Secret Attack in 1981!'

Groups of delegates, including Ricky and Mimi, were reading The Satanist amidst general merriment. Even Mimi's face, always serious in Ricky's presence, was on this occasion wreathed in smiles. When Ezra arrived, he grabbed Ricky's copy to read the article responsible for putting everyone in a light-hearted mood. Even Ezra, who had other things on his mind, could not maintain his composure. He roared with laughter.

'You know who the author of that scurrilous document is,

Ricky? Do you? He wrote it at Santa Maria Maggiore and it was passed round. And these idiots really think it was one of our official documents!'

'Who did write it, Ezra?'

'Someone who has abandoned our ranks, but is still a member of your editorial committee. And you Ricky have failed in your duties. There is no longer any restraint on your colleague's irresponsible sense of humour. I shudder to think what he might do to both of us one day. I know you think he's much more impressive in conversation than on paper, but I'm not so sure. Wounded comrades can be dangerous.'

Just as Ricky was about to reply his face darkened with anger. He had sighted his daughter and Terry Contraband walking towards them. Terry was attired in a suit and a tie, part of a desperate attempt to conceal his age and the shape of his decrepit and flabby body. Terry had known Ezra from the Algerian War days and the two men exchanged greetings. Terry introduced his companion, who was stunningy dressed in a pale-blue linen designer suit, the colour of her eyes, and was exuding warmth and good will, to Ezra, while Lavinia hugged and kissed her parents. As Ezra walked in to deal with more important questions, Ricky, without saying a word to Contraband, began to walk away. Mimi followed him.

'Might as well accept it gracefully, Ricky. She seems happy enough.'

'He's after her money. I know the type well. Canny and tight-fisted. Anyway I'm off. I have to prepare three lectures for Brazil next week, not to mention the seminar I've been inveigled into introducing at the Spanner Institute in Berkeley. I'd better go and prepare them now. I've seen enough. That bastard Contraband turning up like this with Lavinia is the last straw. What is she doing here anyway? This isn't a fashion show. Has he converted her to some brand of Trotskyism already?'

Mimi knew these moods well. They had dominated her life for three decades. She knew that his lectures were already prepared, since he had spoken on a similar theme only a few months ago in

Adelaide. She also knew that argument, when he was in one of his irrational moods, was pointless. So she helped him find a taxi and waved her farewell as the car drove off. An explanation of the internal and external forces which moved Ricky Lysaght would make a fascinating saga, but is best left to a trilogy which deals with little else.

Mimi thought that Ricky had over-reacted. It was not that she liked the old hustler from Dublin any better, but felt it was simply a question of live and let live. This had been Mimi's philosophy of life ever since she was appointed editor of the *New Life Journal*. She felt that Contraband must have a good side or else Lavinia would never have fallen for him. She had been present one evening when Contraband recounted an absolutely delightful story. She heard his heavily accented tones again and could not help smiling.

'My brother Frankie, he's a building labourer in Birmingham. He was working as a casual for the firm which got the contract to build a new mosque in a suburb. It was at the time of all the trouble over *The Satanic Verses* and Frankie got very upset. He had read all Rushdie's books and thought he was as good as Joyce. I don't, mind you, but Frankie does. Well, he bought an extra copy and went down with two mates the very day they had laid the foundations. He undid the brickwork and laid a copy of *The Satanic Verses* underneath. Then the three of them rebuilt the foundation wall. They celebrated by finishing off a whole jug of black velvet . . .'

After this story, which had young Lavinia in hysterics, Mimi began to see the charming side of the old scoundrel, but she still wondered what he was like in bed. Somehow or the other she could never pluck up enough courage to ask Lavinia, and wondered whether the girl would ever divulge the secrets of her bedchamber voluntarily.

Inside the Congress hall itself, the Cuckoo had gone up to the platform and was informing Ezra of what had taken place at the factional caucus organized by the PISPAW/Robot/Burrower gangs to prepare an alternative to his line. The Cuckoo somewhat pompously pledged the support of his Swiss followers. Ezra, who had automatically assumed that the Swiss would vote for him, suddenly began to see the Cuckoo in a new light. Simon was announcing the Congress agenda, which consisted of a counter-report by Jim Noble on behalf of PISPAW, the Burrowers and the Robots, and then a vote on all the proposals. The agenda was accepted by the Congress without dissent. Then John Justice stood up and demanded the floor. Simon asked him politely what particular point he wished to raise. At this point the Satanists, who had deliberately seated themselves in twos in different parts of the hall began to shout in unison.

'Let him speak. No bureaucracy here. Let John speak. Let John speak . . .'

Simon told them to restrain themselves and gave Justice a minute to speak. Justice suffered from a fevered and tormented ego which was in a process of permanent expansion. A megalomaniac, he basked in the security of self-imposed isolation. An avalanche of words now began to pour out of his mouth. It was a torrential downpour not unlike the speedy emptying of genteel English bowels as they tested the native cuisine during the early years of colonizing India. Such was the nature of a Justice-Satanist rant.

'On behalf of the International Satanist Tendency I challenge the legitimacy of this Congress. I challenge the right of Einstein to bring us all here under false pretences. I cannot and will not betray our sacred principles. Everything our movement has stood for is being betrayed by Gorbachev in Moscow and Einstein in Paris. Of course we have problems – as Satanists we are aware of them only too well – but nothing justifies the craven capitulation that we have witnessed today. You are a disgrace. I am off to make sure that International Satanist candidates contest the elections in the German Democratic Republic. We will defend that East German workers' state against all its detractors. West German capitalists, social-democratic scum, Einsteinian revisionists, Gorbachev's German droppings are all abasing themselves before the false consciousness of the backward elements in

Dresden and Leipzig. We will win them back. (*Sarcastic laughter and applause*.) Laugh, laugh, you miserable pygmies. Into the dustbin of history. Long live the Great Satan! (*At this point all the Satanists in the hall chanted: "Long Live the Great Satan!"*) Einstein is anything but inconsistent. His entire history is one of permanent betrayal and now he wants to sell the Trotskyist movement, but not even for a mess of pottage. He is a traitor who should be expelled. The Satanists withdraw from this disgraceful gathering. We will not stay here a minute longer . . .'

The signal having been given, the Satanists left the hall in a flurry of slogans. Justice, who had wanted them to sing a song he had titled 'Ezra and his Dog Went to Suck the Pope', had been outvoted the previous evening because the French Satanists had opposed the suggestion as vulgar and apolitical. Justice had consequently worked out how he would destroy them as an organization before flying to East Berlin.

Just as the Satanists were leaving, old Renard walked into the hall. He looked at them and smiled. He had witnessed this scene too many times in the preceding fifty years. Ezra signalled his joy on seeing Renard and beckoned him on to the platform. The hall became silent. What had the old devil discovered? Renard stood up and informed them that some documents had been discovered, but of a personal nature, which the family of Trotsky did not wish to make public. There was another document, but this had decomposed so completely that there was no possibility of deciphering anything.

Ezra's opponents smiled as he decided to have a small coffee break with Renard and debrief him thoroughly. Both of them left the chamber and walked to a nearby café so that they could converse without interruption.

Jim Noble, who was walking to the platform to present his counter-arguments and introduce the comrades to Chrislama-sonism, went white with anger as he observed the departure of the two veterans. Einstein often walked out during his speeches. He always claimed later that no insult had been intended and it was pure coincidence. Jim Noble counted this walk-out as the thirty-seventh such coincidence. On previous occasions he had administered self-therapy in the form of a string of abuse which questioned Ezra's paternity, accused him of Oedipus' offence, and stated that he was a male organ, a female organ and the orifice of a camel. The reference to the ship of the desert remained obscure and Louise-Carol, when questioned about it by admiring younger comrades, never had an explanation.

Simon repeated for the fifth time that 'Comrade Noble has the floor' and Louise-Carol walked up to him and gave him a little push. Noble tried to shake himself out of his hate-trance, but failed. Finally he reached the podium, where he paused for what seemed an eternity and then began to speak.

'Comrades, I bring you fraternal greetings from Comrade Fidel Castro, Comrade Raul Castro and the Cuban leadership. You know that I have been to Havana many times and discussed with these comrades how to deal with the problems posed by the Gorbachev turn in Eastern Europe. You know what Fidel said to me. He said: "Jim, for us it's not a game. Washington is our backyard. For us it's Marxism-Leninism or death." Comrades, I thought about that a great deal. I discussed it with Louise-Carol and other members of the PISPAW Politburo. They agreed with me that our role had to be the same as that of *Granma*, with this exception. *Granma* was the daily organ of the Central Committee of the Cuban Communist Party. We could not replicate that in the United States. But what we could do is become Fidel's own daily organ and carry out the functions which such an honour entailed . . .'

Louise-Carol, horrified by the turn of events, was sending him one note after another. Finally she walked up to him and whispered in his ear. He nodded and stepped down. What had happened was very simple. Noble, enraged by Ezra's behaviour, had gone from trance into dream-sequence and the fantasy had taken him over. This had happened before, but never in public. Most PISPAW Politburos had, over the last ten years, been taken over by similar occurrences. The week before they had all left for Paris, Jim had pretended that he was Fidel and the others had taken on other parts. That had been good fun, but this was embarrassing. Simon sent Pedro Rossi to the café to inform Ezra of Noble's performance and return immediately. Pelletier and Burrows both demanded the floor. Simon recognized his countryman and it was left to the Robot leader to explain the significance of Chrislamasonism.

Pelletier was an exceptionally gifted demagogue, and he soon had the attention of his opponents with his anticlerical diatribe. Even Ezra and Renard, now back in their respective chairs, smiled occasionally. Few, however, were taken in by the new religion idea until Pelletier challenged them in a very bold fashion.

'I have a small suggestion. Let us interest you in the daily ritual of Chrislamasonism. After that we can vote. You don't have to join in, but you are all welcome to do so.'

At this stage the lights we dimmed and the Robots, Burrowers and some, but not all, PISPAW delegates threw off their coats to reveal pink and black gowns. In unison, led by Pelletier and Jed, they began to whirl, chanting the mystical word 'transitional' and working themselves up into a rare old ecstasy. Then Jed cast off his gown, followed by Pelletier. Their supporters followed suit and the last phase of the ritual began. They touched each other's ears and then the eyes. This had been Jed's idea to stress the importance of watching and listening as the main functions of believers. He did not realize that a precondition such as this excluded those without sight or hearing, and when this was pointed out to him he agreed to consider the problem. The ritual over the Chrislamasonites, dressed themselves and returned to their seats, their every movement a model of discipline.

Much to their surprise nobody had joined them and Diablo and Renard had still not stopped laughing. Renard was still laughing when Simon put the motions to the vote. To Ezra's amazement it seemed that half the Congress was voting for Chrislamasonism. The situation in the hall became very tense as the realization that the vote was very close spread throughout the hall. There was a count: it was a split vote. Simon and Ezra looked at each other in despair.

Suddenly Renard's voice was heard. 'Excuse me, comrades, but I was laughing so much that I did not cast my vote. I now do so and for the proposals of comrade Einstein and against the Chrislamasons.'

In fact Renard had voted before and his vote had been included, but nobody challenged his assertion. His second vote gave Ezra and his supporters the majority they needed. Having helped Ezra score yet another victory in the never-ending war with the forces of evil, Renard, who was very tired by now, put his head on the table in front of him and went to sleep.

A sigh of relief discorded uneasily with the shouts of angry Burrowers and Robots deprived of their victory. They marched out of the hall, followed by the PISPAW brigade. A few Robot hoodlums could not resist beating up some Swiss delegates who they held responsible for their defeat. Some of the Cuckoo's own supporters were angry with their leader for changing his mind and voting for Ezra. They stood up, denounced the Cuckoo as a renegade and left the hall, which was now more than half-empty. Pedro Rossi smiled. He had seen the Cuckoo in similar situations elsewhere and the pattern never altered. It was as though the Cuckoo were fated to behave like this for the rest of his life. Rossi wondered whether he had been too hasty in dismissing theories of predestination. He knew now that he could not give up the priesthood simply in order to marry Lina. Ezra had sounded the tocsin, the gauntlet had been thrown, and it was now necessary to prove conclusively that they were correct and decisively smash the Chrislamason heresy.

At this precise moment, just as Ezra was beginning to think that his life's work had been wasted, Laura Shaw entered the main hall, accompanied by Pierre Kosminsky and followed by fifty people of varying ages and sexes, but all dressed in jeans and leather jackets. Laura had delayed her entry to the Congress because her entire staff had been held up on the estate as the result of a freak hurricane which had damaged the mansion itself and wrecked the garden. A two-hundred-year-old walnut tree had collapsed and brought down the conservatory. One of the dogs had died of a heart attack, or so the vet had decided. Laura was distraught, but she could not go back without finding a resting place for the embalmed Frankie in Siena, especially now that his mystic member had provided her with a speech.

On the other hand, she could not go to the Congress all on her own. So she had instructed the major-domo, a lifelong Tory voter, to make sure everything was organized before leading the rest of the employees to Paris. Instead of waiting for them at the Crillon, Laura left Hood, safely plugged in, in her suite and accepted an invitation from Kosminsky, whom she had run into when he was engaged in an errand on behalf of his employer's wife at Verbizier-Ligougne's, the most exclusive designer boutique in the country. Kosminsky recognized Laura and invited her to dinner at the country house of a government minister. It was an exciting night and a half. Her presence was greatly appreciated and she did not even mind Kosminsky tiptoeing into her bedroom in the early hours and entering her without a word being said. Having spent his passion he withdrew discreetly and returned to his own bed, there to await the return of his wife.

Laura was annoyed by the speed of arrival and departure, but this gave way to amusement and a pleasant recollection. Frank had been just like that when she had first known him, before he had acquired the iron appliance. Nor was that the only comparison. On their way to the Congress, Kosminsky asked Laura for a substantial loan. From his tone she realized that he wanted to be permanently in her debt. So she agreed to the request and added him to her already large list of retainers. She was remarkably coy the next day when the penis had questioned her about her nocturnal activities.

'You know me well, Laura. If I'm here what need is there for allowing some French ponce to soil your body?'

This remark had excited Laura and she was now desperate to get the Congress over and leave with her oak chest for Italy.

Now, with her supporters present and oblivious to the fact that the Congress was over and people were leaving the hall, she demanded the floor. Simon explained that the decision had been taken and they were only deciding where to meet next year. He pointed out that everyone was tired and indicated old Renard, still sleeping soundly, but now silently, without snoring; there had also been a split . . . But before he could go on Laura stood up and insisted on being heard. Kosminsky had prepared her speech and she was determined to deliver it so that it could be published in her daily paper back in London.

Ezra, who had always had a soft spot for Laura as an opera star and as a woman and had envied Frank Hood for having recruited her to his faction, told Simon to let her speak. Laura gave him the smile, the same which had wrecked the heart of many a male lead. She had led them on, but at the key moment, instead of allowing them access to her own chamber, she had thrust a Hoodlum membership card before them and insisted they join the Party. Some had thought that this was the way to receive her favours and had joined and donated a great deal of money, but Laura Shaw had eluded them.

Now she took out her speech and went to the platform.

'I will not be long. I have a motion I want to put to you. It reads like this. This Congress of the world Trotskyist Movement sends its warmest greetings to Mikhail Gorbachev on his decision to send troops to Azerbaijan. We strongly support this decision to defend the Soviet workers' state, which is not just the property of the Soviet people, but of the world proletariat, especially the oil workers in Libya and Iraq. What we saw in Azerbaijan was a conspiracy by the international banks and Zionist agents to destabilize the Soviet Union's oil-producing zone. What they have done to Libya and Iraq, they are now doing to the regions of the Soviet Union.

'Comrades, the Hoodlums have backed the just cause of the Libyan and Iraq anti-imperialists for nearly fifteen years. The whole world supported the Romanian people against the hated Ceausescu, but when the Iraqi regime punished some dirty Stalinists a decade ago, the Hoodlums were the only political tendency to defend the executions. This was not simply because of our organization's important trade links with that country, but because . . .'

Before she could continue, Simon stopped the Congress. Ezra had attempted to wake Renard and realized that the old man had died peacefully in his sleep. The Congress was informed and all the people who had rushed out to avoid the Shaw monologue came back immediately. Simon paid a warm tribute and the Congress rose spontaneously and sang the Internationale. It was endgame for the man and the song. They would be singing other hymns in the future.

Ezra was weeping. He had now lost virtually all the comrades of the old generation. Wu had been taken ill during the Congress and was on his deathbed, the tough little organizer who had fought bravely in Shanghai in 1927 only to be imprisoned by Mao after the Revolution. Gelder was missing, one of Tamarinda's many disappeared husbands. Diablo and he were the only survivors, and even poor Diablo was beginning to look very frail. Renard's funeral was announced for a fortnight hence.

Laura Shaw shook hands with Ezra, collected Kosminsky and her staff and left the hall. Renard's body was lifted and laid on the bench which, till recently, had been occupied by the veterans. Ezra was soon left alone, deep in thought on the platform of the now deserted and gloomy hall. He suddenly shivered, even though the temperature was ultra-mild for March. It had all ended in anticlimax. But, thought Ezra, he had got a majority. That was important. Hands raised. A decision taken. The cadres ready to occupy new positions inside the religions. PISPAW defeated, Burroughs made to look a fool, Pelletier exposed as a Freemason. A new period had begun. True, some might ask whether the Congress had been necessary in the first place. Let them. He, Ezra Einstein, was not dissatisfied with the results.

Outside, Paris was glowing and radiant. Above the Latin Quarter there stretched a sky of skilfully illuminated blue silk, without a single grey spot. Amongst the indolent and carefree youth who were enjoying the day and the sights, a strikingly handsome woman was wheeling her baby towards the Mutualité. She parked the pram outside, lifted Ho, who was dressed in a silky ink baby-grow, and opened the door. The sun flooded in and from the platform Ezra, disturbed by the intrusion, looked up and saw an amazing scene. Maya and Ho were both backlit by the sun, and from a distance they gave the appearance of a Renaissance painting, Mother and Child. Ezra blinked. He could not believe what he was watching. He looked again. There could no longer be any room for doubt. It was still there. A little halo was clearly visible above Ho's head.

Maya's voice disrupted the idyll. 'Come on Ezra. Why are you still sitting there?'

Just as Ezra began to collect his briefcase bulging with manuscripts and unfinished internal documents he heard another voice and looked up. It was unformed, but very clear.

'Come on Ezra. We're tired of waiting.'

Ho had spoken. But it didn't make sense. She was only a week old. Ezra rushed towards them like a man possessed.

'Did you hear that? Did this child actually speak? Maya?'

But Maya did not reply. She smiled, took him by the arm and pushed him outside into the sun. Unlike her husband, Maya was feeling on very good terms with life.

26

Funeral in Paris

It was a very special cold spell, slightly sinister, which hit Paris on the day they buried old Renard. Everything was done according to the old man's instructions. The urn containing the ashes would be buried in a special spot in the Père Lachaise cemetery. Here lay the remains of the Communards of eighteen seventy-one and it was here that Renard had marched when the centenary of that defeated uprising had been marked by the PSR and related initials from all over Western Europe, who carried red flags and banners with interesting slogans like, 'For a Red Europe', 'For a thirty-five hour week', etc. Renard had marched with a group of Latin American exiles chanting, 'Armed Road, Only Road. One Solution! Revolution.' And now many of the same people were here to pay their last farewell to one of the most colourful characters of this movement, which had produced more oddities and eccentrics than even the Jesuits?

That very day, *Le Monde* had reported the death in Romania of Nutty Shardman. The story was hardly credible. It had transpired that the Rockers' cell inside the Securitate had been an elaborate and cruel ploy. Ceausescu's orphans, looking for a safe way out, had put on a show of being ultra-hard proletarians, extremely worried by the danger of capitalist restoration, and obliged for that reason to remain clandestine. They asked Nutty Shardman to provide them with money and passports so that they could go and sit at the feet of the great Rock himself. *Le*

Monde published details of how this had been done. Then as six Securitate agents were attempting to escape with forged British passports in a van driven by Nutty, they were stopped by border-guards. Nutty panicked for no reason and began to drive through the barrier without waiting for the passport check. The guards opened fire and the van exploded.

Nobody referred to this ghastly happening at the funeral. The mood was sombre and very different in tone from the Congress itself, let alone the commemoration ceremonies of 1971. For one thing the Triplets were in priests' robes and the PSR members were dressed in the fashion of Trappist monks. Ezra was in a suit with the famous braces, but he had donned a tiny skull-cap, which symbolized the new turn-around. Emma Carpenter, who had stayed behind for the funeral, was dressed in a smart black track-suit in which she had jogged to the cemetery. The Chrisla-masonites were boycotting the event. It was Renard's vote which had denied them their victory and they saw no reason to become sentimental simply because he was dead. The Cuckoo was there, of course, with a Lutheran collar, but his wife, now a novice at a nunnery outside Rheims, had donned a Carmelite nun's outfit for the occasion. She was looking very attractive.

Renard's non-political admirers were also there in force, among them the sons of the old Renard Taxi Service employees, one of whom had driven up from the South in a convertible custom-built Rolls-Royce and had ordered several dozen wreaths, whose combined scent was overpowering. There were also several collectives of prostitutes, or body-workers as they now called themselves, who were present to pay homage to one of the pioneers of the first war against the pimpocracy. They had refused to dress in black, since there was nothing to mourn. The laws of biology had triumphed at just the right time. He had gone in the best possible way, after helping his side win an important factional struggle. What did surprise them was the amazing number of priests and religious people. Everyone knew that Renard was an old Communist. Whey then so many priests and nuns and skull-caps and even a few mullahs? The women were puzzled, but thought that possibly, at some stage of his life, Renard must have helped the religious orders as well.

Initially, the PSR had wanted to organize the wake, but given that their cadres were dispersed they had finally agreed that it should be left to the Body-Workers' Collectives, who had been insisting all along that they, more than anyone else, were best suited to take full charge of any social occasion which marked Renard's departure. They had booked the Cirque d'Hivers, and organized the most exquisite food and wines as well as live rock bands and a cello concert. No expense had been spared and several hundred people were expected.

But now the urn was being laid to rest and wet earth was covering the ash which was all that remained of Renard. Tears were shed and dried. Then Father Pedro Rossi cleared his throat and delivered his funeral oration. It focused on the activities of the departed veteran in Latin America. Pedro maintained an elevated note and left out the more picaresque aspects of Renard's many-sided life. The RTS contingent and the Collectives were a bit displeased by this omission. If it had not been for their services there might not even have been a movement, since poor old Trotsky might have starved to death on that tiny Turkish island. This was a slightly exaggerated view of their own importance, but their role should not be underestimated.

Rossi was still droning on. 'As I have said repeatedly, the Ancients, four centuries before Christ, raised every major problem both in theory and practice, with the exception, naturally, of nuclear destruction. And it is because Life continually poses the same problems, albeit in different forms, that utopian scholars and philosophers arise to try to cut the Gordian knot. Jesus, Buddha, Lao Tzu, Confucius, Mohammed were all trying to connect the spiritual with the political and the political with the spiritual. Renard understood better than most that our passion and our intellect are always in disequilibrium . . .'

On hearing this last sentence the Collectives collapsed into laughter, which began to border on the vulgar. Rossi hurriedly concluded his remarks, and a singer hired for the occasion by the man with the Rolls-Royce led the assembly in singing the Te Deum. The Collectives frowned because they knew Renard had been a staunch atheist, but they stood still till it was all over.

As Pedro Rossi was walking away, chatting to Ezra, Lina came and took his arm. Even though he was in official garb he did not shake her off, but smiled, a clear sign that he needed her that afternoon to recover from the humiliation inflicted on him by the Collectives. She understood and pressed his arm. Maya winked at her as if to say 'I know' and Lina dragged her priest away.

Ezra had no desire to attend Renard's wake that evening, but he encouraged Maya to go without him. She refused. 'I'm not going without you. You must attend.'

'Listen my dear. Death is not alarming at my age. Renard died happy because he died fighting. I want to see the victory of true Socialism, but it may not come in my lifetime. *That* saddens me.'

The knowledge that he was alone was bad enough, but it was the situation in the Soviet Union which had put Ezra in a very bleak frame of mind. He did not really believe that the restoration of capitalism in most of Eastern Europe would necessarily be a disaster. He thought that the combination of a memory of certain collectivist gains with the experience of actually existing IMF capitalism would be the best education possible for the unfortunate citizens of these countries. But the Soviet Union was different. Ezra recalled the heroic period of the Revolution. Azerbaijan was not simply the remnant of a Tsarist colony. There had been a very strong Bolshevik current present in 1917 and after, but they had been driven to nationalism by the experience of almost half a century of Stalinism. Ezra also noticed the growing number of anti-semitic currents in that country, whose public aim was to drive all the Jews out of Russia. Why was history fated to repeat itself? These were the questions preoccupying him today, and he did not wish to spend the evening with his own comrades dressed as priests and a collection of prostitutes and *nouveaux riches* entrepreneurs.

Back at their apartment, Maya fell into a deep sulk. She wanted to go to the Cirque d'Hivers and join in the fun. They argued.

Ezra lost his temper with her for the first time. She was impressed by his outburst and convinced by his polemical skills. She decided to go alone, leaving Ho with her father.

'But what if she wakes up and needs to be fed?'

'I'll be back before midnight in any case, but if I'm a bit late, unbutton your shirt Ezra! You've done it before.'

He did not smile any longer when reference was made to his amazing feat. When a television programme offered him a great deal of money to discuss the issue and demonstrate his skills, he had refused. Maya was angry with him for denying Ho her first television appearance, but he displayed an obstinacy which she found incomprehensible. She raised her voice and told him that if he had lactated on the box it would have won him a much larger following than he had at the moment, at which point he had laughed and felt her breasts. Now he wanted to forget about the whole business as quickly as possible. He had already begun agitating for her to try to wean little Ho, but she would have nothing to do with any such notion.

An agreement was finally reached with regard to that evening. Maya promised that she would feed Ho at nine-thirty, put her to sleep and then go to the wake. She would return at midnight. Good humour was restored and all talk of male lactation conveniently forgotten.

When Maya arrived at the wake it had already been going on for three hours. A great deal of champagne and smoked salmon had already been consumed. She arrived in time for the main course, which was being served by flunkeys dressed in black and silver. It was tiny portions of filleted beef, served with 1983 Châteauneuf du Pape, an appropriate choice given the very large number of priests present, despite the fact that they were behaving in a most unpriestly fashion. The Triplets were cavorting on the dance floor with their partners, a group of nuns were dancing with each other, and the only real priest among them, Pedro Rossi, had not yet arrived. Nor, for that matter, had Lina, and the wilder elements were beginning to dominate the proceedings. Maya was approached by a white-haired Romeo, who asked her to dance, but she turned him down. She had noticed that since her relationship with Ezra every old guy around the movement imagined that she was available, as if they thought that old men were her particular perversion.

At that point she saw two couples arriving from separate entrances. Over there were Ted Spanner and Mimi Wilcox, who looked as if they too had spent the afternoon in bed. Mimi was looking unnaturally flushed and wore a black ribbon round her neck, held together by a silver brooch. On the other side came Pedro and Lina, looking incredibly happy. Clearly something or the other had been consummated. Whereas there was something very jaded about Ted and Mimi, the priest and his Bulgarian companion looked positively youthful and in a sixth or seventh heaven. Maya went and hugged them both. Pedro blushed, readjusted his moustache and walked away as he heard Lina describing the afternoon. Pedro was a liberation theologist, but he was certainly not a follower of Wilhelm Reich, and he found the ability of women to discuss sex openly both embarrassing and distasteful.

'Well?' asked Maya.

Lina laughed. 'It was great. Makes you think.'

'What?'

'Well, if he really hasn't done it for ten years all I can say is that he is remarkably disciplined. His eagerness did not outflank mine!'

'Hard and slow?'

'Exactly.'

Mimi had walked over to them. 'What are you two giggling about?'

Maya was in one of her devilish moods. 'We're giggling about what you should be, but aren't giggling about. Eh? Tell us all.'

Mimi frowned, but she could not stop herself reddening. 'I really don't know what you're . . .'

'Mimi, why pretend. That horny Yanqui has been eyeing you ever since he arrived. Emma told me about it. What did happen?'

Another voice entered the conversation. Emma had arrived, dressed to kill in a very chic grey trouser-suit, with a creamy silk shirt and a black cravat.

'What is going on?'

'Er . . . nothing at all, my dear Emma . . .' muttered Mimi, who wanted to run away, but felt that if she did so she would not be able to offer any antidote to the poisonous gossip Maya Einstein was on the verge of spreading.

Their attention was diverted by sounds of raucous laughter and loud singing from the nearby tent. It sounded as if a ritual were in progress. They walked towards the noise and were greeted by a horrific sight. The Body-Workers' Collectives were dancing round a naked figure who was covering his private parts with his bare hands, thus leaving his bum unguarded. Every body-worker was running into the ring, slapping his behind and running back. The aim was to attempt to make him guard his posterior so they could glimpse him frontally, but he was immovable. To their horror they realized it was Pedro. Lina, Maya and Emma charged through the ranks of the Collective with a primal scream that halted everything, rescued Pedro and took him away, but not before Maya had translated the choicest Brazilian abuses into French and shocked the Collective into an admiring silence. Mimi should have joined them, but she had been simply paralysed by her Englishness.

The wake itself ended soon after that episode, which Pedro felt had done a grave disservice to Renard's memory. Pedro was not aware that the punishment administered to him by the tipsy members of the Collective had been devised by Renard in the old days for dealing with recalcitrant taxi-drivers who hankered after the old ways and tried to entice some of the members of the Collective back to the *ancien régime* of the pimpocracy.

Maya went back with Lina and Pedro to discuss their future. They both convinced Pedro to become a real father and then celebrated the decision with some old Spanish brandy. He would, of course, remain a priest. Given the momentous decision which had been taken there was no question of discarding the cowl, but he wanted to be the father of Lina's baby as well, and he saw no contradiction whatsoever in aiding both processes. When Maya had left Pedro's apartment and decided to walk back home she caught sight of a very drunk Ted Spanner, a member of the Body-Worker's Collective on either arm, headed for a night of activity.

Alas, poor Mimi, thought Maya. To be deserted by that rake of a West Coast professor for two stale tarts could not have been very nice. With this thought in her head, she began to walk back home.

27

Conversations with Ho, who will be ten in the year 2000

It was after midnight. Ezra was at his desk, where he had been writing a special journal for Ho to read when she came of age. Ezra was a realist. He knew that he would soon join the fathers of the movement in the happy hunting grounds and so he wanted to write something for his daughter, explaining his ideas and his own history, the circumstances in which he had met her mother, and how Ho herself should look towards the future. He had written about his own youth, his arrest by the Nazis during the Second World War and his escape from the camps.

I managed to escape not because of my own superhuman skills which are non-existent or my courage which would not have helped, but because of my interminable and incorrigible curiosity about human beings and how their minds work. I was the only prisoner who did not treat the warders at one camp as if they were beasts. I started talking to them and I discovered that prior to Hitler's victory most of them had been social-democrats and still had their party cards hidden somewhere. Others had been Communists. I talked to them a great deal and learnt a lot that way.

  I was only sixteen, Ho, still six years older than you will be when you read this. Well they were so impressed that I treated

*them like human beings that they helped me escape. It would
have been impossible otherwise. This was in a transition camp
from where all of us were destined for Auschwitz. Always have
faith in the power of reason, even in times which give the
appearance of doom.*

His account of his meeting with Maya in Brazil was sanitized for
his daughter's benefit and was at variance with the description
contained in this book. There was, for instance, no mention of the
incidents on Copacabana Beach. Instead he spoke about how
they had held hands in a tiny cinema in São Paulo, an incident
which had not taken place at all. This fiction, however, was not
without interest. It offered a version of history which was false,
but which is how Ezra would have liked things to happen if the
choice had been his alone.

Ho began to cry. Ezra rushed to pick her up. She stopped crying
the minute she saw him and gurgled with pleasure. Ezra went
straight to the point. 'Hello, little Ho. I know you want some
milk. Maya will be back soon. Hmmm? Don't worry. Everything
is under control. Your Papa Ezra is here. All right?'

He stayed there shaking the cot, but himself began to shake
when he heard a tiny voice.

'Why is our world so cruel?'

Ezra steadied himself. On the last occasion Ho had talked,
Maya had claimed that she had not heard a single word. Her face
had adopted the Mona Lisa look, and whenever this happened it
was impossible to get a syllable out of her.

Ezra began to wonder whether he was going mad, but decided
in any event that he must answer little Ho's question.

'Our world is run by tiny groups of people whose only method
of dealing with popular discontent is to resort to intolerance and
persecution. Bad people are in charge of most of the world, little
Ho. The Iron Chancellor of the new Germany frightens me.
There you have an example of a sinister politician, whose political fathers collaborated with Hitler. Do you see how he plays the
nationalist card once again? It's enough to chill the brain. It will

change, my lovely daughter. I'm sure of that. When you grow up things might be different.'

There was no further sound except that of a tiny brain ticking. Then Ho spoke again. 'When will you die?'

Ezra was surprised at the turn in the conversation. He had been busy preparing another explanation on the state of the world. He often thought of death these days, but never in a worried or sentimental fashion. His only concern was that he might not have written a total of fifty books before his corpse entered the incinerator. He was almost there, but to write twenty odd books over the next ten years was not so easy. That is, of course, if he lived to be eighty. The little voice repeated the question.

'I don't know, little Ho. I think during the next ten years, or so.'

'Now can I have some of your milk? Please! Please Ezra!'

Ezra was so touched that he felt the milk flowing again. He took off his shirt and held little Ho to his breasts. Maya had told him that there was a semi-erotic side to this process, but he did not feel any stirrings below or above. He just thought that it was a sign from heaven that his new strategic thrust of moving the cadres towards religion was being rewarded by the big brain above the sky. He tutted at his own stupidity. A frown appeared. What if the comrades who became cardinals or ayatollahs became so attached to their new positions that they turned their back on the movement? This had happened with members of parliament in Sri Lanka, Australia, Bolivia and Britain. Why should the appeal of spiritual power be any less attractive than the temptations of bourgeois politics?

Then Ezra chuckled to himself. Those idiots who had launched Chrislamasonism would probably pick up some kids, but they would have been better advised to devise something on the pattern of the pre-Christian cults. The problem with modern religions was that they needed a string of martyrs before they could take off. If he had gone for something like that he would have synthesized the Sceptic and Epicurean philosophies. Ezra suddenly nodded his head as if he were agreeing with someone else present in the room. In fact Marx had entered his head and reminded him of the importance of Epicurus' theory of the atoms, which explained clearly how the gods could not interfere with life on earth. Epicurus excluded his possibility. Hence his rejection of the afterlife. Epicurus, thought Ezra, had provided arguments to liberate humanity from the grip of superstition and religion. And yet over two and half thousand years later, the deadly diseases were still going strong. He satisfied himself that the only antidote to religion was to enter and implode the beast from within. And yet . . . and yet there was that ethical, spiritual component. That they must capture for the new movement.

Ezra had spent the past few months immersed in his mighty new endeavour. If his plan was carefully implemented it could turn out to be a ruthless success which would both enrapture the faithful and shatter the bourgeoisie. Heaven, Ezra told himself, was not alone in realizing the necessity that underlay this task. The very thought of a possible triumph in twenty-five years' time cheered him up enormously, and his quivering nerves were calmed by a wild and uncontrollable surge of the imagination. His mood, which had hitherto been dominated by the sordid and anticlimactic end to the Congress, changed to a mixture of yearning, confessional fervour and a desperate desire to sing as he floated upwards and outwards.

Oblivious to the thoughts in her father's head, little Ho sucked away, first on one and then the other nipple. But suddenly she sensed the change in Ezra's internal bodily rhythm patterns and her drowsiness disappeared completely. Her tiny oracle-like tones echoed slightly in this room with a wooden floor.

'Ezra, I think your Congress was a failure.'

Ezra sat up in the bed. 'Why?'

'It ended in a break-up.'

'But all Congresses of the movement end like that, my little Ho. You will learn this as you grow older.'

'Perhaps, but I see evil in front of me now.'

'What? Where?'

'I see that Cuckoo man, sitting in an office with other men. He is telling them your plans, Ezra, so they are ready for you in the Church.'

Ezra was in complete suspense. 'But who are the men? What do you see and hear little Ho? Tell me, please!'

'The Cuckoo is a police agent, Ezra.'

'NO . . .'

Ezra's scream was straight from the heart.

'But don't worry, Ezra. He will die next year when they send him on a mission to Hungary. I have seen him die.'

Ezra stroked his daughter's head with a distant expression on his face. 'Little Ho. Tell me one more thing. The future of our movement. Is it there? Can you see anything?'

'That is beyond even me, Ezra. I don't see anything connected with your movement. No. Nothing.'

'What do you see, Ho?'

'I see the beginning of this century. I see one single political force. Social-democracy. Many currents were visible in the flow of that mighty river. Then there came a horrible war. The movement split. Tiny rivulets began to flow against the stream. The war was followed by a great revolution. The rivulets merged into a single river once again, but one flowing in the opposite direction. Two contending currents of thought fought each other to win the hearts and minds of the workers' movement. One of these has now been extinguished, and with it your movement, which was only a footnote to its history. The light it generated has gone out in most of Europe. Since most of this light was artificial, Ezra, it doesn't really matter. The other movement, social-democracy, is still very much alive. Do you know what this means, Papa Ezra? Have you ever asked yourself that? It means that social-democracy has once again become hegemonic.'

'Social-democracy is far too compromised with the crimes of Capital.'

'But it exists. Everything else is dead.'

'No, not everything. I refuse to believe that we have wasted this century. I can never accept that. Never! Social-democracy has no claws at all. It will need to wear less delicate fabrics than the tailored creatures we see on television all over Europe. Designer social-democracy would be even more powerless in the face of a new Hitler than its predecessors. That's the problem, Ho! Never forget that!'

'You asked the question. I gave you the answer. You see, a great deal of debate about the future will now take place inside or on the fringes of social-democracy. Gorbachev, Yeltsin, all these people are, basically, social-democrats. Gorbachev has already made a proposal to end the historic divide. They have won, Ezra. Your side has lost. Everything has changed and Europe will be dominated by variants of social-democracy. For the next twenty or fifty years, it will be like that. I'm sorry, but history is like that and well, at least it's something. Imagine becoming like the United States. A country without a past or a future.'

Ezra was speechless. Oh please, he pleaded to his new-found ally in the sky, don't let it end like this. Give us another break. Please. Not just social-democracy. Come on. One more chance.

Then little Ho continued to suck and somehow, somewhere towards the end of the feed, both of them fell fast asleep, Ho satisfied and Ezra in the aftermath of a unique erotic glow which had taken him over only when his eyes had closed.

Ezra is dreaming now. A strange disembodied figure is staring hard at him from the sky. Is it the creator? Strange. It is half-Zeus, half-Marx, clothed in a white robe, which matches his white beard. He is frowning. Why is he so irritated? What could have gone wrong?

'Einstein,' the voice says. 'Come up for a minute, will you?'

Ezra is floating in the sky, when Zeus-Marx extends a hand and pulls him up. Then he roars with laughter. Ezra suddenly finds himself sitting on a hard bench. Facing him across the table are Lenin, Trotsky, Kautsky, Rosa Luxemburg and, yes, old Renard. Zeus-Marx is filling their glasses with an amber liquid. Renard grins at him and says to the others: 'He's the one I was telling you about.'

'He's mine,' shouts Trotsky.

'No, no, no.' Rosa Luxemburg is adamant. 'This one really belongs to me.'

'What's going on down there, Comrade?' asks Lenin.

'We know what's going on down there. No socialism without democracy. I've won! Haven't I, Lenin? Trotsky?' and Kautsky laughs like a mischievous schoolboy.

Uncharacteristically, both Lenin and Trotsky remain silent. Bewildered by this, Ezra keeps looking from one to the other. Then, in a quiet voice, he speaks a single word.

'Why?'

None of them reply till Renard turns to Zeus-Marx.

'Should we bring him up permanently?'

They vote, but Renard is in a minority of one. Ezra is giggling with joy at winning a reprieve.

'Comrades, speak to me. Has it all melted into air? We have lost, but historical materialism? That can't be lost, can it? Will religion re-establish its clammy grip? Is progress dead?'

They smile and each speaks in turn to show their approval of the framework within which he has posed this question.

ZEUS-MARX: Man makes religion. Religion does not make man.

LENIN: But man is no abstraction squatting outside the world. Man is the world of man. State. Society. This state and this society produce religion, a reversed world-consciousness, because they are a reversed world.

LUXEMBURG: Religion is the general theory of that world, its encyclopedic compendium, its logic in a popular form, its spiritual *point d'honneur*, its enthusiasm, its moral sanction, its solemn completion, its universal ground for consolation and justification.

KAUTSKY: We could never compete with all that! Religion is the fantastic realization of the human essence because the human essence has no true reality. The struggle against religion is the fight against the other world, of which religion is the spiritual aroma.

TROTSKY: Religious distress is at the same time the expression of real distress and the protest against real distress. Religion is the sigh of the oppressed creature, the heart of a heartless world, just as it is the spirit of a spiritless situation. It is the opium of the people.

RENARD: Where have I heard that line before?

KAUTSKY: The abolition of religion as the illusory happiness of the people is required for their real happiness.

LENIN: The demand to give up the illusions about its condition is the demand to give up a condition which needs illusions.

LUXEMBURG: The criticism of religion is therefore in embryo the criticism of the vale of tears, the halo of which is religion.

TROTSKY: Criticism has plucked the imaginary flowers from the chain not so that man will wear the chain without any fantasy or consolation but so that he will shake off the chain and cull the living flower. The criticism of religion disillusions man to make him think and act and shape his reality like a man who has been disillusioned and has come to reason, so that he will revolve round himself and therefore round his true sun. Religion is only the illusory sun which revolves round man as long as he does not revolve round himself.

ZEUS-MARX: The task of history, therefore, once the world beyond the truth has disappeared, is to establish the truth of this world. Thus the criticism of Heaven turns into a criticism of Earth, the criticism of religion into the criticism of right and the criticism of theology into the criticism of politics. It's simple.

RENARD: Well, Ezra?

EINSTEIN: But all this is taken directly from Marx's *Contribution to the Critique of Hegel's Philosophy of Right*.

RENARD: Exactly! Exactly!

They are all laughing at him now. Rosa comes close and kisses his cheeks. Ezra is overwhelmed. Then Zeus-Marx lifts him and throws him down. He sees debris floating past him. And? No. It can't be. But it is the Cuckoo, or rather the Cuckoo's head. Then there is a sound of a key turning in a lock, a door opening and being slammed. Ezra turns over and this dream disappears.

When Maya entered the apartment she peeped into the bedroom and smiled at the scene. Then she looked more closely and saw the milk stains on Ezra's body and his partially erect member, nodding to and fro like a bar-drunk. She understood and was relieved. Little Ho had not gone hungry.

Maya walked in to Ezra's study where the lights were still on and saw his journal for Ho's tenth birthday. She sat down at the desk and read the last entry:

Often in my political life I was called a utopian. I don't mind that title. Some of the most practical human beings on our planet from the dawn of humankind to this very day have been utopians. They too, like me, have often been confronted with defeat. Too many of them have in the end caved in to despair. That I refused to do. I had lived through two horrible periods of this century: Hitler and Stalin. My best friends and comrades had been destroyed by one or the other of the dictatorships over which these men presided. For me nothing could be worse than that and so as I write these words for you I note that the world is changing again. For the better or the worse it is still too soon to say. We shall know by the time you are twenty, and if nothing has really changed then you will fight again. At least I hope you will. I know the outrages of history only too well, my lovely little Ho! I have been fighting them with my pen for the last fifty years. Do I sometimes lose hope? Yes! A million times and more. But I peer over the abyss and then return. Without doubts and struggles the spirit loses its resilience.

I hope that you, my beautiful daughter, will speak many languages. Chinese, Japanese, Russian, Portuguese and then the three great languages of our continent: English, German and Spanish. I was brought up in German. It was my mother tongue. My parents stopped speaking in that language during the war. But the last words they heard were in German as they were pushed into the gas ovens at Belsen. I have always loved German. I identify it with Goethe and Holderlin and Schiller and Beethoven and Marx and Peter Weiss and Wolf Biermann and Christa Wolf.

I am closing these few pages with my favourite lines from Goethe, in the translation that my own father gave to me. One day I hope you will read it in the master's own language:

> Alas, alas!
> Thou hast smitten the world,
> Thou hast laid it low,
> Shattered, o'erthrown,
> Into nothingness hurled
> Crushed by a demigod's blow!
>
> We bear them away,
> The shards of the world,
> We sing well-a-day
> Over the loveliness gone,
> Over the beauty slain.
>
> Build it again,
> Great child of the Earth,
> Build it again
> With a finer worth,
> In thine own bosom build it on high!
> Take up thy life once more:
> Run the race again!
> High and clear
> Let a lovelier strain
> Ring out than ever before!

There were tears in her eyes as Maya closed the book. Then she went and put out the lights. The apartment was engulfed in darkness.

All Pan books are available at your local bookshop or newsagent, or can be ordered direct from the publisher. Indicate the number of copies required and fill in the form below.

Send to: **CS Department, Pan Books Ltd., P.O. Box 40,
Basingstoke, Hants.   RG21 2YT.**

or phone: 0256 469551 (Ansaphone), quoting title, author
and Credit Card number.

Please enclose a remittance* to the value of the cover price plus: 60p for the first book plus 30p per copy for each additional book ordered to a maximum charge of £2.40 to cover postage and packing.

*Payment may be made in sterling by UK personal cheque, postal order, sterling draft or international money order, made payable to Pan Books Ltd.

Alternatively by Barclaycard/Access:

Card No. ☐☐☐☐☐☐☐☐☐☐☐☐☐☐☐☐☐

Signature:

Applicable only in the UK and Republic of Ireland.

While every effort is made to keep prices low, it is sometimes necessary to increase prices at short notice. Pan Books reserve the right to show on covers and charge new retail prices which may differ from those advertised in the text or elsewhere.

NAME AND ADDRESS IN BLOCK LETTERS PLEASE:

....

Name————————————————————————————

Address————————————————————————————

————————————————————————————

————————————————————————————

————————————————————————————

3/87